RHAPSODY

RHAPSODY

MITCHELL JAMES KAPLAN

THORNDIKE PRESS
A part of Gale, a Cengage Company

Copyright © 2021 by Mitchell James Kaplan.
Thorndike Press, a part of Gale, a Cengage Company.

Thorndike Press® Large Print Basic.
The text of this Large Print edition is unabridged.
Other aspects of the book may vary from the original edition.
Set in 16 pt. Plantin.

LIBRARY OF CONGRESS CIP DATA ON FILE.
CATALOGUING IN PUBLICATION FOR THIS BOOK
IS AVAILABLE FROM THE LIBRARY OF CONGRESS.

ISBN-13: 978-1-4328-8674-5 (hardcover alk. paper)

Published in 2021 by arrangement with Gallery Books, a division of Simon & Schuster, Inc.

Printed in Mexico
Print Number: 01   Print Year: 2021

*In memory of my father
and for Annie*

July 11, 1937, 7:43 A.M.

So dreadfully wet outside. Water spraying down like Morton's salt in the *Ladies' Home Journal* advertisement. The one with the little girl who clutches an umbrella three sizes too big. *When it rains, it pours.*

The office Kay shares with Al Stillman: a dolphin-gray cell, sensible and efficient. None of the art deco flourishes that have brought fame to the RCA Building's lobby thirty-four stories below. Who needs all that ornamentation anyhow, way up here?

Way up here, where the music blooms. She smiles nostalgically, glancing around in appraisal of the moment.

The black file cabinet; Al's oak desk with its three-footed swivel chair; his Royal typewriter. A few half-typed pages, fragments of someday songs, legs and heads awaiting torsos, faces, and minds. An unfinished letter to Al's cousin in Frankfurt urg-

7

ing her and the *kinder* to get out, to come to America. "It is time, Ester."

It is time. It is 1937. It is summer. A long, soggy summer of waiting.

The clock high on the wall, its red second hand slowly turning. The ebony Bechstein upright piano below. The magazine on the piano, *Popular Songs,* open to the two-page spread that features a photograph of Kay in a plastered bob. "She Is the Envy of Songwriters Everywhere."

Tin Pan Alley puffery. What good, really? A momentary thrill. A burst of fireworks and then the black nighttime sky. A lingering residue of smoke.

The office mirrored in the rain-streaked windows, where she stands in a black sheath and heels. Her face reflected in the glass, less fresh than in the *Popular Songs* photograph. Her dark eyes gazing at the sea of umbrellas thirty-four stories below.

Thirty-four stories. Not sixty-six but also not one, three, or ten. In New York City height is eminence, which correlates with the number of people who pretend to be one's friends and the larger number who claim to be *their* friends. Circles around circles all the way to the island's jagged periphery.

The figures cowering under the umbrellas: men, almost all. Their cuffed slacks and black oxfords briefly visible beyond the edges of their umbrellas as they step forward, then retreating again. Working people. Each one, a story. A man starts here and wends his way there. Another begins over there and darts off somewhere else. A life. A burst of activity and then — *poof.* A trace of scent, perhaps — cologne, sweat, garlic.

Men shuffling resigned and courageous to their offices, others hurrying ambitiously into buildings, riding elevators up and down. Hundreds, thousands, millions of individual trajectories: melodic lines. Harmony. Dissonance. Counterpoint. Zigzag rhythms against the unheard ticking of the universal metronome.

But there, in their midst, slipping through and between them: a little girl! A child in a lavender raincoat with a matching broad-rimmed hat. What is she running from?

Kay wipes steam from the glass and peers. *Couldn't be. Same stride . . . similar raincoat and hat . . . Just a girl.*

Her youngest daughter, Kathleeen, is in Washington, D.C. So are Kathleen's two older sisters, April and Andrea. They boarded that train more than two years ago. White-gloved, in pearls, Kay waved and blew a kiss from the platform. She never learned whether they saw that kiss.

Kay shakes away the vision. She is sapped, having worked all night. The Roxyettes will have their boogie-woogie leg-kicker. It is time to go home.

But in this deluge Kay hesitates. She takes her trench coat and clutch, steps into the hall, and locks the door. The elevator dings and whooshes her down thirty-two floors.

She strolls through a carpeted corridor to the projection booth, a closet teeming with metal canisters and sprocketed strips of plastic that magically combine with light to conjure tall, elegant men and women who are always in possession of the *mot juste,* the precise witty rejoinder that the occasion calls for, and the right moves. The projectionist beams, a young buck two years out of college, round black glasses, slicked black hair. "I got it, Miss Swift!" He brandishes a film can. "Just for you they flew it out. Now a good time?"

Crayoned on the can: *Shall We Dance,* Reel One. Kay smiles.

Shall We Dance opened two months ago and closed after a brief run. She delayed seeing it, pretending to be too busy. After all, George was too busy for her, was he not? But she fooled no one, least of all herself.

Then, last night, her phone rang. It was

George. What he told her changed everything.

She is frazzled and spent, but it is raining. Better to remain indoors, in the glow of the movie screen, in the afterglow of that conversation. "Now's a wonderful time," she tells Marvin.

He glances at the clock. "We got two hours exactly, more or less."

The International Music Hall: its hollow immensity, its six thousand seats, its four-thousand-pipe Wurlitzer. Desolate and dim, the ultimate monument of music-hall impresario Samuel Rothapfel, and his sepulcher. Poor Sam, with his soaring ambition and his weak heart.

No windows. No street sounds. Rain? What rain? To stroll down the right-hand aisle under these gold-and-aluminum-leafed telescoping ribs, which taper to a focus at the one-hundred-foot-wide stage, is to relive Jonah's adventure in the belly of Leviathan, swallowed by the sea and a world away from everything.

Leviathan, the Moby Dick of Israelite antiquity . . .

Years ago Kay taught herself to remember dreams. Now a fragment drifts into her mind. She is standing in a crowd before the

11

gangway of an ocean cruiser. The sign, indicating its destination, reads "Nineveh," where she is to perform. Not on the piano. She is to sing. Her dreaming mind conflates the word *cruiser* with the name of the famous tenor, Caruso. A poster on a building across the street showcases her face, under his name. She does not belong there, a woman in a man's poster. She is no Caruso and so, instead of excited anticipation, she feels dread. Her voice is weak and of all the places in the world, Nineveh is the one she most fears visiting. The gates open. Passengers flood aboard the SS *Leviathan* and the next thing she knows she is descending a metal staircase alone, into its bowels.

Another memory, this one all too real: Zilboorg, the psychoanalyst who interpreted her dream of the SS *Leviathan.* His glasses askew on his nose. His tweed jacket falling off one shoulder. She wishes she could erase this image. Undo its existence. But she has no choice. The memory-Zilboorg speaks to her: "Nineveh. Does that evoke nothing for you?"

The memory-Kay shakes her head.

"Nineveh is where God sent Jonah, to prophecy to its citizens. But he refused, and ended up in the belly of Leviathan."

She nods, recalling the story of Jonah that

12

her pious Grandma Gertie used to tell her at bedtime.

"Leviathan," repeats Zilboorg. "The out-of-control sea monster. The id, swimming in the ocean of the unconscious mind. And Jonah, the ordinary man — or in your case, woman — who runs away from her prophetic powers. Her inspiration, her passion, her aggressive urges, dare I say her repressed sexual urges. The woman whose *voice* is *weak*. But in the end that irrational monster gets the better of her, doesn't it. It swallows her whole. You see, we're all helpless against Leviathan."

Zilboorg. Brilliant, of course. But she longs to forget. To forget his tweed jacket. To forget his glasses. To forget his brown Ukrainian gaze. The tendrils of the past shoot up through the soil of the present. They wrap around your consciousness and tug it down, down into the earth.

She takes a seat in the sixth row of this leviathan, the International Music Hall. Up front and center, the way she has lived her life — perhaps for better, arguably for worse. The lights dim. Marvin switches on the dream machine. And with a sigh of relief Kay feels her dark mood seep away as George Gershwin's unmistakable overture spills into the theater.

Shall We Dance is precisely what she expected, a lighthearted, crossed-stars romp, hardly worthy of his talent. But then, George, like Louis Armstrong, like Scott Fitzgerald, has always refused to think that way. "Why only fluffy entertainment, or only serious art? Can't a great chef grill a hamburger now and then?"

The leading man dances out of the shadows: Fred Astaire, a plain, reedy, middle-aged fellow, neither an exceptional singer nor a gifted actor. His loopy smile and aw-shucks eyes call to mind a down-on-his-heels encyclopedia salesman. But Fred is as nimble and weightless as a kitten. Kay knows him, not terribly well but well enough that she sees not only the screen icon, bigger than life, careless and self-assured, but also, lurking behind that image, plain old Fred, George's dear friend since they were scruffy kids with dreams as wide as a Nebraska cornfield.

Which is where Ginger skips in, the corn-fed Midwestern blonde, the embodiment of a concept of America, the audience whose adulation both George and Fred crave. Together Fred and Ginger float and spin, twin feathers in a breeze. They twist, dip, and fly across the screen, acrobats illustrating George's music with their feet and arms.

14

Fred plays Peter, who has achieved fame under the pseudonym Petrov, a Russian ballet dancer. Peter has two problems: he secretly yearns to tap dance to American jazz and he is infatuated with Linda, the New York showgirl played by Ginger Rogers. Linda oozes contempt for Peter but worships his alter ego Petrov. Familiar thematic territory for the man who composed *An American in Paris* and *Show Girl:* European loftiness, secretly craving American authenticity; the New World party girl worshipping at the altar of Old World sophistication.

Despite the pat story line, tears pool in Kay Swift's eyes when Fred croons to Ginger that he will never forget her, the way she wears her hat, the way she sings off-key. And again when, in the finale, he sings the title song to a troupe of Ginger Rogers look-alikes, from which the real Ginger emerges like Aphrodite from the sea. As Fred and Ginger sashay, swirl, and reel with romance, an invisible hand reaches into Kay's gut, or is it her heart, and gives it a squeeze.

Invisible but not unfamiliar. Through these characters, this music, these songs, a lanky man with dark hair and a disarming nonchalance speaks to her. To her alone, soliloquizing on his past and present, his longings and misgivings. The same man who phoned her last night, changing everything.

Again she feels her mood slipping. A dissolve-to-darkness answers the opening fade-in. What is this knot in her gut? As if someone punched her. Something is wrong. Somewhere. *It's about him. It's about George.* She rises and stumbles to the street for air.

She spots a black DeSoto taxi, the new model, the Airflow, with its oversized, swept-back grill that guzzles rain and air the way a largemouth bass gulps water. She waves and the cab lumbers to the curb. Its portly driver splashes over. Water dripping from his cap, he tugs on the chrome passenger door handle and holds an umbrella for her as the long door swings rearward. Kay places one high-heeled foot onto the running board and ducks into the velveted passenger compartment. The door clunks closed. She leans forward, slides open the window to speak to the back of the driver's head, and mumbles an address.

"Yes, ma'am," and the car rumbles off, water spraying from its tires.

Still she struggles to breathe. *Something is wrong, awfully wrong.* She sinks into the bench and closes her eyes.

16

George flew to Los Angeles following the box-office failure of his magnum opus, *Porgy and Bess.* Kay urged him not to go. New York City was home. He owned the city but by the same token, it owned him. George knew this. He did not like it.

He clasped her hands: "It'll be swell, Kay. Fred's kicking up a storm out there. Someone needs to save him from himself. Ginger's begging me. It's been too darn long."

Seven years ago he had plucked Ginger Rogers out of a chorus line and anonymity for *Girl Crazy.* One leg-and-arm-flinging, give-me-my-break moment, supported by musicians Benny Goodman, Gene Krupa, Glenn Miller, and Jimmy Dorsey in the pit, transformed Ginger into a star. And then, in a New York second, she abandoned Broadway and Gershwin for Hollywood. Now, desperate for the unforgettable dance numbers only he could pen, Ginger was yodeling and waving to him from the Pacific coast. And George's ears were pricking up.

As he looked into Kay's cloudy eyes his face softened. His smile fell away. "I'm goofy for you, kid. You know that."

She let her cigarette fall and smashed it

with her toe. "Then why the hell are you flying off, George?"

He waved as if greeting someone in the sky. "This isn't a pair of wings, Kay. This is a tin can rolling down the road."

But it was a pair of wings.

He touched her cheek. "Besides, you deserve a break."

"Whatever you say, George," she said bitterly. "You're the genius."

Now, from her handbag in the back seat of the DeSoto, Kay fetches her monogrammed ivory and silver cigarette holder, a gift from George. She lights a Marlboro, cranks her window down a slit, and sighs. Rain mists her face as she smokes.

She knew even then that what George longed for he would not find in Los Angeles: his boyhood, the sense that his future lay before him, escape not just from New York but from a variety of entanglements. From Kay herself. *How did it come to this?*

Somewhere a horn honks — once, thrice — a slightly underpitched A-flat. Below it, like a supporting bass line, the rumble of tires against asphalt, an occasional shout.

"Watch it, buster!"

"Extra! Extra!"

She looks. A newspaper boy on the corner.

A crowd has gathered around him. They reach excitedly for the information he is peddling. *What has happened?*

Another horn, lower, F-sharp. She cannot help identifying the tones. She was born that way. She smiles, remembering the rubber-bulb taxi horns George brought back from Paris. He sat at the piano in his Riverside Drive apartment playing his new composition and shouting "Now!" when she was to toot one or the other. A bold touch, evoking the bustle and chaos of the French capital through off-key honks. His was not the Paris of Puccini-esque garrets and Monet's soft-hued Gare St.-Lazare but the urban jungle of towering ironworks and exuberant primitivism.

In the distance, the rising howl of a siren, calling to mind another of his sonic gags, the klezmer-style clarinet wail at the beginning of his earlier *Rhapsody.* And in that lament, so much humor, so much melody, so much pain.

PART ONE

PART ONE

CHAPTER ONE

Thirteen Years Earlier. Winter 1924

The Aeolian Hall on the third floor of 29-33 West Forty-Second Street: a spacious room with a broad stage and fan-shaped lamps that supported the side balconies. Kay, or Katharine as she was then known, thought of it as the home of the New York Philharmonic, but Paul Whiteman, the P. T. Barnum of New York's music scene, promised a different experience.

Whiteman was a big man in every way, with a basso cantante growl that he modulated as if riffing in the low range of a flügelhorn. He had telephoned her to insist that if there was one concert she and Jimmy could not avoid this year, it would be this one. "An experiment in modern music," he drawled. "New sounds. New rhythms."

"New pieces?" asked Katharine, sucking on a cigarette. "Or old pieces, newly arranged?" The former might interest her. The

23

latter might upset her. Some modern arrangers, imagining themselves superior to composers, disregarded their intentions.

"Entirely new pieces, Katharine," Whiteman assured her. "We open with a series of short works, sassy and moody and sweet to establish the mood. And then a big, spacious, exuberant piano concerto. The heart of the thing. George Gershwin."

"Gershwin? The songwriter?" *How could a songwriter compose a piano concerto?* The idea seemed ludicrous.

"Yes, that Gershwin," said Whiteman. "But no, not that vocation. We are not talking about a mere song, my dear Katharine. We're talking about Brahmsian lyricism, Joplinesque ragtime, rip-roaring Souza band music, all stewed together in one luscious gumbo."

Really? And just what does George Gershwin know about orchestration? Or counterpoint? The study of music, its intricate machinery, had been the focus of Katharine's youth. Of her entire life. If a song was a hot-air balloon, a piano concerto was a locomotive. Ask a balloon maker to build a train engine, he will not have a clue.

Whiteman, meanwhile, was charging ahead. "What we are talking about, Katharine, is jazz. Clarinet smears, muted trum-

24

pets, blue notes, misplaced rhythmic accents, rubbing up against modern chords and Gershwin's dizzying melodies. You of all people will appreciate this, with your perfect ears. Oh, and did I mention? Jascha will be there. And Sergei. And Igor. The warmth and good spirits of a family reunion. But even with these dear friends in attendance, what pleasure would there be without you and Jimmy? Where the gaiety, the wit, the sheer delight?"

"Oh, dry up, Paul," Katharine chuckled.

That was how he did it, though. Paul Whiteman thrust people together the way he hammered sounds together, with a brashness that bordered on boorishness, delivered with a wink and a smirk. Heifetz, Rachmaninoff, Stravinsky — anything but a family. More like a zoo. The carnivore division. How could anyone herd a grizzly bear, a Siberian tiger, a Eurasian wolf, and a *Tyrannosaurus rex* into one cage? Together with a few feral cats and a brood of starving rodents. Somehow, though, Whiteman got away with it.

"I'll have to check with Jimmy," said Katharine. But she knew they would go, if only for the illustrious company. They always did.

The trouble began before it actually started. Or vice versa. It commenced with the preparations. She and Jimmy were running late. Her strap pumps were too tight. One of the hidden buttons at the side of her silk column gown flew across the room and burrowed into the rug. Olga, her chief domestic, squinted and fumbled as she tried to align the clasps of Katharine's jet and crystal choker. Together they dug through hatboxes searching for her matching cloche. "You must have misplaced it," Katharine snapped. But then regretted her tone. Olga deserved better. She was one in a million.

"Here we are, madam." Like a magician Olga extracted the hat from a silver box. "And here is your velvet wrap."

"Oh, what would I do without you?" Katharine pulled the hat low as Olga draped the cloak over her shoulders.

Wearing a bespoke worsted wool suit that he had picked up on Savile Row four months earlier, reclining into the back seat of their chauffeured car, Jimmy opened the window a slit. "What's on the program?"

"Music." Katharine dabbed her lipstick with a handkerchief. "Music that Paul

Whiteman thinks terribly innovative and exciting."

"Well that narrows it, doesn't it," said Jimmy.

"*New* music," said Katharine, "brassy and lively, according to Paul. And finishing with a piano concerto that doubles as a New Orleans gumbo." She replaced her lipstick in her clutch and stretched her legs. "George Gershwin."

Jimmy frowned. *"La La Lucille?"*

"*La La* someone or other," said Katharine. "As if I followed these things." Which was misleading. She had seen the posters, if not the shows.

The theater doors were swinging shut when their driver released them. Jimmy escorted Katharine to their third-row places like a window dresser wheeling a mannequin. Katharine removed his hand from the small of her back and smiled as she waved to Jascha Heifetz's sister, Pauline.

They took their seats two rows behind Igor Stravinsky. Such a large head for a man who stood five-three in elevator shoes. Thank heavens, though, it was Igor and not Sergei. Rachmaninoff was taller, with a fuller head of hair than his rhythmically and harmonically more adventurous compatriot. Katharine opened the program.

George Gershwin has written a "Rhapsody in Blue," which he has consented to play accompanied by the orchestra. Delicacy, even dreaminess, is a quality he alone brings into Jazz music. His sense of variation in rhythms, of shifting accents, of emphases and color, is faultless.

Consented to play. She sniggered at Whiteman's too-clever wording. She had never met George Gershwin; indeed, never set eyes on him. But one thing she knew even then: the fellow did not shy from the spotlight. During the last few years she had seen his name clambering higher and higher on broadsheets for *George White's Scandals,* the long-running series of musical revues on Broadway.

Katharine did not care for popular music. She found it predictable and trite, boring really. She was certain Igor, Jascha, and the rest of Whiteman's validators shared her feeling. By inviting so many serious musicians, financiers, and politicians — no, not inviting them, corralling them — Whiteman was pegging expectations skyscraper high. But what fresh notions could show-biz hacks like Irving Berlin and George Gershwin possibly plant in the febrile mind that had birthed *The Rite of Spring*? And to lecture about "dreaminess, shifting accents, emphases, and color" with Sergei Rachmaninoff sitting in the front row — now that was what one of Jimmy's relatives might call *chutzpah.*

She closed her program as the audience lights dimmed and Whiteman waddled out to polite applause. She liked that word, *chutzpah,* probably because her husband loathed it, along with every other grimy expression his people had hauled through Ellis Island in their battered cardboard suitcases. (*My people? Perhaps,* Jimmy would grudgingly admit. *But not my immediate kin. Not any Warburg or Loeb. Our suitcases were crafted of Florentine leather, and we did not carry them. Our servants did.* Except that he would never actually utter such words. He would transmit them with a glance and a raised eyebrow.)

The concert began, essentially a series of popular songs without voice, scored for wind ensemble. Saxophones, clarinets, and trombones delivering squiggly marginalia to melodies by and large carried by the other horns. Dixieland spread its messy tentacles everywhere in banjo twangs, whistling, *oompah-oompah* tuba bass lines, and grandstanding solos, all delivered in strict four time and diatonic scales. How could anyone

29

express anything new and original, as Whiteman had promised, with such a paltry musical vocabulary?

It was celebratory music, entertaining, at times vaudevillian. She did, indeed, hear evocations of New Orleans brothels although she had never set foot anywhere near such an establishment. And of course, it went without saying, there was not a Negro in the house.

At intermission Katharine sipped a sarsaparilla, lemon, and cream soda; James clutched a tumbler of dry ginger fizz. Pauline Heifetz, in a knee-length print dress, sucked a pink beverage through a paper straw. Around them other guests chattered about mundane trifles, but no one mentioned their collective ennui or its cause, Whiteman's overhyped dud. Katharine enquired whether Pauline and her brother were free to join a group of mutual friends for dinner next Tuesday. "*Century Magazine* picked up one of Jimmy's poems." She slung her arm through Jimmy's. "It's so terribly exciting, we have to celebrate."

"Well done, Jimmy," said Pauline. "But I'm afraid Jascha and I will be traveling next week."

"Where?" asked Katharine.

"Oh, only everywhere east of New York."

Pauline sipped. "Everywhere that matters, that is. London, Paris, Rome, Berlin."

"Nice," said Jimmy in a tone that sounded, to Katharine's ears, more than a little patronizing.

"Jascha's touring," said Pauline. "Me, I'll be shopping. Shopping and drinking. *Il vino*'s still legal over there, you know."

"You must try a Biondi-Santi Brunello di Montalcino." Jimmy smiled at a memory. "Exquisite."

"Not everyone's a banker," said Pauline. "We'll settle for ordinary Frascati."

"Just you wait 'til they hear what Jascha does with Bach's D Minor Partita," said Katharine. "He'll be a smash. You'll be stuffing your trunk with Brunellos."

"Brunellos and shoes," said Pauline.

"And maybe a boyfriend or two?"

"You are so wicked." Pauline tapped her hand. "But no, I'm fine in that department. At least for the moment. I think."

"Who is it?"

Pauline smiled. "I'll give you a hint. He's in this theater right now."

"Then why are you standing here, gabbing with me and Jimmy?"

"He's busy. That's all I'm saying. You'll find out soon enough."

The room lights dimmed and they ambled

back to their seats. Katharine braced herself for continuing boredom. The stage lights rose and Paul Whiteman bowed. Everyone applauded politely.

George Gershwin strolled out, a tall man with pomaded black hair and a prominent nose. Attractive, certainly, but it was not about his features. It was the way he held himself; his bemused, blasé expression barely masking an underlying restlessness; his dark, soft eyes. All in all a coolness tinged with vulnerability and warmth. He wore his tuxedo like a shroud of sobriety. The finest evening attire, however, could not transmute a Tin Pan Alley tunemeister into a classical pianist. He lowered himself to the Steinway shoving his tails behind the bench. Whiteman raised his baton and that klezmer clarinet embarked upon its crazy discourse, complaining, wheedling, sulking. A hush fell over the audience. They had never heard anything like *this*.

At first, Katharine was not quite sure what to make of it. Then she realized she was holding her breath and wondered why she was doing so during a piano concerto, or whatever this was. How many concertos had she heard performed on this very stage? She could hardly count them. She exhaled. She inhaled again, and repeated the exercise until it felt natural. As natural as . . . as breathing. Or almost.

Gershwin played like a self-taught virtuoso. Everything was wrong, his posture, his fingering, the distracted expression on his face. But when Katharine closed her eyes and set aside all she had learned since early childhood about the code-bound ways in which individual notes, rhythms, melodic figures, and harmonic progressions were supposed to cavort with each other — when she allowed the music to justify itself — somehow everything sounded right, too. How could that be? She opened her eyes.

His fingers tapped the keys repeatedly; scurried up and down, passing each other; meshed together; flew apart to opposite corners of the keyboard. Swaying, smiling to himself, Gershwin appeared not to be thinking about his hands or the sounds they produced. Yet despite his apparent mindlessness each note sounded confident, even the phrases that conveyed wistfulness, longing, and sorrow. At times Katharine wondered whether Gershwin was improvising or performing passages he had meticulously composed.

She failed to notice the moment when the music persuaded her to stop thinking and just listen. What she heard then was a man pouring his heart out to the world. At the height of the soaring, lyrical passage two-thirds of the way through, Katharine forgot about the funny parts, the exuberant parts, the piano-against-orchestra quipping and cajoling parts. The sadness and beauty of it enveloped her.

She closed her eyes again and leaned back. For no particular reason she imagined herself drifting in a rowboat. The wavelets softly smacking its sides. Ribbons of undulating moonlight.

That was the moment when Katharine Warburg, née Katharine Faulkner Swift — and still Katharine Faulkner Swift deep inside — realized that something was lacking in her marriage. She tried to ignore the absurd claims of her heart. She did not know George Gershwin or what he intended to communicate with his music. This was lunacy. By all accounts, her husband was an extraordinary man.

She and Jimmy drifted the half block to their car. He tapped the window to wake the driver and opened a rear door for Katharine.

She slid open the window of the driver's compartment. "Twelfth Avenue. Across One-Hundred-Tenth. Down Fifth."

34

"Good lord," said Jimmy sliding in beside her. "It's a straight shot up Fifth Avenue and you want to drive over to the port, up to Harlem?"

"I'd like to see the water."

"At this hour? When I have a meeting with Andrew Mellon in the morning?"

"May I remind you?" asked Katharine. "The last time you met with Mellon, he was two hours late."

Jimmy shook his head and let out a deep sigh, his hands clasped on his overcoat. The driver twisted the key and the Duesenberg shook to life.

As the Hudson River came into view under a crescent moon, Katharine looked over the water to the Jersey shore, its lights, its Ferris wheel. She placed her hand on Jimmy's. He twisted toward her.

"You're going to get lucky tonight," she whispered.

Jimmy responded with a thin smile. "And to what do I owe this good fortune?"

She looked out toward the water, the Ferris wheel, and the crescent moon. "To that," she said.

The next morning, Paul Whiteman's *Experiment in Modern Music* was no more than a fleeting dream. Or so Katharine told herself as she glided down the curved stairway of their five-floor townhouse in her white robe, and through the main salon and hallway into the tiled kitchen with its high ceilings and tall windows.

"Morning, Misses Warburg." Lionel, their majordomo, poured a cup of coffee, with cream.

"And it is a lovely morning, isn't it, Lionel."

"Couldn't be better, ma'am. Couldn't be better."

Katharine sat down and peered at the news. It was Jimmy's habit to browse widely before heading to the office. On top, a one-week-old copy of the *Berliner Börsen-Zeitung*. It took that long for a newspaper to travel across the Atlantic, which made gazing at Europe through this lens somewhat like studying a distant star. What you were observing was the past of the universe, at least if you believed the famous theory of that disheveled whiz in Germany, Albert Einstein. Or what the newsmen wrote about it, anyway.

She saw splashy headlines about the legal woes of a young upstart named Adolph Hitler, whose coup plot had fizzled but whose trial was a smash. For Herr Hitler, it seemed, the courtroom was a stage on which to prance and strut, blaming "Jew bankers" for Germany's predicament. By *Jew bankers,* Hitler meant the Warburgs and a few other families whose offices filled fashionable belle époque buildings in Hamburg, New York, and London. For Jimmy, this news was personal.

Under the *Berliner Börsen-Zeitung* lay this morning's copy of the *New York Times.* She leafed to the Arts section and skimmed the review:

Rhapsody in Blue shows extraordinary talent . . . irresistible vitality and genuineness . . . a young composer with aims that go far beyond those of his ilk.

It had not been a dream, after all. The music surged back. She reread the article. But for all its praise, it failed to explain why the *Rhapsody* had moved her. Was it the music itself or something within her, a yearning that for some inscrutable reason attached itself to Gershwin's melodies? *It could not have been the music. George Gershwin! Just a songster.* Even the title, *Rhapsody,* was a dodge, as if to imply, *sure, it doesn't conform to the rigid structure of a classical concerto. That is deliberate.* But she had to admit, Liszt and even Brahms were

37

guilty of the same evasion.

And what of that other word, *Blue*? Synaesthesia, wasn't that the term? Associating sounds with colors? A reference of course to the blues, the musical style and the mood. Also, perhaps, to Picasso's famous *Blue Nude,* further suggesting sadness and modernity.

Leaving her cup half full, she went into the salon. She sat at the piano, attempting to retrieve portions of the composer's long solo.

Katharine possessed not only perfect pitch but also an unerring musical memory. To these aptitudes her parents had added the finest musical education money could buy, although in her case there had been no exchange of currency. Her conservatory schooling had been financed with scholarships and grants. Not that her father would have hesitated to support her ambitions, had he been able. Her technique meant more to him than his own. Her dreams were his.

Katharine could ramble through almost anything on the piano after hearing it once. The *Rhapsody,* however, proved different. So much of it was *wrong.* Although she still heard it, she found herself unable to reproduce it and grew frustrated with the effort. She had never learned how to play *wrong.*

38

She tried again; a different portion. The part that made her think of horses racing around a track. Failing to reproduce Gershwin's style, she bit her lip and gave up. She opened her book of Chopin's nocturnes and meandered through his thoughtful, introspective opus 9, number 1, a piece her father used to play when she was a child.

As Katharine's mind floated on the warm pond of Chopin's nocturne, her daughters April and Andrea dashed into the room accompanied by their governess, Miss Louisa, and Andrea's nurse, Miss Lainey. Katharine's hands paused midmelody above the keyboard.

April clutched a doll. Miss Lainey cuddled Andrea on her shoulder. Both girls were dressed up, their curls brushed, their shoes shined.

"Go ahead, say it," Miss Louisa instructed little April.

Sucking her thumb, April looked up at her.

"Say 'Good morning, Mama.' "

"Good morning, Mama," April recited.

"Come here, you little ragamuffin, so I can give you a smooch," said Katharine.

April glanced up at Miss Louisa, who nudged her forward. Katharine gave her a peck on the forehead.

Two-year-old Andrea struggled and

pointed. Miss Lainey set her down. Katharine opened her arms, but Andrea darted toward the gray cat on the corner table. The cat leapt off, dashed away, and squeezed under the sofa. Startled, Andrea began crying.

"It's all right," said Miss Lainey crossing to pick her up again. "It's just a kittie."

"We was going to go to the park," Miss Louisa informed Katharine.

"That sounds delightful." Katharine glanced at the window. "The weather is perfect, isn't it."

"It most certainly is," agreed Miss Louisa with a toothy smile.

After they went out, Katharine stared at the piano feeling blue and unfulfilled, chiding herself for resenting her children's interruption. *They are not that disruptive. They are adorable.*

She resumed playing, allowing her hands to guide her away from the present. She dipped into a Mendelssohn sonata, and another by Brahms, and finally traveled back to Beethoven. Music she found celebratory rather than contemplative.

Celebratory of what? Of their early days together. Hers and Jimmy's. Of their courtship. Of a languid summer day, seven years ago.

CHAPTER TWO

Summer 1917

A heathered sky. Sun-drenched grass and flowers. A sweeping lawn. Rolling hills. A sculpted garden of roses, hydrangeas, and peonies. Her short dark haircut and bangs framing her saucer eyes and high cheekbones, Katharine sat at a Steinway grand that had been rolled onto a plank dais for the occasion. Her friends Edith, holding a violin, and Marie, cradling a cello, wore long neo-Grecian dresses similar to hers.

On Katharine's nod they began plucking, bowing, and hammering: Beethoven's Opus 97, a piece Katharine cherished for the way it wove melancholy and playful motifs into one unified whole. Beethoven had composed it while recovering from an ill-starred love affair at a friend's lakeside retreat. Katharine heard this in the music: its composer's solitude, his slow healing, rambles along flowering trails.

The guests clustered in small groups under a vine-clad pergola and on the lawns and walkways. Under towering top hats, New York's bankers and politicians discussed the war in Europe, the price of steel, and *The Immigrant,* a new celluloidal dramedy by that diminutive British wunderkind, Charlie Chaplin. Between movements, as she glanced into her audience, Katharine noticed a striking young man with wavy black hair. He wore a naval reserve pilot's uniform that stood out in the sea of tailored suits.

At the break, Bettina Warburg approached. She was three years younger than Katharine but seemed older in her dowdy dress and hair bun. "How about a drop of giggle water for the keyboard whiz?" She led Katharine down the promenade. "Everyone is positively drooling over your performance."

"As long as they don't drool into the giggle water," said Katharine.

"We have measures to prevent that," said Bettina.

"Such as?"

"Corks." Bettina raised a bottle of Dom Perignon and handed it to a sommelier, who twisted it open with a muted pop.

"Is Margaret here?" Katharine glanced around.

Margaret Seligman, whose grandfather had financed the Union during the Civil War, had studied with Katharine at the Institute of Musical Art. Evidently burdened by a social-class obligation to master the rudiments of piano performance, Margaret had learned to execute a baroque trill and a legato slur with finesse, if not bravura. A dear friend of Bettina, she had recommended Katharine and the Edith Rubel Trio for today's entertainment.

"Margaret is attending an event at the art museum," said Bettina. "Invited me but museum appetizers bore me to tears." The sommelier poured the sparkling wine. "Anchovy canapés, celery olives, crabmeat croquettes, and whatnot." She handed Katharine a flute of champagne.

"Oh yes, museum events, terribly boring," agreed Katharine. "Unless you happen to fall into that small contingent of humanity, only about ninety-nine percent, that has never set eyes on a crabmeat croquette. Is that something they hit with a mallet over in England?"

Bettina laughed. "You are exactly as Margaret described you. Petite, proper, and *pétillante*."

Katharine understood the French term. *Pétillante* meant "sparkling, bubbly," and in certain contexts "quick-witted." And it was true that she enjoyed the challenge of a brisk verbal duel. In a contest of wits, the sparring partners, no matter their social milieu, stood on a level stage. Like piano performance, that was the kind of contest in which Katharine could excel. And although terms like *pétillante* hardly defined her, her public persona was all that the likes of Bettina and Margaret needed to know. Self-doubt and struggle were not concepts they could understand, but merriment and naughtiness they grasped with ease.

"Is that all she told you about me?" asked Katharine, remembering the time she and Margaret were caught smoking in a bathroom.

Bettina smiled. "She also said you were pretty, steel and silk, and tralala tralala."

"Steel and silk?"

"Graceful. Charming. Determined. It's a compliment."

Determined. Just the kind of thing a rich woman would say about a social climber, thought Katharine.

"We're cousins, you know," continued Bettina. "Margaret is a Loeb as well as a Seligman. And I'm a Loeb on my mother's side as well as a Warburg on my father's. And of course, Margaret will soon be a

44

Lewisohn, as well. Marrying Sam in February. Well, I'm sure you've heard about it. Sam's a lawyer. Went to Princeton. Also fancies himself an author. His sister Adele married Arthur Lehman, of the Lehman Brothers family."

Katharine nodded. Margaret Seligman's engagement to Sam Lewisohn had lit up the society pages. The monstrous stadium up at 136th Street was named for Sam's father. Not that Katharine bothered with the society pages — but her mother did. Aloud.

Much more important, for Katharine, was the involvement of Bettina's parents, Margaret's, and a few others in the financing of the Institute of Musical Art. The ink on Katharine's diploma had been purchased with Warburg, Seligman, Lewisohn, and Kuhn *gelt* — as had all her scholarships and grants. And here she stood a couple of months after graduation participating in their private affair, albeit not as an equal but as an entertainer.

And with good reason. She had been a star at the Institute. *The* star. Everyone expected her to become its first celebrity graduate. She still recalled the remark of the visiting German composer Gustav Mahler to her instructor, New York Symphony Conductor Walter Damrosch, following her command performance of Schubert's C Minor Sonata D. 958 at the age of ten. *"Dieses hier,"* said Mahler, pointing at her and nodding. "This one." Coming from the conductor of the Vienna Opera — and the composer of *Das Liede Von Der Erde* — those two words were as powerful a compliment as one could hope for in a lifetime. *No, not just a compliment,* she told herself. *A prophecy.*

The very idea of an American pianist ascending to the stratosphere of world-class musicians seemed outrageous to many. But that was precisely what her sponsors expected of her. For if the Warburgs, the Loebs, the Lewisohns, the Schiffs, and the Seligmans were passionate about any cause, it was the cause of American culture. Everyone agreed that America was emerging as the world's dominant economy, but if America sought the respect of the old continent, she would have to raise her unique voice above the din. And that could only be accomplished through artistic excellence. This was their mission, their pet charity, as Katharine knew. Indeed, through her trained hands, she was to be their emissary.

"Excuse me."

Katharine turned. The lilting voice belonged to the young man in the naval reserve uniform.

A handsome gentleman. No, *gentleman* was too grown-up a word, what with his boyish cheeks. His long thin mouth conveyed a *soupçon* of amusement. Katharine also detected a gravitas and energy in his fiery blue eyes, his square cleft chin, his assertive eyebrows.

"I wanted to express my gratitude, Miss Swift. And to thank Tina for luring you here." He held a tumbler of whiskey. It seemed too strong a drink for such a young mouth. "I'm an admirer of the Archduke Trio."

So he knew the nickname for Beethoven's Opus 97, which the composer had dedicated to his favorite student, Archduke Rudolf of Austria. Katharine cocked her head. "I didn't know navy boys fancied Beethoven trios."

He smiled. "Don't believe what you hear about navy boys. Especially officers."

"Oh, gee, so you're an officer now?" cracked Bettina.

"Soon enough, Tina. Or I should say not soon enough." He sipped his whiskey. "But sooner than not."

Bettina turned to Katharine. "Jimmy's

twenty, going on thirty-five. Always in a hurry."

"Well, isn't that grand," said Katharine. "Twenty is my favorite number. One of them, anyway. Matter of fact," she turned to Jimmy, "I happen to be twenty, myself."

"For me, being twenty is a disease, like mange or dropsy," he replied. "But the good news? We'll recover."

"Oh, did I mention? Jimmy fancies himself a champion tongue-wagger," added Bettina.

"Jimmy — ?" Katharine fished.

Bettina wiped her forehead with her napkin. "James Warburg, Katharine Swift. *Voilà.*"

"Your brother," said Katharine, looking for a resemblance.

"So they say."

"And they should know," observed Jimmy glancing at a gentleman with a wide, thick moustache, who wore a sober black suit and who was refilling his glass with soda water. His glistening bald dome, and the thinning black hair at the sides of his head, made it appear as if his forehead stretched all the way to his crown. Katharine recognized Paul Warburg, father of Jimmy and Bettina. She had seen him from a distance at a couple of Institute events. Like every student there she knew he was a director of the Wells

Fargo Bank and the chief architect of the Federal Reserve system, although she had no inkling what that was.

"Come here, Dad." Bettina waved him over.

"Thank you," Paul Warburg told Katharine, taking her hand and bowing. "We all appreciate your playing." In his German accent, *playing* sounded like *plenk*.

"Jimmy was just explaining how naval officers fancy Beethoven," said Bettina, covering Katharine's momentary loss as she tried to decipher what the older gentleman had just said.

"Bitte verschone mich," Paul Warburg told his daughter. Katharine, who knew some of Wagner's librettos by heart, understood his German more easily than his English. "Please, spare me." He bowed again to her. "Excuse me, I don't want another dispute *mit* mine son." And strolled away.

Katharine frowned. Until she realized she was frowning. And then she smiled. She did not wish to be caught frowning at anything Paul or any other Warburg had to say.

"The patriarch's in a flap," remarked Jimmy over the top of his whiskey tumbler.

"Why?"

"I suppose because out of all my various and sundry outfits, of which I own at least two, I happened to select this uniform." He pinched his lapel.

"He doesn't like the navy?"

"Oh, he has no beef with the navy. He just doesn't like what they do."

"What do they do?"

"They fight wars."

"Dad grew up in Germany," explained Bettina as if it were not obvious. "We have relatives there. Oodles of them, apparently. Wilhem the Second's one of his best friends."

"Or so he thinks," Jimmy said. A calico cat, wandering through the yard, rubbed itself against his leg.

"You don't think so?" asked Katharine.

"My opinion?" Jimmy picked up the cat and stroked its neck. "The Kaiser's hardly worth the effort. To quote Shakespeare, or to misquote him at any rate, he may have more wealth than hair, but he has more hair than brains."

"Misquoting Shakespeare should be punishable," said Bettina. And to Katharine: "It's a naval officer thing. Or should I say, a future naval officer thing."

Jimmy laughed. "A Harvard thing, actually."

Katharine smiled again, amused as much by Jimmy's arrogance as by his wit.

"You mean a Harvard crime," Bettina said. She turned to Katharine. "Well at least the Harvard part is real."

"Which part isn't real?" asked Katharine.

"The costume," said Bettina.

"You're not in the navy?" Katharine asked Jimmy, utterly confused.

Jimmy smiled. "I will be, soon enough."

"Well, you had me fooled," said Katharine. "Or your uniform did, anyway."

"I'm in training."

"What do they teach you in that training?" asked Bettina. "How to shine your buttons?"

"How to ignore insults," quipped Jimmy.

"A lot of good that'll do at ten thousand feet, with German fighter pilots shooting at you."

Katharine was starting to feel like an accessory to family discord. "Perhaps we should be winding up our break," she suggested, glancing across the lawn toward Edith and Marie, who stood talking to each other shyly.

The trio reassembled on the dais, adjusted their tuning, and launched into Schubert's Trio no. 1 in B-flat Major. Katharine performed with renewed spirit, hoping at least one person in her audience was actually listening.

So often she felt her role at events like this was to provide ambience. People associated classical music with aristocratic taste. As a result, the newly rich and the newly almost-rich, who aspired to an appearance of nobility, surrounded themselves with it, at least in society functions. Usually their appreciation stopped there. This crowd, though, was not newly anything. And Jimmy Warburg had recognized the Archduke Trio. So she played, perhaps, with a tad more sensitivity than usual.

Katharine's father had bequeathed to her a mission, to use sound for exploration as others might use a lamp, a compass, a machete, or a scalpel. Sounds could serve many purposes, but the one that had interested Sam Swift, and which fascinated Katharine, was a finely balanced tool, nuanced, elegant, and complex, for probing the human soul. Schubert had understood the capabilities of this tool. So had Chopin and Beethoven. To recreate their discoveries was to peel back the layers of human experience and expose its moist, pulsing heart. For this gift, and for a thousand memories, she felt gratitude to her departed father.

Glancing at Jimmy near the conclusion of the scherzo, she noticed him in spirited conversation with a woman whose hand lingered on his arm, a statuesque blonde whose back was turned to Katharine.

Jimmy's eyes, past the woman's shoulders, wandered to Katharine's. Her fingers delayed a run of triplets by a quarter beat. Nothing anyone would notice, other than Edith and Marie. And perhaps this young man in the navy costume.

"Do tell me everything," demanded Katharine's mother, Ellen, in her singsong Leicestershire accent.

Her hair swooped up and piled high, she reclined on the faded damask divan in her blue and pink kimono, which almost matched the old-fashioned flowered wallpaper. Although Ellen worked as an apartment décor consultant for well-heeled Upper East Side clients, she exerted little effort improving her own accommodations. In her left hand she held Booth Tarkington's latest novel, *Seventeen.* The upright piano, the bookshelves, the cupboard, the dining table, and the rug were shrouded in shadow.

All this, and the sweet, peculiar scent of Ellen's homemade furniture polish, a mixture of boiled linseed oil, turpentine, and vinegar, were as familiar to Katharine as her reflection in the mottled wall mirror. This was Katharine's home, the one place where she had always felt almost as comfortable as at the Institute of Musical Art. Until her father's death. Now these stodgy rooms felt as restrictive as an old corset.

"Everything about what?" she asked.

"Oh, come now, Katharine. A sip of verbena?" Ellen refilled the cup on her side table. "Why, your garden party, of course. The masters of this mysterious banking empire. Their great hall, or hilltop castle, or whatever extreme architecture such people dwell in."

"You make it sound so Gothic." Katharine put down her satchel and plopped into a dining chair.

"Well it is Gothic, isn't it. Very Bram Stoker, I'd say." Ellen handed her the cup.

"More like, the *Wall Street Journal*."

"Same thing," snorted Ellen. "Dreary fortunes; ominous accents; bloodthirsty old fogies."

"Otherwise known as gentility."

"Oh, they're gentile, are they?" asked Ellen.

Katharine sipped her infusion, choosing silence over a pointless dispute; preferring not to allow Ellen the pleasure of getting her goat.

"Why don't you tell me about their pooch," tried Ellen. "I judge gentlemen by

54

their dogs, you know. Do they even have one? An English setter, is it?"

Katharine shook her head. "They're German."

"Not bloody German shepherds, I hope, or those brutish Dobermans. Dachshunds?"

"I did spot a cat," said Katharine.

"Siamese? Abyssinian?"

"Calico."

"How terribly pedestrian. I suppose they figure if you have enough money, you can get away with anything. Which, alas, happens to be true."

Katharine set down her teacup. Her mother pretended to peruse her novel, looking up again as Katharine crossed toward her bedroom. "Any eligible gents?" she asked in feigned afterthought.

Katharine sighed. Her mother saw no contradiction in her contempt for bloodsuckers, on the one hand, and her desire to see her daughter advantageously wed, on the other. "It was a job, Mother. We performed. They paid us."

"Well, fine and dandy," said her mother. "You were paid." The unstated implication: *a lot of good your paltry, sporadic income does for us.*

Katharine went into her bedroom, shutting the door more loudly than she meant to. It was a tiny chamber crowded with a bed, a chest of drawers, and a padded bench. She did not bother rotating the Bakelite switch to the On position but removed her dress in the dark, slid under the sheets, and stared at the ceiling.

Maybe I should get a job, she thought, not for the first time. They were hiring at Wanamaker's. A meager salary but a regular paycheck. Maybe all her training was for naught. Perhaps the aspirations her father had instilled in her were mere vanity. After all, they had not served *him* too well, had they. She tossed in bed trying to quiet her mind. To sleep.

CHAPTER THREE

As Katharine sleeps, the memory of her beloved father, Sam, strolls into her dream, his features resembling the death mask he wore in his coffin a few years ago: chestnut hair, a gray-stubbled cropped beard, forehead lines smoothed in serenity. Although Sam Swift died abruptly at the age of forty-one, he had long before acquired an older man's wisdom and weariness, which remained visible in his eyes even in death.

Wearing lace-up boots, knickerbocker pants, a pleated jacket with leather buttons and a fabric belt, he sits on the bed. "Things look different from here," he tells his daughter as if gazing over the Hudson Valley from the Poughkeepsie Railroad Bridge.

"What do you see?" asks Katharine.

"The past. The future. Mountainous landscapes melted in a glassy uniformity. Men and women naked, shorn of the badges of consequence." He crosses his legs.

"How I wish I could be with you, Papa."

"You mustn't think that way. Not until . . ." He glances down, pursing his lips.

"Until? Do you know when I'll die? Do you know how?"

He lifts a flap of his jacket, removes a gold watch, and studies it. "The problem is that word, *when.* The hands move backward and forward and stand still all at once."

"But if there's no time," says Katharine, "there can be no music. That must be unbearable." She cannot conceive of a melody in which all the notes are played simultaneously, or not at all. Nor can she imagine her father dwelling in a world that has no operas.

"I didn't say there's no time." He sets the watch on her night table. "There are all sorts of time, an infinite variety, all at once or never. It's hard to express this in the language of the living."

She sits up on her bed propping the pillow in her back. "Do you know how I'll die?"

"You'll die of heartache, as everyone does. It spreads through one's days and years of stumbles, bruises, and scars and in the end one simply melts into the earth. But that's not why I took the trouble of visiting with you."

"You missed me."

He strokes his chin. "I do miss you terribly but that's not why I came, either. Do you remember the day you performed for my workers?"

She thinks back to that day ten years earlier, in 1907. "How could I not remember, Papa?"

And now she is a young girl in her father's factory in New Haven, the one that *his* father bequeathed to him. The One-Lock Adjustable Reamer Company.

During the train ride to this place, Sam has explained the purpose of the performance. He yearns to prove to his workers that he is a different kind of owner. He wants to show respect for their intelligence and sensitivity. He wishes to share his passion for music. Katharine knows however that more than anything, what he desires is to offer his daughter her first public stage. She has performed Mozart sonatas for her classmates' parents but this will be an opportunity to communicate across educational and social barriers. Even at ten, Katharine understands that although her father may possess no more money at month's end than his workers, he moves in a different milieu. He is, after all, the respected opera critic of the *New-York Tri-*

bune, a position that earns him little in pay but a great deal in honor. At least within a certain, admittedly small, social circle.

Having organized the transportation of a Baldwin upright to the factory floor, Sam allows the workers an extra hour of lunch break. They slouch in rusting chairs in five rows wearing smudged blue coveralls. Katharine enters in a new white dress, with bows in her hair, and curtsies.

Immersed in the stench of machine oil and men's sweat she performs Beethoven's *Moonlight Sonata.* A flawed rendition but a sincere one. When her fingers slip she glances at her father, who nods, *keep going.*

The workers listen respectfully, but little by little she loses control of the music. It develops a life of its own. Her hands cannot keep pace. Anxiety and panic seize her as she attempts to recapture and tame the notes.

Katharine hears the distant voice of her father's ghost. "When I look back on scenes like this, I see . . ." he searches for the word. "Leitmotifs. Music made of light that connects people and events."

Leitmotifs?

"Let me give you an example. Among the workers that day, in the fourth row of your audience, sits a man named Max Levant."

Katharine glances up from the keyboard and spots him. He smiles and winks at her. "He's the uncle of a boy about your age, Oscar," continues the voice of Sam Swift. "Your performance inspires Max, who in turn influences his nephew. Oscar grows up in Pittsburgh and becomes a brilliant pianist. Years later he enters your life, a friend of a friend who provides advice in a moment of confusion, when your life can veer one way or another. Neither of you knows that this moment flows from your performance at the One-Lock Adjustable Reamer factory. This is just one example. These leitmotifs, which connect distant people and events, they stretch everywhere, invisible to the living."

As in opera, thinks Katharine. The ten-year-old version of herself rises and again curtsies. The workers applaud, remove their chairs, and return to their lathes, grinders, and drill presses.

"These leitmotifs, these waves of light," says Sam. "The nodes they form where they meet."

The nodes?

And again she is riding in the New Haven Local, returning home. Sam is not with her but she still hears his voice. "A node. Where small vibrations that emanate from remote times, places, and beings encounter each other and give birth to harmonies that reverberate through the universe. Not a terminus but a station in a network of stations."

Katharine imagines piano strings vibrating simultaneously, creating overtones, chords stacked upon chords stretching all the way to heaven, some heard, many unheard.

"Sometimes, you're riding in the train of your life," says Sam, "and you come to a station."

The train stops. She disembarks and wanders along the platform. Another train squeals to a halt releasing a final puff of smoke. Katharine looks at the schedule board but the letters are garbled.

"You're not sure which one you're supposed to take. All you can do is guess. What are the criteria? Perhaps you should slip into the most comfortable train? Or the one that's departing soonest? Why not? You have to go *somewhere.* You see, you've lost your way, and it hardly matters what you do because until you remember your destination, if you ever do, you will remain lost."

Sam Swift kisses her forehead and leaves her bedroom. She hears him shuffling to the piano in the other room, where he begins playing Chopin's Nocturne, opus 9, number 1. The moonlight streaming through her window dims to blackness.

In the morning Katharine awoke feeling disoriented. At first she recalled only the tail end of her dream, wandering in a train station. But when she reached for her father's pocket watch some of the earlier portions drifted back. She remembered playing the Baldwin upright at her father's One-Lock Adjustable Reamer Company.

It had never actually taken place, that performance, had it? Although her father had indeed inherited the factory, tried his hand at running it, and failed.

That recital, though, was the kind of event he could almost have organized. Her dreaming mind may have hatched it but the egg of logic was all his: providing a stage for his daughter; dressing her for the occasion; trying to express himself to his employees through music, the language of the men he revered.

Katharine rarely prayed. If God existed, He surely had more pressing business than the yearnings of an unsettled young woman on the Upper West Side. But this morning she knelt at her bedside, clasped her hands together, closed her eyes, and confided to any spirit who might be listening about her yearnings. She did not desire wealth. She merely wanted to reach her destination as an artist. This was the train in which she was meant to be riding. She had to find the right track. Was that too much to ask? And if it was, why had she been given this burning sense of destiny?

She and her friends Marie and Edith waltzed and scherzoed through the most gossiped-about circles, but they were not her circles. Music was the only power she possessed, but although the Edith Rubel Trio had acquired prestige on the salon circuit, it might never provide her a living income or independence.

Among the wealthy, some owned Victrolas but no one would use one to entertain. That would be deemed vulgar and disrespectful. The use of a music machine would preclude the vital interaction between musicians and listeners. It would be tantamount to stepping into a respectable restaurant and ordering *homard à l'Armoricaine* or *coquilles Saint-Jacques* from an automat.

Thus, opportunities for musicians abounded. Wherever people congregated they expected sounds, organized according to the harmonic and rhythmical grammar of their place of origin, to set a mood and reinforce a sense of kinship. The Irish enjoyed their jigs, bursting with panache and gaiety; the Italians their soaring arias; the Poles their triple-time mazurkas and polonaises; the Jews their half-impromptu, minor-key clarinet and violin colloquies. Those who were partial to the tastes and manners of the modernist French elite opted for the tonally ambiguous aural poetry of a Debussy or a Fauré.

Katharine, Edith, and Marie performed in the salons and gardens of politicians, actresses, and playwrights. In the sprawling Madison Avenue apartments of Alva Erskine Smith Vanderbilt Belmont, well-heeled women congregated for a rally supporting their right to vote. Mrs. Vanderbilt Belmont, a stout lady with the nose and eyes of a Brueghel peasant, boasted of having shared exquisite moments with numerous gentlemen and more than one husband, most of them dim-witted. "Men are in no way superior," she assured her guests, rolling her *r*'s. "And as much as they need our guidance in the boudoir" — an observation that elicited titters — "how much more so in matters of the economy and warfare."

She introduced "the undisputed leader of our national movement," Carrie Chapman

Catt, who defended the women's suffrage movement against the accusations of those who claimed it was pro-Negro. "White supremacy will be strengthened, not weakened, by women's suffrage," Catt proclaimed.

Katharine had grown up in a pious Christian family. Grandma Gertie had composed hymns that were still sung in her church. Katharine's father had played the organ there. And there she had learned the stories of Abraham and Isaac, of Jonah and Leviathan, and of a Jesus who had suffered and died to atone for the sins of *all* humanity.

Of course women should have the right to vote. They were entirely equal to men. Why did people like Catt deny the rights of one group to buttress their credibility in supporting another? It came down to politics. Whatever Carrie Chapman Catt's personal feelings about Negroes, she needed the support of white supremacists.

Politics. Katharine despised the idea that to promote justice, one had to appease thugs. Tammany Hall, the corrupt political machine that ran New York, offered citizens some of what they desired but in the end their diligence was self-serving. Politics divided the nation and stoked enmity. Politics made a mockery of democracy.

The answer to the division and rage that politics fostered, she felt sure, was *shared culture.* The memories of a people, pickled in melodies. On a nod from Edith, the trio dove into Katharine's arrangement of the suffragist anthem, "Eliza Jane," and the room hushed.

Another afternoon, a half hour up the Hudson River Valley by chauffeured motorcar, they performed Brahms's Piano Trio no. 1 in the thirty-four-room Italianate mansion of Madam C. J. Walker. A colored woman who manufactured hair care products, Madam Walker had distinguished herself as the world's first self-made female millionaire. *Now that is something to be,* thought Katharine.

No less husky of frame than Madam Vanderbilt Belmont, Madam Walker had invited her neighbors the Astors and the Rockefellers, but as she told Katharine with a laugh, "unfortunately they had more pressing engagements. They did send their wishes. Not that I care a hoot." Several of her guests were more famous and venerated than any industrialist or real estate tycoon, including the man known as the greatest entertainer in the world, Al Jolson.

In an impeccably tailored suit, Jolson seemed to tower over everyone although he was of average height and build. Katharine sensed he was so in love with himself and his success that his face emitted some kind of invisible light. His booming voice, affected speech, outgoing manner, and hearty laugh stole his listeners' attention. Everyone gathered to hear his stories of travel by luxury liner and private railcar to San Francisco and Berlin, and of his audiences' fervor in those far-off venues. Her hands folded on the keyboard cover, Katharine participated in their collective dream of exotic realms, blinding limelight, and raucous applause.

But of all these soirées the most peculiar, to her mind, was a reception in the Lower East Side for a diminutive man with unruly raven hair, a goatee, and a flamboyant moustache, who hailed from Russia. The dignified woman who introduced him, Emma Goldman, told her poorly attired guests that "Leon Trotsky is terribly famous throughout Europe, where he is despised as well as adored as the irrepressible *enfant terrible* of the workers' liberation movement as well as their most persuasive advocate."

Trotsky climbed onto a crate. Frowning, he belted out one or two sentences at a time, waited for his translator, and resumed full-throttle about the servitude of the proletariat and their masters' weakness. Rather than sweep his eyes through his audience, he stared at one member at a time. Like Katharine's mother, but far more eloquent, he denounced the international bankers who sucked their lifeblood, mentioning among others the Rothschilds, the Schiffs, and the Warburgs, some of the very people who had recently hired Katharine, just a few hours' ride from the Lower East Side but a world away. Although he thought of himself as utterly unlike Paul Warburg, Trotsky too vehemently opposed American intervention in the brutal European War, which seemed endless in the late summer of 1917.

Trotsky's listeners, many of whom toiled in sweatshops for a dollar a week, spoke Yiddish, Ukrainian, Lithuanian, Polish, and Russian better than English. Katharine realized they must have stretched their resources to pay for her incongruous engagement, desiring to honor their illustrious guest with an up-tempo performance of Borodin's Piano Trio in D Major. A klezmer band would have been more appropriate, she thought. While Borodin's earthy, passionate music held undeniable appeal, it was infected with Russian nationalism. But then, these men in their ill-fitting suits, these women in their patched Saturday best, who could not afford the garments they manufactured, heard klezmer at bar mitzvahs and other religious celebrations nearly every weekend. They wanted to mark the distinctiveness of the occasion and its secular European flavor.

Trotsky's eyes alighted on hers. "But of all these injuries and illnesses," he was saying, "the worst violation perpetrated in the name of capital is the robbing of men's and women's very lives. Reduced to despair, they have no choice but to sell their souls."

His gaze roamed elsewhere but his words chilled her. She understood these people's apocalyptic dreams. No one gets to choose the conditions of their birth. Some grow up in mansions and others in tenements. Rare and far-between are the impecunious souls upon whom society bestows opportunities. Therefore society itself must be the problem, or a big part of it.

She had shared enough champagne and banter with millionaires, though, to know that being born rich was not in itself necessarily a moral stain. Perhaps John Rockefeller Jr., so often blamed for the Ludlow Mineworker Massacre, was indeed a scoundrel. But Jimmy Warburg seemed merely naïve.

Naïveté is not absolution, Trotsky would say, if he could hear her thoughts.

But as the image came back to her of Jimmy awkwardly clutching his whiskey, or chatting with a blonde admirer but gazing past her toward Katharine, she wondered whether Trotsky's reasoning was sound. If the poor bore no inherited moral burden, why should the rich? Weren't these revolutionary Socialists, rejecting the Bible in favor of *Das Kapital,* just substituting one form of original sin for another?

She smiled inwardly at the memory of Jimmy's lopsided grin and the way he petted his calico cat. The silliness of his pretentions. *Naval officer, indeed.* She smiled at her own foolishness for devoting even a moment's thought to him after all this time. How long had it been? More than two months, at least.

Following their brief encounter with Lower East Side socialist fervor, Katharine, Edith, and Marie walked to J. Ross Confectioners, where they topped off the evening with egg-cream sodas and schoolgirl titters. Their friendship required neither profundity nor wit. They had grown up together in the tight corridors and practice rooms of the Institute of Musical Art. When they performed, angels flitted between their hearts.

During bursts of inspired musicality, they dwelled harmoniously in the estate of the composer whose work they were performing. He — always a man, always European — had built his domain with his own hands. They were his guests.

In *real life,* though, Katharine, Edith, and Marie had their differences. For one, Edith and Marie found little to admire in the crowd that cheered for Leon Trotsky.

"Those fools," said Edith, sipping through a paper straw. "Don't they see? The socialist revolution is just another power grab."

"They don't want equality," said Marie. "They want revenge."

"You could say the same about the French Revolution," said Katharine. "But that Trotsky, he had this . . . this raw power, don't you think?"

Edith shook her head. "I thought him positively ugly."

"No one is asking you to marry him," said Katharine.

They giggled. Perhaps nervously, because the thought of it, any thought of marriage actually, posed a threat to their fragile consortium. Matrimony and its inevitable harvest of children and housekeeping might stress their triumvirate, their shared and exclusive dedication to music, their readiness to travel far away together, if necessary, at any time. *If only that time would arrive . . .*

Katharine's eyes wandered to the window and the gaslamp-lit street. All the white-hot discussions of inequality, war, and injustice had only made her feel peripheral and helpless. She would never reach her destiny, or contentment, in soirées, champagne, and propaganda although she might momentarily escape sadness and penury. The Edith Rubel Trio was at best a vehicle, not a destination.

Between her musical engagements, while her mother was out matching silk moiré wall panels with Jacquard-upholstered settees for newspaper tycoons and surgeons' mistresses, Katharine applied herself to her piano technique. As she sat at the keyboard cutting a trail through the forest of chords, a trance-like feeling washed over her, a refined blend of elation and melancholy. It almost felt as if her father were leaning against the wall behind her, his arms crossed, listening.

The brass doorbell jangled, signaling a telephone call — a real-world event. She sprinted for the hallway, where the candlestick telephone sat on a wooden stand. Mrs.

Grissom, a neighbor, cracked open her door, peeked through, and closed it again. Katharine pulled the earpiece from its holder and, clutching the stalk in her left hand, spoke into the mouthpiece. "Hello?"

"Soon-to-be naval officer Jimmy Warburg here. Remember me?"

She smiled and thanked heaven he could not see her smiling through the telephone. "How could I forget? No one in a navy uniform has ever misquoted Shakespeare to me before."

"Don't you worry, I can misquote more than that," said Jimmy.

"I'm all ears."

"Let's see. *Non so più cosa son, cosa faccio* —" His Italian accent was preposterous but the words were correct.

"Or di foco, ora sono di ghiaccio," Katharine completed the line. "But I'm afraid that's not a misquote. That's just a quote. 'I no longer know what I am, what I do; now I'm all fire, now all ice.' Mozart, *Le Nozze di Figaro.*"

"So it doesn't count?"

"Depends what you're counting."

"I'm counting other passionate opera lovers of my generation," said Jimmy. "And unfortunately I can count them on one hand. On one finger, in fact."

74

"That would be *moi,*" said Katharine.

"For better or worse. But the former, I hasten to add."

Katharine leaned against the wall. "My father was the *Tribune*'s opera critic. I spent my childhood playing backstage with Louise Homer's daughter."

"The contralto?"

"Among others."

"Well, that's swell. As a matter of fact, I happen to have an extra ticket for *Le Nozze di Figaro,* Thursday. Sorry, so last minute. Care to join me?"

"Thursday, Thursday . . ."

"The day before Friday and after Wednesday."

"Oh, that Thursday." Well, she was free — of course she was free — but she had her pride.

"Why don't we meet beforehand? Sam's Deli, Thirty-Eighth and Broadway. You know the place?"

"I lunch there all the time, pretty often anyway," she lied.

"It's settled, then. Six-thirty, sharp. Enough time to chat before the show."

"Va bene," she agreed.

As she hung up, Mrs. Grissom's door creaked open again. Enough that Katharine could make out the blue flowers of her housedress and her loose hair. Katharine smiled defiantly and the door slammed shut.

CHapter Four

Sam's Deli: wood-paneled walls; high, pressed-tin ceilings; fans; cigar smoke; waiters in stained, loosely tied aprons. Katharine arrived on foot and stood inside the big front window watching the carriages, the horse-drawn trolleys, the motorcars, the pedestrians' hats. The hard felt bowler, perched askew, denoting middle class aspirations, raised with a slight bow when its wearer greeted a woman. The wool cap, low on the forehead, of the working man with no pretensions. The flat straw boater with a seersucker jacket and a cane to twirl, indicating leisure and insouciance. The top hat, frock coat, and beard of the man of consequence. That was New York, for better or worse: rich and poor, Italian and Jew and Irishman, rubbing elbows at the intersection of tradition and modernity.

Jimmy pulled up in a five-passenger vehicle with robin's-egg-blue wheels, wide curved fenders, and a black cloth roof. The automobile vied for space curbside with two buggies, then halted in the middle of the road. As other drivers cursed, Jimmy stepped down to the street looking like a high school boy dressed for a class dance in his silk hat, black tailcoat, and patent pumps. Katharine glanced down at her long, plum-colored dress, the best she owned but a little dated. Would he notice? She smiled and adjusted her posture, trying to project confidence.

Jimmy navigated past a horse's rump to the sidewalk and through the pedestrians. The bells hanging on the door chimed as he stepped in. He waved away the driver and the passenger in the motorcar, which honked like a goose and rumbled off.

"Navy pals," he told her. "Both shipping off to officer school next week. Boy, will I miss those flyboys." He escorted Katharine to a dark-wood booth.

"And when are *you* shipping off?"

They sat down.

"They never tell you, no matter how much you bribe them." Jimmy placed his hat on the bench. "I've completed ground training. Go ahead, ask me about the ailerons on a Curtiss Jenny."

"Okay. Are they good?"

He laughed. "I certainly hope so."

"So . . . a couple of weeks? A month?"

"At most."

Well, that answers that. Not that she was expecting their camaraderie to lead anywhere. What a preposterous idea. Just about the only thing she knew about Jimmy Warburg was that he had access to more money than anyone she had ever met. And that he was handsome, of course. And funny, in a way. And a tad pretentious, like a boy posing with a serious expression in a suit that was a half size too large.

She wondered, though, whether there was the hint of a possibility in his mind that their nascent friendship might evolve into . . . something. After all, he had called her three and a half months after meeting her. He must have been thinking about her. He must have asked his sister for her number, perhaps even pestering Bettina until she dug it up.

"Why do you want it so much?" Katharine asked.

He scratched his cheek. "The navy?"

She nodded, although that was perhaps not what she really meant.

Jimmy leaned forward slightly, crossing his arms on the table. "An overbearing, aggressive empire has attacked our allies. Are

79

we supposed to avert our eyes?"

"And that empire would be . . . ?" This war was such a bloody mess. So many nations were involved. No one wanted it. Nevertheless, everyone had piled onto the fray.

"The Austro-Hungarian one." Jimmy allowed the waiter to pour their coffee. "A slice of apple pie, à la mode?" he asked Katharine.

"Sounds far too pleasurable," Katharine weakly protested, "to be entirely moral."

"What did Nietszche say about morality?" asked Jimmy. "A fiction used by inferior human beings to hold back the superior ones."

"Apple pie it is," agreed Katharine.

The waiter nodded and stepped away.

"There are personal reasons too," said Jimmy.

Katharine stirred sugar and cream into her coffee. "For going to war?"

He nodded. "I came to America as a child. This great country adopted me. Now she's asking for my help. Frankly, I consider it my duty to answer that call."

She sipped. "Your father disagrees."

"He sees no heroism in defending one's country." He tasted his coffee black.

"Ah. Heroism."

"Well, yes," insisted Jimmy. "Ever since

ancient Rome and even before that, the idea that there's virtue in exposing oneself to danger, to defend one's people — that has always been the highest calling, upon which civilization rests. The notion that the individual life, even one's own life, matters less than the culture, the history, the civilization."

The waiter set their pie with vanilla ice cream on the table.

"I suppose I can see merit in self-sacrifice, under certain circumstances," admitted Katharine. "But what about killing? After all, the people you're fighting share the same sentiments as you. Defending their culture, their history, all that business. Why should they die?"

He glanced at his wristwatch, a delicate jewel-like rectangle of gold with a beveled crystal. Katharine, who had never before seen a wristwatch, marveled at its compactness and beauty. "You're quite right," said Jimmy, slicing into the ice cream and pie with the edge of his fork. "Both of us are placing our destinies in the hands of the gods, as the Romans would say. Letting *them* choose the victor. That's the whole *enjeu*."

"The *enjeu*," echoed Katharine. It sounded French, but it did not appear in any Bizet libretto.

81

"The sport of it."

"So you see war as a game?"

"In a manner of speaking. Although that does trivialize it, doesn't it."

"Like a gladiator fight?"

"More like the *Ludi Romani,* scaled up to the proportions of modernity."

"You do have a way with words, Mister Warburg."

"Jimmy. And thank you. Poetry happens to be my passion."

"I didn't realize we still lived in ancient Rome." Katharine tasted a forkful of pie and ice cream. "That explains a lot."

"We're all heirs of Rome," said Jimmy.

She grinned, finding this statement even more ridiculous than the Lower East Side Trotskyites' predilection for the music of Borodin.

His face eased into a lazy smile. "Let's enjoy each other's company while we can, shall we?" He placed his left hand atop hers on the table.

And what precisely did he mean by that? She withdrew her hand. No well-bred lady would accept such a proposition without questioning her companion's intentions. But she did not wish to discourage him, either. "That would be lovely. Within the constraints of my schedule, and of propriety, of course."

"Your schedule?"

"The Edith Rubel Trio. Some of us work for a living." To soften the sarcasm, she returned his smile.

He nodded but she suspected he did not understand. How could he imagine what it was like to be the daughter of a working mother who could never earn enough to cover rent, food, and other necessities?

They strolled afterward to the opera, where they sat close to the stage and centered. The music and spectacle entranced Jimmy, who laughed full-throatedly at its inspired silliness and briefly clutched Katharine's hand at the end, when the count begs forgiveness of his wife, whose affections he has so doggedly tried to betray. After the show, Jimmy hired a horse-drawn phaeton and accompanied Katharine home. As the horse clipped north on Broadway, he sang aloud: *In qual laccio cadea?* "What trap have I fallen into?" His pitch was so wavering that Katharine had to suppress a grimace, but she answered good naturedly with an aria of her own:

Porgi, amor, qualche ristoro,
Al mio duolo, a'miei sospir!

"Oh, love, give me some remedy for my sorrow and my sighs." Jimmy laughed, delighted, as the carriage trotted to the curb in front of her mother's apartment. *We can have a jolly time together, can't we,* thought Katharine as she bade him good night. He held her hand as she stepped down, bathed in the warm glow of a gaslamp.

They met again a week later at the spacious, crowded, noisy Café des Beaux Arts on West Fortieth Street. It was the second time Jimmy had seen her in her plum dress but he hardly noticed.

They sat at a small table. The waiter approached. "Chablis and oysters," said Jimmy. Then, as if realizing he was not alone, "will that be okay?" he asked Katharine.

She had never tasted oysters. But she nodded.

Resuming the conversation they had begun at Sam's Deli, Jimmy mused about his ambitions and frustrations. "America's about to roar into this conflict in Europe. They need me in the cockpit, not on the ground in Delaware. I should be buzzing over Pensacola. Hell, I should be on a boat heading to Belgium. What are they thinking?"

"I'm glad you're here," tried Katharine, who thought it absurd to see war as a social event or a rite of passage. At the same time she enjoyed Jimmy's candor, especially perceived through a haze of Chablis.

"Well if I have to be on the ground, I can think of no better company."

That was Jimmy. Occasionally he would say something that would melt her stockings, and then move on.

The waiter returned, and Katharine tasted raw oysters for the first time. Salty and acrid with a slimy, runny texture. She grimaced and washed them down with wine.

"In college," Jimmy told her as the waiter refilled their goblets, "my focus was history, but music and English literature vied equally for my affections."

"A man of many loves," observed Katharine.

He nodded. "My classmates elected me class treasurer. Why? I never asked for the honor. Economics wasn't my passion."

"It must be tough, being a Warburg," she said in a tone of mock pity.

"Well, it is, actually. Anyway, that was yesterday, and the skies of Belgium are tomorrow, and now is now, so there's nothing to do but celebrate our youth." He held up his glass, she held up hers, and they clinked. He sipped. "Do you enjoy dancing?"

"Why, yes, of course. Doesn't everyone?"

Jimmy charioted her not to a ballet or cotillion but up to a Harlem ballroom crowded with sweaty Polish, Italian, and Irish immigrants, colored folks, blaring saxophones and trumpets, and an out-of-tune upright piano used primarily to emphasize the beat and to gesticulate in tinkling musical adornments. A palace of commercialized leisure where people who worked hard could play hard. More specifically, the dungeon of that palace, a basement bursting with cheap liquor, socially stratifying brawls, and furtive dalliances. The last place where Katharine would have expected a Warburg, a Harvard man, to unwind.

Her fox-trot left something to be desired, as did his, but the wine they had enjoyed with dinner, combined with the vigor and agitation around them, made it all more than tolerable.

"Boy have we got a treat for you," announced the bandleader, who looked so juvenile Katharine wondered how he had slipped past the bouncer. He introduced a colored lady in a hat and flowing long dress just up from Atlanta named Bess Smith.

"And she's gonna yodel a toe-tapper by a fella calls himself Irving Berlin." He pronounced the name *Oivin Boylin.* "I think ya know the guy."

Everyone cheered. The band started playing. Hands and feet flailed. And then the bandleader stopped them, waving his arms. "No, no, no," he told them. "That ain't what we're doin' here tonight. We ain't here to dance. That we can do any night. We're here to *crazy dance!*"

The band resumed playing, more up-tempo, and this plump, unprepossessing Southern woman belted out a song called "I've Got to Have Some Lovin' Now."

The beat was as asymmetrical as the rhyme, and the music as lively. Giddy with the scent of booze and Jimmy's Rhineland cologne and the wild primitiveness of the music, Katharine waved away all sense of propriety and decided to make a fool of herself, flinging her arms and feet like a drunken frog. *Crazy dancing,* the recent discovery of a culture in flux. Perhaps not Katharine's culture, or Jimmy's either, but that made it all the more exhilarating.

Her exposure to dance had taken place solely within the context of musical instruction. The pedagogues at the Institute had emphasized the physical basis of musical rhythm. In order to perform Telemann, Vivaldi, and Bach, one had to master the seventeenth-century bourrée and gavotte; for Liszt and Schubert, the nineteenth-century quadrille and the waltz. In a spirit of magnanimity and with a nod to modernity, her teachers had also introduced their charges to risqué newer dances, the tango and the fox-trot. However, Victorian restraint had cast its shadow upon these academic gyrations. No one had mentioned the correlation between musical pulse and sexual thrust. Females danced with females; males with males. Within such pairings, physical attraction was unthinkable.

"How do you know this place?" she shouted to Jimmy after Bessie Smith finished, while everyone was clapping, stomping their feet, and whistling.

"Navy fliers know how to whoop it up!" he shouted back.

"I'll say!" But she wondered what he meant, what kind of dissolute life he was leading at the naval reserve's air pilots training camp in Delaware.

When a man, wobbly with giddiness and booze, bumbled into her, she fell into Jimmy's arms. They looked into each other's eyes and broke out laughing.

■ ■ ■ ■

"Katharine, a gift from your beau!"

She opened her eyes. It was morning. How early, she was not sure. But too early, anyway, based on the street sounds and the blush of light on her wall.

"My beau?"

"Mister James Paul Warburg," chirped Ellen. "I'm setting it on the table. Quite sumptuous, really."

Katharine heard her mother close the door and traipse downstairs.

She tried to fall back asleep but the Angel of Curiosity, an old and irritating acquaintance, grasped her dangling hand and yanked her out of bed. As she tightened the belt of her robe she noticed the spray of roses and tulips on the dining table. The swirled crystal and silver vase that held them. And, tied around it with a ribbon, James Paul Warburg's calling card.

That's it, she thought with a grin. *I've snared the rascal.* And then: *Or has he snared me?*

Although it was an expensive long-distance call, she tried to telephone him at the training camp in Delaware to thank him. The male operator took the message. She fixed herself tea, sat contemplating the vase, and attempted to lasso her febrile imagination and pull it down to terra firma. But lassoing, like riding bucking mustangs, remained a foreign and exotic art. She imagined herself on a horse, riding through the desert in Nevada, then smiled at the inanity of her random thoughts. Where did such thoughts come from? Random thoughts were like dreams. They came from somewhere faraway.

Like music. Another random thought — which she hurriedly dismissed. Music was rational. Otherwise, what was the purpose of her entire education?

As she gazed at the vase on her table her thoughts returned to Jimmy. She had shared memorable moments with a young man who valued music and poetry, who enjoyed life, and possessed the means to do so. But where would it lead? If Jimmy was infatuated with her, as his occasional sidelong glances and this crystal ornament suggested, the consequences were insubstantial so far: a plate of oysters, a carriage ride, a few songs.

Mulling over Jimmy's possible intentions, she walked to the New York Public Library, where she had spent countless hours as a student poring over musical scores by Bach,

Mendelssohn, and Richard Strauss. There she found the name *Warburg* peppered throughout the vast card catalog. With five books under her arm, and as many periodicals, she located a seat in the reading room.

As Bettina had mentioned, Jimmy was the scion of three powerful banking families, the Warburgs, the Loebs, and the Schiffs. The Warburg branch traced its lineage back to Anselmo del Banco, the most successful moneylender in 1500s Venice. Today, they occupied a lofty but precarious position at the pinnacle of European society. After immigrating to America, Jimmy's father Paul had helped create the Federal Reserve System. That made him one of the most influential bankers in his new country. Even in the land of freedom, however, powerful voices objected to the notion that an immigrant could wield so much sway. At issue was the question of loyalty. Foreigners might retain affection for their homelands. To empower them was to expose America to vulnerabilities.

Katharine appreciated the Warburg family's role in cofounding and supporting the Institute of Musical Art. But like other students, she had regarded them as aloof and mysterious.

The person seated to her right was peering through his wire-rimmed glasses at a battered copy of Thorstein Veblen's *Theory of the Leisure Class,* taking notes. Katharine smiled, remembering how her father had cherished that book, and often alluded to it.

Sam Swift had inserted aphorisms into her piano lessons. "They need to spend, you see. They really have too much. Spending confers status. Let them disburse their excess on your work. Let them see you as a *marque de prestige,* but never become a slave of fashion."

She returned her reading materials to the circulation desk, wondering how Sam Swift would have reacted to the thought of her dating Jimmy Warburg. Sam had so many qualities: his idealism, his devotion to music, his restless intellect. But his disdain for conspicuous affluence and power was deep-rooted, perhaps more emotional than rational.

His position as a connoisseur of *serious music,* his accomplishments as an opera critic and church organist, had conferred upon him a limited sense of achievement. Now Katharine wondered whether one of Sam's fundamental beliefs was valid, after all. Did artistic freedom, integrity, and pride necessarily imply poverty? And if they did, was the trade-off worth the indignity?

"Did you need something else?" asked the librarian as Katharine lowered the books to the counter with a thud. With a pencil moustache and a gold watch chain dangling across his tweed vest, he gazed over the rim of his narrow glasses.

"Oh, no — I mean, yes," said Katharine.

The librarian smiled and waited for her to continue.

"You see," said Katharine, "I've spent a great deal of my life in this library. It's like a second home for me. The staff has always been so kind. And so I was wondering . . . I'm a pianist, you see. But work has been terribly inconsistent, or perhaps it's the war in Europe, or . . . well, what I'm saying is, do you think there might be a position for a girl like me in this place?"

The librarian's lips curled, revealing tobacco-browned teeth. "This isn't how you go about procuring a position in our storied establishment, darling. Telling me your saga will land you precisely nowhere because as much as I might be inclined to help, I have no say in that matter — or any other matter, for that matter. But you're free to hop down to Personnel if that would tinkle your chime."

Katharine nodded. "Thank you."

She had never ventured to the library

basement, a labyrinthine crypt devoid of wainscoting, windows, and the dusty odors of decaying manuscripts. In Personnel a single Edison bulb dangled from the ceiling, insufficiently lighting the brick-and-mortar walls. A cloud of stink drifted from a cheap cigar, which hung on the lip of a stocky man who hunched over an oak rolltop desk staring at a handwritten page while pecking at a Williams typing machine. "Yeah?" he grunted.

"I . . ." She swallowed. "I wondered if there were any employment opportunities in the music department?" She smiled. "I'm a pianist, you see, and —"

He pointed to a basket of application forms and pencil stubs and turned back to his task. So preoccupied with transcribing words, this man did not seem to enjoy uttering them. She scribbled her name and address. When she reached the Skills section, she gazed blankly at the page in front of her:

☐ Knowledge of Dewey Decimal Classification System
☐ Phone Switchboard Operation
☐ Stenography
☐ Typing
☐ Alphabetical Filing

A mischievous fairy took hold of her hand, preventing her from applying pencil to paper. Another of those invisible creatures with whom she was all too familiar, like the Angel of Curiosity. She bunched up the application form, tossed it into the wood-slatted trash basket, and strutted out.

Fifth Avenue thronged with motorcars, buggies, and elegant shoppers, some already wrapped in furs. She ogled a store window that featured a set of Lenox dishes described as Gold Ground Botanical Service Plates. Lilies, anemones, and wisteria adorned this refined dinnerware, their leaves streaked in the hues of one-hundred-dollar bills. Along the edge of each dish was a thick, veined band reminiscent of Nefertiti's bracelets. She felt as if she were gazing through a telescope at a distant continent where flowers never faded, gardenias exuded no fragrance, and beef gravy never smeared porcelain. *Who could eat on such a plate?* she thought. *But why, oh why, am I staring?* She pried her eyes away and dragged herself toward the Fifty-Third Street subway.

A steamy aroma of lamb chops, onions, butter, and potatoes suffused her mother's apartment. Ellen sat at the table spooning mint jelly onto her pink stoneware plate. As

Katharine stepped in, she looked up and smiled. "Just in time!" Ellen pointed to an empty chair. Katharine lowered her satchel, slumped into the chair, and helped herself to a lamb chop.

"Lately you seem distracted, dearie." Her mother's eyes softened. "Did something bite you?"

"It's nothing," said Katharine.

"A vampire," said Ellen. "That's what bit you."

Katharine served herself mashed potatoes and onions.

"What was his name again? Warburg, that's it." Ellen glanced at the vase on the mantle. The roses and tulips were long gone. "James Warburg."

Katharine sawed at her lamb chop. Overcooked, as usual. She chewed.

"Has he proposed to you yet? I had an inkling it'd come to this. More than an inkling. A presentiment."

"Please, mother."

"Well what is it, then? Out with it, or I'll be conjuring castles and pumpkins 'til midnight."

"Oh, that will help."

"You're my only daughter, Katharine," Ellen pleaded, shooting her a what-else-am-I-to-do? look.

"Guys like him . . ." Katharine shook her head.

"They're just human," said Ellen.

"There are lots of girls out there," said Katharine.

"Not like you, luv. Warburg or no Warburg, he damn well knows it. Where'd he take you this time?"

"I went to the library. I thought maybe . . . a job . . ."

"Hah! The future Misses James Warburg shelving books, organizing card catalogs. That's a jolly one."

"Honestly, Mother."

"What else am I to make of *that*?" Ellen glanced again at Jimmy's gift. She rose, took the vase in her hands, and turned it upside down. "Glasfabrik Johann Loetz Witwe," she read. "That's the place of manufacture. And this is the signature of the artist, Karl Witzmann. An authentic German treasure. Even a wealthy man wouldn't gift such a masterpiece to a mere friend. Especially a wealthy man."

Katharine chewed.

Ellen replaced the vase. "You're going to do it, you know. You're going to tie that knot — around your neck. Or should I say, that diamond choker. And then, whatever post you've managed to hitch yourself to in the meantime, assuming you do find a position in a boot factory or at a makeup counter, or entertaining Tommies at the front — they adore Fauré, you know — will seem as meaningless to you as a newspaper that's been left in the rain, with its ink running onto the sidewalk. And however much small change you've eked out, you'll stare at it in your hand and giggle at the foolishness of it all. The sad joke that is the condition of the laboring class."

"I have absolutely no idea what you're jabbering about," said Katharine.

"Mind you," her mother went on, regaining her place at the table, "you'll be wrong. There's nothing foolish about hard work. The muddy laborer who hauls home his deer hide and his pack of Gauloises at the end of a backbreaking day is going to savor that pittance every bit as much as you will enjoy polishing your pearls."

"His deer hide and his Gauloises?" repeated Katharine incredulously. "You've been reading too many French Neanderthal romances."

"Actually he'll enjoy his pittance more than you'll enjoy your pearls, because it was acquired honestly."

"Since when did you become a Socialist?"

"We're not debating economics," said El-

98

len. "We're discussing psychology. How are the onions?"

"Mmm," said Katharine.

"I know you love them fried in lard with pepper." Ellen chewed absently for a moment, glancing at the door. "You'll miss that, won't you."

"I'll miss what?"

"Why, my cooking. The wholesomeness of it. The warmth. The . . . the lard." Ellen smiled.

I won't miss it one bit, thought Katharine. But she returned her mother's smile.

One foggy morning in late November she received what at first seemed to be a monogrammed invitation: "Mister and Misses Felix Warburg request the honor of your presence at a gala soirée to be held at their Fifth Avenue residence."

She realized soon enough that this was not a request to attend, but a professional engagement. At the bottom of the card, Bettina Warburg had scrawled, "Just piano, please. Same terms as the Trio. (Except all for you.) Game? Hugs, Bettina."

At the library, Katharine had come across the name Felix Warburg, Paul's brother and associate and Bettina and Jimmy's uncle. She would have preferred to have been invited as Jimmy's guest. But a gig was a gig, and what felt like an indignity was in fact an honor.

The trees were bare and Central Park dreary and chilly, but as she crossed on foot she felt increasingly resigned, and by the time she reached Fifth Avenue she had managed to convince herself that the evening should be pleasant. And if it wasn't, the money would be.

The French Renaissance Revival mansion stood six stories tall and stretched the entire block from Ninety-Second Street to Ninety-Third. Large carriages and motor vehicles lined the street, bathed in radiant new electric lights. Footmen offered white-gloved hands to ladies stepping down to the sidewalk.

Silk-upholstered Louis XV furniture and oil portraits adorned the marble-floored entrance. A liveried doorman announced the arrival of "Miss Katharine Faulkner Swift." Felix and Frieda Warburg shook her hand. Unlike his dour brother Paul, Felix had a full head of hair and a sardonic twinkle in his eye. His moustache was bushier than Paul's and his smile warmer, but Katharine was not sure he or his wife knew who she was. Bettina hurried over.

"Where's your music?" she asked.

"In here." Katharine tapped her head.

Relieved, Bettina pulled Katharine to the Bösendorfer grand.

She decided to play Franz Liszt's *Un Sospiro,* a beguiling étude fit for a spacious, bright room with tall windows and chattering guests. Soon she lost herself in the music, the piano notes weaving themselves into and through the guests' words. As she raised her hands at the last chord the butler mumbled into her ear. "Mister Paul Warburg would like to have a word with you, Miss Swift."

She followed his gaze across the room. Jimmy's father sat on a window bench, studying her. She recognized his bald pate and big moustache. Rather than loom above him, or risk impropriety by crouching in front of him, she dragged a chair over.

"Thank you for this, Miss Swift." He gestured toward the piano.

Katharine smiled.

His dark eyes fixed hers. "I believe my son has taken a fancy to you."

He paused, waiting for an answer, but she was stumped.

"You come from such different backgrounds." He shook his head. "He is young. So are you. I want to know your thoughts."

"We've shared some interesting conversations, Mister Warburg," said Katharine. "We saw a couple shows. Shared a couple meals. Discovered mutual interests." And she added, "I sense you're worried."

"You hardly know my son. He is impulsive and sometimes . . . *flüchtig.*"

"Volatile?"

"It's not that I do not think you're a nice girl. You seem to be good-natured. Polite. A skillful pianist. But Jimmy and you?" He shrugged.

"Isn't Jimmy heading for the front?" she asked.

"We shall see about that."

Katharine attempted a smile. "Mister Warburg, just so I understand, are you suggesting Jimmy and I shouldn't be friends?"

He did not smile back. "I have nothing against friendship. But what you see as friendship may not be what James has in mind."

"You're asking me to warn him that romance isn't in the cards?"

"Not in the cards?" He shook his head. "I'm asking you to throw away the deck."

She detected a hint of superiority, even contempt in his tone, in his inability to accept his son's potential interest in her, in his confidence in his powers of observation and persuasion. But she simply repeated his words. "Throw away the deck?"

The slightest nod, but an authoritative one. "Never see him again."

Katharine was at a loss for words.

"To be perfectly clear," he added, "we are discussing a financial transaction." *Trenssection,* as he pronounced it with his German accent. "One that can free you to focus on your ambition." *Embition.* He lowered his face and looked her in the eyes with the flair of a poker player engaged in a high-stakes bluff. "For many years. The time a wonderful artist like yourself needs to develop her reputation. And I will personally help you with that, as well."

Stunned by Paul Warburg's injurious proposal, Katharine glanced across the room toward Jimmy's mother. Taller than her husband, Nina Warburg wore a single strand of gray pearls and a sapphire-and-platinum wedding ring — together, surely worth more than all of Ellen Swift's worldly possessions. Mrs. Warburg's posture conveyed assurance and elegance. She clutched a tumbler of sparkling water as she earnestly listened to a guest, who was relating some long-winded story. Her face expressed both intense interest and utter boredom.

I could never hope to be that kind of woman, Katharine thought. And Jimmy's father was discouraging her from trying. Besides, Jimmy had never actually suggested their friendship might point to romance.

All that on one side of the equation. On the other, a financial *trenssection*. One that would enable her to focus on her *embition*. More time to devote to music. Resources to rent her own flat. Yes, his offer was insulting. It implied that Katharine's emotional entanglements were just another commodity to be bought and sold. The dignified response would be to reject Paul Warburg's conditional patronage. *But to hell with dignity.* At stake was her mother's well-being, not to mention her own, and perhaps her career as well.

As she mulled all this, the front door swung open and Jimmy stepped in wearing pin-striped brown slacks, a brown vest, a Harvard club tie, and a white shirt with a high collar. His jaw set, his eyes lit with fury, his hair disheveled, the tall young man looked dashing, especially in contrast to the other guests, who in addition to being older were all attired in black, navy, and gray. As a servant closed the door, Jimmy scanned the room and steamed over to his father.

"I thought you were in Delaware," said Paul Warburg.

"I left," Jimmy told him, "after my commander admitted I was wasting my time, that I would never be drafted into the officers' corps. That it was beyond his control. Beyond his control, Dad!"

Paul Warburg blinked. Twice. "More than ten million dead, James. Ten million! And for what?"

Jimmy crossed his arms. "So you admit it, darn it."

"I spoke with some people. How could I not, my son?"

"And you don't see anything wrong with that? Thwarting my ambitions? My independence?"

Paul Warburg averted his eyes and combed his moustache with his fingers. "I do see something wrong with it," he admitted. "But I see something wrong with silence as well."

Jimmy stormed over to the bar, where he demanded a whiskey. Paul turned back to Katharine. "You see?"

The other guests pretended not to notice as Jimmy stomped back outside, squeezing his tumbler like a perfume vaporizer. In that moment Katharine forgot about Paul Warburg's offer and about decorum and rose to follow Jimmy outside.

He glanced at her as if he had expected her. "That's it." He leaned against the wall staring across Fifth Avenue, where a big motorcar lumbered by. "It's over."

"Your father is right. You could have died."

He turned and looked at her, his eyes vibrant and probing. His mouth twitched. His hair fell on his forehead in a rebellious side bang. In his moment of exposure, of weakness, she yearned to touch him. Before she could act upon this impulse, however, he pulled her close and kissed her.

She squirmed. This was not acceptable behavior in her circles. At least, not under the glaring city lights.

Then she yielded.

CHAPTER FIVE

As a girl, Katharine had been an early riser. The crank-start grindings, scrapings, honks, and whistles of a great, still-young city bursting to life had roused her. In autumn the first rays of dawn pinked the far wall of her bedroom. Every new day was a territory to explore.

Since graduation, her morning routine had changed. Her mother took appointments first thing, visiting clients' lodgings to assess their taste and their pocketbooks. Having invented the vocation of apartment décor specialist, Ellen had few competitors, but the upper middle class, her clientele, had not quite caught on. The very wealthy bought their furniture in Europe, where graduates of the École des Beaux-Arts, affecting admiration and friendship, solicitously guided them through museums and explained the difference between a Louis XV chair and a Mucha print. The less wealthy yearned for furniture that suggested luxury without the hassle or expense. Ellen's British accent lent her cachet and authority, but no one had heard of an apartment décor specialist and half her job consisted in explaining the concept and its utility.

When she had no appointments Ellen strolled to Eliza's Tea and Biscuits, a picturesque refuge on the other side of Central Park. Despite her professed sympathy for the downtrodden, Ellen preferred to take her Ceylon Black in elegant neighborhoods. As a result, if Katharine lingered in bed until eight-thirty, she had the flat to herself.

And so she perused *Anna Karenina* or *Madame Bovary,* drifted back to sleep, contemplated her uncertain future, and ruminated about the song or string quartet she was composing — the obscure mathematics of harmony, the clever ways she might twist and spin a melody. Sometimes, in this semiconscious state, she felt she was gliding on a lake on a sunny day. Other times she was gulping water. She cherished the solitude and peace but chided herself for her laziness, then congratulated herself for it.

Beauty, or the contemplation of it, was a leisure-time pursuit, a luxury. What would

108

life be, devoid of such little sins? She thought of Débussy's "Rêverie," the self-indulgence and dissipation implicit in the title itself. Had music of more exquisite clarity, evocativeness, and lavender fragrance ever been penned? Beauty and Idleness were fond companions, Pleasure and Sensuality their love children. When the ancient Greeks contemplated Beauty they visualized naked human forms: Aphrodite, Adonis.

This was the sort of circuitous path her thoughts took on a typical morning. It led to no destination. But this was not a typical morning. This morning her ruminations led her back to Felix Warburg's mansion, Paul Warburg's gall, and Jimmy's kiss.

At the age of twenty Katharine Swift remained a virgin, emphatically so, but she could hardly help imagining what lovemaking would be like, or should be like. A summer picnic on a mountain top. Diving off that summit and sailing in the wind. Wild and extravagant, natural and invigorating.

A sharp *click* interrupted these musings. Then another.

She peered at the gold pocket watch on her nightstand. It was ten fifteen, technically rather late to be lingering in bed no matter what justifications she could invent. She pulled on her white kimono, stepped out to the parlor, and glanced around: the wallpaper, the divan, the table. She was alone. Again that rapping. The window. She tightened her robe and looked down to the street.

In a gray suit and a sky-blue shirt that matched his pin-dot bow tie and his striped fedora band, Jimmy Warburg hurled an object. Katharine opened the window. "Just what do you think you're up to, Mister Jimmy Warburg? Some gentleman you are!"

"Gentleman, shmentleman," he called back. "Gentlemen are dull. Besides, they're usually four-flushers. I would suggest you avoid them like the devil." He flung another object.

Katharine ducked as a half-dollar coin sailed into the room. "What's a four-flusher?"

"One card short of a winning hand." He tossed another coin.

"Have you nothing better to do, Mister Jimmy Warburg, than hurl coins at unsuspecting, half-sleeping maidens?"

"Half-sleeping?" He checked his wristwatch. "Why, it's only ten twenty. How impertinent of me!"

Others were looking from their windows and storefronts. "Ten fifteen, three thirty — it is always too early, Mister Jimmy War-

110

burg, to be —"

"Will you please quit it with this Mister Jimmy Warburg business?"

"That is your name, isn't it?"

"First name, Jimmy, yes. That's what the flyboys call me. Last name, unnecessary."

"It's always too early, Mister Jimmy Warburg, to be loitering on a public sidewalk, shouting inanities at a self-respecting girl in her a.m. kimono."

"In that case, why don't you invite me in? Did you say kimono?"

"I said a girl in her kimono, yes. But she could just as well be perched in a madrono, talking on the telephono. What's the difference? Point is, she deserves a modicum of privacy." Katharine tried to close the window but it resisted.

"What's a madrono?"

"A beautiful tree. A leafy retreat for thrushes and quail."

"Why don't you flit down from that beautiful tree?" suggested Jimmy.

Finally, she managed to slam the window shut.

I'm in no hurry! If Jimmy Warburg wished to visit, that was swell. She had been hoping for another encounter. Perhaps an opera or dinner. But she did not appreciate the notion that he might call upon her whenever it struck his fancy or that she should interrupt everything to accommodate him. Yes, there was a power differential between them. A wealth gap wider than Central Park. But he should not call attention to it, darn it.

It took her ten minutes to slip on her long black skirt, buttonless blouse and lace-up boots and boil water for tea, but there was no cream in the icebox so she stepped out for the corner grocery. Any witness to her banter with Jimmy would have vanished by now or would at least pretend not to have noticed. She slapped on her mother's wide-brimmed hat, with that silly peacock feather. Not the way she usually dressed for a morning cream-fetching excursion, but not too fancy, either.

Fifteen minutes in all by the time she reached the street, and there he was still, leaning against a brick wall, his nose in a newspaper. "I knew you'd come up for air sooner or later." He folded the paper.

"The flat does not lack oxygen, thank you."

He looked up to her apartment, squinting. "That right?" He threw the newspaper into a trash bin and they began walking.

"And I did not come up for air. I came down for cream."

"Ah, I know just the place." He led her to

a buggy that was waiting at the corner and helped her in.

The Century Theatre was closed to the public during the day. But the doorman recognized Jimmy, whose family had financed construction of the building, and the elevator operator whisked them up in his polished-brass cage to the enclosed portion of the Roof Garden Pavilion, where a disk was spinning on the Victrola while maintenance employees swept the floor and set tables. Eddie Cantor, backed by an orchestra, sang —

Every lyric writer since the world began
Has put in overtime in raves about the
    moon.
And when the animals descended from
    the Ark
They sang a song that rhymed with June
And tune and spoon.

Apart from the restaurant staff and the invisible singer and his orchestra, Jimmy and Katharine had the spacious glass room to themselves. As they proceeded to a table at the far end of the room, Katharine wondered whether Jimmy had not prearranged the entire scene, including the music. It all seemed too picturesque and dreamlike to be entirely spontaneous.

"I should apologize," said Jimmy as they sat down.

"For throwing coins at my window? Darn right, you should. You could have cracked it!"

He shook his head. "For last night."

"Oh." She smiled, feeling heat rising in her cheeks. "That was nothing. Just a . . . a moment."

"The state I was in. I didn't fancy your seeing me like that."

The waiter brought a teapot, cups, and a plate of petit fours. Jimmy tasted one of the miniature cakes. "So the mystery is solved," he announced. "I won't be flying. They're dumping me in an office in D.C."

"What will you do there?"

"At the base in Delaware, I designed a new kind of compass in my spare time," he said with uncharacteristic modesty, as if announcing he had discovered a clever way to knot his tie. "Specifically for aviation. They had the damn things mounted on the floorboards. You had to take your eyes off the windscreen and wait for your irises to adjust so you could read the compass, and then if you could even see the darn thing, you were squinting like a bag of nails when you turned your eyes back to the sky. I figured out a way to mount a rotating magnetic card inside a glass ball and position it right in front of the pilot's eyes. So he's looking at the horizon rather than his feet." He waved the waiter over. "Bruno, would you mind bringing me a foot or so of butcher paper?"

Eddie Cantor had ceased singing and the shellac disk was spinning noisily. Before going back to the kitchen, the waiter lifted the needle. He returned a moment later with a length of torn-off paper. Jimmy removed a Parker Lucky Curve pen, black with gold filigree, from his breast pocket and sketched. "Imagine a snow globe, sans castles and reindeer." He illustrated the sphere and rotating magnetic card, added a perspective view of the Curtiss panel, and pushed it across the table. "Now they want them on all the military planes, and they've put me in charge of having them mass-produced and installed."

"Why, that's terrific. Here you are, all of twenty years old and —"

"Twenty-one, thankfully."

"Twenty one and already in charge of . . . Jeepers."

"I'll be buzzing down to Washington this afternoon. Which is why I took the shocking liberty of rousing you so early."

She smiled to conceal her disappointment. "That's how you bid a girl adieu? Pelting her window with pennies?"

"Half-dollars. And no."

"No, what?"

"That's not how I bid a girl adieu." He pushed a lock from his eyes. "I guess, well, yes, I needed to see you. But not to say goodbye." He collected her hands in his. "I've decided I want to see you every day of my life. If you consent, that is." He blinked twice, just like his father — an unconscious gesture that pinched her heart. *So Paul Warburg was right, darn it.* "What do you say?" he pressed her.

In addition to his intelligent good looks, Jimmy was adventurous, always ready with a quip, and a smidgen vulnerable. This latter quality touched her particularly.

"Your father was right about you," she teased.

"That I'm a blight on my family name? Or that I'm crackers?"

"Does it have to be one or the other?"

He reached for her teacup and sipped. "I suppose it could be both."

"He's right that you're impetuous. You get an idea and act upon it, just like . . ." She pointed. "Like sipping from my teacup. How do you know I don't have some exotic

116

disease?"

"If you do, I want to share it with you. I want to share everything with you." He drained the cup, refilled it, and pushed it back across the table.

She chuckled. "You hardly know me, Jimmy Warburg."

"I like what I see," said Jimmy. "I like what I hear when you play the piano. I like your accommodating ways as well as your contrarian ones. You're a bit of a caged lynx. Also, Katharine Warburg has a ring to it."

She laughed. "What kind of ring?"

"Why, diamond, of course. Or any stone of your choosing."

She rested her chin on her hand. "Can I give it some thought?"

"Why don't you think about it until June." He uttered it like a statement, a directive.

"June?" She had no desire to think that long. Maybe a day or two, or a few minutes. "Why June?"

"Because it rhymes with moon, and tune, and spoon." Jimmy leaned closer. "In the meantime, I'd like to take something from you. Something that will keep me dreaming."

My virginity? Is that what you're implying? Would I allow you, on nothing but a promise? You bet I would!

It would be the most momentous decision of her life.

"Katharine?"

"Yes?"

"A pose," he corrected her as if he knew what she was thinking. He signaled to someone at the far end of the room. Katharine turned to see two men entering: a mustachioed gentleman in a black suit with a silk neckerchief, and his assistant in baggy cotton dungarees, wheeling a wooden tripod, a large camera with a hood, and a flash.

CHAPTER SIX

Sunday morning, Ellen rapped at Katharine's door. "Out of bed! We're heading to church."

Katharine shuffled out of her room and poured herself tea. "We haven't sat in a pew in months. Why all of a sudden?"

"They're honoring your grandmother."

Decades earlier Katharine's paternal grandmother, Gertrude Swift, had composed and published a book of devotional songs. Katharine's father, who occasionally played the organ at St. Ignatius of Antioch, had taught the hymns to the choir.

Father Ganter delivered an impassioned gloss on a passage — "be ye therefore sober" — from the First Epistle of Peter. "As in the time of Saint Peter, so in ours," he warned, peering at his congregation through horn-rimmed spectacles that reflected the gem colors of the stained-glass windows. "Never before have we seen the family in such a shambles, our fathers so ambitious, our mothers so neglected, while our youth dance and carouse as if there were no tomorrow." He pushed his glasses back on his nose. "Drink is the scourge of our time. Women come to me in tears. Their husbands guzzling, squandering their vitality. Ultimately sacrificing their positions and reputations as well as their souls. The answer to this wickedness, the path to healing, lies in Prohibition. I urge you, brothers and sisters in Christ, for the sake of our communities, our families, our church, and our country: support Prohibition."

Several congregants muttered amens.

Prohibition. Katharine had followed the fiery debates in newspapers. Prohibition signified everything she had not been doing with Jimmy. She glanced at her mother. Was this why Ellen had dragged her here?

His voice rising, the reverend resumed: "I know, I know, you've heard the sophistries of the Papists, the Germans, and the beer barons. I urge you: pay them no heed. If you want to see where that *Hofbräuhaus* philosophy leads, look at what's happening in Europe." He swallowed and sighed, clasping the lectern. "Let us now join together in Gertrude Swift's eloquent arrangement of 'Christ Our Passover.'"

The organ played a few introductory chords. Choir and congregation sang:

> Christ our Passover has been sacrificed
>   for us.
> Therefore let us keep the feast,
> Not with the old leaven, the leaven of
>   malice and evil,
> but with the unleavened bread of sincerity
>   and truth.

"The leaven of malice and evil." The words reverberated in Katharine's mind. Her grandmother, whose memory Katharine honored, had composed this music. She remembered Grandma Gertie's laugh, the dresses she sewed for her, her piety, evenings spent at her piano. The thought that she, Katharine Swift, might soon be leaving home to join a clan with foreign traditions saddened her. But she also remembered that during her father's last years, doubt had crept into his heart and metastasized into an inverse faith. Much to his wife's dismay, Sam Swift had died an atheist.

Although Katharine cherished her heritage, she refused to let it shackle her. She knew that Jimmy Warburg, coming from a very different background, held similar views. America no longer belonged to Sam

Swift's Puritan ancestors, if it ever had. America encompassed steel and farming, the telephone and moving pictures, women's suffrage, the assembly line, and the Silent Parade. America was the bustling city with its odors of garlic, seared beef, borscht, fried chicken, cabbage, soy sauce, horse manure, and automobile smoke. On her meandering coasts, in the Appalachians and the Rockies, and in the wide-open prairie, there was plenty of room for historically incompatible traditions to mingle — room for the Irish as well as the English, the Germans as well as the French, the Poles and Ukrainians as well as the Russians — provided they set aside the sectarian ways of their Old Countries, the tribal dissonances of their tired Old World.

Thoughts of the Old World and the new brought Katharine's mind back to Jimmy, who had immigrated at a young age, who remained fascinated with the idea of America, who had so fervently sought to fight in her naval air force. And to the question he had posed in the Roof Garden Pavilion of the Century Theatre.

Now he was in Washington. Was he thinking of her? Would his father's objections hold sway? If Katharine accepted Jimmy's proposal, would she be stumbling into a hornet's nest?

CHAPTER SEVEN

Jimmy. Washington

Wearing his naval reserve uniform, Jimmy looked out from the sliding door as his train rolled into Union Station. There was his driver, in a seaman apprentice uniform. Jimmy waved and the driver saluted him. Two porters, also sailors, rushed to help with his trunk.

A long car waited at the curb. The rear door swung open and a tall man in a dark suit stepped out. A shock of brown hair, neatly parted; a long, thin face; gray-blue eyes that assessed Jimmy through wire pincenez spectacles. He shook Jimmy's hand. "Franklin Roosevelt. Let me help you with that." He reached for Jimmy's briefcase.

"Thank you, sir." Jimmy preceded him into the back seat of the sedan.

Jimmy knew the name, as did every Harvard graduate. The Roosevelts were American patricians, members of that elite group of alumni families whose association with the university justified its exorbitant tuition fees. Franklin's cousin Theodore had recently served as president of the United States. He had been a progressive, a Republican who cared deeply about America's natural environment and who was known for challenging the power of large businesses. He had lost reelection to Woodrow Wilson, a Democrat with strong support in the South, who allowed segregation based on skin color, resisted taking sides in the Great War — and then finally took sides and advocated for entering the war, despite the objections of his friend and advisor, Jimmy's father, Paul. Now Franklin Roosevelt, an attorney, worked for President Wilson as assistant secretary of the navy and declared his fealty to the Democratic Party. *When you can't beat 'em, join 'em.*

"I wanted to meet you here personally," Roosevelt told Jimmy as the Packard Twin Six rumbled to life. "Heard quite a bit about you."

"Not *too* much, I hope," said Jimmy.

Roosevelt patted his knee. "Only things a proud father would say."

Jimmy watched the stately buildings passing along the Mall. He knew Washington well enough to notice they were taking an

125

indirect route. Roosevelt wanted to impress him.

The car slowed to a stop at the Latrobe Gate of the Navy Yard. They ascended wide, worn marble steps to the third floor. Roosevelt led Jimmy into his front office, where a stylish secretary sat typing. "Miss Porter, James Warburg, your new tormentor," he introduced them.

She smiled. Jimmy touched his hat. "Charmed."

"Miss Porter is one heck of a typist," said Roosevelt. "She also brews a mean cup of java, which is crucial the morning after one of our disreputable sausage parties." He winked.

Jimmie nodded.

"She has a report to finalize, then she's all yours." Roosevelt opened the door to Jimmy's inner office. Tall, arched windows with views of the shipyard, where construction of several large battleships was under way. "That is what war looks like, from here," said Roosevelt. "Your contribution will be crucial. Just the technological edge we need." He turned to Jimmy. "Make no mistake about it, Warburg —"

"Jimmy."

"— war is the means by which mankind tests new technologies. That's why President

126

Wilson invited Tom Edison to lead our unit."

"That's an interesting take," said Jimmy, dropping his briefcase on the desk. "I thought war was the means by which we tested moral systems."

Roosevelt shook his head. "Morality is propaganda. Best technology triumphs. That's how it's always been, at least since Archimedes invented the catapult."

"He didn't invent it, sir," Jimmy corrected him. "But he did improve it."

Roosevelt smiled. *Yes, I took Classical History 101 same as you. Good ol' Professor Hornsworth.* "We've got to get our birds back in the sky as soon as possible." Roosevelt tapped the sheaf of papers on the rolltop desk. "Our contractors. Sheet metal fabricators, glass fabricators, compass manufacturers, riveters, installers. Fire up their competitive spirit. That's your mission. But first, let's nail down the finances. Work up a budget, walk it down to Room 374, we'll get it approved. Let's get these compasses built and fitted to the entire air fleet within three months. Can you pull that off, Warburg?"

"I can certainly give it a good Harvard try," said Jimmy.

Roosevelt nodded, smiling. "You do that."

Jimmy knew how to write up a budget. After all, he had been class treasurer. And he understood the mechanics of his compass. But no one had ever served him so much responsibility all at once. He thought it astonishing that the navy would entrust so critical a task to a cadet. It daunted him a little and thrilled him a lot.

"Have at it, boy," said Roosevelt turning to leave. "Need anything, I'm down the hall." He stopped at the door. "And let's get you out of that naval reserve monkey suit. Your lieutenant junior grade uniform is being steamed and pressed as we speak."

"Yes, sir," said Jimmy with a salute.

Roosevelt went out. Jimmy sat down in the oak swivel chair and leafed through the papers. Names of companies all over the East Coast and the Midwest, with phone numbers and contact people. A budget form. He picked up the telephone earpiece.

"Navy operator."

"Just checking. Thank you." He hung up.

He swiveled. He glanced around. His first office — on the third floor of this Greek Revival monument, which had been constructed during Thomas Jefferson's presidency. Clearly, Assistant Secretary Roosevelt wanted Jimmy to feel important. Jimmy could almost hear his father's voice pleading with Roosevelt's superior, Secretary Daniels. *A delicate operation. He wanted to be flying, you see.*

He opened his briefcase, removed his framed photograph of Katharine and set it on his desk. In a large hat with a peacock feather, a long black skirt, a buttonless blouse, and lace-up boots, Katharine was sticking her tongue out. Jimmy shook his head, smiling. *What am I getting into?*

Girls were after his money. That was a given. Wealthy girls, whom he had met at dances at Wellesley, lusted for even more wealth. To secure their patrimony. To build a bigger domicile, with more architectural flourishes. To ascend to higher levels of society. Above all, to avoid status slippage. That was the nightmare of the wealthy. Status slippage.

Jimmy abhorred any overt preoccupation with wealth. He regarded his condition as an accident of birth, like the blue of his eyes. Everyone's circumstances presented not a pedestal on which to preen but a unique set of challenges.

Naturally Katharine was impressed with his family's position, like the others. But money and social standing were not her unique preoccupations. Chopin meant as much to her as sapphires; probably more.

She knew who she was, and she was exceptional. And lovely. The curve of her lips was as disarming as the shape of her body. Effervescent and witty, she held her own with anyone.

He picked up the photograph and wiped the glass over her face. That spontaneity. None of those ladylike Wellesley beauties would have stuck out her tongue like that. Yet Katharine needed no lessons in decorum. She was sharp, delightful, and slightly rebellious. A stimulating companion.

In the society into which Jimmy was born, a woman's purpose consisted of patronizing charities and presiding at social functions. The idea that a woman should entertain professional ambitions was viewed as selfish if not downright self-aggrandizing. Jimmy's mother and her friends thought labor degrading for females of their rank. Let the men, the poor darlings, earn their livelihood. Wives were meant to facilitate their husbands' ambitions, not to compete with them. The life of a society wife was quite busy enough without such distractions. To Jimmy's mind, however, if a woman sought to contribute something of value to the world, be it a chunk of radium or a piano concerto, society as a whole would benefit.

He glanced at his watch. It was lunchtime

and he had skipped breakfast. No point trying to make those calls until two o'clock. He stepped out to his outer office. "Miss Porter?"

His secretary looked up from her work, her fire-truck-red lips slightly parted. "Bette."

"Bette, is there a galley, or a canteen, or a mess hall, or however you refer to a room where naval employees dine, somewhere in this cavernous building?"

"For you, it's called the Officers' Dining Room."

"Are you allowed to show me the way? And perhaps, as a reward, to accompany me for lunch?"

"If you invite me," she told him.

"Come on, then. You can give me the lay of the land."

She rose, picking up her handbag.

She smelled like gardenias, Jimmy noticed as they walked down the corridor. Other men in crisp navy uniforms glanced at them, he in his smart suit, she in her red dress.

CHAPTER EIGHT

Jimmy's position in Washington devolved into a multitentacled headache. "I'm arguing with aviation engineers in New York, negotiating with a compass manufacturer in Boston and riveters in Pittsburgh, and meanwhile we've got fleets of grounded planes in several states, as well as Europe," he wrote to Katharine.

In an angular script on linen stationery, his weekly letters ran to ten or twelve pages. The ink, always Carter's blue, carried a chemical odor but Katharine detected a hint of his European cologne as well. He wrote of his work, the war, the operas and exhibits he attended, and his future with Katharine. In their salon they would host gatherings of New York's literati and musicians. They would raise real American children, for whom concepts like *monarch* and *ghetto* would be as abstract as imaginary numbers. Jimmy would chomp on hot dogs and cheer with their son at baseball games. Their daughter, with satin bows in her hair, would perfect her *croisé* in ballet class. Occasionally, tired of the hustle-bustle, Jimmy and Katharine would retreat to their estate in the country, where they would ride horses and play tennis.

Not quite prepared to dwell upon the prospect of raising children, Katharine folded these letters back into their envelopes. Music remained her focus. Music was her future. That was not negotiable. But she comforted herself that in the highest echelons of society, nurses and nannies usually attended to the young ones.

She wrote back: the Edith Rubel Trio was attempting a new direction, performing with a mezzo-soprano who sang folk songs from around the world. Katharine arranged the material, assigning harmonic and melodic support to the cello, violin, and piano. "No rehearsal necessary and the audiences eat it up." What she did not mention was that even the enthusiasm of twelve or twenty amateur ethnomusicologists left her feeling irrelevant. In her moments of frustration, thoughts of Jimmy soothed her. "I couldn't sleep last night, thinking about you."

"Great to know I'm not alone. Keep dreaming that, my love," he urged.

Katharine remembered their evenings together, their mischief, and as time passed, her reveries acquired an erotic hue. "Mother is asking to meet you," she wrote. And a few weeks later: "The next time you're in the city why don't you stay at our place? Mother agrees!"

"Why, that would be heaven!" Jimmy wrote back. "Simply to breathe the same air as you."

After reading these words she folded the letter and held it to her breast. Life was full of twists and the most stunning of all was love, that crazy, blood-heating mélange of discovery and certitude.

She had never seen her mother so flustered as on the day of Jimmy's visit. He had provided two weeks' notice but Ellen acted as if two years would not suffice. All talk of vampires and strange accents vaporized and in its place, "help me push this divan, will you, Katharine? What we need is a fresh coat of paint. Are you listening? And these floors," she groaned. Then, snapping her fingers, "a rug, we need a bloody rug!"

Nor had her mother ever devoted so much attention to the preparation of a meal. Ellen, who had hitherto professed to dislike everything French, borrowed a tattered copy of *Easy French Cookery* and selected a recipe for baked loin of lamb and potatoes. Due to war rationing, potatoes were scarce and costly. That made them all the more delicious. Ellen mumbled something about advance payment for her work, but Katharine suspected she had pawned an inherited jewel or two. Her mother fussed over the oven while Katharine beat cream and castor sugar for the baked apples and whipped cream dessert.

The knock came twelve minutes sooner than expected. Still in her apron Katharine opened the door. The young man standing before her, in a tweed suit, holding a leather suitcase as well as a shopping bag, was taller and more alluring than the Jimmy she remembered.

Her mother's voice broke the spell: "Katharine, where are your manners? Please do come in, Mister Warburg. I am so very pleased to make your acquaintance. Charmed. As they say in Spain, *mi casa es su casa.*" She chuckled.

Jimmy produced a bottle of 1915 Beaune Premier Cru "Les Aigrots" and a box of Jean Neuhaus chocolate truffles. Placing them on the table, he asked how he could help with the preparations.

"Now, now, none of that," Ellen chided

him. "Katharine, offer Mister Warburg a glass of Madeira, won't you?"

Over dinner Ellen reminisced about her childhood in Leicestershire, her career as an apartment décor specialist, and her taste in music. Katharine glanced at Jimmy, a little embarrassed. The purpose of the meal was not to honor Ellen, after all. But she knew her mother's volubility reflected nervousness rather than self-centeredness.

Jimmy listened, his chin on his fist, and posed questions. He learned that Ellen was fond of Gilbert and Sullivan, Offenbach, and Kern. Jimmy nodded as if he knew of no greater composers. He refilled Ellen's wine glass as soon as it emptied. By the end of the meal, he had conquered her.

She insisted on lending him her room. "The bed my dear departed Sam slept in. He would approve, I assure you, my Sam would." She offered to sleep on the divan in the parlor, and would not be talked out of this arrangement.

Katharine lay awake much of the night, aware of Jimmy in the next room. She imagined he was awake, too, thinking of her.

In the morning, while pouring coffee, Ellen related her dream. She took great stock in dreams and loved to ramble on about them. "You were riding in a train, Katharine.

I must have been sitting in the seat opposite because I was watching you. It was the loveliest train. The Orient Express perhaps. Walnut, brass, leather, crystal. And you in a white organza dress, with a hat and parasol. Looking out the window at the passing countryside." She smiled, pushing the coffee cup toward Jimmy. "That's all I remember. But that's plenty." She served Katharine. "You're on this train. You're going somewhere."

"On what train?" asked Katharine, annoyed by her mother's veiled prognostication.

"You may not know what storms lie ahead," said Ellen, "or what land you're heading to. That is precisely what makes the journey so thrilling. But at least you're riding in a nice car."

"Speaking of going somewhere, and despite this delightful conversation and memorable coffee, I'm afraid I'm expected elsewhere," said Jimmy glancing at his wristwatch. "I have a meeting downtown in forty minutes."

At the door Katharine kissed him goodbye, feeling suddenly settled despite herself. As if they already lived in matrimony and he were running to the office.

On a treadle table in the bedroom she had shared with Sam, Ellen kept her Singer sewing machine, black with gold-and-red painted-filigree adornments and a big stop-motion wheel. She handled this contraption the way Katharine played piano, with resolve, reverence, and pride. After purchasing yards of satin and lace and a bag of beads, she devoted her free time to designing and sewing a fashionable gown that would showcase Katharine's figure without sacrificing her mystique, as well as a beaded headpiece.

The Warburg clan requested that Katharine convert to their Jewish faith but neither Jimmy nor Katharine would hear of it. "I will not ask you to be anyone other than who you are," he wrote. "And we can do without the mazel tovs and the pageantry, as well."

"What is a mazel tov?" she wrote back.

"They insist on throwing these silly terms around," Jimmy replied, "like passwords in a defunct language. I told them we are planning a simple civil ceremony. In your mother's flat, perhaps? With a justice of the peace. This wedding will be ours. On our terms. Not theirs, for Pete's sake."

"My mother's flat? Why not?" Katharine wrote back.

Why not was that although Jimmy's parents cared little about religiosity, they were seen as leaders of the Jewish community in New York City. The idea that their son would be marrying a gentile woman, in a humble apartment on the Upper West Side, appalled them, although they knew better than to say so.

Jimmy's father hoped at least to participate in the selection of an officiant, perhaps a Supreme Court justice or the mayor of New York City. But as fate would have it, the man they settled on fell victim to an attack of the gout the day before and everyone had to scramble for a replacement. Rather than see a confounding omen in this complication, Jimmy and Katharine found it amusing. Deflating, in a way that Jimmy in particular enjoyed.

They had cleared the furniture in Ellen's front room, except the upright piano, and set up folding chairs. In a nod to Jewish tradition, and for its exotic touch, Ellen draped flowers and sprigs over an embroidered canopy. To hold up this baldachin, and to complement it with Greco-Roman flair, she placed four art-nouveau caryatids representing Venus and Adonis and wrapped with branches, sprigs, tendrils, and flowers.

The Edith Rubel Trio, including Katharine in her striking wedding dress, performed Mendelssohn, Richard Strauss, and Mozart as guests entered. A few of Jimmy's Harvard friends, in naval and air force uniforms, acted as ushers, seating twenty-three members of the Warburg, Schiff, and Seligman families, as well as seventeen relations and friends of Sam and Ellen Swift. A handful of Katharine's fellow graduates of the Institute also attended, and two of her instructors, including the celebrated German orchestra conductor, Walter Damrosch.

The judicial officer who hobbled up the stairs to Ellen Swift's crowded apartment on that blistering afternoon of June 1, 1918, was the magistrate of New York City's Domestic Relations Court, whose daily task was to preside over marital disputes. "And the amazing thing," he told the guests after sipping cold water and wiping his sweat-beaded brow, "is how similar most of these stories are. It always comes down to a lethal combination of too much booze and too little money. And that is why I am the bearer of good news for you today. You see," he looked at Katharine and Jimmy, "although I don't have the pleasure of knowing you personally, I do know enough about both of you that I can assert with confidence that I won't be hearing that familiar complaint — too much booze, too little money — from either of you any time soon. And that fact alone is surely a powerful incentive to take delight in pronouncing you" — he rotated his head from one to the other — "man and wife."

Katharine felt Jimmy's palm on the back of her head and realized she was expected to perform in a public demonstration of their bliss. Her lips met his. Everyone applauded or honked, blowing their noses into linen handkerchiefs. She inhaled the sweet Rhinewater of his eau de toilette, tinged with perspiration and longing.

PART TWO

Part Two

CHAPTER NINE

Six Years Later. February 1924

Katharine stood in her walk-in cupboard, adjacent to the kitchen, looking over the plates, saucers, and cups. A kaleidoscope of the finest American and European designs. She had never hoarded china. Her collection had simply materialized, starting with her mother's wedding gift of Johnson Brothers semiporcelain, adorned with roses and garlands, which remained untouched behind the cabinet doors as a reminder of everything Katharine disliked about Victorian fussiness; proceeding through a modern Viennese porcelain collection with black-and-white semicircles and gold vertical and horizontal lines; all the way to a miscellany of abstract designs by Nikolai Suetin, which the artist had shipped to Jimmy after their meeting at the 1920 Olympic games in Antwerp.

People showered the Warburgs with gifts.

It was one of life's vinegar ironies. When Katharine was penniless, no one had offered a dime's assistance. Six years into her marriage with Jimmy Warburg, strangers burdened her with everything she no longer needed. She selected a hand-painted Wedgewood fantasy collection with insets of gardens, fireflies, and castles. Her favorites. Numbered, signed, and irreplaceable.

Tonight, they would celebrate. Jimmy, who had long aspired to become a romantic poet in the tradition of Keats and Tennyson, had finally seen his work published. Just one poem, but a respectable launch. A vindication. He was proud of his entrée into the Western literary canon and Katharine aimed to support his glee.

"No lace tablecloth tonight," she instructed Olga.

"Lace would detract from these dishes, I quite agree, madam. Something simple. Elegant. Maybe this one with the gold stripes. How many guests?"

Katharine counted on her fingers. "Dottie, Marc, George, Averell, plus Jimmy and me. That makes six, at eight thirty." She had considered inviting her old friends from the conservatory, Edith Rubel and Marie Roemaet, but the last few times she had asked them over they had mumbled excuses.

Katharine understood: her former school-mates felt out of place in the company of smug bankers and fame-chasing literati. "And also the beverages, Olga. Port wine, claret, gin."

"Naturally, madam."

Prohibition was now the law of the land, so what was there to do but drink? Prohibition had made drinking more risqué and pleasurable. It had driven intoxication out of public places and into residences and speakeasies, private living rooms and remote, lawless outposts, where, lubricated beyond inhibition, a distinguished merchant might shout obscenities and an otherwise well-mannered married woman might kiss another woman or disrobe without shame or fear of arrest. Katharine did not ask how Lionel and Olga obtained the liquors and spirits. Gangsters were surely involved, if only indirectly. That was another achievement of the Prohibition: it made gangsters rich. And power followed wealth as surely as blood followed a fusillade. She smiled at the irony of it. *I suppose I do support Tammany Hall, after all, if only indirectly.*

Her guest count was off by one. Jimmy had invited Elizabeth Lange Donahue, an office secretary. Liz was all glistening green eyes, dimples, and black ringlets, but Katharine worried the other guests might prove heady company for a girl of twenty-two — forgetting that she herself had been two years younger than twenty-two when she met Jimmy.

They dined at table like a family. A family that skewed artistic and a bit eccentric, to be sure. Marc Connelly and George S. Kaufman, the satirical playwriting team, could not have appeared more ill-matched. Connelly was bald and gregarious. Kaufman, who wore his dark hair straight up and slicked back, elongating his already lengthy face, fidgeted with his napkin or spoon. Their friend Dottie Parker, famous for her cultivated poverty, sultry gaze, and passionate love affairs, had published several oh-so-clever ditties and vignettes in *Vanity Fair* and *Vogue.* Dottie, Connelly, and Kaufman took inordinate pleasure in jibes, barbs, and insults, which they incessantly hurled at each other, at others within their sights, and at more established authors, whom they regarded as competitors but who never bothered to acknowledge their existence in return.

Jimmy's other guest, Averell Harriman, had recently inherited the largest fortune in America and looked the part in his pin-striped wool suit. Like Jimmy, he worked in the banking sector, with expertise in financing railroads. Unlike Jimmy, and an unending source of ribbing between them, he was a graduate not of Harvard but of Yale.

The preponderance of artists at the table was no coincidence. Katharine was a respected pianist and an aspiring composer; her husband fancied himself a poet. "As a matter of fact," he announced while pointing to Liz's wine goblet and nodding to Lionel, who refilled it, "I don't know whether you've picked up the new issue of *Century Magazine.*" He brandished the prestigious journal. "After all these years wandering in the literary desert, at long last . . ." He flipped it open and displayed a sonnet entitled "The Dark Star" and signed, "James Warburg."

"Bravo!" Connelly raised his glass.

"I have a wicked idea," said Kaufman, folding his napkin into a triangle. "Why don't you read it?"

"Since you're dying to anyway," put in Dottie in her dark, cloudy voice.

Jimmy stood, cleared his throat, and began:

Thou art the sun, Love; I am but the
     moon,

That palely glows with thy abandoned
  light,
Absorbed and hoarded for my lonely
  night —

"Say, I have an even better idea!" Dottie
interrupted.

Jimmy frowned. "Excuse me?"

"Why don't you *not* read it?"

"Bravissimo!" exclaimed Connelly with a
laugh, applauding.

Katharine bit her lip. Although nearly as
capable of a sharp quip as some of his
guests, Jimmy sometimes took criticism personally.

He handed the magazine to Lionel and
sank into his seat. "What did Ovid say about
envy? Oh, yes: *Summa petit livor: perflant al-
tissima venti.*" Marc Connelly registered no
recognition. "Oh, forgive me," said Jimmy.
"They don't teach that where you went to
college? 'The winds howl around the highest peaks.' Freshman Latin."

Dottie jumped in. "Unfortunately, the
good Lord endowed me with a handicap far
more distressing than mere envy." She
touched her earlobe. "Delicate ears."

Jimmy sliced into his beef. "I guess I'm
fortunate, then, that the editors of *Century
Magazine* are tone-deaf."

"Tone-deaf? I doubt it," said Kaufman, toying with his peas. "That name, Warburg, has a certain ring to it."

Dottie smiled. "Rather reminds one of the chimes in a cash register, doesn't it."

Connelly held out his glass, and Lionel refilled it. "I hear *Century Magazine* may have to close shop if they don't find benefaction."

"Unfortunately, though," remarked Kaufman, "trying to buy one's way in rarely works in the long run."

"You get to be a moneyman or a scribbler, darling," Dottie confided to Jimmy. "Not both. It smacks of insincerity."

"Leave the arts to those who suffer," said Connelly.

"And who doesn't suffer?" Jimmy shot back. "You think misery is the unique privilege of the poor?"

"Not their unique privilege," admitted Connelly. "But the poor are pretty good at it."

Averell cast a murderous glance in his direction. "Meanwhile, you don't seem to mind the free filet mignon."

Through all this rapid-fire verbal one-upmanship Katharine had watched Jimmy, who pretended to take the taunting in stride. She feared any overt defense would

151

backfire so she offered a weak smile that, in his pride, he refused to acknowledge.

"You got lucky, darling," Dottie told Jimmy, "long before *Century Magazine* printed your sonnet. Your birth manger was a gold mine. I say, make the most of it! Why squander your glorious intelligence on silly poetry, anyway?"

"Banking is an entirely reasonable occupation," Kaufman concurred. "While the arts are madness. How can one be practical and insane at the same time?"

"Well, there go my ambitions!" said Katharine, trying to change the subject.

Connelly poured himself a glass of water. "Weren't you writing a song cycle? Or was it a symphony?"

"Oh, no you don't." Katharine shook her head. "I'm not falling into that trap. Not after what you just did to my husband."

"I quite liked Mister Warburg's poem. Loved it, actually." Liz had been watching this exchange, and especially her boss's face, with concern.

"What did you like about it?" asked Dottie. "The part about the moon, or the part about hoarding?"

Liz gazed at Jimmy with what seemed to Katharine a blend of adulation and guile. "It was sincere. That is precisely what a poem should be. Not cocky. Not clever. Sincere. Was Wordsworth cocky? Was Tennyson clever?"

"Checkmate," said Dottie. "Wordsworth was never cocky. Nor, by the way, could he dance the Charleston."

"Maybe Jimmy hasn't quite found his voice," said Katharine, determined to show no reaction to Liz's brazen coquetry. "Maybe he's still searching. But isn't that how art works? It's about searching."

A frown creased Jimmy's brow and vanished. Katharine regretted her comment.

"Voice, shmoice," said Liz. "Mister Warburg's poem was touching. Romantic. He is every bit as brilliant as he is debonair. And you are all quite insensitive."

Jimmy smiled.

"If you have other poems, I for one would love to hear them," purred Liz. "You know, I write poetry, too. I believe everyone should write poetry. It cleanses the soul."

"I'd be happy to hear some of your work," said Jimmy.

Katharine thought his tone condescending, but Liz failed to take it that way. "Say, why don't we read each other's poetry on the boat to Germany?" she asked Jimmy.

As Katharine sipped her water she felt the blood draining from her face. "You're traveling together to Germany?" Her husband had never invited her on a trip abroad.

Jimmy scratched his chin. "Liz's mother is German. She speaks fluently, and . . ."

"Habe ich etwas Verletzendes gesagt?" Liz whispered. "Did I say something wrong?"

He smiled and shook his head. *It's nothing.*

"Ich verstehe auch deutsch," Katharine warned her with a smile. "I too understand German."

Dottie exchanged a look with Connelly. Kaufman walked his fork on the table. Averell cleared his throat.

It was anything but *nothing.* That wag of Jimmy's head sharply twisted the valve of Katharine's mood. She looked down, trying to calm herself. Jimmy was no angel but this public display? With a little *Schlampe,* a slut? It was insulting and injurious. "Oh, to hell with it!" Katharine swept her one-of-a-kind, hand-painted Wedgewood Fantasy dessert plate off the table. "I'm done." She flitted out of her chair and flew upstairs like a wounded sparrow.

She lay down in the dim bedroom. As her eyes adjusted, she could make out the contours of the crown molding and the Venetian glass chandelier. Downstairs the chatter resumed muted but unvanquished. Katharine inhaled, exhaled, and instructed herself to relax.

Jimmy traveled often, spending months abroad. He delighted in sexual escapades. This he had confessed four years ago, after Katharine happened upon evidence. A slow earthquake had begun rumbling through their domestic life. It had never ceased despite her attempts to ignore it.

She remembered the incident all too vividly. Four years younger but a lifetime more naïve, she was lying on this same bed flipping through a copy of *Harper's Bazaar*. He stepped into the bedroom from the shower, a towel around his waist. "Would you mind digging through my steamer for a pair of shorts?"

"You got it, sailor." Katharine pulled open the leather-and-wood trunk. Inside the lid, someone had scrawled a heart in lipstick. Stung, Katharine looked at him.

"Oh, that's awful," he admitted.

She flung the underwear at him and stormed out of the room.

A half hour later he asked her to join him for a walk in Central Park, away from servants and children. She still recalled the overcast late-autumn day, the leaves breaking free, the rumbling thunder announcing an oncoming storm, the sound of horses' hooves in the park, and that cold, haze-obscured sun. Jimmy walked with a contemplative stride, looking down.

"What does she look like?" Katharine demanded. "Does she flatter you? Is she clever? Does she squeal like a pig?"

"Please, Katharine."

"Don't *please, Katharine* me! What does she look like?"

She imagined a statuesque blonde like the one she had seen from behind on the day when she first met Jimmy. She visualized high cheekbones blushed with the Prussian chill. Icy, sparkling eyes. A body as curvaceous and heated as an Edison bulb but perhaps a smidgen softer.

"What difference does it make? By God, Katharine, the whole affair was as inconsequential as . . ." Jimmy looked at the horizon. "As a flash of lightning."

"*Inconsequential?* Not to me, Jimmy. Not to your little girl's mother."

"I suppose Helga was pretty enough," he conceded. "But that isn't the point."

"The hell it isn't."

"It is the point," he admitted. "But it's not important." He took her hands in his. "I chose you to be my wife, Katharine. Not her. And I would do it again."

She withdrew her hands. "Then why?"

Jimmy sat on a bench and patted its wood slats, inviting her to sit beside him. "I can't help it if I'm a romantic," he said. "I was born that way."

"A romantic!" spat Katharine, still standing. "A romantic is just a fellow who needs women to admire him. No, not to admire him, to worship him. To idealize him. And when he meets that kind of woman, the fool mistakes her coy smile and playful eyes for love. She's not in love with him. How could she be? She doesn't even know him. Certainly not the way his wife does. She's in love with a fantasy."

"She was a sweet girl." Jimmy stretched his legs, crossing them. "Innocent and morose. What I offered was a moment of escape."

"How charitable."

"Not charitable. But not a lifetime either. A moment."

"An innocent, sweet girl does not have an affair with a married man. She runs the other way. Oh, God." She sat down, away from him.

"You're being awfully dramatic, Katharine." He looked at the gleam of his polished oxfords beyond the pressed wool cuffs of his trousers.

"Why did she smear your trunk with lipstick?" asked Katharine. "Probably while you were in the bath rinsing off the residue of your lust. Who was that message meant for — you, or me?"

"That was vulgar," Jimmy admitted. "And terribly unfair. But you can't blame me for her indelicacy."

"I wouldn't call it *indelicacy*. I would call it deliberate and calculating."

"Perhaps, but you can't blame me for that, either, can you?"

"Oh, yes, I can blame you. How stupid I've been!"

"I wouldn't say stupid. A bit ingenuous? But that's part of your charm."

"My trust and ignorance are part of my charm?" she asked. "Well, kiss them both goodbye."

"I'm sorry if this caused you pain," said Jimmy. "But Katharine, I can't be sorry for being who I am."

"Oh," she assured him, "I can make you sorry for that, too."

He looked at her with a side smile "Ha! You're plotting revenge."

"Lust is a disease, you know," affirmed Katharine. "And, dare I say, it's catching."

"You're threatening to stray?"

"Not threatening. Promising."

158

He chuckled and shook his head. "As long as our union remains our priority, I don't see why you shouldn't. Marriage isn't about ownership, it's about sharing."

She looked at him hard. "It's chilly. I'm heading home."

That was four years ago. Now as she lay on her bed listening to the conversation downstairs, the tinkle of silverware and dishes, she acknowledged to herself that although something remained between Jimmy and her, a bond of sorts, it was not what she had once expected.

Footsteps. A knock at the door. Repeated. "Come in."

Dottie entered, sat down on the bed and took her hand. "Men are swine."

"What do you have against swine?" asked Katharine.

"You're right. I didn't mean to insult our charming porcine zoological neighbors."

"The problem is not pigs," sighed Katharine. "Or even men. The problem is marriage. The fire dies . . . and then it's dark. And you're in a room by yourself." Her eyes searched Dottie's in the obscurity. "The only thing worse than marriage, I suppose, is being single."

"Oh dear, dear Katharine, I shall never get married," said Dottie. "I shall fall madly in love. I shall drink myself silly on love and sing and dance on tables and shout with joy and make love with some rogue just as tortured as I am. And when it's over, really over, I shall sob into my pillow like a girl whose kitten just fell off a cliff. Rinse, towel-dry, repeat."

"Do you ever feel like running away?" asked Katharine.

"All the time," said Dottie. "And when I do, I smear on some lipstick, screw on a hat, and dart out to the theater. Maybe a light opera. Maybe a tragedy. A distraction. Someone else's sorrows and laughter. A context for our own. That's what this thing they call culture is really about, darling. That's how we cope with our substratal anguish."

Katharine had no idea what *substratal* meant but understood the gist of Dottie's complaint and prescription. They held hands in silence, listening to the monotonal music of the indistinct voices downstairs.

In her sleep, once again a scrubbed girl wearing a white dress and ribbons, Katharine revisits her father's One-Lock Adjustable Reamer Company. She is aware that she has experienced this moment before, but each time with dramatic differences.

Looking at her hands on the keyboard she notices blemishes. Bruises. Her dress is stained and tattered. The music has turned strange. The audience, her father's workers, are laughing.

Awaking with a start, Katharine wondered why this dream recurred. The event never happened, did it? Even the underlying circumstance, her father's ownership of that factory in Connecticut, had been ephemeral. From the time *his* father bequeathed the enterprise to him until the time it failed, little more than a year had elapsed. But the failure of the One-Lock Adjustable Reamer Company cast a shadow over the rest of Sam Swift's life. Even if he never mentioned it.

She felt queasy. It was too early to rise. She tried listening to her breathing instead of her thoughts.

When she opened her eyes again, her dyspepsia had intensified into nausea. Her face in the bathroom mirror had paled three shades. *No,* she thought, realizing she had missed her menstrual flow. *Not again. Not now.*

For Katharine, pregnancy had never been a time of exhilaration. *Discomfort* and *dread* better described the mood. The first two times had been semivoluntary, an exigency of wedlock. But *this,* arriving *now,* could only be characterized as negligence, a mistake. She felt a pang of guilt as she descended to the parlor, admitting to herself that neither pregnancy nor its consequence, maternity, had ever been her ambition.

On the breakfast table she discovered a pearl-and-ruby choker. Jimmy's note read, "You're my gal. Never forget that, Katharine." She brought the note to her nose to smell Jimmy's Carter blue ink and eau de cologne.

CHAPTER TEN

April 17, 1925

A rainy morning. A day to remain inside. Katharine found a book on the mail table. *Porgy,* by DuBose Heyward. It had arrived the previous afternoon. As she opened it, a handwritten note fell out.

Dear Katharine,
We hope you enjoy reading DuBose's novel.

Dorothy

Below the signature, Dorothy Kuhn's phone number and address.

Katharine remembered the gangly young actress from Ohio who had studied theater at Radcliffe, won a prize for her dramatic comedy, *The Dud,* and seen it produced on Broadway retitled *Nancy Ann.* Based on Dorothy's life, the play drolly depicted the awkward social adjustments of a girl from

Midwestern high society, who leaves proms and debutante balls behind for the adventure and unpredictability of a life in theater.

It was the first — and remained the only — Broadway-produced play written by a woman. Unfortunately, *life mirrors art,* the play had been a dud, closing after forty performances. But Katharine and Jimmy enjoyed it. And the fact that a female playwright had managed to get her work produced on Broadway thrilled them. She telegrammed Dorothy, in care of the theater, inviting her for dinner. They conversed over roast beef and Chablis, but Dorothy was already packing for South Carolina to marry DuBose, an aspiring novelist. Since then, not a word . . . until *Porgy* tumbled out of the mail slot a year and a half later.

Katharine sat in an armchair by the window and opened the book. Soon she was strolling through Catfish Row, a tiny ghetto in the heart of Charleston, South Carolina, and a world unto itself. Laughing and gabbing with its inhabitants, the Gullah people, whose dialogue was challenging but whose hearts were bursting with humanity; seeking shelter in tenements from an impending storm; weeping over the body of a murdered man; resenting the foreign, white hand of law enforcement. Written in a lofty, refined style, rich with description, detailed shading, and compassion, *Porgy* represented the probing regard of an educated southern gentleman exploring a culture not his own, which burgeoned under his eyes with love and violence.

A few hours later, the wailing of her infant Kathleen jolted Katharine out of her South Carolina sojourn, followed by the pitter-patter of April and Andrea's feet and the *clump-clump* of clogs. That would be the nursemaid, Jo. Finally the squeals died down.

When she and Jimmy had purchased the adjacent townhouse and opened doors between the two structures, she asked the architect to provide acoustic insulation so she could practice piano at night. He shrugged, raising his hands. "Eh? One can only do so much in this regard, Madam Warburg. If I may speak in a — how shall I say? — in a Mediterranean manner; which is to say, candidly . . ." He raised his bushy eyebrows.

"Please do," said Katharine.

He glanced at the piano and back to her. "When one decides to have children, one invites chaos into one's acoustical environment. It cannot, if I may say so, be helped, my dear Madam Warburg."

Chuckling at the memory of this rotund Frenchman's pomposity, she pulled on her robe and shambled down to the kitchen, where she finished the room-temperature coffee Jimmy had left and looked at his newspapers. Jimmy received five or six of them daily, air mailed in paper-and-string packets from M. M. Warburg Bank offices and affiliates in London, Hamburg, Mexico City, and elsewhere.

This morning, it seemed, he had focused on several back issues of a Detroit broadsheet, the *Dearborn Independent*. The typed letter that accompanied this package, from a law firm in Detroit, commented that the paper was more widely read than any other in the country except the *New York Daily News*. Its owner and publisher, Henry Ford, required every Ford Motors dealership to carry it and provide it free of charge to customers. As Katharine browsed, it became clear why Jimmy's lawyers had brought the *Dearborn Independent* to his attention. In a series of headline articles, Henry Ford had fashioned Warburg-hatred into a *cause célèbre.*

As far as Katharine knew, Ford had never met Jimmy, Paul, or any member of Jimmy's extended family. He studied them from afar and his animosity derived not from knowledge but from ignorance and fear. The unreality of his perceptions, however, did not render his accusations less brutal or painful. Katharine could only imagine how Ford's public, vociferous, and relentless denunciations affected Jimmy, his family, and their associates. She scanned the front-page headlines:

JEWISH IDEA IN AMERICAN
MONETARY AFFAIRS:
The Remarkable Story of Paul Warburg

JEWISH IDEA OF CENTRAL BANK
FOR AMERICA:
The Evolution of Paul M. Warburg's Idea

HOW JEWISH INTERNATIONAL
FINANCE FUNCTIONS:
The Warburg Family and Firm Divided the
World Between Them and Did Amazing
Things Which Non-Jews Could Not Do!

JEWISH POWER AND AMERICA'S
MONEY FAMINE:
The Warburg Federal Reserve
Sucks Money to New York

THE ECONOMIC PLAN OF
INTERNATIONAL JEWS:

An Outline of the Protocolists' Monetary Policy, With Notes on the Parallel Found in Jewish Financial Practice

Ford's articles were poorly constructed, meandering, and devoid of serious thought but as she perused them, a few themes emerged: the Midwesterner's animus toward East Coast privilege; the self-made American yokel's envy of European refinement, education, and gentility; and especially, the manufacturer's resentment of the class of people who had provided him, at a cost, with the means to build his empire. But Ford did not direct his ire toward the entire class of New York bankers, nor even to all the recent immigrants among them. Ignoring the power and influence of Amadeo Giannini, Charles Edward Merrill, or the house of J. P. Morgan, he focused on the Baruch and Warburg families — and on their ethnic identity, which he confused with religious faith.

Part of the irony was that the Warburgs' religiosity was faint, in fact hardly detectable. When they bothered to attend synagogue, once or twice per year, their motivation was social, a form of *noblesse oblige.* Katharine's family had been far more pious than any of the Warburgs. But the absurdity

168

of Ford's contentions hardly ended there. For Henry Ford, one of the richest men in the country, to rail against the privileged class on behalf of the honest, hardworking, common American was so ludicrous it would have made Katharine laugh, had it not been so pathetic. And although Paul Warburg had played an important part in the creation of the Federal Reserve, he had not done so for his own gain but out of devotion to his new country. Paul admitted privately, with pride and regret, that his efforts in Washington had cost him a fortune in lost revenues due to the time and effort involved.

The most ridiculous and alarming of all Ford's accusations, from Katharine's point of view, was that Paul Warburg and other German Jews had dragged America into the Great War, in effect murdering millions of Christians for personal gain. Had Ford researched the question even minimally, he would have learned that Katharine's father-in-law had argued — personally, to President Wilson — against American involvement in the war. She could not help wondering: was Ford deliberately lying, or was he just insane?

Henry Ford was hardly alone, as Katharine knew all too well, in his distrust of the

Warburgs and their ilk. Such attitudes were, in fact, increasingly fashionable. Katharine had read Frank Norris's celebrated novel *McTeague*, which portrayed the Jewish Zerkow, "groping hourly in the muck-heap of the city for gold, for gold, for gold. It was his dream, his passion." Sitting beside Jimmy in the Provincetown Playhouse on MacDougal Street, Katharine had winced during a production of Theodore Dreiser's *The Hand of the Potter*, in which a Jewish man murders an eleven-year-old Catholic girl and his Yiddish-accented family covers up his crime. And in several of T. S. Eliot's contemplative, modernist creations including *Gerontion* and *Burbank*, the famous poet — who worked at a bank, himself — had molded lower-case derision into verse.

The rats are underneath the piles.
The jew is underneath the lot.
Money in furs.

But Henry Ford's diatribes were neither fiction nor poetry. They were accusations; they were personal; they were obsessive; and they were public.

M. M. Warburg and Company, or any of its affiliates, could have created its own publishing organs. They could have hired

170

journalists to refute or counterattack their accusers. But to do so, to amass and exercise that much influence, would be to vindicate the claims of people like Henry Ford. In the age-old tradition of court Jews, Jimmy and his family preferred to distance themselves and their operations from the public view.

As Katharine sipped a second cup of coffee she remembered when, shortly after moving into their townhouse, Jimmy and she had invited his parents, Paul and Nina, for dinner. Much of the animosity between Paul and Jimmy had faded, but when discussion ran to questions of identity, the truce broke down.

"Don't believe me," Jimmy told his father. "Believe the Scriptures. How do they characterize the Hebrews? A *tribe.* And what is tribalism? Whom do you trust? Whom do you not trust? You don't trust the *goyim.*"

"Everyone takes pride in their group, as they should!" said Paul. "It is only human. Why should we be different?"

"The world is changing," said Jimmy.

"Those who say the world is changing, they are a group, too," insisted Paul. "They imagine their club is superior to all the others, but it's just another ghetto. And let's hope you never have to leave it. You might find yourself pretty lonely."

The subject had come up again during subsequent family reunions. Jimmy wanted to change the culture of the bank and its reputation. Paul resisted in principle but little by little yielded control to his son. One by one, Jimmy let the *alter kockers* go, replacing them with Harvard friends who had names like Rutherford and Howe. So far, though, Jimmy's strategy had not made an impression on Henry Ford and his comrades in journalistic arms.

Katharine turned to the European papers. There at last she encountered pleasant news. Following Jascha Heifetz's tour of Europe, a year ago, the French and the Germans had clamored for him to return. He had finally done so, a brief whirl through the most glamorous concert houses, and the reviews were ecstatic.

Katharine asked the telephone operator to connect her with Roosevelt twenty-three seventy-two. She picked up a pack of Marlboros, the luxury smoke for ladies that featured a red band to hide lipstick smudges, and flicked a cigarette out of the box. "Miss Heifetz, please. Katharine Warburg." Lionel lit her cigarette. "Thank you," she whispered. She inhaled and blew the smoke upward.

"Oh, Pauline darling, so delighted I caught

172

you. I hear your gifted brother is back. That his tour was a smash. Jimmy was dying to see him in Berlin." Another puff. "He did catch the headline, of course." She read from a battered newspaper. *Der größte lebende Geiger."* The greatest living violinist. "That's the *Berliner Tageblatt* but from what I gather they all agreed. Paris, Rome, Vienna. Pauline, our Jascha's on top of the world. Isn't that wonderful." Another puff. "Listen, we ought to celebrate. Especially with this dreary weather. Oh, absolutely! Of course you can bring a companion. Who is it?" Another cloud of smoke. "Surprise me, then!"

In addition to Dottie Parker, Marc Connelly, George S. Kaufman, and Averell Harriman, the Warburgs' circle had ballooned to include the playwright Robert Sherwood, the satirical columnist Franklin Adams, and the drama critic Alexander Woollcott. Nor was a group of fifteen or twenty, including a handful of strangers, unusual these days at 34 East Seventieth Street.

A gossip columnist or two sometimes slipped in as well. The drinking and antics of banking magnates, stage stars, and writers guaranteed the sales of morning papers. Indeed, terms like *creative people,* as used in William Randolph Hearst's gazettes, implied that common rules of decency did not apply. "Creative people" possessed or thought they possessed the power to invent their own moral codes. Their vainglorious, seemingly continuous celebration of freedom fascinated the masses, who traveled and worked within inherited bounds of decency, honor, and virtue — or at least pretended to.

Katharine hoped Jascha would bring his Stradivarius. Just one partita would set her soirée aflame. "Of course. Check with him and get back to me. Kissy kissy." She blew a final puff, hung up the phone, snuffed out her cigarette in a silver and crystal ashtray, and headed upstairs to get ready for a long-overdue lunch with Edith Rubel and Marie Roemaet at the conjoined Waldorf and Astoria hotels.

The three musicians sat in the bright lobby-restaurant at Fifth Avenue and Thirty-Fourth Street. A careless pianist, wearing an ill-fitting suit, exhibited Tchaikovsky's Waltz in E-flat Major as if sloppily hanging aural wallpaper. Katharine, Edith, and Marie nibbled on radish roses, shrimp cocktails, and lamb roast seasoned with rosemary and mint jelly. Katharine had planned the get-together and all three understood she would foot the bill. Although they had not performed together in years, she hoped they would share enthusiasms about the musical scene, maybe even revive their collaboration.

"Did you hear Jascha at Carnegie Hall in December? What a delight."

"Jascha?" asked Marie.

"Jascha Heifetz," said Katharine.

"We know who Jascha is," said Edith, glancing at Marie.

Katharine regretted referring to him by his first name. What a terrible *faux pas.*

Marie smiled and with a sideways nod admitted that neither of them could afford it.

And thus the lunch proceeded, mournful rather than gay, as if they were memorializing rather than celebrating their friendship. Although they smiled and attempted a few giggles, the restaurant ambiance and inflated prices heightened Katharine's sense that she now dwelled in a rarefied social stratum where wastefulness was *de rigueur* and elegance a matter of means rather than taste.

She wondered whether her friends envied her. Perhaps the desire for wealth and conspicuous consumption was universal, and martyrdom for Art merely the self-protective posture of romantic misfits like Katharine's father. She inwardly cringed at the thought.

She suggested that the Edith Rubel Trio try new material. Perhaps something original. "I've been composing, you know."

"We would love to." Edith smiled. "But . . ."

"But what?"

Again Edith glanced at Marie. "We're working with another pianist."

"Lillian Abell," said Marie.

"Oh yes. Lillian." Katharine smiled. "She's quite adequate." She realized she sounded bitter. But again, she *felt* a little bitter.

"She needs the income as much as we do," said Edith.

Katharine considered donating to the coffers of the Edith Rubel Trio but dismissed the idea. It would only bruise her friends' pride.

"The last times we called you, you were out of town," apologized Edith.

"We were in Boston. And then D.C." Katharine tasted the Waldorf Salad. "I understand, really."

Her mind did understand. But not her heart. For Katharine, their musical partnership had been more than a business. It had been a sisterhood. Even if she *had* taken time off to bear children and attend to family obligations.

The pianist hacked his way through Chopin's Mazurka in B-flat Major. Katharine, Edith, and Marie moved on to profiteroles, musing about old times and the more affordable of the recent concerts and operas. But their mood had collapsed. Their friendship no longer felt natural.

She asked herself how money, social standing, or marriage could degrade something as vital and supposedly resilient as friendship. Was true friendship, meaningful connectedness independent of worldly circumstances, an illusion?

That's what culture is for, Dottie Parker had told her. *To distract us from these sad truths.*

If intimate friendship and shared memory were nothing but tattered illusions, revelry and drunkenness were ready to step in to fill the gap, or at least to divert one's attention. The Warburgs' guests no longer gathered around the dining table; those days were long past. The idea that everyone might participate in one conversation now seemed stodgy. Food, champagne, and chatter flooded the dining room, kitchen, parlor, library nooks, sitting room, even the bedrooms. In the inebriation and noise, some smooched with their friends' lovers on sofas, played the fiddle, or danced a Charleston. Groups of two or five, sitting or standing, formed and re-formed, trying to outcompete each other in tall tales and exuberance. They smoked, drank, noshed, and soiled the furniture. One drunken man embraced another, who socked him in the jaw. He fell backward onto two women, who screamed. An ingénue with Broadway ambitions allowed men to lick champagne off her dainty ankles and calves, giggling.

The bartender fixed Katharine a Gin Rickey. She noticed Jimmy leaning against the wall by the door, sipping white wine and observing his guests. He seemed thoughtful, a bit distracted. She tasted her drink and approached him. She had been meaning to ask him about those articles she had seen. She wondered how Henry Ford's attacks were affecting him, and wanted to let him know she cared.

"Not at all," said Jimmy. "I understand why he feels that way. He built his fortune with his hands. He distrusts people who earn money without creating physical objects. It rings false to people like him." He sipped his wine. "Besides, no one likes feeling dependent on others. Least of all, industrialists. They resent bankers precisely because they need them. None of this is new, Katharine." He smiled.

Jimmy's eyes told a different story — or rather, a variety of stories, all at once. One of those stories was a tale of caution. The subtext was fear.

There was a knock at the door. As if to change the subject, Jimmy opened it. There stood Alexander "Aleck" Woollcott, the drama critic, next to a smaller man. With a high forehead and circular glasses — his nose, moustache, mouth, and chin scrunched into the lower portion of his face — Aleck cut a bulky, slovenly figure. He wore a cape, dripping with rain, over his suit and spoke in a growl. "Jimmy, Arthur," he introduced his friend. And, to Arthur: "If capitalism is the font from which all evil flows, this fellow's the Bernini of fountain architecture."

"Thank you for the tribute, though I'm afraid it's unmerited," replied Jimmy as he studied the face of Aleck's guest. "I've seen you somewhere," he said to the stranger.

"You'll recognize him if I stomp on his foot," bellowed Aleck.

He did so, and Arthur's mouth gaped in a magnificent, silent howl, which seemed to take over his head. His face tilted backward. His cheeks shot up to his forehead. His round eyes shrank to slits.

"Harpo!" exclaimed Jimmy.

The silent shriek vanished. Arthur Marx grinned. "Pleased to meet you." He shook Jimmy's hand. His voice, unfamiliar to Jimmy and the Marx Brothers' theater and movie audiences, was mellow and ingratiating. Without the battered top hat, the loopy wig, and the shabby coat, Arthur Marx looked uncannily serious. It was difficult to imagine him honking a rubber horn and, stooped, chasing girls around cluttered drawing rooms.

Jimmy ushered them in. Aleck pursued the theme he had evoked when introducing Jimmy to Arthur, discussing economic systems, the Russian revolution, and the ascent of Joseph Stalin. Dottie Parker, Marc Connelly, and George S. Kaufman joined in with the occasional quip. Arthur Marx listened.

"I haven't the faintest idea how I became mired in this bastion of capitalist excess," Woollcott declaimed. "It's one of the many less-than-amusing pranks that Providence has played upon me. I'm a tear-it-down Socialist at heart."

"Olga, tell them how that worked for you," Jimmy instructed his housekeeper, who was serving drinks.

180

Olga threw her shoulders back and announced proudly, "My family were *dvoryanstvo*. Nobility. We owned a residence in St. Petersburg and a dacha in the Tula *oblast*. We had so many servants. One whose task was to polish the silver. Another to dust the chandeliers. The Bolsheviks, they stole it all, the work of generations, and murdered many of my relatives. Savages."

"The devil's children inherit the devil's luck," said Aleck.

Olga ignored him, serving Arthur.

"Now Aleck, that's out of line," said Jimmy. "And, need I say it, ungentlemanly. You don't know her, let alone her lost kin. Olga is a gem."

"I was jesting," Aleck apologized. "You know me. All buzz, no sting."

Olga ignored his apology. "Thank you, Mister Warburg." She huffed off to serve other guests.

Marc Connelly and George S. Kaufman pitched in with *bons mots* about the swollen stock market, social decay, and revolutionary utopias. Jimmy smiled, shaking his head. "I'm all for people struggling against oppression. But when the envious rise up against the privileged, they always go too far. Look at the French Revolution. The Red Terror. The Taiping Rebellion. They all beat the drum of egalitarianism. What they're really after is blood."

"You're just saying that because you're rich," thundered Aleck.

"On the contrary," insisted Jimmy. "I'm quite concerned with the moral implications of my work. So is everyone I work with, including — especially — my father."

"I haven't a clue which system is better," said Dottie. "But I do know one thing about capitalism. It's terribly *démodé.*"

Other guests knocked at the door. This time Katharine opened to reveal her friend Pauline, who stood with a man Katharine recognized all too well, though she had never seen him quite this close. He stood about five-foot-eleven in a tailored, pin-striped suit; but his presence exceeded his physical stature. Katharine noticed the eyes. Dark with a faraway softened look as if focusing on something beyond the party, the people, or the place. They met and acknowledged hers but floated away again, finally alighting on the Steinway grand in the center of the room. He smiled as if he had spotted an old friend stepping off the New Haven Express in Grand Central Terminal.

George Gershwin.

"Jascha was beat. I let him sleep," said

Pauline.

Katharine escorted them in. "I'll have a Biondi-Santi Brunello di Montalcino," said Pauline.

Katharine laughed. "Would you settle for a Frascati?"

"Whatever." Pauline took a flute of Perrier-Jouët from one of the waiters' trays.

As they glided toward the center of the room, Katharine turned to the composer. "And you, Mister Gershwin? Some brandy?"

He shook his head brusquely as if the thought had dampened his hair. "Something fizzy."

"How about a sparkling gin lemonade?"

"Sounds swell. But without the gin, and without the lemonade."

"Just the bubbles?" laughed Katharine.

"That would hit the spot. Mind if I — ?" He completed his question with a wave at the piano.

"Of course not. Please!"

He sat down and began playing a rousing anthem. The conversations and laughter subsided. Gershwin's hands swept across the keyboard brushing into the air a multiplicity of simple tunes that wound through or bounced off each other, disappeared, reemerged, and recombined in the treble or

183

bass register adorned with grace notes and triplet flourishes. Sometimes he hammered on one tone while moving chords in surprising patterns underneath, contrasting simplicity with sophistication. Other times he flattened the climactic note in a series, layering in a shade of nostalgia or regret.

Pauline leaned close to Katharine. "He can play, all right. Trouble is, no one taught him how to stop playing."

"Is he your date, or a friend?" asked Katharine.

"He was my date. Now he's a friend."

"What happened?"

"Nothing. That's the problem." And then she corrected herself. "I don't mean nothing. But, well, nothing."

The music pivoted. The mood shifted. A sorrowful melody tinged with philosophical, big chords that slid through half-step gradations, implying key changes, like a man drunk on love swaying and lurching through a gaslamp-lit alley. The room held its breath as the guests congregated around the piano. Olga set a glass of seltzer near the music stand.

Leading that intoxicated personification of his melody from the alley into a wide-open field, Gershwin ragged-up the same romantic tune. The melody man danced into the middle of the meadow, kicked up his legs, and flailed his arms, throwing back his head. He crouched, spun, and whirled. And slowly crumpled to the ground in a graceful heap.

Katharine had no idea how long Gershwin had been playing when he paused to sip his seltzer, oblivious to the enchanted crowd. But he could not ignore them long, for they broke into applause. He turned to Katharine, a gleam in his eyes. "Say, I hear you've got a wicked left hand, yourself."

"Both of my hands are wicked, Mister Gershwin," said Katharine.

"Why don't you serenade us with something you picked up at the Institute?" He rose, clutching his highball glass and ceding the bench.

"What did you tell him about me?" Katharine whispered to Pauline.

"Only that you're blessed with two of the finest ears in the city, and fingers to match."

Katharine grimaced and headed to the piano, where she played the portion of the *Rhapsody in Blue* that she had worked out. The slow portion. After several bars Gershwin lowered his half-empty glass to a side table and crouched behind her, extending his arms on either side of hers. His scent teased her nose, cigars and an eau de toilette mélange of citrus, sandalwood, and bergamot. He began embellishing and soon their melodies intertwined. Katharine glanced up at Jimmy, who stood near the end of the piano watching and smiling in his ambiguous way.

Gershwin added notes in other implied time signatures, triplets against eighth notes in exotic keys, and bumped up the rhythm so that Katharine soon felt she was his accompanist rather than the other way around. Nor was she adept at this style of accompaniment, which involved reading the other player's mind rather than looking at notes on a printed page. Flexibility and instinct rather than calculation and precision. Together they waded further beyond her waters. She tried to swim but flailed. It may not have been noticeable to the others but Gershwin knew. She felt uncomfortably warm. A flush she did not care to name or recognize. She worried others might notice but glancing around the room saw no sign they did. As her eyes returned to the keyboard, her fingers stumbled. *That* was mortifying.

As if sensing she needed air, Gershwin crossed his left arm over to the treble end of the piano, providing her with a means of escape. The gesture dismayed her but she

186

took the hint and rose. He played on insouciantly while sliding back to the center of the bench. The *Rhapsody* theme had mutated into a Scott Joplinesque rag. His listeners remained silent, mesmerized.

The style changed again. "Here's one we dumped from *Lady, Be Good!,* our show at the Liberty. If you haven't seen it, you should bolt over there 'cause they're beating the doors down." His fingers relaxed into long, large chords. Quieter harmonies under his New York–inflected voice. "It's called 'The Man I Love.' Too slow for the stage, but we'll find a place for it."

He played the tune as a piano solo, without words. A dialogue between a left hand that descended in half steps, bringing to mind a tight spiral staircase, and a right hand that yearned for ascent in parallel chords yet slowly sank downward as if under the weight of the left. Overall, the minorkey melodic fragments conveyed a mood of pensive longing, if not downright sorrow.

Which shifted again as Gershwin's right hand began strumming chords and his left produced a swinging bass line. Instead of playing the new melody, little more than a ditty, Gershwin sang it. His voice soft and murky, untrained but, unlike Jimmy's, on key.

It was chance, not romance.
Now you know, I must go.
I'm leaving now,
But wish somehow
That we had met before.

Katharine thought his look-at-me show-business ostentation brash and graceless. Her guests' surrender seemed too automatic, inevitable, and unthinking — the swoon of giggly cheerleaders for the cocky quarterback.

Not only had he taken possession of her piano but he had cunningly engaged her in a competition. It rankled her that he had controlled the terms and that his victory was so resounding. After all, she was the classically trained professional. Still she had to admit that performing with him had been a jolt. Exhilarating. Intimate, even.

His song wound to a conclusion. His hands sprang from the keyboard and flipped down the piano lid with finality. *Now that I have performed, no one else dare touch it.* He stood up and as everyone applauded again, he bowed. Glancing at his Cartier wristwatch he announced, "Well, I'm afraid the ship for Europe isn't going to wait for me."

"Not even a goodbye peck," Pauline

groused as Gershwin shut the door behind himself and the room once again filled with chatter. "That's George. It's all about him."

Katharine's feelings mirrored her friend's. But she wondered whether he too had felt that awkward warmth while they had played together, prior to rushing off as if nothing unusual had occurred. "Why is he going to Europe?"

"He's supervising the London production of his new musical play, *Tell Me More*."

"I thought his new show was called *Lady, Be Good!*, and that it was playing locally."

"That's what I'm saying. He's a juggler."

Katharine considered sitting again at the piano and performing something by Lizst or Strauss, if only to break the mood. Instead she grabbed a cocktail cracker, smothered with caviar. She bit into it and wiped her lips while Pauline prattled on about the cloud of unhappiness that George Gershwin had blown into her life.

Katharine glanced around the room, lost in thought. Her eyes met Jimmy's. He was drinking, his back to the wall, watching her. She smiled.

Alexander Woollcott heaped contumely upon middlebrow Broadway confections, mercilessly burying them and reserving his praise for melancholy drama and silly farces. He boosted Eugene O'Neill and the Marx brothers with equal fervor. But the principal subject of his theatrical criticism was his own wit and erudition. The Gershwin impromptu at the Warburgs' dinner party must have impressed him, for the following week Woollcott reviewed *Lady, Be Good!* for the *World.* His column sparkled with references to Restoration Comedy, Jules Moinaux, and even Mozart.

Perusing this column during Saturday brunch at the Gotham Hotel, Jimmy remarked to Katharine that he considered their friend an intellectual bully. "Woollcott's an elitist. That's why he throws in all those references. Which is fine, but rather ironic coming from a Socialist, don't you think?"

"Socialists aren't allowed to be sophisticated?" asked Katharine.

"Don't ask me. Ask Stalin," said Jimmy. "That's the whole point of socialist realism." The term was new to Katharine. "To be Socialist and claim sophistication," Jimmy pontificated, "is hypocritical as hell. Because Socialism means egalitarianism, or claims to anyway, while sophistication suggests hierarchy."

"Jimmy," said Katharine, "have a mimosa,

will you? Or better, a double shot of bourbon." She peppered her omelet. "Aleck
doesn't necessarily agree with Stalin on
everything."

"No, he's only a member of the economi-
cally ignorant masses, whose misplaced
idealism plays into the hands of dolts like
Stalin." Jimmy tasted the melon in port
wine.

"All the same," said Katharine, "I'd like
to see what this ballyhoo is about."

"What ballyhoo?"

"*Lady, Be Good!*"

Jimmy raised an eyebrow.

Katharine smiled. "Aleck may not be an
economist, but according to just about
everyone he's a brilliant critic. And he says
Lady, Be Good! is a thrill. Why not?"

While Jimmy took his coffee and read the
Sunday World, Katharine strolled to the new
mercantile behemoth, Saks Fifth Avenue.
She picked out a sleeveless peach shift in
silk chiffon. Silver stitching and crystals in
stylized floral patterns accented the bust,
waist, and sides.

That evening she wore it with nude silk
stockings, a possum shawl, a silver-mesh
clutch, and a pearl-and-rhinestone hair
band. Jimmy dressed in a pair of satin stripe
trousers, a white wing-collar shirt with a

matching bow tie, a white vest, and a single button jacket accessorized with sterling cuff links, white gloves, and a top hat.

The show was sold out. The crowd outside chirped with anticipation. Ticket hawkers shouted inflated offers and negotiated with desperate Gershwin fans. Arc lamps and the headlights of passing automobiles added an electric buzz. A few minutes late, the doors swung open and the public spilled in. Katharine and Jimmy located their seats in the middle of the eighth row.

She had spent the most memorable moments of her childhood in first-tier seats at the Metropolitan Opera at Thirty-Ninth and Broadway. When her father reviewed performances of *Lohengrin* or *The Marriage of Figaro* for the *New-York Tribune,* she tagged along. She loved the elaborate fantasy of opera. In Wagner's mythological world of gods and beasts, whose turmoil mirrored that of an adolescent girl, she sought refuge from the banality of her parents' endless financial and social predicaments.

The Liberty Theatre was no Metropolitan Opera. The room was smaller, the décor plebeian, the seats hard, the audience casually attired. She sensed the energy in the room but felt out of place. The lights dimmed. The curtains parted.

To watch a Wagner opera was to pluck leitmotifs out of the air and braid narrative strands into shimmering, dark myths. A Gershwin musical was sparkly and wild. The show blended Ziegfeldesque spectacle, legs kicked high, tout ensembles choruses, with the pathos of songs like "Oh, Lady Be Good!" and the throb and swing of "Fascinating Rhythm." She recognized some tunes and harmonies from those Gershwin had whisked through at her piano. The audience rode a Coney Island roller coaster of absurd storytelling that played on primal emotions: risqué lust, poverty dreaming of wealth, orphans craving family, fraudulent love and true love, alliances and enmities forming and vaporizing, all delivered with a knowing leer as if exploiting and ridiculing the previous generation's Victorian tastes. The composer, the book writer, the choreographer, the dancers, especially the gravity-defying stars Fred and his sister Adele Astaire, and the invisible boys who followed them with a tight spotlight, had conspired to make the audience forget their troubles and to erase their consciousness of time.

In addition to being the world's most acclaimed dancing duo, the Astaires were comedians. Adele's laughter was lighter than air. Sometimes she threw a playful jab at her brother that he seemed not to anticipate. He turned to the audience with a puzzled expression, raising his index finger to his closed mouth as he thought up a rejoinder, then poked her right back, and the orchestra served up another dance number. It was magic, Katharine admitted to herself, but of a ridiculous kind. On reflection, though, no more preposterous than Wagner's lugubrious *Sturm und Drang* or the dreamworld forest and castle of Debussy's *Pelléas et Mélisande.*

When the show ended Katharine and Jimmy floated out of the auditorium, flotsam on a wave of song. Everyone was humming, singing, and whistling. Fans queued in the lobby where representatives of Harms, Inc., Gershwin's publisher, sold printed sheet music. Katharine pulled Jimmy to the end of the line. "I want to try my hand at these."

They reached the table, where piles of sheet music, songs from *Lady, Be Good!* as well as other Gershwin hits including the *Rhapsody in Blue,* covered the counter. "Whaddya want?" the sales clerk demanded. "This? Ten cents. Thank you. This? Ten cents. Thank you. This? This?" Katharine glanced at the titles: "Do It Again!," "The Man I Love," "Soon" . . . Had other male songwriters, she wondered, composed so prolifically and touchingly about female longing? Perhaps this was a clue to Gershwin's mystique.

"Come on, we don't have 'til Christmas."

"One of each," said Katharine.

The salesman's eyebrows shot up. "All of 'em?"

She nodded.

At home she propped "Fascinating Rhythm" on the music stand and attempted its wacky, lopsided jangle. Its subject was nothing more serious or meaningful than the composer's obsession with his own tune, and having observed Gershwin perform, especially at her party, she believed every word. She wondered whether his melomania was not a form of self-love, a vicious-cycle celebration of his power over his audience.

A half hour later, she spread open "The Man I Love." Contemplative and bluesy, a hymn of solitude and longing. The dialogue between the right and left hands mirrored the singer's hope-in-the-face-of-despair conversation with herself as she wondered what such a man might be like, when he would appear.

Jimmy stepped downstairs in his pajamas to ask her to stop playing. Unlike her, he pointed out, he had work to finish in the morning.

"Tomorrow's Sunday," she reminded him.

"Yes, but I'm taking Monday off. I have something to show you."

I have work, too, thought Katharine as they trudged upstairs. But that was playing with words. Most people understood *work* to imply *remuneration* and *predictability,* neither of which applied to aspiring composers. Jimmy had once understood the value of music and poetry, devoid of practical utility as they were. She was no longer sure he did.

She listened to his breathing as it slowed toward sleep, a train approaching some faraway station. As she attempted to join him in that station she thought about her education, popular music and serious music, and her unfulfilled ambitions. She listened to the songs that still rang in her head. Her fingers twitched as if bouncing across an invisible keyboard. Fred and Adele Astaire gyrated, pivoted, and dissolved in shadows.

Jimmy whisked in from the office at eleven the next morning. "Lionel, telegram Benjamin Fairchild. Tell him we'll be arriving at two."

"Yes, sir."

Looking up from the novel she was reading, Katharine searched her memory. "Benjamin Fairchild?"

An hour later, they were heading north in a coal-powered New Haven Railroad train. With his monogrammed leather satchel on the wooden bench beside him, Jimmy gazed out the window as the brick buildings of upper Manhattan yielded to forests, fields, and glimpses of the Hudson River.

"Where are you taking me?" asked Katharine.

He just smiled.

They disembarked at the small Greenwich, Connecticut, station. A reedy older gentleman in loose clothes and a lopsided hat approached at the exit. "All ready?" Jimmy nodded and the man led them to his Model T.

They rode over bumpy cobblestone and dirt roads into back country and then followed a river through a wooded gorge. They turned up a path to an isolated farm and passed a stone dam, an ancient mill, and a lofty chestnut tree. Up ahead, an old house with dormers and a shingle façade. Behind the house, a cliff. Off to the left stretched a pasture and an old red barn. Sparrows were chirping.

Benjamin Fairchild unlocked the door and escorted them into a large room. The furniture predated the American Revolution. The

197

wide oak floorboards were dulled with use and age. Dust covered everything. At the far end of the room stood a cast-iron Franklin stove. Jimmy motioned for Katharine to sit on the wooden settee. He sat beside her as Fairchild spread open the creaky shutters.

Fairchild took a sheaf of papers from the corner table and pulled up a Windsor chair, unmindful of the poorly repaired spindle in its back. He placed the papers on the pedestal table between them. "You have what we discussed?"

"I have more than that, my man." Jimmy removed a large envelope from his satchel.

"I don't need more," grumbled Fairchild. He pushed a page toward Jimmy. Katharine craned her neck to read it. She saw the word *Deed* in florid lettering. Below that, *the property known as Bydale,* and — she looked closer — *fifteen hundred acres.* "Jimmy," she asked, "are we buying this place?"

He nodded. While he read and signed papers, Katharine walked around. No one had updated the house in decades, but the floors were sturdy and the plaster walls, though patched in places, were free of cracks.

Fairchild joined her at the kitchen sink, a rectangular zinc basin. The shelves and cupboards were unpainted, graying oak.

"Seventeen forty-one," he told her. "In case you were wondering."

"I was," said Katharine.

"A gentleman named Silas Mead built her. A turncoat. Fled to Canada with Benedict Arnold."

"Charming."

They returned to the salon, where Jimmy joined her at the window. "How did you find this?" asked Katharine.

"I've been searching," said Jimmy.

"As in, visiting places?" she asked, astonished,

He nodded. "All over the coast. Bydale stole my heart."

Katharine looked at the aspen leaves shimmering in a breeze. "And all that time, you said nothing?"

Jimmy smiled.

"You rascal," she said, shaking her head. But as they looked at each other, they acknowledged something in each other's eyes. Something they rarely spoke about these days. Something almost embarrassing in its poignancy. Especially now.

That first night at Bydale, in a creaky bed on the second floor, Jimmy took her in his arms and kissed her. She held him, looking into his eyes, and allowed him to make love to her. Comfortably. Warmly. Fervently.

Afterward they lay on their backs. "A penny for your thoughts," said Jimmy.

She was thinking about their lovemaking. About its meaning. Its sweet nostalgia. Its sadness. But that was not what she said. "Just now? I was listening to the frogs," she improvised. "And the crickets. And I was thinking, from their point of view, this is *their* land. We're just squatters."

"That's what I love about this place," said Jimmy. "It puts everything in perspective." He kissed her on the nose and turned onto his side.

In the morning, while preparing breakfast with Katharine, Jimmy expanded upon what Bydale meant to him in the context of his family's historical aspirations, or frustrations. "For centuries — millenia, actually — the European aristocrats forbade us to own land. Did you know that?" He struggled to light the gas stove. One of the valves was stuck. "We could trade. We could send ships across the oceans. We could finance their dreams of power and conquest. We could negotiate treaties on their behalf. But *they* owned the land. *Their* serfs worked it. That was the bottom line." A second valve finally twisted and *whoosh,* he lit the flame.

Katharine squeezed orange juice. "So that's what this is about?" she asked. "Getting even with European aristocracy?"

Jimmy placed the glass percolator on the flame. "I should rather say, healing."

We could all use some of that, thought Katharine.

She looked at the trees through the kitchen window. Their bright leaves announcing rebirth and hope and the warmth of summer. She leaned over the counter and opened the window. In a nest under the eaves, new-hatched sparrows were cheeping to their mother, all at once but hardly in unison, the music of hunger and love. Their mother flapped down to the nest, a worm in her beak. Katharine thought of her daughters, of her husband, and of what Bydale might come to mean to all of them.

CHAPTER ELEVEN

December 1925

Once upon a time, Katharine cared where her husband was traveling, how long he would be away, but it had all grown so complicated and mutable. She no longer paid attention. He was somewhere in Europe, or on the sea, or elsewhere. He would return when he returned.

She was composing an étude. She was attempting stride piano. She was playing Gershwin songs. Not the way their composer did, loosey-goosey, with shifting tempos. She struck the notes properly, intentionally. But through the music she had gained insight into the man. In his chords, rhythms, and melodies, Gershwin's moods played and fought like unsupervised youth in the back alleys of the Lower East Side.

Now, in the music she was composing, she inserted a Gershwinesque key change here and a bouncy rhythm there. She was breaking rules, or at least bending them — but Chopin and Schubert had defied the rules of their era, too. The bigger question concerned not the evolution of her style but her need for an audience. She experienced it as a dark hole in the center of her life. What was the point of artistic expression in music, or any other medium, if it affected only the artist herself? That kind of exercise was akin to self-pleasuring. It might provide release but what she craved was contact, through her music, with other souls.

She attended the premiere of Gershwin's *New York Concerto* alone. The composer, at the piano, wore a fitted beige suit, defying Carnegie Hall tradition, which dictated that black was *de rigueur* for soloists. Even more eloquently than his attire, his music argued — as he had done in the *Rhapsody* — that the freedom, spontaneity, and verve of jazz could be captured on the page and translated into an orchestral setting, just as new photographs froze the motion of a horse. But a picture of a horse was not a horse, and some critics heatedly maintained that Gershwin's sound was not jazz. Whatever it was, his way of blending Rachmaninoff-like lyricism with bumpy-road rhythms captivated her and carried her all the way to the big dissonant chords and soft coda at the end of the *New York Concerto.*

Because drinking was still not permitted in restaurants, the conductor Walter Damrosch had organized a celebration in his apartments, which were crowded with Old World oil paintings and sturdy German furniture. He had invited twenty-three friends and students, including Katharine, and provided one beverage per guest, beer he brewed in a dedicated room according to family recipes. Katharine strolled through Damrosch's flat holding a frosted stein. She recognized orchestra musicians, showgirls whose painted faces and long legs she had admired in *Lady, Be Good!,* and impresarios she had seen profiled in pencil-sketch busts in the *New York Times* or the *World.* Sam Rothapfel was talking with a pretty showgirl. "No, no, contrary to my reputation, I don't build theaters," Katharine heard him tell her. "I build dreams." From time to time Katharine glanced at Gershwin, who stood chatting with a handful of associates.

He seemed intense and preoccupied. She wanted to reassure him, to tell him how much she had enjoyed his performance, that she had found the *New York Concerto* brash, bluesy, poetic, and soaring. That his orchestration was inventive and that despite her initial skepticism, his grand project of fusing folk-musical modes, beginning with the blues and klezmer, with late-romantic symphonic structures and harmonies, now struck her as brilliant and original. Most of all, she yearned to share her own musical ideas with him.

His bearing beckoned no such exchange. Whether deliberately or not, he turned his back to her.

The hell with him. She approached his older brother, Ira, instead. Squat and pudgy, with a soft face and glasses, Ira reminded Katharine of a factory accountant. He seemed too serious to have co-penned the lyric,

I won't say I will, but I won't say
   I won't!
I don't say I do, but I don't say I don't!
Kissing of any kind
Never was on my mind.
Maybe I can arrange it —
It's my mind, and I can change it.

They talked about, what else, words and music. Ira was an avid reader of Tennyson and Byron, appreciated the witticisms of Gilbert and Sullivan, Irving Berlin, and Cole Porter, but loved the simplicity and emotion of Puccini's librettists, Luigi Illica and Giuseppe Giacosa.

"What do you think of Richard Wagner?" she asked him. "When I was a girl, his operas were my fantasy world."

"I can hardly sit through them," admitted Ira. "The overture of *Tristan and Isolde*? It's out of this world. So's the "Liebestod." But in between? The fella needed someone to tell him, 'hey, Dick, not every note that pops in your head is brilliant. And not every word, either. Put your *tuchus* in the seat of the listener once in a while, for Chrissakes.' "

Katharine laughed. "Geniuses sometimes become infatuated with themselves. Why not? Everyone else is infatuated with them."

Ira cocked his head and rubbed his chin as if to ask, *what are you trying to imply?*

Katharine shrugged as if to say, *nothing at all.*

Ira noticed a tall gentleman in a tweed jacket who stood uncomfortably by himself, and waved him over. "Al Stillman, Katharine Warburg. Up-and-coming lyricist, meet up-and-coming composer."

Katharine shook Al's hand. His eyes exuded gentleness and shyness.

"What do you think of the Wagner libretto?" Ira asked him.

Al frowned. "Is that that new Italian bicycle?"

"Built for long distances, but not great for speed," quipped Ira.

"But beautiful to behold, soaring through the Alpine wilderness," said Katharine.

Al sipped his beer. "All of Vienna was delirious with Johann Strauss's *oom-pah-pah*. Why mess with the tried-and-true?"

Appreciating his irony, Katharine smiled. And glanced at George, whose back was still turned to her.

Weary of cocktail patter and miffed by George's indifference, she left early. *Sure, the man's music hits a nerve, but what of it? The gall, to ignore me like that. After what we experienced at my piano.* As she opened the elevator gate and exited to the ground floor she heard a door slam several flights above. The elevator whooshed back up. She buttoned her coat, bracing for the winter chill, and pulled on her gloves. As she was about to leave the building, the elevator slid down and Gershwin stepped out, wearing a wool coat and hat.

"Kay," he grinned.

"The name's Katharine."

"I know. But to me you're Kay."

"Since when am I anything to you, Mister

Gershwin?"

"Since now. And it's not Mister Gershwin. It's George. Hey, what do you say we head uptown?"

He escorted her to the sidewalk, stuck his pinkies into the corners of his mouth, whistled, and hailed a cab. He opened the rear door for her. *Well,* she thought, *why the hell not? Jimmy's out of town. Jimmy's always out of town. Probably drinking, or whatever, with some* fräulein *in Berlin, or wherever.* The thought of spending the evening with another man — with *this* man — letting him lead her wherever he wanted, within limits of course, thrilled her. She slid into the cab and he followed, jerking the door closed and leaning forward. "One Thirty-Fifth and Lenox." His mood seemed to have lightened. "Did I mention how much I enjoyed your playing?" he asked.

"At my party? It felt like I was pitching to Babe Ruth."

"Nah. We're on the same team. We're both musicians, aren't we?" From his pocket George removed a pale-blue-and-black package of Black Jack chewing gum. "Like a stick?"

"Why not?"

He gave her two. She unwrapped both and folded them into her mouth. The sweet bite

208

of licorice. "Look," said George, "I know jazz isn't your thing. You attack the keyboard like a mathematician attacks a blackboard."

"A sensitive mathematician, I hope."

"Me, I play like a trapeze artist," said Gershwin.

"A sensitive trapeze artist," said Kay.

He chuckled. "Hell, you can't do what we do without sensitivity, can you? But there's sensitivity and there's sensitivity. That's why we have so much to learn from each other."

Whatever that means, she thought. "Where are you taking me?"

"Nowhere you'd mind," said Gershwin.

"That's not an answer."

"A friend's throwing a rent party. Wait 'til you hear his glissandi. It's like the keys melt into each other."

His hand covered hers on the seat. Her heartbeat syncopated uncomfortably, *dada-badump, dada-badump.* "A rent party?" she asked.

"There's quite a few talented pianists, especially in Harlem," explained Gershwin, "who can't rub two dimes together. So they put on these shows in their apartments and charge admission. Best stride you'll ever hear for a couple clams."

"A couple clams?"

"Two dollars. Even one'll get you in but the point is not to save money."

Harlem felt like the flip side of the world. George paid the driver, instructing him to wait all night if need be. "Head up to a Hundred and Forty-Second Street, the Cotton Club. You know the joint? Open all night, and you can park in front. Tell 'em Gershwin sent you. They'll treat you right. Have a drink on me. Hell, have three. The music'll cost you nothing. We'll meet there later."

The driver swung his beefy face around. "Gershwin? You're George Gershwin? Holy moly. My wife won't believe it. She's crazy about you. Can I have an autograph?"

"Later." George patted his shoulder. He and Katharine stepped out to a low-rise brick building that shook with music and chatter. The crowd spilled onto the sidewalk and the Negro partiers brazenly ignored Prohibition, guzzling, gabbing, and kissing in the stairwell — and narrowing the path to the third floor so much that Katharine's hips touched Gershwin's as they climbed. *That certain feeling* washed through her as she crossed an invisible boundary, ignoring the warning signs: excitement, anticipation, a tinge of fear. The third-floor apartment

210

roared with piano-playing, hoots, and laughter. Cake-walkers wiggled their hips, slapped their thighs, and shook their hands toward the heavens. The man at the door knew George, who stuffed not four dollars but forty into the collections hat.

"Hey, Georgie, I knew you'd make it! How'd it go, boy?"

"It went okay," said George with uncharacteristic modesty.

"The *New York Concerto*? Oh, it went exceptionally well," Katharine corrected him.

"Who's the lovely lady?"

"Luckey Roberts, I'd like you to meet Kay Warburg," said George. "A pianist and composer, like you. Like me. Like him." He pointed to the big fellow at the piano.

"Katharine," she corrected him again.

Luckey Roberts rose and kissed her hand. George reached into the ice bucket, grabbed a seltzer and a bottle of gin, and mixed drinks for Katharine and Luckey. "Luckey taught me so much when I was a kid," he told her. "I used to ditch school and roller-skate over to his place."

"That ain't no lie," said Luckey. "Only now you're playing Carnegie Hall and your teacher's still working the bars. And that's when things are rolling."

George handed him a glass. "Luckey, I can get you into private parties. I can get you into clubs. I used to play that circuit myself, you know that. But Moses himself couldn't part the stage curtains of Carnegie Hall for a colored man."

"Moses and Jesus together," laughed Luckey.

George handed Katharine her drink. "I remember when Jolson sang 'Swanee' at Carnegie Hall in blackface. My first big break. Management was beside themselves. A colored man on the Carnegie stage! And the crowd's going wild! Al thought they might change their policy."

A scowl etched Luckey's expressive face. "He wasn't tellin' 'em that, Georgie. He was just showing 'em one more time that white folks can mock the Negro and get paid for it."

"That isn't how Al meant it, Luckey," said Gershwin.

"Maybe that ain't how he meant it. But that's what it meant anyway, ain't it."

"Maybe to you."

"Look at it this way," said Luckey poking George in the chest. "Say a white man put on a long black coat and side curls and a fake nose and — what do you call that little hat?"

212

"A yarmulke."

"And say this fellow rubbed his hands together hunched over like an ape, counting his money. And all these fat white men watching him, these Stanleys and Freds slapping their thighs and laughing 'til tears rolled down their cheeks. How would you feel about that, my friend?"

Gershwin's face fell, his lips pursed. He stared at his feet, deep in thought, then placed his hand on his mentor's shoulder and nodded his understanding.

"Moses and Jesus can't do it?" said Luckey. "Well, I'm gonna do it. They're gonna let me on that stage sooner or later. They're gonna beg me — or someone just like me."

"I'll drink to that," said George, and they clinked glasses.

The gentleman at the Chickering upright sang in a melodious tenor punctuating his lyrics with chuckles, wiggling his eyebrows, and joshing with the dancers. His right hand raced over the keys with uncanny alacrity while his left jumped like a grasshopper. "Who is that?" asked Katharine, sipping her drink.

"Everyone calls him Fats." George smiled. "I call him a genius."

Fats Waller's technique was even more

virtuosic than George's, but drew on a narrower range of styles. There was little or no Debussy in his fluid, extroverted, blues-soaked tunes. His playing resembled nothing Katharine had studied at the Institute. Her teachers either had no idea such music existed or willfully ignored it.

"Hey, Georgie!" Fats cried out. He continued playing with his left hand while he waved with his right. "Come on over here, you crazy man. Put your twitchy fingers where they want to be. I feel like shimmyin'!"

George and Katharine waded through dancers to the piano, where George took over hammering out one of his earliest tunes, "The Real American Folk Song." An elegant woman with a radiant smile, a long teal dress, and pearls approached the piano. "Ladies and gentlemen," George shouted. "The great Sara Martin from Louisville, in the green state of Kentucky!"

As Sara Martin belted out the lyrics, Fats Waller dragged Katharine into the dance zone at the center of the crowded apartment and started flailing his arms and feet. She tried to emulate his vim and elasticity. Fats pulled her close and released her. The gin was doing its job and she was starting to enjoy the scene. She sent her shoes flying across the room and swung and flapped and thrashed with him. Sweaty and flushed she jumped, twisted, and finally collapsed to the ground, laughing.

George stopped playing, stood on the piano bench, and clapped his hands. "Hey, all of you want to hear something? We hit the jackpot not once but four times tonight. We got a highly trained classical pianist with us. Get your ears ready for something special now. Kay, swing over here, will you?"

Fats led her to the piano.

"Show 'em what you're made of," George said into her ear.

The room quieted. Katharine caught her breath, lowered her hands to the keyboard, and began playing Chopin's soft, haunting opus 9, number 1. If she had given the matter a moment's thought, she would have chosen any other piece for this night, this crowd. A rousing Beethoven piano sonata, perhaps? But Chopin's quiet contemplation was what burst out of her.

She felt her father's presence. Sam was guiding her fingers. As the notes drifted from the upright piano, the chatter and hum of the room quieted and the partygoers, glistening with sweat, succumbed to the Polish composer's mood. She finished to applause, whistles, and whoops, then stood and curtsied. Tears shone in her eyes.

She had never before associated with colored folks other than her servants, never sought out their company or requested their friendship. The warmth and unabashed sentimentality of people like Luckey Roberts, Fats Waller, and Sara Martin touched her. And the talent! Their ability to snatch moments of exuberance from lives filled, she presumed, with toil and penury. Their courage to laugh in the face of despair. Unlike the snide titters of so many of her friends, theirs was not the laughter of derision or mockery, but an uncowed celebration of life.

She and George stumbled giddily up Lenox Avenue. Although Katharine harbored no ill will toward others, regardless of their origins, she would have felt uncomfortable in this neighborhood prior to this evening, if only because it was so unfamiliar. But walking with Gershwin, who had spent part of his childhood in Harlem, she felt privileged and at ease, as if she had discovered a window that offered a different view of their surroundings. "That's the thing about music," she told him. "You grew up primarily on the Lower East Side. I can't imagine your childhood. What did you do?"

"I broke rules," said George. "I guess I'm still doing that."

"I spent mine on the Upper West Side. Museums, operas, and my home away from home, the Institute of Musical Art."

"That's not a childhood," said George. "That's a miniature adulthood."

"And Fats Waller and Luckey Roberts, all they knew was Harlem, right? But then the music starts, and everyone's legs and arms are flying, and in that moment whatever we've experienced, all our grudges and resentments and rivalries, it all vanishes. And that's priceless."

"You think so?" asked George hopefully.

"I know so. That's why you and I do what we do, George."

"And I thought I was just in it for the money."

"No you didn't, you lying bastard." She looped her arm through his, feeling giddy.

A beggar slammed his palm onto George's coat and pitched forward. "Can ya help a man's got nothing? I came up here five months ago. I was a sharecropper down in Louisiana. It's rough down there. The farmers in Louisiana, they're starving, brother."

George opened his wallet, handed the man ten dollars, and patted him on the shoulder. The beggar stared at the bill. "Buy "yourself a coat," George told him.

"Praise Jesus," muttered the man.

"He's only going to buy himself booze," said Katharine as he stumbled away.

"Same as us," George remarked as the Cotton Club came into view.

Fancy automobiles — Chrysler B-70s, Oakland Sixes, Packards, a Bugatti — lined both sides of Lenox Avenue, the storied vehicles of gangsters and show business executives. Inside, at almost two in the morning, Harlem's prime watering hole was swinging. Piano, blaring brass, tomtoms beating African rhythms; dancers in sequin-fringed outfits; beer and moonshine, Prohibition or no Prohibition.

"How do they get away with it?" Katharine shouted over the din.

"It's all politics," George shouted back. "Money. Guns."

The celebrated gangster Owney Madden, proprietor of the Cotton Club, emerged from the noisy crowd to greet George, who introduced Katharine, again calling her "Kay."

"There's a couple of folks waitin' for you," Owney said as he led them to the back. On the way, George returned friends' and admirers' smiles. At the table of Al Jolson, who sat with three young women, he stopped and introduced her. "Kay Warburg, Al Jolson. The man who gave me my start in show business. I'll never be able to repay him."

Jolson wore a fitted silky-gray jacket, a crisp white shirt with onyx cufflinks, a matching tiepin, and a geometrical necktie. He stood to kiss Katharine's hand. "Pleased to meet you."

She smiled. "I met you once before. Well, almost met you, at a party. Madam C. J. Walker?"

"Of course I remember," said Jolson. "A beautiful face like yours."

She smiled. *Professional charmers — that's what these fellows are.* It hardly mattered whether Al really remembered her. That portion of her life was so far away. She was no longer that person, the young woman who fell in love with Jimmy Warburg.

Owney Madden escorted her and George to a corner booth, where Mayor-elect Jimmy Walker sat engaged in tipsy conversation with the cab driver who had escorted them uptown.

"You two know each other?" George addressed the cab driver as the mayor rose unsteadily.

"We do now!" Jimmy Walker pumped George's hand. "So pleased to make your acquaintance, Mister Gershwin."

Goodness, Katharine wondered, *what do the mayor-elect and the cab driver have in common, that they spent their evening guzzling together?* Then she realized. Walker must have been told that the cabbie was waiting for Gershwin and decided he was as worthy a drinking partner as anyone. And his vote as good as anyone's, too.

Katharine had not voted for Jimmy Walker. She had not voted at all. She had been thrilled when women earned the right to vote in 1920, and she agreed with much of the Tammany Hall chicken-in-every-pot agenda, but she despised their reputation for thuggery. She tried to hide her contempt as she regarded Jimmy Walker's glistening teeth and obsequious smile. A dandy with the handshake of a machinist, he looked into her eyes and then George's, simpering tentatively like a charlatan who felt demeaned in the face of achievement and grace. "Anything I can do for you, George. You just let me know." He winked.

She awoke in George's arms. Sunlight flooded her bedroom. He still wore his undershirt and tweed trousers. She had retained her silk slip.

She remembered returning home with

him the night before, both of them flushed with desire and fatigue as dawn approached. "You probably find yourself in this situation fairly often," she had surmised aloud.

"Often enough," admitted George.

"Well, keep your trousers buttoned. I'm not one of your showgirl floozies."

"They're not all floozies but I'll try to be a gentleman," he agreed drowsily. "Just this time." And he drifted off to sleep without so much as touching her.

She listened to his quiet breathing. She felt his warmth. *Go to sleep!* she told herself. And then, an hour later, *go to sleep,* again.

That was last night. What time was it now? She glanced at her father's gold pocket watch on her nightstand. Ten-thirty. Katharine wrapped herself in an organdie robe. George opened his eyes, smiled, and clambered to his feet. He slipped on his shirt and tied his shoes.

"You don't need to get dressed," she told him. "You're not going anywhere."

"You're a doll but I can't stay," he said.

Disappointed, she led him down to the kitchen. At the threshold she stopped in her tracks.

Dressed for work, Jimmy sat at the table sipping coffee and reading the *New York World.* Just like any other morning although much later than most. He glanced at her and George. George smiled sideways uneasily. Katharine's heart pounded.

She did not however avert her eyes. *Freedom in our marriage, isn't that what you wanted?* Jimmy nodded as if reading her thoughts and returned to the news.

Katharine marveled at his self-restraint. *Well, that's that,* she thought. But then she asked herself, *that's what?* That one stumped her. She had to say something. Anything. "When did you get home?" she managed.

Jimmy glanced at his watch. "Before you."

"How was your trip?"

He turned the page of the newspaper.

Lionel poured an additional cup of coffee. "Lots of sugar," George told him.

He and Katharine fiddled with their beverages at the counter. "Did you sleep well?" she asked.

Jimmy allowed the question to linger. "Are you asking me?" he asked finally, his eyes still buried in his newspaper. "Could have been worse."

"How about some music?" Katharine proposed in a tone of forced enthusiasm.

"That's a swell idea, Kay," mumbled George.

Jimmy turned. "Kay?"

"Kay," she confirmed.

Jimmy nodded. "Kay." His eyes met George's. "Mister Gershwin."

"George."

"I'd wager ten dollars you haven't read this yet." Jimmy pointed to the paper.

"I don't gamble."

Jimmy read aloud from Samuel Chotzinoff's review of the *New York Concerto* début:

> The truth is that George Gershwin is a genius. He is the present, with all its audacity, impertinence, its feverish delight in motion, its lapses into rhythmically exotic melancholy.

George stepped to the table and leaned over the article. "I would have been delighted to attend," said Jimmy.

George read the review, sipping his coffee. Kay stood behind him looking down over his shoulder. When he reached the end she gripped his hand. "Come, George. Let's play some piano."

He cocked his head and looked down his nose at Jimmy as if asking permission. Which seemed a surprising thing for George to do. Jimmy returned his glance with the hint of a nod, not so much offering his blessing as accepting the inevitable. Which also seemed strange.

Kay led George into the drawing room. On the music stand, her work in progress. She sat down and patted the bench. "I'd love your take on this." She began playing.

George listened attentively, rubbing his cheek with the back of his hand and studying her notation. "It's swanky, the way you dodge cadences," he commented as the last chord faded. "Clever, the tonal ambiguity. You learned your lessons well at the Institute."

She sensed he was holding back. "But?" she asked, bracing herself for more not-so-subtle irony.

"But Kay," said George, "music isn't just . . . machinery."

She frowned, wondering why he would say such a thing.

"Don't get me wrong," added George. "I love a well-built machine. But there has to be something else. I don't know what to call it. The mainspring. No — the energy in the mainspring. The spark of life in the heart of the song. It comes from somewhere else."

A part of her took umbrage at his lofty attitude. Another part appreciated his unabashed honesty, and wanted more of it. "From where?"

"You just have to listen." He looked at his watch. "And I have to run."

Kay touched his arm. "Right now? Is it . . ." She pointed toward the kitchen.

He shook his head. "I've got work to do. If I pounded the keys from morning 'til midnight, and wore my pencil down to my fingertips, I'd never reach the end of it."

"I could assist you, George." Still seated at the piano, she picked up her music pad and pencil. "I'm good at transcription. How much time would that save you? Go ahead, whistle something."

He whistled the first ten notes of "Somebody Loves Me," one of his early blues-inspired tunes. She jotted them down, tore the page from the pad, and handed it to him.

He looked at it and gave it back. "I'll keep that in mind. Meanwhile, I'll be touring the *New York Concerto*. You won't see me for a while."

"Where are you going?"

"Anywhere they'll let me near a stage."

I could accompany you. She said it with her eyes.

He turned to leave, then turned back. He pulled her up from the piano bench and hugged her. She closed her eyes and allowed herself to feel the warmth of Gershwin's body, the prickle of his unshaven cheeks, the pressure of his hands.

There are hugs and there are hugs. Some represent closure — *so nice to see you* — while others fling open doors. This hug was one of the latter. He held her tightly, with unanticipated conviction. It was brief but as expressive as some of his best songs. As if to say, *don't worry, this is just the beginning.*

The door closed with an irrefutable snap of metal against metal. A vault swinging shut in a tomb. She felt the air being sucked out of the room and gasped. As she stood staring at the closed door, Jimmy sauntered in.

"What was that piece you were playing?" He smiled as if to say, *nothing has changed, there's still plenty of air in here, take a breath.*

"Oh, just a little something I've been, you know . . ." she told him.

"Can I hear it again?"

Kay sat at the piano and again played through her composition. Jimmy listened, his arms crossed.

"Katharine . . . Kay . . . That is lovely." Jimmy took a moment to collect his thoughts. "To be that gifted and get no recognition."

She looked at him sideways.

"I'm not due back at the office until

Thursday," said Jimmy. "What do you say we ride up to Bydale for a few days? I swear I was dreaming about that place the whole time I was abroad."

"In the middle of winter?"

"I'll have Fairchild heat the house. Let's get it in tip-top shape for spring."

She appreciated her husband's self-mastery. *He knows he did this to himself.* And yet, she no longer wished to nourish feelings of resentment. Jimmy loved her composition. She appreciated that — even if, deep inside, she knew he was wrong. And George was right.

She smiled. "Why not?" A break to Bydale might do them both some good.

Jimmy smiled back, tousling her hair.

CHAPTER TWELVE

Lionel reserved a train car. He and Olga secured five trunks of provisions to the luggage ties. Miss Louisa and Miss Lainey brought coloring books, story books, and crayons but April and Andrea ran up and down the car hiding behind seats, shouting, and occasionally falling down. Jimmy joined in their mischief and when he caught one of them, pinned her to the bench and tickled her. Jo, the nursemaid, rocked little Kathleen on her knee.

Kay smoked Marlboros and watched the scenery, reliving her evening with George. First, Fats Waller's rent party, then the Cotton Club, then home, feeling his closeness in bed. And finally, his fervent hug.

Jimmy returned to his seat. April and Andrea settled, pointing out the window and babbling. Kay showed them pictures from *Raggedy Ann's Alphabet Book,* her mind still elsewhere.

At the station a man named John Becker awaited them. His beard reached the top pocket of his overalls. He drove a Model T flatbed. The children and their caretakers jostled and shivered in the back.

The woodburning stove at Bydale radiated heat, which spread through the house. While Miss Louisa and Miss Lainey escorted the girls to their bedrooms, and Lionel and Olga stocked the larders, Jimmy and Kay consulted in the front room with John Becker, who opened a large sketch pad in which he had drawn the house and property. "Tennis court." He pointed to an open area and added charcoal strokes. "Swimming pool." He pointed again. "Corral. How many horses?"

"Two, for now." Jimmy glanced at Kay.

John nodded. "Barn."

"You're a builder," Kay deduced.

"Landscape architect," Becker corrected her.

"John studied classics at Harvard," added Jimmy. "We took Ovid and Virgil together, then he moved on to Petronius while I lingered in Hades."

"Which turns out to be not too shabby, from what I can tell," said Becker.

"Landscape architecture was an afterthought, right John?" said Jimmy. "But don't worry, Katharine —"

"Kay," she corrected her husband. *Katharine* now felt like a discarded dress, ill-fitting and out-of-date.

"Don't worry," said Jimmy. "John's meticulous in everything."

"Especially in my genitives and ablatives," said Becker.

"Ah, yes, Latin grammar," said Kay. "Such a fond memory."

"You studied Latin?" asked Becker.

"Of course," said Kay. "Early church music and all that. I remember precisely three words. *In vino veritas.*"

"Just one sentence," Jimmy told Becker, "but she learned it well."

Becker laughed as April came bounding down the stairs. Little Andrea followed, shouting. Miss Louisa tromped after them but they were faster. Andrea ran to Kay and grabbed her skirts, cringing.

Kay clapped her hands. "Girls!"

Andrea stopped in her tracks. So did Miss Louisa.

"You can be down here," Kay told them. "But no wildness. The grown-ups are trying to have a conversation."

No sooner had she uttered these words, however, than the wildness resumed. Andrea jumped on a bench, shouting. April tried to grab her.

Miss Louisa struggled to calm them. "Now, Miss Andrea, you know that's naughty."

Jimmy walked across the room, took Andrea in his arms, and placed her on the floor, kissing her forehead. "Let's go into my office," he suggested to Kay and John.

They closed the door of the bedroom that Jimmy had designated as his office. Kay and John sat on a leather sofa. "Kay, why don't you take charge of the décor," proposed Jimmy, settling into an armchair. "Make this place your sanctuary."

"We need a piano," said Kay. "A Steinway."

Becker scratched his head. "Not an easy find around here. New York. Maybe New Haven if you can abide a serviceable second-hand instrument from Yale. But first we refinish the floors, paint the walls."

She looked at her husband. He nodded. *Your call.* "Let's prioritize the floors, then," said Kay. "I'll try out pianos in New York."

Jimmy walked briskly these days. Kay took long strides to keep up as they trudged together through the naked, frozen woods, talking about their plans for the house and considering Becker's suggestions.

"What's the hurry?" she asked, panting.

"Race up the hill, beat the chill," said Jimmy.

She looked down. *Don't fall in the gorge. Don't fall for George.* "It's just that . . . I remember when we used to stroll more *andante.* When walking wasn't just about getting there."

"*Andante,* I don't recall," said Jimmy. "Maybe *andantino.* Or *rubato,* on occasion."

"*Andante,*" insisted Kay. "Even *largo.* When you still wanted to be a poet."

"Who says I gave up on that?"

They looked out over the frosty, leafless landscape, a study in shades of brown and gray with patches of white. She remembered the spring day when she had first come to Bydale with Jimmy, the bright leaves shimmering in the breeze whispering of rebirth and expectation. Now those leaves were gone and the birds had winged their melodies to a warmer climate. *Yes, we age,* the trees told her. *Our leaves fall and the birds no longer chirp in our boughs. But we're still standing.* She mentally mocked her cheerlessness. *Silly, sentimental trees!* She was far too young to be attributing such long-suffering, mawkish ponderings to the vegetation of her Connecticut getaway. Her skin was still smooth, her step sprightly. For the young, life was not supposed to be about resignation, but dreams.

Jimmy rubbed his arms to warm himself. "Do you imagine," he asked, "that because I've managed to find merit in my banking activities, I've lost my sensitivity to language, or beauty?"

"You don't talk about poetry, these days. Or opera, for that matter."

"I've been focusing on providing you and the children with a certain quality of life." He offered her a weary, accommodating smile. "But let's see if we can't invite poetry back into the mix." She thought her husband courageous and stoical. "My poetry and yours," he added.

"Mine?"

He nodded. "You have an enviable talent, Katharine. Kay. What you need is exposure. You've written enough music to fill an evening. The problem is, no one has heard it. Why don't we rent a stage? The Grand Ballroom at the Hotel Astor has excellent acoustics. We can post an ad in the *Times*. You'll perform your best pieces and two or three classics, and we'll see what kind of response we get."

His offer moved her, more for its intent than for the opportunity. She took his hand.

That afternoon their distant neighbor

Benjamin Fairchild drove up with a salted ring-necked pheasant. Olga stewed it with puréed carrots, which she served with rice, baked asparagus, and a stout Bordeaux. Jimmy and Kay decided to allow the children at the dinner table. "After all," said Jimmy, "the family that eats together —" he searched for a rhyme.

"Cheats together?" tried Kay.

Jimmy shook his head. *Not quite what I was going for.*

Jo snuggled the sleeping infant, Kathleen, in a rocking chair. Andrea picked at her rice. April refused to eat altogether. "I hate pheasant." She rose to look in the pantry. "Do we have cookies?"

"April," Kay said, "come back to the table and eat what we offer."

April rejoined them but crossed her arms refusing to eat. Andrea threw a bread roll at her, laughing.

"Miss Louisa. Please," said Jimmy, giving up.

Miss Louisa removed the children to the upstairs den. Jimmy refilled Kay's wine glass and rose to place a record on the Victrola.

"Ah," said Kay raising her glass as her husband regained his seat. Rachmaninov's swelling strings might not be a panacea, but they were a damn fine Band-Aid.

That night, Kay and Jimmy again shared a bedroom. This time, though, Bydale failed to shine its magical torch upon them. He desired her with an earnestness she had not experienced in years. She acquiesced. It amounted to playacting but it was also a release.

Their lovemaking left her feeling torn and guilty. Torn, because she had married Jimmy with hope in her heart and retained a remnant of that optimism. Guilty, because she visualized another man. She lay on her stomach, but he noticed her shaking as she burst into a muted sob, her face in her pillow. "What is it, love?" He stretched his arm over her trembling shoulders.

She turned onto her back. He ran his index finger over her cheek. "Oh, darling," said Kay, "I fear I've been a terrible wife. And mother. I'm so sorry."

Jimmy moved his finger to her lips. "Hush. You're every bit the wife I had in mind. And our children are receiving a first-class upbringing." He stroked her hair.

Kay peered into the darkness. She tried not to think about the failure that the evening's dinner *en famille* represented. She tried not to think about George Gershwin. About his embrace, that twinkle in his eyes, and the way he used the piano as an exten-

sion of his soul.
  She tried.

CHAPTER THIRTEEN

April 1926

Desire, it seemed to Kay, was like a chocolate Grand Marnier soufflé: given enough heat and alcohol, it would expand and satisfy, but it had to be savored warm. Allowed to cool, it would collapse. If she ignored her emotions and waited, they would deflate.

On her twenty-ninth birthday Jimmy invited his wife out for brunch. On their way to the restaurant, their driver stopped at Cartier on Fifth Avenue and Fifty-Second Street. The doorman admitted them to an elegant room dressed *à la Française* in white with gold trim, mirrors, and chandeliers. Not a watch or necklace in sight. *This place is not about commerce,* the room whispered. *Heavens, no. We are about urbanity and refinement. Any business that is consummated here is entirely incidental.* A distinguished gentleman with a pencil moustache

237

looked up from his walnut marqueterie secretary. "Monsieur, Madame."

"Jules Glaenzer?" Jimmy glanced around. "He's expecting us."

"*De la part de . . .* If I may ask?"

"Mister and Misses James Warburg."

"Naturally, Monsieur Warburg. Would you care for a *Flor de Naves*? Perhaps some claret?" Even in these times, Cartier offered complimentary wine to select customers.

Jimmy glanced at Kay, who shook her head. "No, thank you."

"Of course. If you please." The man escorted them down a carpeted hallway to Jules Glaenzer's office. His accent and manner, and the scent of lilac-oiled wood, smacked of theatricality. Kay loved it, she had to admit.

Julie Glaenzer lumbered around his French Empire desk to greet them. "Katharine." He kissed her hand. "Jimmy." Glaenzer shook Jimmy's hand. "Here to collect my gambling debt, I presume?" A slight British accent coated his Brooklyn inflections.

"You presume well, Glaenzer."

"Jimmy slayed us last Tuesday," Glaenzer told Kay. "Woollcott's poker party." He opened a drawer in the wall revealing a diamond-and-emerald necklace on velvet

238

and removed it carefully. "Let's have a look at this, shall we?" He moved to Kay's back. "If you don't mind." She lowered her head for him to fasten the clasp. Glaenzer held a mirror to her face. The necklace sparkled on her milky skin above her square-neckline dress.

Jimmy grinned. "Happy birthday, Kay." And to Glaenzer: "We're even, pal."

"Delighted to be acquitted," replied Glaenzer. "I so despise gambling debt. I dare say, you have quite the diabolical poker hand."

Jimmy chuckled. "I assure you, that was chance."

Glaenzer cocked his head skeptically.

"You know as well as I do," said Jimmy, "Woollcott's card games are just a way he fundraises for his literary ventures, without overtly begging."

"All of which is predicated on his presumption of poker superiority, which we are supposed to reinforce," laughed Glaenzer, regaining his seat behind the desk.

"I tried to lose," said Jimmy. "Just as you did, I'm sure. Instead, I broke the bank. The goddess Fortuna played a trick on all of us."

Glaenzer leaned forward, folding his hands. "What is not chance?" He turned to Kay. "Where did the two of you meet, if I dare ask?"

"Oh, do dare," said Kay, still looking in the mirror. She turned to face him. "His father's country estate. I was the piano girl."

"There you have it. Chance. You could have been anywhere. But one thing led to another and *voilà*. You certainly do justice to this piece, Kay." He smiled.

"You look splendid." Jimmy kissed her forehead.

She wore the necklace as they exited Cartier for the Waldorf-Astoria. "If I ever forget your kindness and generosity, Jimmy Warburg, please lock me up," she said as they took a table.

"And why would I do that?" He nodded to the waiter, who poured coffee. "If marriage robs us of freedom, what good is it?"

She smiled. But she was thinking: *If freedom robs us of marriage, what good is that?*

In preparation for Kay's performance at the Hotel Astor, Jimmy's secretary purchased advertisements in the *Herald Tribune* and the *Times.* It disappointed Kay to learn, two weeks prior to the event, that Jimmy had to leave again for Germany. A new automobile manufacturer, Daimler-Benz, was planning its first factory and hoped M. M. Warburg & Co. might contribute to the financing. In

240

such ventures Jimmy invested a great deal of energy. Perhaps, if the German manufacturing sector regained ground lost during the Great War, Germany's economy could be saved and further social decay avoided. "You don't need me at your recital," he assured Kay. "I already know how brilliant you are. Let's keep that seat for someone who doesn't."

"Of course." She nodded. His change of plans would not affect her performance. She studied the fast third movement of Beethoven's *Moonlight Sonata.* The very piece she had performed so many times, with disastrous results, in her recurring dream of her father's One-Lock Adjustable Reamer factory. Perhaps, if she mastered the *Moonlight,* its misshapen dream avatar would stop harassing her.

She tried her hand at her own compositions, old and new. The most recent were perhaps salvageable, but needed work. She fiddled with them. Played them faster, slower, and upside-down, in different keys. *Why do they sound unconvincing? Did they always sound that way? Have they changed, or have I?*

Gershwin was right. Something was missing. More than that: she concluded that her old compositions were unsalvageable, the lot of them. She crumpled them, one page and then another, and tossed them into the trash. Years of work. Rubbish.

You just have to listen, he had told her. She lay on the sofa and listened. She heard nothing other than muffled street sounds and an occasional creaking of floorboards, and eventually, she fell asleep.

When she awoke she remembered imagery of water, fragments of melody, and an unfamiliar feeling — a vague sense of imminence. She hurried to the piano but when she sat down, those melodic bits escaped her.

Her fingers searched the keyboard until she recovered them — or invented melodic twists, dips, stretches, and curves that resembled them. Something unusual was happening, an interaction of imagination and memory predicated not only on resolve, technique, and energy but also on relaxation and openness and dreams.

It reminded her of the long mornings she had spent reading in bed as a young woman, before she married Jimmy and life became more complex. Of Debussy's "Rêverie" and visions of Greek gardens, Aphrodite and Adonis.

She toyed with the musical figures she had rediscovered, fitting them together this way and that, or one on top of the other, or inverting them. A new piece began to take form. It came out raw but she heard something in it. Something she never would have imagined composing. Something not entirely her own. A gift.

She spent hours and days revising. When it was finished, and polished, and then burnished, it glowed. She titled it "Something Different."

The evening of the performance arrived. She had instructed Lilly, Jimmy's secretary, not to inform her about ticket sales. *Numbers don't matter,* she told herself. She was steeling herself. She hoped to elicit the fervent audience response she had witnessed at *Lady, Be Good!* But as she approached the Grand Ballroom of the Hotel Astor on West Forty-Fifth Street her heart sank.

The crowd that had gathered . . . No, *crowd* was not the word. Group, perhaps? Cluster? New York City was not storming the gates to hear Kay Swift perform. The box office was not bursting. She was not yet the star that her instructors at the Institute of Musical Art had predicted she would become.

Of course not. Yet she could not help feeling she was disappointing them. Walter Damrosch. Gustav Mahler. Her father. *Yes, of course* these feelings were irrational. But weren't *all* feelings, by definition, irrational?

By the time she stepped over to the piano fifteen minutes later, perhaps a third of the seats were occupied, most of them by her friends. They smiled when their eyes met hers. But they were scattered. Her goal was to inspire them, to carry them on a zephyr of music to new places. She wished she could wave them down to the front rows, where enthusiasm might spread like ink in water, but that was not the way classical musicians behaved. A jazz musician, perhaps. But jazz was not on the menu this evening.

Wearing a black shift and her Cartier necklace, she bowed to light applause and sat at the Steinway, feeling a little unnerved. This was no high society cocktail party. Nor had she ever before played her own compositions in front of a paying audience.

On with it.

She raised her hands but before she began playing, out of the corner of her eye, she noticed two people strolling down to the front row: George Gershwin, accompanied by Adele Astaire, the most revered danseuse on Broadway, who lugged a capacious Gladstone leather bag.

No one had reached out to George. His

decision to attend Kay's performance, in a venue where he could not insert his hands onto her keyboard and mess everything up, was personal. It had to be. And he had brought along one of his closest and most glamorous friends.

In addition to being so fleet and spontaneous in dancing shoes that she sometimes threw her brother off, Adele was tall and svelte with a pert nose and large eyes. She wore crimson lipstick and face powder the palest shade of apricot. Kay knew she had befriended George as an adolescent vaudevillian soon after she and her brother had come to New York, years earlier. The three of them had rejoiced in each other's triumphs and matured together. *Then again,* thought Kay, *perhaps "matured" was not the right word . . .*

With no written music on the stand, she began playing. A tad nervously at first, but then closing her eyes and allowing the music to speak for itself. To sing and dance for itself. She had planned the evening so that one piece would contrast with the next, waves of intensity breaking upon sands of repose and reflection. Her fingers skipped and capered across their ivory-and-ebony proscenium. She played for an hour that felt like mere minutes, and concluded with

"Something Different."

Her audience applauded vigorously. Kay smiled and bowed. Someone threw flowers. Small and large blooms in a variety of colors, tied together with a yellow string, from which a card dangled. And then another bouquet, this one composed of lilies, encyclias, and cattleyas with large leaves that caressed Kay's neck as she hoisted them for everyone to see, and maws so gaping she feared they might bite her.

George and Adele rose to their feet, still clapping. The rest of the audience followed suit. Flushed with joy, Kay smiled at George. She saw a glint in his eye. *He heard it.* Her new piece. "Something Different." He had recognized its unusual quality.

She noticed Adele Astaire's leather bag on the seat beside her, open and empty. So that was how they had snuck the flowers in! The famous dancer smiled at Kay with all the warmth of a new best friend.

When George had hugged her that certain way, the morning after Fats Waller's rent party, she should have known what awaited them. Actually, she did know. She knew the what. And she had done some pretty serious thinking about the why. As for the how, that was just mechanics. What she did not know, but itched to find out, was the when.

The night of her performance at the Hotel Astor. That was the when.

In her apartment they banged on the piano and drank Prosecco for an hour and a half. He improvised melodies, she played chords, and they switched around, and around again.

Perhaps it was the alcohol. Maybe just giddiness. Her mind floated. Her fingers erred recklessly. Now her hands and his were not competing, but playing in harmony, adorning each other's musical statements, offering witty comments and asides, predicting each other's moves.

"Wait," George called out, waving. "That progression! What the hell was that, Kay?"

"G seven, C seven . . ." She tried the chords as they came back to her.

George twirled his index finger counterclockwise. "Before."

"Hmm. D seven, and then . . . D diminished seven . . ." *Why'd I do that?* she wondered.

"Do it again."

One chord more dissonant than the other, on top of which George struck two notes. D to E and back again. The second note, present in neither chord, added more dissonance so that when he returned to the D it sounded like a resolution — though an incomplete one, since diminished seventh chords suggested restlessness and further motion. "You hear that? Again."

She played the chords. He repeated the two-note melody. Now she heard it. It was little more than a hint. A door ajar. But it made her wonder. *What is inside that room?*

In his ebullience, George took her in his arms and kissed her. Kay stared at him, tears in her eyes. "George, where have I been, all these years?"

"Write that down," he said.

They both knew, though. She had been in purgatory, waiting for the clouds above her to part. So had he. It had begun the evening they met at her party, when they first sat at the piano together. A tear spilled onto the music. She had no idea why. He gently kissed another off her cheek.

Later, in her bedroom, he undressed her one button at a time until she stopped him, gathering his hands in hers. "George, I've never —"

He pushed her hair aside and kissed her. "Forgive me, Kay. I'm such a cad."

She held him close. "No. That's not —"

He interrupted her, caressing her hair. "With Jimmy gone so often, I assumed the two of you —"

"Jimmy does play around," said Kay. "Me? I'm not playing. That's the problem."

George looked at her, his dark eyes warm, his expression unreadable. "Neither am I," he said.

Well, that's that, Kay thought as the thrill of sexual climax dissolved in a calm euphoria. There was no going back. But the question remained, *what does forward look like, from here?*

She lit a Marlboro as they lay together. "I'm taking the train to Bydale next weekend. Care to join me?"

"Bydale?"

"Our country home, in Connecticut. Can you ride a horse?"

"Long answer or short answer?"

"Long answer," said Kay.

"No."

"It isn't complicated. You just sit."

"That I'm good at. Ask my piano bench."

"We have two Arabians, Klyde and Ella. But with Jimmy away, poor Ella's bored out of her little equine head."

"I have a date with the Coney Island roller coaster."

"Who are you going with?" Her voice was tinged with anxiety. Coney Island had lost its title as the world's capital of first kisses, having ceded that laurel to movie theaters everywhere, but it remained a privileged venue for laughter and romance.

"Let's see, there's my brother Ira; his fiancée, Leonore; my pal Dick Rodgers; and his girl, Dorothy Feiner. Dick's an Institute boy, like you. And then there's his songwriting partner Larry Hart. Larry's blue as a Curaçao Monday. The whole point? To cheer him up. You see *The Girl Friend*?"

She shook her head.

"Oh, you gotta see it. These guys are on their way."

She blew a cloud of smoke. "After Coney Island, head up to Bydale. Spend two weeks with me." She ran a finger over his cheek. "No butler. No maid. Just the two of us."

He scratched his head. "Two weeks, you must be goofy. Four, five days maybe."

"Eight days and we seal the deal."

"You got a piano up there?"

"A new Steinway grand. Bright and lively. And a tennis court. You play?"

"Only racket I ever got near? The music racket. And that one's rough enough."

"Perfect," said Kay. "We'll learn together."

She held his head to her breast as he drifted into sleep.

In the morning she reached for him. "Good

morning, George." Where his head had been, her hand detected its imprint in the pillow. He had risen, dressed, and slunk out without saying goodbye.

As she went about her morning routine — robe, coffee, news — she remembered her concert, the audience's enthusiasm, the night with George. She wanted to exult in the memory but something was troubling her.

Jimmy had organized the evening, rented the theater, and attempted to lure an audience. And how had she repaid him?

Damn these scruples, and damn my Christian upbringing! He gave me permission, she reminded herself. *More than gave me permission, he led by example.*

And then again there was the exploding conundrum called George. What did last night mean to him? Why had he crept out like a thief? Or had he? Maybe he had considered waking her. Maybe he kissed her goodbye while she slept. She closed her eyes and thought she remembered the touch of his lips on her eyelids. But perhaps that was wishful thinking, or wishful remembering.

She tried to practice piano but her fingers were stiff. She attempted reading but her mind loped away. She napped, half dreaming of her night with George, especially the comfort they had felt with one another, as if they had known each other all their lives. Then she noticed Adele Astaire's calling card dangling from the vase in the drawing room.

"I am positively delighted to hear from you," said Adele through Kay's dumbbell-and-cradle salon telephone. "George thinks the world of you. We so enjoyed your performance."

"I was wondering," began Kay. "Forgive my presumption . . ."

"Not at all!"

"Perhaps you're free for lunch?"

"I'm afraid lunch isn't possible," said Adele. "But why don't you trot over to my place this afternoon, say four thirty? I'll let the doorman know."

Kay showered. She sat at her vanity wearing a towel around her chest and a second as a turban. She applied cream and makeup and chose a dress and hat. She walked to the Park Avenue address on Adele's calling card, announced herself to the doorman, and rode the elevator up.

Adele's apartments were swathed in Persian rugs and silk curtains with braided ropes. A painted frieze of grape clusters and leaves in faded gold edged the tops of the high walls. She wore a sheer maroon robe over a green tunic. Her demeanor was as flighty and sparkling off-stage as on. She addressed Kay with an easy familiarity, as if their mutual friendship with George justified an instant affinity. "Let's play a game," she suggested as they sat down in the parlor, where her butler served tea and cookies. "You tell me one thing you know about me, and I'll tell you one thing I know about you."

"That sounds amusing," Kay acquiesced, stirring sugar into her tea. She preferred milk in her tea as well but dared not ask. "I know you and your brother are George's closest friends," she said.

"And I know you are in love," said Adele.

Kay sipped. "What makes you think that?"

Adele giggled, covering her mouth. Kay had heard her cackle pouring down from the stage at the Liberty Theatre but her drawing-room laugh differed, much as the sound of a harpsichord differs from that of a piano. "Oh, just the tinge in your cheeks, darling," she said. "Not to mention that sparkle in your eyes."

"Darn," said Kay.

"What could possibly be wrong with being in love?" asked Adele.

"I'm married."

"How shocking!"

"Go ahead, make light of it," said Kay. "But really, my husband doesn't deserve this."

"Well, what *does* he deserve? Surely he deserves something. All husbands deserve *something.*"

"He deserves a moment of jealousy," said Kay. "All right then, more than a moment. But not to lose my affections entirely."

"*Has* he lost your affections entirely?"

"Well, no. No and yes. But yes. And no."

Adele tasted her cookie. A nibble, more a gesture than a gratification. "The way I see it," she said, "we're given a choice. We can embrace life's complications — sorrow, joy, laughter, even treachery on occasion — or we can lead safe lives. We can't do both, though."

"And which do *you* choose?" asked Kay.

"Once upon a time I chose the former, but now I yearn for the latter."

"I suppose once upon a time I chose the latter, but now I yearn for the former," said Kay.

"You see," said Adele, "we always want what we can't have. Which leads to my next question."

"Which is?"

"Would you like milk for your tea?"

"Why, that would be marvelous."

Again, Adele tittered. "I'm sorry, we're out of milk. This isn't a full-service restaurant, you know. Oh, Bobby!" she called to a servant. "Would you mind running downstairs to fetch a jug of milk?" She turned back to Kay. "Now do tell me more about how miserable you are."

"What good is talking about it?" asked Kay.

"Probably no good at all," said Adele. "But you need to anyway, don't you. And I enjoy hearing about it."

"You enjoy hearing about my suffering?"

"Why, yes," said Adele. "It helps alleviate my envy."

"*You* envy *me?*"

Adele smiled. "Why should that be surprising?"

"Because *I* envy *you*. We can't very well both envy each other, can we?"

"You have nothing to envy, foolish girl," said Adele. "You are exceptionally talented and elegant. And you're rich. Well, yes, that counts too. If it's my celebrity that impresses you, I assure you it's nothing but hocus-pocus. Teasing the world into admiring you, when they're the ones with families and stable lives and beautiful children. And all you've got is bunions and a painted mask staring back at you from tired backstage mirrors late at night."

"Then why do you do it?" asked Kay.

"Because unfortunately, I have no choice," said Adele. "Just as you have no choice about being in love with George. We artists are powerless against our passions."

Kay tasted her tea. "I love Jimmy, too," she said sadly.

"How could you not? But you have to choose. It's your marriage and stability, or George and music." Adele snapped her fingers. "As simple as that. But no looking back. Keep moving. I know, I know. It's heart-wrenching."

Kay finished her tea just as Bobby arrived with a pitcher of milk. He refilled her cup but Kay was feeling dizzy and thought the caffeine might be part of the problem. *As simple as that,* she told herself. *No looking back.* Except that not looking back was not simple. She visualized Jimmy tossing coins at the window of her mother's apartment, reciting Keats's ode "To Autumn" as they walked in the park, reading to the children. And she remembered that night, outside Felix Warburg's mansion on Fifth Avenue at Ninety-Second Street, when Jimmy learned that he would not be flying over Belgium with his friends in the Naval Air Force. His passionate disappointment. The way he looked at her. His kiss.

passionate disappointment. The way he looked at her. His kiss.

CHAPTER FOURTEEN

Bydale. July 1926

Kay and George wandered on horseback through the leafy canyon. They crossed the brook and climbed into craggy hills. "Do you hear that?" George pulled back on the reins. His horse, Ella, snorted, shook her head, and paused.

"Hear what?" asked Kay. She stopped hers, Klyde.

"That music," said George.

She listened. "I hear the stream. The leaves in the breeze. Is that what you hear, George?"

He stared into the forest. "All that, yes," he said. "And that damned music."

"As in . . . a melody?" asked Kay.

"An entire orchestral setting," said George.

She shook her head. "It's in your mind."

"All music's in your mind," said George. "Otherwise, it's just sound."

They spread their blanket on a cliff over-looking the gorge and the creek. "Think about it," George elaborated. "What is a melody? A string of notes. But you only hear one at a time. By the time you hear the next note, the one before is gone. And the rest of the song doesn't exist yet. The whole song never actually exists, except between your two ears."

"And on paper," observed Kay.

"Yes, but that's not *music*," insisted George. "That's a *representation* of music."

"And a painting is a representation of a thing," said Kay. "But that doesn't make it not art."

George shook his head. "No. A painting is not a representation of a thing. A painting *is* a thing."

Kay shook her head at the absurdity of this debate. "In any case, if there are no instruments, there's no music."

"That's not true, either," said George. He bit into an apple and changed the subject. "I paint, too, you know. One day we'll fill a gallery with my oils. And folks will flock to it. Don't laugh."

She did not laugh. She smiled.

He set up an easel in the front room and began work on a new portrait. "I'm going to paint someone everyone will recognize," he told Kay, propping a mirror next to the easel while she warmed up at the piano playing scales and arpeggios.

As the painting took on the form of a self-portrait, Kay had to admit he had talent. Using broad strokes in blues, grays, beiges, and maroon he sought to shed light not on his playful nature but on his darker, contemplative side.

While George painted he wondered aloud: What was the role of hero worship in the appreciation of music, or any of the arts? Would Beethoven's music be the same without that face of his? His scowl had so much to do with the myth that surrounded and enhanced his music, in George's view.

"Maybe he used his music to sell his delusion of grandeur," said Kay.

"It's not a delusion when it's true," said Gershwin.

"Would it be true, if he had written the same music but the world didn't recognize his genius?"

"No," said Gershwin.

She hired a high school athletics coach to teach them tennis, and they practiced an hour each day after their lesson. They shared an unsuspected trait: they both hit the ball hard. They played piano mornings, afternoons, and whenever in the bright front room. He composed — assiduously, furiously — an overture and songs for a new show that he decided to call, *Oh, Kay!* She transcribed melodies and chord progressions and commented on his counterpoint. He ingested her knowledge like a famished schoolboy at a banquet.

George demonstrated compositional tricks he had learned from Jerome Kern and Irving Berlin, both innovators in his estimation, and from private teachers he had hired over the years, Charles Hambitzer, Rubin Goldmark, Henry Cowell, and Joseph Brody, who had introduced him to new, sometimes contrasting ways of thinking about harmony, counterpoint, orchestration, and rhythm. Despite his reputation as a self-taught genius he had continuously studied music theory since his youth, though never in recognized institutions.

He never claimed, however, to understand music. Its essence remained a mystery to him. If he was humble about anything, it was this.

In the evening, they found German editions of Heine's poetry and Kafka's *Der Prozess* in James's bookshelf, as well as a copy of *Ulysses,* printed in Paris. The latter was banned in the United States and the controversy had only enhanced its reputation. Late at night Kay and George slogged through it aloud. George judged *Ulysses* a dazzling experiment, virtuosic, at times fascinating, but just as often trying and exhibitionistic.

"One thing it's not," said George. "It's not *storytelling.* Just like Wassily Kandinsky isn't painting *pictures.* Just like Schoenberg isn't writing *melodies.* It's something else."

Much as he wrote modern but melodic music, so in painting George chose a middle ground between realism and abstraction, but erring on the side of realism. He cared about his audience and his first audience was his own ear. Modern harmonies, rhythms, and instrumentation provided freshness if not innovation. But a melody had to seize the listener's attention and hold it captive or the entire effort collapsed. He knew that much of musical academia disagreed. He did not care.

They talked in semidarkness about the Great War, a wound that had not healed. George wondered whether the war had been a cause, or a symptom, of changes in the culture. Kay asked him to elaborate. "Well," George mused aloud, "not so long ago, the idea of Europe meant something. It meant certain attitudes about music, and painting, and religion — which is storytelling on the biggest canvas, isn't it? — and then it all collapsed. It all turned out to be so fragile. What I'm saying is, maybe the change happened first in the culture — Wagner, Debussy, Schoenberg — and the Great War was just the final implosion."

"So where do we go from here?" Kay wondered. "Beyond abstraction in painting, non-linear narrative, and atonality in music?"

"That's when your steamer docks at Ellis Island," said George.

"And what do you find?" asked Kay. "A different scale?"

"A different rhythm," said George. "Jazz."

They decided to read something else. Kay went into the salon and came back with the copy of *Porgy* that Dorothy Heyward had sent.

Sales of the novel, Heyward's first, had soared, fueled by the near-unanimous enthusiasm of reviewers. The *Nation* had praised its "poetry and penetration." The *New York Evening Post* had described *Porgy* as "a series of throbbing moments, a ghost of Africa stalking on American soil." Ellen Glasgow, the prestigious author of the novel *Barren Ground,* declared that *Porgy* was destined to become "a classic." The poet Langston Hughes appreciated "the poetic qualities in the inhabitants of Catfish Row that make them come alive."

With George, Kay entered the Gullah tenements of Charleston a second time. They took turns reading aloud in bed. The setting reminded George, in ways, of the Lower East Side of his youth. Entranced, they allowed *Porgy* to occupy them through the night.

The following afternoon Kay found George wandering through the house in his slippers, holding *Porgy* and looking for something. "You got a phone?"

"Who do you want to call?"

"DuBose Heyward. You got his number?"

"It's on that note we're using as a bookmark."

A few minutes later, the telephone operator rang the line of the author at his home in the Smoky Mountains of North Carolina. "DuBose Heyward, George Gershwin here. My friend Kay Warburg and I cruised through your novel last night, title page right through to . . ." He flipped to the last line. "Mariah left Porgy and the goat alone in an irony of morning sunlight." He placed the book on a side table. "I was hoping for some shut-eye but Catfish Row kept calling me back."

"Why thank you, Mister Gershwin, mighty honored," DuBose Heyward answered in a thin, wheezy voice.

"Your Porgy, what a fella," gushed George. "A cripple, dirt poor, no education, a rough seven-card-stud hand, but he knows he's worthy of this doll. Deserves her more than Sporting Life or Crown. And she knows it, too, but she's not as strong as he is."

"Why, thank you kindly, Mister Gershwin. That was precisely my intention."

"Tell me how you came up with this story, these people."

"Well," drawled Heyward, "I used to work the docks in Charleston. I was one of the few whites and many of the others were Gullahs. That is the way I spent my adolescence. As different as the Lord made us they were like family to me and I was always fascinated with the rhythms of spoken language, so naturally I absorbed their dialect." He paused. "Then one day a few years back I came across a story in the local news about a crippled man who tried to flee the police using his goat cart. The story filled me with compassion and I knew right then that man would be the subject of my first novel."

"Your compassion hit me hard, Mister

Heyward."

"That means a lot, coming from you, Mister Gershwin."

"You see, Mister Heyward," George told him, "I've been wracking my brain for a subject for an opera. Any chance we could meet?"

"Why that is a fascinating idea. But I must tell you, my wife is working on a stage adaptation. *Porgy* has been such a surprising success, she swears there's a Broadway show in there."

"I would hate to interfere with your wife's plans," said George. "Why don't you just go ahead and see if you can throw that show together. Let's talk later, one way or the other."

"I will very much look forward to that, Mister Gershwin," said DuBose Heyward. "I am so honored."

Hanging up the telephone, Gershwin chuckled and shook his head at some inner thought. But his smile dissolved into a frown as he sniffed. "Do you smell that?"

"Smell what?" asked Kay.

"Burning rubber," said George.

Kay shook her head, laughing.

Olga brought the children for the holiday weekend. Andrea and Kathleen ran around

266

outside, shouting and yelping. But April, the oldest of Kay's children at seven, shut herself into her room. "Something's bothering her," said George.

"That's how she is," said Kay. "I'm not happy about it but what am I to do?"

He went upstairs and knocked. Kay followed.

April sat on her bed studying a scrapbook. George entered and sat beside her. "*Little Orphan Annie,* eh," he said.

"She cuts them out every day," said Kay. "And glues them in."

"What's it about?" George asked April.

"A girl."

"How 'bout I read to you?" He moved to take the album from her but she clutched it tightly.

"I didn't give you permission."

"April!"

April ignored her mother. "I'd rather be with my dad," she told George.

"I'll leave you alone then," said George. He rose and left, closing the door behind him.

"She's going through something," Kay told him, as they went downstairs.

"The kid feels orphaned," said George.

"There's a man all over that scrapbook," said Kay. "Daddy Warbucks. *Daddy War-*

burg, get it? He saves her from the orphanage. Not Mommy Swift. Daddy Warburg."

Andrea adored Gershwin, whom she called Uncle George. She tromped with him through the forest when he ventured out with his Leica camera. She sat next to him on the piano bench when he improvised. Sometimes the music made her giggle. Sometimes she rolled on the floor laughing. He looked down at her, smiling, while his hands increased the tempo, as if tickling her. Then he stopped and let her recover.

On the afternoon of July Fourth, wearing a beret, George rolled up a newspaper and used it as a megaphone, refereeing a footrace between Andrea and Kay. That night, Benjamin Fairchild drove them all into Greenwich except April, who refused to leave her room. The ice cream shop was offering two double-scoops for the price of one. They sat on the grass and watched star pods burst over the water. They watched flowers of light bloom and fade. Andrea draped her arm around George's shoulder and leaned into him. Kathleen drifted to sleep. Ice cream melted onto her skirt. Before they left, George asked: "What's April's favorite flavor?"

"Strawberry," said Kay.

He returned to the ice cream parlor,

where he bought a half-gallon container of strawberry, a dozen cones, and a bag of Abba-Zaba candy bars.

CHAPTER FIFTEEN

November 1926

Having just returned from another three-month trip, Jimmy asked Kay to join him for a stroll in Central Park. "Top of the morning, Mister and Misses Warburg." A police officer tipped his hat.

"Good morning, Officer McGinty." Jimmy slowed his pace to match Kay's. "The oddest thing happened while I was away," he told her.

"Your pants stayed buttoned up?" asked Kay.

He turned to her, raising his eyebrows. "Why, yes, precisely."

"Hah!" said Kay. "You've become celibate?"

"Celibate? Heavens, no. Monogamous, possibly." Two nannies passed, pushing black prams. "What if we were to take this over from the beginning," asked Jimmy. "To just pick up the needle and drop it back

270

down at the start of the record. Wouldn't that be grand?"

She shook her head. "We can't, though. We were so naïve. We had to be, or we never would have tried. And naïveté, that's not something you can get back."

They passed an amateur artist who was painting the trees and the lake. "I didn't sign up for a lukewarm marriage," said Jimmy. "I want to fix this."

"Suddenly? Now?"

"It's obvious, Kay. You've taken the dive. You and Gershwin."

She laughed. "Aren't you the one that said marriage isn't about ownership, but sharing?"

"Sharing, certainly. Not giving everything away. Not giving away your heart."

"I can't perform without feeling," said Kay. "That isn't music. That's just notes."

"I appreciate that," said Jimmy. "It's why I was drawn to you in the first place." He took her hand. "Speaking of sharing, maybe we should resume sharing a bedroom."

"I've grown used to sleeping alone. You know how much I move in bed," said Kay.

"You've grown used to sleeping with Gershwin."

She freed her hand. "What do you want from me, Jimmy?"

"A pinch of reassurance, perhaps?" he tried. "Just tell me everything will be fine and dandy."

"You want little white lies?"

"They wouldn't cost you a thing, would they," said Jimmy.

A cycle-skater zipped past wearing boots bolted to narrow ten-inch wheels, flinging himself forward with ski poles. "Everything will be fine and dandy," said Kay with a smile.

Children were running, shouting, sliding, and swinging in the playground. Jimmy watched them, contemplative and sullen. "Let's catch a musical tonight," he suggested. "How about *The Girl Friend*? Word is it's a delight."

The Girl Friend, by the new team of Rodgers and Hart, was indeed a pleasure. Its bare-bones plot treated themes of ambition and love, the temptation to get ahead by cheating, and the ultimate reward for honest labor. It illustrated the essential mythos of the aspirational American middle class: that success is to be measured not in peerships, freedom from labor, or other privileges, but in sincerity and diligence.

"I guess Gershwin isn't the only talented songwriter out there," Jimmy remarked as they walked down Forty-Second Street for after-the-show refreshments.

"As far as I know," said Kay, "Irving Berlin, or Richard Rodgers, never composed a *Rhapsody in Blue* or a *New York Concerto.*"

"I can't deny he's a wunderkind of sorts."

"And I can't deny it's invigorating to work with him," said Kay. She slung her arm through his. "Jimmy, I always needed to write music, you know that. But my compositions . . . I went to bed every night fearing no one would ever hear them."

"I know," said Jimmy.

"The best thing about my Hotel Astor recital? George Gershwin showed up, with Adele Astaire."

Jimmy held the door of Molly's Sweets & Sundries. "I worry he might exploit you," he said. "Your brilliant musical mind. Your perfect ear."

Kay went in. "Perhaps," she said as they approached the counter. "Or maybe *I'm* using *him.* I'll have a Sundae Decadence," she told the fountain jerk. Vanilla with crumbled cookies and melted chocolate fudge.

The ice cream boy turned to Jimmy. "Yes, I'll have a Dreamland." Vanilla with fresh peach slices, walnuts, and whipped cream. "Just give me those little white lies," he repeated to his wife as the shop boy busied himself with their desserts.

"Everything'll be fine and dandy," said Kay with a smile.

These days, Kay enjoyed working at night. But Jimmy was a morning person. She was touching up a song she had begun at Bydale when he sauntered into the room in his pajamas and robe, smoking a pipe.

"What do you think?" She ran through the wide-ranging melody she had composed. The style was her own, a broader, more sweeping line than the typical Gershwin song. But like him she added off-key notes and broke the rhythm into uneven beats.

"Catchy. Lyrics?"

She shook her head. "Just a title. 'Little White Lies.' I might ask Ira."

He crossed to the liquor cabinet. "Gin Rickey?"

She smiled.

He set her drink on an aluminum tray on the piano and stood watching while she played a few more chords, then modified them and tried again. He poured himself a tulip glass of Armagnac.

Later that night he appeared at her bedroom door. She was reading the new issue of the *New Yorker,* the magazine founded and published by Aleck Woollcott's house-mate Harold Ross. "That tune you wrote. It's driving me batty."

She looked up.

"Couldn't sleep. Some words came to me." Jimmy whined in his wandering tonality:

> The ancients, they touted the virtue of
>   honesty,
> But ask any modernist: that was a fallacy.
> Just give me more of your little white lies,
> Your lily-white smile and sparkling green
>   eyes.
> Tonight I intend to sleep like a kitten,
> Atop a silk blanket in a castle in Britain.

She lowered her magazine. "Not shabby! Let's try it."

They raced downstairs. She sat at the piano and played as he sang the lyric, adding a second verse:

> Let the moralists boast of their permanent
>   truths.
> And the leaders of Europe, their delicate
>   truce.
> Just give me more of your little white
>   lies . . .

"You made that up on the spot?" asked

Kay, astonished.

He nodded.

"Why was I not aware of this talent?"

He stepped closer and leaned to kiss her forehead. "Just don't say, lyrics by James Paul Warburg. I'm a banker. It wouldn't fly."

Like Kay, Jimmy had been trained to appreciate Victorian styles in poetry and music. In the Romantic vein, he had written poetry that idealized love. It had come off as stilted and inauthentic. Kay deemed his lyrics to "Little White Lies" refreshing and poignant. She had conceived of it as a gloomy ballad but he had inverted her intention with tender irony. And now, far from craving recognition, he did not even want his name on the lyrics.

"What name do you have in mind?"

"Why don't you reverse my middle and first names. Paul James."

"Sounds rather Episcopalian."

"Precisely."

"And I'll be Kay Swift," said Kay.

James smiled past her shoulder. Kay turned to see their daughter Andrea standing at the foot of the stairway in her pajamas. "I had a bad dream."

"Come, little nut." Jimmy took her hand. "I'll tell you a bedtime story."

276

CHAPTER SIXTEEN

June 1927

A month earlier, Charles Lindbergh had flown from New York to Paris in his custom-built monoplane, the *Spirit of St. Louis*. His daring, so soon after two Frenchmen had perished in a similar attempt, defined him as a symbol of American pluck. Everyone understood that his proof-of-concept adventure would change the world. A parade welcomed him home to New York, and the crowds that gathered paralyzed the city.

M. M. Warburg & Co. sought no visible role in the celebration, but Jimmy did want to witness history. He asked Kay to walk with him to Fifth Avenue. As the throngs waited and brass bands passed — then the mayor's convoy, then that of President Coolidge, and finally the convertible in which the boyish Mister Lindbergh stood in his top hat, waving — the crowd erupted in waves of cheering. Ticker tape flew from apartment balconies.

Kay noticed the expression on the young aviator's face. He looked both drained and astonished. Of course what he had accomplished was courageous. All that signified was that, like every soldier who dashes bayonet-in-hand to the front line, he was young enough to have no concept of death. And yes, the technological triumph was impressive — but it was not his. The intensity of the throng's worship seemed to puzzle the gangly Midwestern aviator himself, even though it was the fruit of his endeavor and aspiration.

"It's about pent-up sexual energy," Jimmy told Kay, with the confidence of a devotee of the latest intellectual trends as they returned to their apartment.

Kay shook her head, smiling and frowning at the same time as if to ask, *where do you come up with these crazy ideas?*

"Sigmund Freud," said Jimmy. "The Viennese neurologist."

"Oh, that one," said Kay. "Everything is pent-up sexual energy, isn't it. At least everything we're passionate about, right? Only problem? I've been passionate about music since before I even heard of the sex drive."

278

At the top of the stairs he kissed her forehead. "You stay that way," he said.

Kay rode a cab down to Twenty-Eighth Street, the historical beating heart of the popular music industry, known as Tin Pan Alley because in the summer, when all the "song pluggers" were demonstrating new compositions in different keys and rhythms on pianos, with the windows open, the cacophony reminded sarcastic pedestrians below of children beating on tin pans. It was here that T. B. Harms had invented the concept of publishing popular music, an outrageous proposition in 1875, when only classical music and religious hymns were deemed worthy of printing. And it was here that George Gershwin, as a sixteen-year-old pianist, had first set foot in the music industry.

Since that time, many of the music publishers had shed their Yiddish accents and moved uptown, but some still maintained offices on Twenty-Eighth Street. Kay sat in a waiting room with other aspiring songwriters. A peppy blonde introduced her to Sonny Remick, a nephew of the founder of Jerome H. Remick & Co.

"We don't manage singers here," he told her as she entered his office, without bothering to remove the toothpick from his mouth.

"I'm not a singer," said Kay. "I'm a song-writer."

"You look like a singer," he said, eyeing her bust and her trim figure.

"Unfortunately, I don't sound like one," she said.

He removed the toothpick. "A lady song-writer. That's a new one. Why not? Long as you know what you're getting into. The music biz can be pretty rough."

"I can be plenty rough, myself," said Kay, sitting at the piano.

He laughed. "All right, let's see what you've got."

"This song is by me, Kay Swift, and my lyricist Paul James." She played and sang "Little White Lies."

Sonny Remick removed the toothpick from his mouth. "You got something else?"

She played the other two songs that she and Jimmy had written. "And we have others," she lied.

"Okay," said Sonny. "You seem like a nice lady. Classy. I'm not sayin' no and I'm not sayin' yes. You can play piano, I can tell. The lyrics are sharp. That's why I'm not sayin' no. Do I see a show for this tune, or the one before, or the one before that?" He twisted his mouth. "That's why I'm not sayin' yes."

She tried other houses, who praised her talent but found excuses for not signing her. Some complained that the piano part was too busy; others, that it was too simple. Some explained that the market, at the moment, was finicky. Others offered versions of, "it's good, real good, but not my thing personally."

The songs she and Jimmy were now writing were catchier and more clever than many that the big publishers *interpolated* into shows and promoted with posters, radio spots, and star power. That was the verb they used: *interpolate.* An important-sounding word, as if the process of inserting a song into a Broadway revue were a delicate surgical procedure, when in reality the numbers *interpolated* often seemed unrelated to the vaudeville antics and dance acts that enveloped them. The publishers' mind-set eluded Kay and Jimmy.

How, then, was one to break in? What cosmic principle justified the power these people wielded over the dreams and careers of aspiring artists? Did any of them even know the difference between a pentatonic scale and a dry-goods scale?

At the end of a balmy Sunday, George rang.

Kay and Jimmy were burnishing another song. George listened, his hand on his cheek. Kay ended the song with a jazzy coda. "You lucky S.O.B.," George told Jimmy.

"And I intend to remain that way, Gershwin. Will you join us for dinner?"

Jimmy and Kay ate trout, Lyonnaise potatoes, and string beans, and drank a white Puligny-Montrachet. Gershwin requested a bowl of oatmeal and peppered Jimmy with questions about safe investments, developments in European politics, and domestic sports. A chest-puffing fellow named Mussolini, leader of the Fascist Party, had taken control of Italy and turned it into a one-party dictatorship, with impressive popular support. Babe Ruth was on track to hit more home runs this season than any other baseball player in history. Buster Keaton's new motion picture, *The General,* was a smash.

Between dinner and dessert Kay demonstrated "Little White Lies," which Gershwin asked her to play again. He held up his glass. "Mazel tov. Terrific."

Kay described her quest for a publisher. Gershwin laughed. "That'll never work. These people, they don't believe their own ears. They don't even know what they like.

Hell, they don't know what their kids are up to. No, you have to prove it to them." He tasted the cherry pie.

"How?" asked Kay.

"Come around my place noon tomorrow." He removed a business card from a Tiffany case.

"I'll try," said Kay, glancing at her poker-faced husband.

The first-floor entrance at 316 West 103rd Street was ajar when Kay arrived the next day. She heard ragged piano music and peeked inside. A colored boy played ping-pong with a red-haired girl in the center of the front room. A skinny kid with glasses sat at the upright piano. A young couple talked on a sofa. Diffidently she asked, "Is this the home of George Gershwin?"

The pianist stopped. "Upstairs."

She turned back to the street, climbed a few steps to the front door, and rang the electric doorbell. A tall, elegant man of indistinct European origin answered. "Is Mister Gershwin in? Kay Swift calling."

The man bowed. "Pleased to make your acquaintance, Miss Swift. My name is Paul. Paul Mueller. Please, follow me." George's valet held himself like a distinguished member of the family rather than a servant.

"Who are those kids?" asked Kay as he led her into the foyer.

"That's George's idea," said Paul. "The neighborhood clubhouse."

He stopped at the first-floor door. "Papa and Rose wish to meet you, Miss Swift." Paul knocked. A fine-featured middle-aged woman, in a powder-blue dress and pearls, answered. Her head cocked, scowling, she eyed Kay from head to toe. "What are you waiting for? Come in." The accent was Russian. "Morris," she called. "She's here!"

Kay looked at the floral wallpaper and reproduction Catherine II furniture in walnut and maple. A stooped man in a silk bathrobe and slippers stepped in. "Would you like drink? Juice, whiskey, water?"

Kay smiled and shook her head. "Thank you."

"All right," Rose Gershwin told her husband. "We met her."

"We met her," nodded her husband. Paul ushered Kay back out to the stairwell.

Jeepers creepers, thought Kay. As they ascended one flight after another, Paul played the tour guide. "Arthur's apartment," he announced at the third-floor landing, "George's kid brother." And at the fourth: "Ira and his wife, Leonore."

Approaching the top floor, Kay heard

George's unmistakable piano. Paul led her into the expansive drawing room, where George worked at one of two back-to-back pianos, cigar in mouth, pencil in hand, a picture of disheveled elegance in a sweater, open-collar shirt, wool slacks, and socks. He stood and hugged her. "I missed you, Kay."

"Your mother doesn't approve of me."

He laughed. "She's afraid I'm going to marry you."

"Would that be so terrible?"

"For her? A calamity!"

"Because I'm not Jewish."

He pursed his lips.

She kissed him. "And for you?"

"You're already married, Kay. And not just to anyone. Paul, grab those horns, will you?"

George's servant fetched a small suitcase. George opened it revealing two oversized rubber-bulb horns with curled chrome tubing, wrapped in a gray and cream cashmere shawl.

"Where on earth did you dig those up?" asked Kay.

"The music of the Champs-Élysées," said George. "Taxi horns. They reach out with their left hands and squeeze the bulbs, like this." He honked. It was boisterous and offensive. He handed it to her, unwrapped the other, and tooted it. "The shawl's for you. Picked it up in London."

He placed the second horn on the piano and draped the shawl over her head and shoulders. "Wait 'til you get a whiff of this." He sat at the piano. "I've got various parts in my head. It's called *An American in Paris*. When I say honk, squeeze the smaller horn three times, eighth notes. And when I say honk again, do the same thing with the larger horn."

"Honk!" he called shortly after he started playing. And a few moments later, "honk again!"

"It's modern," said Kay, as she listened to the piece, its smashed-together melodic fragments, its leaping bass line punctuated with dissonant chords. "French enough. A little wacky. But where's the melody?"

He grinned. "That's the point! My answer to the scribblers who say I'm just a tunester."

"I thought you didn't pay attention to critics."

"Once I've proved the schmucks wrong, I'll answer my own answer with a contrasting, lyrical B-section. It's all mapped out up here." He tapped his head. "All I need is time."

"You know I can help with that," offered Kay.

Hours later, they awoke in each other's arms. They showered. They strolled in Riverside Park eating Eskimo Pies. George mentioned he had spoken with his friends Dick Rodgers and Larry Hart, who were working on a new musical. "They're hot as spiked chili. Did you catch *The Girl Friend?*"

"We saw it while you were in London. Or Paris. Or wherever you were."

"They'll need a rehearsal pianist. It'll be several months but you've got the gig. That's how I broke in, working for Kern."

"I thought you started as a song plugger."

"I *started* as a plugger, but I *broke in* working for Kern."

It seemed a subtle distinction, but then the music industry was rife with subtleties. "Thank you." Kay wrapped her arms around him and kissed him. Generosity like George's was alarmingly rare. The arts teemed with people who yearned, it seemed, to deny opportunity to talent. Or simply to overlook it. Miraculously, George — their greatest star — was not one of them.

"I'm not doing you a favor," he assured her. "I'm doing Dick a favor."

Ironically, she reflected, had she sought a

tion like this when she needed it finan-
y, she would not have made it through
door. Work was like men. She thought
of George's very first published song,
"When You Want 'Em, You Can't Get 'Em,
When You've Got 'Em, You Don't Want
'Em."

They hailed a cab and rode down to Fifty-
Second Street, where theatergoers had lined
up in front of the Guild Theatre. The
marquee announced Dorothy Kuhn's adaptation of DuBose Heyward's *Porgy,* starring
Frank Wilson and Evelyn Ellis, colored
performers unknown to white audiences.

Dorothy and DuBose had found producers for their play. Despite its all-Negro cast
and the fierce competition of Jerome Kern
and Oscar Hammerstein's *Show Boat* and
Guy Bolton's *Rio Rita,* Dorothy's *Porgy* was
a hit. As with the novel, the critics had taken
the lead, starting with Alexander Woollcott's
praise, in the *New York World,* of its "high,
startling beauty." Such was Woollcott's
prestige that even the lead *New York Times*
reviewer, Brooks Atkinson, had felt compelled to revise his initial pan with a second
article that heaped praise on the show. And
Stark Young, in the *New Republic,* judged it
"one of the high points of this or any other
season."

DuBose had invited George to the opening night, but George had been traveling. Now he led Kay to the front of the line, spoke with the doorman, and stepped into the theater without a ticket.

Kay observed George watching the show, his attention total and unmitigated. The novel had been a detailed, almost anthropological study of Catfish Row. The stage play substituted spectacle, including ensemble set pieces, for the novel's rich character development. It offered the audience a hint of optimism, infused with bitter irony, in place of the novel's poignant ending.

After the show they hailed a cab back to Riverside Park at Ninetieth Street, where they strolled hand in hand discussing the ways in which the play differed from the book. George loved this *Porgy* even more than the novel. The play's director, Rouben Mamoulian, in partnership with the Heywards, had made the story even more suitable to an operatic adaptation.

"But will theatergoers want to see it again?" wondered Kay. "And the novel readers, will they be willing to experience this story in a third format?"

"The world's a big place," said George. "The future's a long time."

They sat on a bench contemplating the

glittering New Jersey shoreline. The same view she had shared with her husband the night of the *Rhapsody* concert, but closer and brighter. She rested her head on his shoulder. "George, would it upset you terribly if I confessed I'm in love with you?"

"Not unless it was a lie." He took her face in his hands and kissed her. She wrapped her arms around his neck. A tugboat groaned on the Hudson River below the full moon and the sparks of the Ferris wheel.

CHAPTER SEVENTEEN

October–November 1927

"I like the octagram." Dick Rodgers stood behind Kay at an upright piano in a Brooklyn warehouse. "Who doesn't like octagrams, Busby? But where's the beat?"

Light filtered through slit windows set high in brick walls above piles of crates, catching dust motes in its path. Fifteen women in rehearsal tights, ranging in age from seventeen to twenty-three, held hands awaiting instructions. Some were prettier than others but all possessed long legs, trim figures, and pert busts. The choreographer, Busby Berkeley, rubbed his cheek in thought.

"Okay, Constance, Bill, you're in front. Look at me." He stepped, twirled, and jumped. They mimicked him. "Everyone else, push it back a little and open it up."

For two weeks Rodgers had been quarreling with Berkeley about the choreographer's new-dance concept. Berkeley visualized dancers as groups forming geometrical patterns: stars, circles rotating within circles, oscillating waves. Rodgers insisted that the sense of individual body motion not be lost. However, neither Berkeley nor Rodgers was the director. The actual director was wrapping another show. The purpose of this rehearsal was to learn the music and sketch out possible dance patterns to present to the director.

"Let's pick it up five bars before the intro. One, two, three, four," Rodgers counted.

Kay played again. The dancers crossed their feet and stretched their arms. Bill Gaxton and Connie Carpenter, the stars, sang. Busby Berkeley clapped and called out the beats.

"No, no," Rodgers waved. He pointed to the score on Kay's piano. "I'm very sorry. Those two eighth notes." He reached down with a pencil. "They should be tied. The second beat in measure thirty-two, accented. Once again, five before the verse."

And so it continued through the afternoon. Repetitive, chilly, excruciating — and Kay savored every moment. For the first time in years, she was working. For the first time in her life, her job lasted more than a few hours.

She worked as rehearsal pianist for Dick Rodgers every day and most nights until the November opening of *A Connecticut Yankee* at the Vanderbilt Theatre. She observed Rodgers rewriting, discarding, and replacing songs. She sat with her arms folded on the closed piano keyboard lid watching the book writer, the choreographer, and the director debate, compromise, and argue more. She absorbed the ambience and learned how the mechanism of a show slowly aligned.

She lunched with zesty flappers and with her fellow Institute graduate, the composer. Unlike George Gershwin, Dick Rodgers was a son of privilege. Prior to attending the Institute of Musical Art, now known as the Juilliard School of Music, he had attended Columbia University. For him, songwriting was a task to be performed methodically, according to a timetable. He glanced at his wristwatch every ten minutes and expected his coworkers to do the same. He dined on roast beef, peas, and mashed potatoes. He slicked back his dark hair as George did. Younger than George, and less experienced in the entertainment business, he dressed more conservatively. He would never think of wearing a sweater rather than a jacket, as George sometimes did. Kay thought Rodgers lacked George's spontaneity, vivacity, curiosity, and charm. But there was no denying his talent or ambition.

In contrast, his lyricist Lorenz Hart was witty, often drunk, anything but punctilious. The two men balanced each other like the Greek Gods Apollo and Dionysus. On one occasion, George joined them for dinner. "Isn't Kay the best, guys?"

Rodgers glanced at his watch, pushed his tray aside, and said, "better be heading back." He rose and walked away.

"He's thrilled with you, Kay," George assured her as they strolled back to the stage.

"Hard to tell, though," said Kay.

George chuckled.

Larry Hart chimed in. "You know how to tell Dick likes you? He hasn't fired you."

During a break, Kay spoke with Hart, who was eating a donut and sipping coffee while looking over hand-scrawled lyrics. A kind, rumpled man seven years Rodgers' senior at thirty-two, Larry struck her as the wisest and most cynical artist associated with the production.

"Larry, I've been working on some tunes and I think they're jim-dandy. But publisher after publisher turns me down. Do you have advice for an earnest ingénue?" She smiled ingratiatingly.

"An earnest ingénue, eh?" said Larry looking up from his notes. "Yeah, I have advice. Don't try to make sense of it. It's a roll of the dice. And then another. And another. Life is a casino." He placed his hand on her shoulder and looked her squarely in the eyes. "That's the advice I'd offer a stranger. But someone I cared about, like a niece or a nonchalant chorus girl? I'd say, why trouble your pretty head? You're better off learning shorthand."

Dress rehearsals started at 8:00 p.m. and lasted well into the night. Kay slept much of the day. As opening night neared, frayed nerves yielded to temper tantrums. Broadway was a pressure cooker. In show business, success bred success but one failure engendered others too, leading to career extinction. The egos of leading men and women were as fragile as their reputations. So were those of the creative team, including the songwriters. And although only the most celebrated actors and actresses felt entitled to vent their anxieties, the future of every other individual involved was also at stake. A hit show would glow on the curriculum vitae of the lighting supervisor as well as the gofer, even if the lighting had been uneven. A dud, no matter how impressive the lighting, and employment would be harder to come across next time.

Dick Rodgers insisted that everyone connected with the production attend the final dress rehearsal, with full orchestra. Additional handpicked guests, friends and critics, filled the theater. Kay heard flutes and violins sound the notes she had been playing all these weeks.

George leaned toward Kay. "You feel that buzz? It's not just what's happening on stage. It's not just the audience either. It's the whole damn room. The walls, the ceiling. That's how you know you've got a hit."

At intermission, he made introductions. "Kay Swift and Paul James, the songwriters," he said to the singer Libby Holman and Libby's lover the DuPont heiress Louisa d'Andelot Carpenter. Tall and shapely, Libby Holman held herself like a diva. "Libby blew in from Cincinnati like a heat wave," said George. "This broad was born to be a star. All she needs is smart, new material."

Kay took George's cue. "I may have some of that!"

"Can I hear it?" asked Libby.

"I certainly hope you can," said Kay.

"How do you know she's going to be a star?" Kay asked as George escorted her back into the theater.

"I feel her hunger. Don't you?"

"So many singers and dancers are hungry —"

"Not like that."

After the final curtain fell and they spilled into the street, Kay turned to look at the marquee. A laborer on a ladder applied the last letters. "Rodgers and Hart," it proclaimed: "*A Connecticut Yankee.*" Pride swelled in her heart. No matter how modest her part, she had contributed to a production that would inspire laughter and song throughout New York, perhaps the world.

CHAPTER EIGHTEEN

January 1928

Kay visited George's apartment almost daily. They improvised duets and composed side by side. She transcribed and took notes. He repaid her with companionship, love, and introductions. Sometimes she played a new tune or asked George's opinion of a musical idea. *Maybe that's what friendship should be,* mused Kay, still smarting from the loss of Edith and Marie and the Rubel Trio. *Not a promise but an opportunity. Not a lifetime but a moment.* Emotional expectation, after all, sometimes melted away in the hot sunshine of social mobility. "Listen to this one, George. Jimmy and I wrote this for Libby."

"Who?"

"The singer. You introduced us. *Connecticut Yankee,* intermission?"

"Oh, sure. Her."

"You thought she had a brilliant future."

"Right," he nodded. "Libby."

Kay propped "Can't We Be Friends?" on the piano and played the intro as a solo in Gershwin's style. "I thought it was sweet and uplifting. But Jimmy came up with this sad lyric." And she sang in her dusky voice:

> I thought I'd found the man of my dreams,
> Now, it seems, this is how the story ends:
> He's gonna turn me down and say, "Can't we be friends?"

The song twisted through a few more verses, the metrically unbalanced lament of a spurned lover delivered on the loopy melody of a drunken nightingale. While she played, George's valet Paul brought in the mail. She doubted that George was listening; he seemed too busy opening envelopes and reading letters. But when she finished playing he looked up. "Kay, that's your best number yet. Libby'll love it. It'll fit her voice like a bathing suit." He read a note and slipped it into his breast pocket. "Let's grab a bite." He fetched his hat. "Bring your song."

They hailed a cab. George mumbled directions to the driver. In the back seat they jostled and bumped south and east and south again, music playing in their minds.

"Where are we going?"

He smiled.

The car bobbled and wove through cobblestone streets past Delancey, finally pulling to the curb in front of a coffee-and-sandwich establishment, Meier's. As they stepped out and George paid the driver, a ragman was pulling a wooden wagon, calling out to prospective buyers. Men in ill-fitting suits and Stetson hats hurried up and down the sidewalk. A woman shouted from her open window to another woman across the street.

"It may not smell like honeysuckle," said George. "More like garlic and brine. But this place makes me feel alive. Look at those kids." A boy zoomed past on roller skates. "That could be me." His eyes lingered on the roller skater until the boy disappeared around a corner. George opened the sandwich-shop door and escorted Kay in. The front window was steamy, the painted wood tables marred with pen-knifed initials.

"Jake, where you been?" The burly, balding man at the counter glanced up from the corned beef he was slicing. "Folks say being famous has turned your cup. That you're so busy doing this and that, running here and there, Paris, London, all the fancy places,

300

who needs the Lower East Side? They call you a genius, 'course it blows you up."

George grinned. "Meier, this is Kay."

Meier's small eyes, set in a bloated face, took in her pearls, her hat, her silk dress. "Have a seat." He waved them toward a bench.

"Jake?" asked Kay as they walked to a table.

"Jacob Gershowitz," George told her. "Everyone has a birth name. I'm no exception." They sat down. "Meier likes you."

"I would never have guessed."

George nodded, beaming. Kay leaned over the table and asked, low, "Why would you care?"

"Meier has a direct line to God. Don't laugh. I could tell you stories. Without him, I'd be a nobody."

"Someone like you could never be a nobody."

George shook his head. "There are plenty of smart, hardworking musicians running around this town. Never insult Fortune, Kay. She's the stage manager. We're just lousy bit players."

Meier brought two pastrami sandwiches. "Two pickles, half-done, lots of mustard, your way."

Kay frowned at the pile of steaming meat

in soggy rye bread. She raised it to her mouth and bit into it with resolve, losing meat and staining her face and hands. George chuckled and leaned forward to wipe her face with his napkin. He removed the top slice of rye from his sandwich and slathered extra mustard onto it. "You only live once, Kay. We're all here on borrowed time, as Meier says. Enjoy the ride is what I'm saying."

"Jimmy would never set foot in this place," said Kay as she glanced around.

He followed her eyes. "Is that right. Ever heard of Eva Gauthier?" He wiped his hand with his napkin, reached into his jacket pocket, and pulled out an invitation.

"Who hasn't?" asked Kay raising her eyebrows.

"Five years ago, before the *Rhapsody,* she sang a few of my numbers alongside Bartók and Schoenberg in the Aeolian Hall. You can imagine the uproar. A classical mezzo-soprano singing Gershwin! That's what gave Paul Whiteman the idea for the *Rhapsody.*"

"It was Whiteman's idea?" asked Kay.

"His idea. My music," George reassured her. "I had two weeks to write it. Planned the whole thing on a train from Boston to New York."

"Did you know it would be a master-piece?"

"Sure," he nodded. "*I* knew. But I didn't know whether *the world* would know."

Kay found his peculiar mixture of over-weening confidence and humility — if that was what it was — positively dizzying. He handed her the card. "In honor of Monsieur Maurice Ravel," it began. And scrawled in the margin: "George, do please join us. Ravel implored me to invite you. Can't wait to see you, mon ami. Eva."

"Out of all the girls that would sell their baby brother to attend this party on my arm," said George, "you're my pick."

"Zowie, George. Ravel!" Kay stared at the invitation. She set it on the table and at-tacked Meier's sandwich with renewed courage. As she did so, she smiled inwardly. An invitation to a private party honoring Maurice Ravel and a battle with this greasy sandwich. All in the same afternoon.

Louisa d'Andelot Carpenter was the eldest and wildest daughter of Lammot du Pont, one of the inventors of blasting powder and, as a result, one of the wealthiest men in America. She had run away from Delaware to New York, where she took pleasure in horse-racing, flying airplanes, dressing like a man in a suit, tie, and top hat, and flaunting her obsession with the singer Libby Holman. She derived glee from the flashes of celebrity hounds' cameras and the venom of Sunday preachers and split her time between her concierged Upper East Side penthouse and her lover's Lower East Side walk-up. Louisa answered the door in her pajamas. "George, what a treat, you rat!" She kissed him on both cheeks and called, "Libby, my love, company!"

"You remember Kay Swift," said George.

"How could I not?" said Libby, emerging from her bathroom in a towel, hair dripping. She slipped off the towel, propped her foot on a chair, and dried her leg.

"Such an exhibitionist," Louisa exclaimed.

"Who's complaining?" said George.

"Don't worry," Libby reassured her lover. "The garden may be in bloom, but the gate's locked. Only you have the key, darling."

Louisa turned back to George and Kay. "What's the occasion?"

"You got a piano here?" asked George.

Wiping down her other leg, Libby shook her head. "Landlord forbids it. But Louisa knows her way around a guitar fretboard." George nodded to Kay, who handed Louisa her hand-written sheet music for "Can't We

Be Friends?"

"Just write down the chords, will you, darling? We'll give it a shot." Louisa fetched a pen and paper, headed to the bedroom to grab her handmade Martin guitar, and sat on a chair to tune it while Kay, at the dining table, jotted down the chords.

"You're slightly sharp," commented Kay.

"How do you know?" asked Louisa. There was no tuning fork or piano at hand.

"Perfect pitch," said George, pointing to Kay with his thumb.

Louisa retuned.

Libby looked at the sheet music and hummed the melody. Minutes later, still naked, Libby serenaded them with Kay's song while her pajama-clad lover plucked the chords. When they finished, Kay applauded. "That was lovely. What a voice!"

"What did I tell you?" said George, beaming.

Libby retreated to the bedroom. "They've cast me in *The Little Show,*" she called.

"That Dietz-Schwartz revue?" asked George, removing a pitcher of tea from the ice box.

"It won't hit the stage for months, maybe a year. And I'm not exactly chuffed with the numbers they gave me." Libby stepped back into the room wearing a tunic. "You mind if

I hold onto your song?" she asked Kay.

"It's yours!"

George poured iced tea for himself and Kay. "Lunch was salty," he explained.

"Maybe Dietz and Schwartz will switch things around," said Libby looking at Kay's music on the table.

CHAPTER NINETEEN

The Canadian mezzo-soprano Eva Gauthier presented herself as French. Craving continental sophistication, America swallowed her pretentions without a burp. She wore Javanese robes that recalled Claude Debussy's fascination with the music of Bali and decorated her New York apartment in *belle époque* opulence, with Lautrec and Mucha lithographs.

Maurice Ravel, who actually *was* French, dressed like an American businessman in a natty suit. A small, wiry man with an oversized head, he begged George to sit at the Pleyel grand and play the *Rhapsody*. George spliced together two handfuls of rapid passages and mixed in a few rags and show tunes. Ravel observed George's fingers like a cat studying a fly. To Kay he commented: "I must say I find his technique astonishing."

"That's because it isn't a technique at all,"

said Kay. "It's more like a seizure."

Ravel sipped his wine. "Precisely."

With uncharacteristic self-restraint, George yielded the keyboard after only a quarter hour. "Why don't you play something for us, Kay?"

By way of reply, Kay turned to Eva. "May I have the honor of accompanying you, Miss Gauthier?"

"I would be delighted!" replied the singer.

From Eva's towering bookshelves Kay removed a song she had studied with George, Ravel's "Deux mélodies hébraïques."

"Ah," commented the composer. "This one has earned me the hatred of many nationalists in France. Their, how do you say, *detestation* is my pride."

Kay sat at the piano. Eva sang *Kaddisch* and *L'énigme éternelle* in her resonant low range. Everyone applauded and the two ladies curtsied.

During dessert with the man generally considered the greatest living composer, Kay found him down-to-earth, contrary to the stereotype of the proud, detached Frenchman. "I am more Basque than French, you see. The French are not fond of me, I'm afraid, especially since I refused their *Légion d'honneur*. Even Erik Satie, whom I had promoted, attacked me."

Kay wiped a dab of *crème pâtissière* from her lips. "Why did you refuse it?"

"I oppose all forms of nationalism."

"Hey, I have a notion," said George. "Duke Ellington's lighting up the Cotton Club tonight. Remember, I told you about him at Le Belvédère?"

"Certainly."

"What do you say we hop over there?"

"Avec plaisir," said Ravel. "I would love to."

Duke Ellington's music saturated the Cotton Club and oozed through its doors and windows. Saxophones and bass clarinets leaped and fell in squiggly parallel motion; a muted *wa-wa* trumpet reached high for the melody and then toppled down; a banjo strummed the rhythm; the Duke chimed at the piano.

Maurice Ravel paused at the entrance to take it all in: the flappers hopping about; the "downtown men," bankers and lawyers, wearing monocles, with watch chains dangling across their chests, at backgammon tables puffing cigars; the women slouching, twisting, laughing, sipping Rittenhouse Rye or Sweet Vermouth, displaying their calves and thighs.

George introduced the French composer to the proprietor, who did not seem to recognize Ravel's name. Owney Madden escorted them to a corner table and ordered drinks on the house. "Tell the Duke to swing by during his break," George instructed Owney.

Ravel concentrated on the music, watching the players. "This is extraordinary," he said. "You must understand, my dear Gershwin, what we are witnessing here — you, the Duke, your friends — it is new, it is brilliant, it is . . . how do you say?" he searched for the word, looking up at the lamps. "Incandescent."

Ravel's words astonished Kay. She had been taught to worship at the altar of European music, and here Europe's greatest living composer was expressing admiration for the American music of George Gershwin and Duke Ellington, both largely self-taught.

"Maurice," said George, "ever since I met you, even before, I've had this nagging idea."

"Yes?"

"Do you take students?"

"A few."

The waiter brought their drinks.

"Here's what I'm getting at," pursued George. "Do you think it might be possible . . . Could I study with you? A few months. Maybe six. Your place, mine, wherever."

Ravel laughed. "My dear Gershwin, why should I endeavor to turn you into a second-rate Ravel when you are already a first-rate *you*?"

"I sop up influences from everywhere," said George. "That doesn't make me not me."

"All I can teach is style," insisted Ravel. "You already have style, which is a far greater achievement than mere technique."

"Right. But I'm sure if you let me dig in your tool chest, I could find a few useful gadgets."

"They say the best teacher in France, for Americans, is Nadia Boulanger," Ravel conceded.

"Well can you refer me to *her*?" On the table, George clutched Kay's hand, perhaps to console her. He knew she yearned to be his teacher, and that she would balk at the prospect of his leaving the country again.

Ravel waved the waiter over and asked for a pen and paper. On Cotton Club letterhead, he wrote the date and "New York." When he finished he handed the missive to Kay, who translated. "My dear Nadia," she read aloud:

311

There is a musician here endowed with the most brilliant, most enchanting and perhaps the most profound talent: George Gershwin. His worldwide success no longer satisfies him. He is aiming higher. He knows that he lacks the technical means to achieve his goal. In teaching him those tools, one might ruin his talent. Would you have the courage, which I wouldn't dare have, to undertake this daunting responsibility?

Ravel

She gave the note back to Ravel, who folded it and slid it into his breast pocket. "I shall mail it from the hotel."

When Duke Ellington approached their table, George introduced him to Ravel. A tall man with a thin moustache, a checked suit, and a black tie, Ellington smiled graciously. "Honored," he said with a bow. George moved to accommodate him at the table and ordered a glass of straight bourbon, Ellington's preferred beverage. "So what do you think of our jazz, Monsieur Ravel?" asked the Duke.

Ravel lit a cigarette. "I do not yet understand what jazz is." He puffed. "Perhaps that is why I love it."

"I'll tell you what it is," said the Duke. "It

is the answer of those of us who grew up admiring composers like yourself, but were denied the right to play in legit theaters. So if we can't perform under Toscanini's baton we'll make our own damn baton. And that baton is beating out a rhythm Beethoven and Wagner never heard of. It's called *swing.*"

"The rhythm of freedom," agreed Gershwin.

The waiter refilled Ravel's wine glass.

"But can you define *swing?*" asked Ravel.

"I will do so this very evening," Ellington told him. "Just stick around."

George waved to a friend. "Hey, Oscar!"

Oscar Levant, frowzled but attractive, spotted him and escorted his taller, red-headed female companion to their table. "George Gershwin, Margaret Manners," he introduced her. "Let's see," Oscar added, pointing to each, "Duke Ellington, Kay Swift, Maurice Ravel: Margaret Manners, the head-turning dancer, singer, and actress who's taking Broadway by storm. Hey, make room for the lady, will you?"

Delighted that a man she had never met knew her name and recognized her face, Kay slid sideways. Levant sat next to her, Miss Manners beside Ravel. "Oscar's a keyboard wiz," said George. "Like Kay here, only he's from Pittsburgh. Which is, of course, no small difference."

"I'm also a composer," Oscar reminded him. "Like you."

"We're all composers, here," said George. "Well, almost all of us," he added with a wink at the sultry Miss Manners.

"Say, Monsieur Ravel," asked Oscar with the nonchalance of a shopper requesting advice on hats, "I've noticed some people play your 'Jeux d'eau' *rubato* while others give it an almost Bach-like mechanical flavor and I'm wondering, which approach do you prefer?"

Kay expected Ravel to say, *why,* rubato, *of course,* meaning with a fluid, variable, dream-like meter in the late-Romantic tradition, but Ravel offered a more cryptic answer. "Bach never marked his music *meccanicamente* so far as I am aware."

Oscar ordered a glass of moonshine for himself and "something sweet and sparkly for the dame, to match her personality."

The dame, Miss Manners, flashed the requisite smile at Oscar and added a sidelong glance at George, who seemed oblivious. Ellington excused himself and sauntered back to the stage, where he dedicated the next number to "Monsieur Maurice Ravel, the celebrated French composer, and my friend George Gershwin, who needs no introduction in this crowd." To his orchestra he added, "Let's show Monsieur Ravel what *swing* means," and struck up a brisk "I'm Gonna Hang Around My Sugar."

George excused himself and wandered off. Minutes later, Margaret rose. Oscar and Maurice concentrated on the music while sipping their beverages. Kay looked for George in the crowd.

When George returned he said, "Forgive me, fellas, but I have to catch some *z*'s." He glanced at his watch. "Early business and all that. Oscar, can you escort Kay to her place, and Monsieur Ravel to his hotel?" He slapped a fifty-dollar bill onto the table.

"How could I say no to that?" said Oscar, eyeing the excessive sum.

"I'm ready to leave, too." Kay started to rise.

"You'll be fine, Kay," said George. "Just don't let these rascals mess with you." He pecked her on the nose and turned toward the door.

Ellington broke into a "Down in Our Alley Blues" that dripped with New Orleans remoulade flavor. But Kay felt increasingly restless. And then: "What happened to Margaret?" she asked no one in particular.

The men exchanged a glance.

"She's a showgirl." Oscar shrugged. "Or should I say, a show-but-don't-tell girl."

With a rising sense of dread, Kay looked down into her drink.

An hour later, in a cab he'd hired to drive the three of them home, Oscar turned to her. "You haven't fallen for this big shot, I hope. I have nothing but respect for George as a musician, a composer, a painter. The guy's an *idiot savant,* what can I tell you. But this settling-down business he has not figured out. He's got songbirds falling out of the trees."

"Are you implying that women are just playthings for George?" asked Kay.

"I'm saying celebrity is a disease," replied Oscar. "And he's got it bad. You and I are lucky in that regard. At least so far. Though I could use a little less luck and a little more notoriety."

With an unsteady hand Kay removed a cigarette from its package. Oscar lit it for her. "I'd hate to see a talented, one-in-a-million dame like you get bruised."

She blew a cloud of smoke out the window.

As the cab drew to a stop in front of her home Oscar patted Kay's hand. "Take a couple aspirin. Get a good night's sleep. This is just a node."

She frowned. "A node?"

"One beat in the magnificent concerto of your life." He winked.

Returning home a little after eleven, Kay found Jimmy in the parlor puffing on cigars and drinking cognac with guests. "Right on cue, Kay." He rose to introduce her. "This is Elisabeth and this is Carl. You know Edgar already. They'd like to hear 'Little White Lies.' "

Carl had a thin moustache and slicked-back hair. Elisabeth's eyes were the hue of Connecticut mud; she wore bright lipstick and a gray dress. Together they presented the appearance of two fashionable individuals of limited means, eager to make an impression on a renowned banking institution. Edgar, impeccable and subdued, was an associate of Jimmy's and a friend from college.

"Of course," agreed Kay, stifling her inner turmoil. *What is George up to?*

As they walked toward the piano, she whispered to her husband, "Why don't you let me do the singing."

Despite her inebriation and fatigue, or perhaps because of it, she played and sang "Little White Lies" in a fluid, Gershwinesque manner. Her fingers felt as sloppy

317

as warm Camembert. No one seemed to notice — except Jimmy. He frowned for the briefest moment. Her fingers stumbled. But when she finished, all he said was, "Now, 'When The Lights Turn Green.' "

Again, she played and sang.

"These are a kick," commented Carl.

"Smashing," said Elisabeth.

"Splendid," said Jimmy. "Then we've clinched the fundamentals. Let's talk again Monday."

After he escorted them to the door Jimmy swung around to face his wife. "What's bothering you, Kay?"

"Nothing," she said.

Jimmy looked at her with concern, then said: "Carl and Elisabeth were looking to finance a show. Normally I wouldn't get within a football throw of this kind of investment. But Kay, it pains me to see your songs floundering like," he searched for a simile, "like flounder. On the shore."

"The Hotel Astor show," she reminded him, "didn't get us far."

"Then let's keep trying, shall we?" He returned to the parlor, where he snuffed out all three cigars. "It's about exposure. And more exposure."

Kay picked up his cognac snifter and drained it. "They have a book?"

318

"That and two nickels." Jimmy turned off the lights and escorted her upstairs. "It's called *Say When,* by Calvin Brown. A Harvard man and a decent wordsmith." Before retiring to his bedroom he added, "I'm under no illusions, Kay. Some shows turn ridiculous profits, others crash and sink. I'm not aware of any way to predict these things. It's on a par with gambling and I'm not going to stake our roof on it. But again, this is not about the money." He held her shoulders and kissed her.

Soon after her head collided with her pillow, the alcohol lulled her into a carefree sleep where thoughts of Margaret Manners and Oscar Levant faded. A few hours later, though, she woke. She tried turning onto her left side and her right side, and staring at the ceiling, to no avail.

Her mind raced. She was not thinking about "Little White Lies" or Jimmy's show business experiment. Not even about music. She was thinking about where she stood and where she was going. About George. About Jimmy.

She would have preferred not to devote a moment's attention to questions of desire, sexuality, intimacy, or love. But now they mattered more than anything. More than melody. More than applause. The paradox involved in loving two men but not being able to love either fully, and not feeling loved in a satisfying way by either, was tearing her apart. Was she at fault, for harboring impossible expectations of others, and of herself?

All three of them — she, George, and Jimmy — had grown up in more-or-less traditional families. Although the customs differed in name and flavor — Protestant Christian, Shtetl Jewish, Court Jewish — their notions of morality were similar. Marriage was a holy sacrament. People strayed. Such errors were shameful but human.

Jimmy saw all this as hypocrisy. In his view, to stray was indeed human but not shameful. Like Prohibition, all the moralistic preaching through the centuries amounted to nothing but ninety-eight-point-six-degree wind. George saw marriage as a distant goal, something to aspire to but possibly never reach. For Kay, physical desire and romantic entanglement were of a piece. That was the problem. That, and an aching dissatisfaction with the status quo that had been increasing since long before the *Rhapsody in Blue* premiere. All this was complicated by the fact that Jimmy was a debonair, decent, generous man. Not without his flaws, certainly. His wandering, geographical and emotional. His smugness. His certitude that his analyses of — well, of everything — were accurate, which his triumphs in school, business, and society had seemed to vindicate. His need to feel admired. His difficulty accepting defeat.

She had to admit to herself, though, that George was a rascal too. Yes, she had plugged herself into him, or him into her, through music. So had millions of others. Such was the power of melody, its universality, its ambiguousness. In the vigor and lyricism of a *Rhapsody in Blue* or a *New York Concerto* his audience discovered a canvas on which to illustrate feelings and dreams. But like dreams, sounds emerge one moment only to disappear the next, as George had observed at Bydale. Not the ideal foundation on which to construct one's hopes. She wished she could stifle her feelings but as Adele Astaire had pointed out, for people like her, emotions always trumped reason. To try to talk herself out of them would be futile. At the same time, she had no claim on George — as long as she was married to another man.

Finally, little by little, these real-world preoccupations yielded again to sleep and dream-world imagery. She was standing in a line at the docks. An enormous ship loomed before her. The placard in front of the gangway read "Nineveh." She had never heard of such a place. Someone was singing somewhere. It sounded like a scratchy record. Caruso, perhaps, or Jolson?

Bleary-eyed in a slim shift, wearing a cloche hat and clutching a matching handbag, she took a cab the next morning to George's apartment. She feared she might catch George red-faced in the arms of that floozy, Miss Manners or whatever her real name was. More likely, George's valet would turn her away. But nothing of the sort happened. Paul escorted her up to George, who was hard at work with his brother Ira just as on any other morning.

"Get an earful of this, Kay!" He played an ascending progression that combined major and minor seventh chords with a dash-dot, dash-dot beat.

"Daah dah-daah dah," Ira sang gayly. He gestured as if turning a wheel.

George played the progression again. "I got some-thing," tried Ira. And he tried again: "I got some-thing." And then he asked, "What do I got? I got *daah-dah.*"

"What you've got?" tried Kay. "You've got music."

Ira tried it. "I got mu—sic. Works!"

"That's it!" shouted George.

They played it through again, with Ira singing "I got music, I got music, I got *daah-dah. Daah da daah daah dada daah daah.*"

That was how they worked. Unlike other songwriting teams, in which one man — always a man — wrote the lyrics, and another devised the music, George and Ira collaborated on every note, every syllable. George invented the melody, which often included a rhythmic hook. Ira found a mood and a few words to match. Then he concocted the rest of the lyrics around that nugget. If Ira's lyrics turned out more rueful than George's music but otherwise fit, they would slow the song down. Other times they would speed it up, or modify the chords or the key. They would further adjust the text, word by word. Matching the music to the lyric was like tuning a saxophone to a flute until no space was left between the pitches.

Kay slammed the keyboard cover, almost hitting George's precious fingers before he pulled them away. "George, did you bed that tramp?"

Ira looked down.

"Who?" asked George with a frown.

"The so-called Margaret Manners, who

has none."

"What are you blabbing about?"

Kay shot him a don't-you-dare-lie-to-me stare. "Well, did you? Did you make love to her?"

He shook his head. *She* made love to *me!*"

Kay stepped closer and slapped him. "I will not have you toying with my heart."

George brought his hand to his cheek. "That's not what I was toying with."

Another cheap joke. Another weak effort to laugh off her pain. "Oh, yes, it was," said Kay.

"See ya later, fellas," mumbled Ira as he left.

George stood up. His dark eyes probed hers. "She's just a girl, Kay. A nice show-girl. Nothing to get steamed up about."

"A girl! Is that how you think about women? About me?"

"What does this have to do with you?"

She stared at him, her hands clenched. "You left with her, George. Everybody saw. Why'd you have to humiliate me?"

George frowned. "Humiliate you?"

"Oh, drop it. You're all the same. How could I have been so blind?"

She collapsed into a leather chair. For the first time, she and he were standing on opposite rims of the gender divide, which sud-

324

denly gaped as wide as the Grand Canyon. They could hardly hear each other.

He sailed across that chasm and landed in front of her, kneeling. "Kay, you're married. Jimmy's an upstanding fellow. I never promised anything, did I? But that dancer last night, I've got no illusions. Hell, she's got no illusions. She's not you, Kay."

Kay covered her face with her hands.

"I didn't mean to hurt you, baby," added George removing her wet hands from her eyes. "My life is a cannonball. Someone fired it in the middle of a war. Always flying and I have no idea where I'll land. But when I do I sure hope you'll be nearby."

She sniffled.

"Meantime," he added hastily, "they're calling me to London. *Oh, Kay!*'s busting the box office over there, just like it did here. Everyone's hollering for an interview. Then, back to Paris. They're asking me to perform the *New York Concerto*. And I'm going to study with Nadia Boulanger."

Oh, Kay! She knew the songs. She had transcribed them. She knew the story, too, which revolved around the romantic misadventures of a certain Jimmy and a certain Kay, set in a milieu of unlimited wealth, drunken revelry, and Prohibition law enforcement. At the show's peak, in the midst of the tomfoolery, Kay soliloquizes:

There's a somebody I'm longing to see.
I hope that he turns out to be
someone to watch over me.

That song was a tease. George knew Kay was waiting, and wanted her to know he knew. In New York, "Someone To Watch Over Me" was the chart topper of the show. The world was celebrating her turmoil.

"I'm happy for you," she said in a small voice. "Have a good trip."

CHAPTER TWENTY

Two weeks later, Elisabeth and Carl were holding auditions for *Say When.* Kay so wanted this to be an exhilarating time for her and Jimmy, but the director and producer stipulated that the financiers were forbidden to assert oversight rights. Precisely two of their songs, "Little White Lies" and "When the Lights Turn Green," would be interpolated.

Having experienced the preproduction of *A Connecticut Yankee* Kay understood the process, which involved ruthless self-criticism and the willingness to alter every detail, depending on what happened when dance shoes hit floorboards.

Dick Rodgers, not a particularly generous man, was touting Kay as the best rehearsal pianist in New York. Nevertheless, the producers of *Say When* barred her and Jimmy from pre-production. Jimmy, ever the optimist, consoled her that their purpose was to hear their songs performed on a Broadway stage.

Only when the night of the dress rehearsal arrived did Kay and Jimmy learn that their two songs had been dropped in, rather than showcased. The audience applauded politely but Kay listened in vain for the uproarious response she had expected. The show as a whole was only mildly entertaining; the audience response, tepid.

Kay wondered how this could have happened, what could have gone so wrong. Everyone involved in *Say When* was experienced, hardworking, and ambitious. How could all of them, pooling their resources, have failed so miserably? Elisabeth and Carl had been convinced they had a hit.

The only answer Kay could come up with was that a show was not a show until it had an audience. Its worth could not be measured prior to that because it did not yet exist. A show was not just a performance; it was more like a collective dream, a collaboration between spectators' minds, singers' voices, and writers' imaginations.

The prebooked eleven-day stint sped by like a snail in mud. Fifteen performances and hardly a notice in the papers. Aleck Woollcott promised Kay he would refrain from reviewing *Say When,* out of mercy.

Kay and Jimmy reconciled themselves to the reality that no hit would emerge. Kay sighed through the last performance. And then it was over.

Just another show, she told herself as she exited the Morosco Theatre. *Another group of theatergoers spilling onto the sidewalk.* Jimmy would survive. So would she.

She thought too about the writer, the actors, the dancers, the comedians, and the director, all praying for that big break. So many careers, so many lives. Where would they all go? How many would give up now, or try again — and yet again — before throwing in the towel? Who would sink into depression, and who would discover a way out? Who would merely survive, and who would find redemption?

When Kay's mother died of breast cancer, in the summer of 1928, she and Jimmy wanted to cover the costs of the burial but learned that Ellen had prepaid the service and burial and left a set of instructions. Even in death, Ellen preserved her pride and solicitude. On a balmy July morning the congregation of St. Ignatius sang hymns composed by Gertrude Swift and the organist played Sam Swift's meticulous arrangements. A handful of Ellen's friends — fellow British expats, former clients, members of her Bible study group — rode in horse-drawn carriages up to the burial grounds, where Father Ganter sermonized not about the departed congregant, his friend, or her exemplary life but about the faith they shared and the salvation they expected. "Because Jesus was raised from the dead," he reminded his parishioners, "we too shall be raised."

His words touched Kay. She remembered that faith. The recollection shrouded her like a shadow, indistinct yet as somber as the suits and dresses that surrounded her. The pallbearers lowered Ellen's coffin into the pit, and grief overcame Kay. Her shoulders shaking, she buried her face in her husband's lapel. Emotions seemed to flow from beyond her conscious mind, through her body, as if her ancestors were using her to express their sorrow. Kay knew they dwelled within her, memories of memories.

Ellen's had been a small life, fashioned of modest ambitions and unassailable loyalties. In many ways, Kay had unconsciously designed her personality in opposition to her mother's. Still, Ellen's devotion had been her foundation.

She could not cease sobbing until Father Ganter tapped her shoulder and handed her a shovel full of dirt. She wiped her tears and, as she poured the final heap onto the mound, felt she was burying not only her mother's life but her own life up to that point.

She shoved the spade into the soil and, looking up, noticed a dirigible above the horizon, hundreds of feet long, glistening in the sky, its passenger gondola suspended beneath. She thought of Ellen's soul hovering above them, silent and watchful. Other mourners' eyes followed hers. A cloud swallowed the airship.

The reception took place at Ellen's Upper West Side apartment, where Kay and Jimmy had been married ten years earlier. As the other mourners nibbled on whitefish and sipped chilled wine, Kay sensed Father Ganter's eyes on her. She approached him at the back of the room.

"We've all heard about your advantageous marriage and modern lifestyle," he told her, glancing through the guests toward James, who was talking quietly with a group of Kay's distant relatives. "We're proud of you, Katharine. We hope you found what you were seeking."

Perhaps it was the emotion of the moment. Perhaps it had something to do with being back in this apartment, among family acquaintances. Perhaps she simply needed someone to talk to. Whatever the reason, Kay spoke more openly to Father Ganter than she might have expected. "I'm not sure I *have* found what I was seeking, Father."

Father Ganter frowned. "Is everything not working out as expected between you and James P. Warburg? By all accounts he's a remarkable man."

"Yes, he is," said Kay. "And I do love him. It's just that . . . I'm no longer certain what that means."

Father Ganter nodded gravely. "It's not just a sentiment, after all, is it. It's a blending of families. Of histories. The two lineages have to be compatible."

"You're referring to Jimmy's religion?" asked Kay.

He nodded. "A religion is not a hat you can take off and put on at leisure. A religion is a moral universe. What does your husband believe about the destiny of man, or our purpose in history?"

She shook her head. She had no idea what Jimmy thought about these matters.

"Does the man believe in anything?"

"He believes in reason," said Kay. "He took a course or two at Harvard. Descartes, Kant, the Enlightenment. Also Schopenhauer and Nietzsche. I can't argue with him.

I never read any of that. I was too busy practicing arpeggios."

Father Ganter nodded. "One thing about reason, though: you can argue anything. Some use reason to support carnal lust. Or to justify killing unwanted babies. Lord have mercy. And then, some use reason to bolster the Golden Rule that our Lord gifted us. But morality does not flow from reason, and the Golden Rule needs no support. Kant was a genius but he was wrong about that. Dead wrong."

Kay felt there might be truth in the reverend's words but distrusted this feeling. She had grown up in his church and been conditioned in it. Of course her gut would agree with him. This observation, however, did not lead her closer to solving her problems. "Jimmy's a good man," she said.

"There's a map for where you're standing," said Father Ganter. "You just can't read the signs." He smiled sadly. "Maybe someday."

"Or maybe I can read them but something in me is resisting."

"Don't blame yourself," he advised her. "The problem isn't you. It's our culture of self-gratification. All the rest — our confusion, our sense of unfulfillment, even the momentary exhilaration of our stock market profiteers — it all flows from there."

Kay smiled.

"Listen to your heart," Father Ganter advised her, placing a hand on her shoulder. "And do keep in mind, no matter what happens, you have a home. God is eager to forgive, if only you ask, Katharine."

She covered his hand with hers, on her shoulder. "Thank you, Father."

"Your mother has moved on," he said. "I myself will be retiring. But our mother church will always be here."

His smile struck Kay as deficient, the pious simper of the professional cleric who earned his bread by displaying bought-and-paid-for compassion. But later, as she and Jimmy rode home, Kay reflected on Father Ganter's words. *The church is your home.* Despite the degradation of her marriage, despite the cynicism born of frustrated hopes, she appreciated his effort. Even if she sensed that destiny would not lead her back to St. Ignatius but somewhere else entirely.

CHAPTER TWENTY-ONE

Jimmy had read Freud's international best-seller, *The Interpretation of Dreams.* The troubles in his marriage, it seemed, reflected unresolved conflicts within himself and his wife. He had no desire to shirk from self-examination. On the most obvious level, his desire for sexual freedom and his expectation of a serene domestic life now seemed at odds with each other, even if upper-class Europeans including his forebears had pulled off this high-wire act for centuries. Although he blamed Kay for taking things too far and for her — and George's — lack of discretion, he had taken things too far himself on more than one occasion. He had flailed in love with two or three helpless paramours. Later, when the sentiments had evaporated and he had found himself stranded on emotional dry land, he had asked himself how in the name of everything he held dear he could have been drawn to such shallow, ordinary women.

None of them compared with Kay. What had he seen in those women that appealed to him, apart from their looks? Kay was on target when she defined a romantic as a man in search of women to idealize him.

Psychoanalysis offered a method to examine the wheelwork of his psyche, perhaps to tune it up and repair its broken cogs. He sought the most renowned practitioner and settled on a short Upper East Side Ukrainian doctor, Gregory Zilboorg.

At first Jimmy treated his sessions with Doctor Zilboorg like a secret diplomatic mission or an Austrian love affair, refusing to divulge their nature or content. Then one evening, returning home after what he described as a brutal double session, he told Kay that Doctor Zilboorg wished to speak with her.

Kay was lying on the floor, working on a coloring book with their middle daughter, Andrea. Kay derived no pleasure from coloring books, nor did she understand how anyone could. But Andrea loved them and Kay was doing her best to take pleasure in the exercise. She looked up. "Doctor Zilboorg? Why?"

"Moiré interference," said Jimmy. "Between our psyches."

"Moiré interference?"

"When two expanding circles of waves collide," explained Jimmy, "creating offshoot wavelets that roll away in many directions."

"Right," said Kay. "I'll keep it in mind." It sounded poetic enough, but trivial. What mattered now was that George was in Paris, and that Kay had no idea when he would be returning. That would be decided by Madame Nadia Boulanger, the famed French teacher of illustrious American composers including Aaron Copland and Virgil Thomson. The woman who was providing George with the instruction in harmony and counterpoint that Kay had offered to provide . . .

"Mommy," said Andrea, frustrated with the effort to color on her own. She had not yet mastered the art of shading within lines.

A metaphor for my own issues, thought Kay as she resumed helping her daughter.

"Please, Kay." Jimmy sat down. "Give Zilboorg a try."

Again, Kay looked up. "I just wonder how this is going to change you. Suppose Doctor Zilboorg does solve the puzzle of your neurosis. What kind of man will you become? The one I married, or some stranger?"

"I don't know that I ever was the man you

married."

That statement gave her pause.

"Mommy." Andrea pulled on her sleeve.

Kay helped her daughter shade the drawing of Pegasus. "We all change, I guess," she said to Jimmy. "In which case, what does commitment even mean?"

Jimmy looked at his watch. "Andrea, it's time to get ready for bed. Mommy and I have a dinner engagement."

Once a month the members of the all-male Harvard Club were allowed to invite their all-female spouses inside. Over a candlelit meal Jimmy informed Kay that . . . well, just that the world's economy was about to collapse. "To pay its war debt to France and Britain under the Versailles Treaty," he explained, "Germany has borrowed heavily, as you know. Now they're devaluing the Reichsmark, so their repayments are worth nothing."

She had read about hyperinflation in Germany, which had drained almost all value from the German coin. "Sounds awful. But Jimmy, Germany is not the world."

Jimmy sipped his bordeaux. "France and Britain also borrowed. To finance their side of the war. And without credible German repayments to *them,* per the Versailles

Treaty . . . You get the idea."

Kay got it, all right. M. M. Warburg & Co. stood smack in the middle of a world-engulfing financial quagmire. How would these developments impact the Warburg-Swift household?

"Added to which," said Jimmy, "we have issues domestically. And not insignificant ones."

"Domestically?" asked Kay.

"In America."

"Are you referring to the floods in Mississippi and Vermont, the explosions in Ohio and Pittsburgh, or the Bath School massacre?" asked Kay. All these two-inch-headline events had involved ghastly fatalities and displacements.

"I'm referring," Jimmy sighed, "to our massive farm debt."

All that was far away, though, was it not? Somewhere in the twangy Midwest? In New York City and Southern Connecticut, people were still celebrating the booming stock market. The waiter brought their *table d'hôte* meals of lobster and rice. "We're going to jettison most of our investments," Jimmy informed her as he dipped a forkful of lobster into butter. "But this is so much larger than us, Kay. I'm afraid I'll have to leave again for Germany," he sighed.

She tasted her lobster. "I'm sorry to hear that."

"You are?" He raised an eyebrow.

"I wanted to get started on our next show. We're not going to let *Say When* knock us sideways, are we, Jimmy?"

He smiled. "Why don't you sketch out the music, then. I'll think about the lyrics. What shall we call it?"

"How about *Fine and Dandy,*" suggested Kay. "Because that's how everything will turn out. The international economy, the domestic —" and she completed her sentence with a flip of her hand — *the domestic whatever.*

Jimmy raised his goblet. "Let's write songs that people will hum in their bathtubs."

Everything would be *Fine and Dandy*. And *Fine and Dandy* would be everything. The little white lie that the occasion required. Like the uplifting music of the string quartet that played on the deck of the sinking *Titanic.* They clinked glasses, drank to their next Broadway production, and dined quietly, absorbed in their thoughts.

Two weeks later, with both Jimmy and George once again out of the country, Kay felt deflated and depleted. She cursed herself for feeling that way. She did not need a man — her father, Jimmy, or George — to provide a sense of purpose and significance. She only had to fill her days and evenings with meaningful activities.

She tried to spend more time with her children. She read to them, taught them piano and do-ré-mi singing, and walked with them in the park. She attended every hit Broadway show, notebook in hand to record her thoughts and snippets of song. Which dramatic or musical devices affected her? Which failed? She invited Adele Astaire to lunch at the Waldorf. The waiter seated them front and center among the tables in the lobby, where everyone could gaze at them.

"Why don't we start with a good rouge," suggested Adele. "How about a carafe of bordeaux? Oh, do you know Kay Swift?" she asked the waiter. "George Gershwin's gal."

"Delighted, Madame," he told Kay. "But as you know quite well, Miss Astaire —"

"Oh, please, Jean-Pierre, I know you have a stash of 'twenty-six Margaux in your cellar, just dying to be savored by your spoiled clientele, who love to be treated like they're unaware of the law."

He nodded noncommittally and strolled off, a towel draped over his sleeve.

"Jean-Pierre is such a putz," said Adele, buttering a slice of bread. "He always protests, but he always delivers."

"I can't blame him," said Kay. "That's precisely what I do with my husband."

"Perhaps," said Adele, and then added, with all the confidence of a certified Yiddish scholar, "but by definition, a woman can't be a putz."

Jean-Pierre returned with a carafe, wrapped in a towel, and two goblets. He leaned down and addressed Adele in a conspiratorial tone. "I implore you, be discreet. If anything should happen, you brought this from home."

After he took their order, Adele turned to Kay with a serious expression. "George will always give more than you ask for," she said. "I don't mean romantically but in other ways. I sure am going to miss him, the scoundrel."

"Miss him?" asked Kay.

"Oh, Kay, I've met someone. Someone terrific." She set her water glass on the table. "Charles Cavendish," she announced in a mock British accent.

The name did not register.

"Lord Charles Arthur Francis Cavendish," Adele expanded. "We literally bumped into each other at a party after the premiere of

Funny Face in London last year. Causing his drink to spill. So I guess I owe this to George." And she softly trilled the title song, "Funny Face," in which Ira humorously and warmly explored the subject of mutual attraction between two people who know they are not outwardly pretty. "Isn't it just darling, how Ira writes for every Joe and Jane?" enthused Adele. "You don't have to be a knockout to be worthy of love. I guess my Charles agrees."

"Oh, kill it," said Kay, laughing. "You're hardly a plain Jane, Adele. Tell me about him."

"He's a banker. Served in the Royal Tank Regiment. Studied at Cambridge. Oh, and his father is, wait for this, the Ninth Duke of Devonshire."

"Sounds like my husband in more ways than one," remarked Kay. "Powerful father. Good college. And Jimmy wanted to serve in the war, too."

"Charles may not be all there, mentally," said Adele. "But then, I'm not all there, either. So we have that in common. And he does have that accent."

"Where will you live?"

"I'm afraid I'll have to hole up in a drafty castle in Ireland. That is, when I'm not moping around Chatsworth, our pied-àterre in Derbyshire. Such are the sacrifices one makes."

"Oh please, do hand me a handkerchief," said Kay. "What about Fred?"

"There's a battalion of nimble-toed gals out there, eager to tap dance up to my tape marks. I'll miss my brother but there's more to life than hopping around on scratched-up stages, taking bows, and reading about yourself in the papers. I'll be delighted to throw all that on the refuse heap of memory and set it ablaze with one of those dainty Blue Britannia matches they hand you with every pack of Wild Woodbine fags. I'm more than ready for private life, Kay. Peace and quiet. A family."

Kay sipped her Château Margaux. "Who else knows?"

"No one except Charles and Fred. And George, of course."

Kay chewed her salad, looking at Adele and reflecting. *It is so easy for someone in your position to deride what others think of as unsurpassable achievement. But look at it the other way. How many people, who already have a family and peace and quiet, really feel fulfilled?* Aloud she asked, "Are you certain you'll be happy in Europe? Far from everything, and everyone who loves you?"

"Charles loves me. And you don't bargain

with love. Happy is a big word," admitted Adele. "Have you been to Europe, Kay?"

Kay shook her head. "Jimmy spends half his life there, mostly in Germany. George is in Paris again. I'm holding down the fort."

"What fort? Last I heard, East Seventieth Street hasn't been under attack since the mid-1770s. Why don't you surprise George? Paris is magnificent."

"I don't know. Seems awfully intrusive." Although, Kay had to admit, the thought of visiting Paris was tantalizing. A change of scene. Famous museums. That Garnier opera house. And to see the expression on George's face when she bumped into him in Boulanger's studio — that would be precious. Nor would Jimmy care that she was gone, or even notice; he was away again for who-knew-how-long. The girls would hardly miss their piano instruction. Andrea would practice even in Kay's absence; April, sadly, would prefer her mother to be gone.

"George adores surprises," Adele insisted. "Especially when they drive the point home, how much he's loved. Tell him it was my idea."

Kay finished her salad, contemplating the prospect of visiting Paris. Its reputation as the world's capital of sensual pleasure — cream-laden food, elegant wines, marital infidelity — *Madame Bovary, Les Liaisons Dangereuses, Thérèse Raquin.*

While at the Institute, Kay had read so many novels set in France: *L'Education sentimentale, Le Lys dans la Vallée, Illusions Perdues, Notre-Dame de Paris, Les Misérables.* She also knew the librettos of *La Bohème* and *La Traviata,* both set in Italian-inflected versions of the French capital. In her conception, Paris's monuments loomed over filthy but lively neighborhoods that teemed with beggars, cripples, sultry gypsies, and destitute painters, and romantic young Frenchmen in love with older, married, society women.

"Kay," said Adele. "Don't look now, but the Morality Police just stepped in. Let's skedaddle."

Despite Adele's warning, Kay looked. Two men in gray suits were standing at the front of the restaurant, their eyes sweeping the room. Kay thought they were probably businessmen waiting to be seated.

Adele rose and flounced toward the bathroom. Kay followed nonchalantly. When they reached the rear wall, Adele ordered the elevator operator, "twenty-three, please," and handed him a five-dollar bill.

At the twenty-third floor Adele broke into a trot, heading for the stairs. Kay followed and they rushed down to the twenty-first floor, where they exited the stairwell and doubled over panting and giggling. It did not matter, after all, whether those two men were ordinary lunch-goers or Prohibition officers. In Adele Astaire's world, everything was make-believe and every path led to mischief.

Including friendship, Kay supposed.

As Kay walked up Fifth Avenue a quarter hour later she could not help feeling a pang of disappointment. It was a social triumph to lunch with a celebrity like Adele Astaire. She had sensed the other diners' eyes on them, and that was titillating. She wanted to believe she had forged a new partnership, intimate and mildly subversive. But Adele would soon be living an ocean away. For all her warmth and charm, Adele Astaire had no need of new friends. That was the curse of celebrity. When everyone in the world craves your friendship, what does friendship mean?

For advice she turned to Julie Glaenzer, who traveled to Paris twice every year on Cartier business. Again she visited him in his office on Fifth Avenue. And again, the concierge offered a goblet of claret.

"My flat happens to be unoccupied at

present." Julie removed a key from his drawer. "A two-minute walk from the cathedral." He handed the key across his desk.

"Notre Dame Cathedral, of Paris? That is awfully generous, Julie."

"Not at all," said Glaenzer, which she interpreted to mean, *this is how I do business, my dear.* "Pascal, my manservant, will help you with your bags, or drive you anywhere. But in my humble opinion, Paris is better experienced on foot. May I ask what is the purpose of your visit?"

"Sightseeing, I suppose."

"May I suggest the RMS *Olympic*? You've heard of the *Titanic,* I'm sure."

"It sank," said Kay.

"The *Olympic,* her surviving twin, will not. In fact," he added puffing on his cigar, "the *Olympic* could have rescued the *Titanic*'s passengers, but was dissuaded from doing so."

"Why?"

"White Star, the owner, didn't believe anyone would die. They wanted to avoid a panic."

"That's reassuring."

He tapped his cigar into the Baccarat ashtray. "Following the event they adjusted their emergency protocol. I assure you, the *Olympic* is every bit as safe as Fort Knox and as elegant as the Ritz. When would you like to sail?"

"How about tomorrow?"

He smiled. "I'm certain she's booked for at least six months but let's see what we can arrange."

He reached for the telephone.

A week later, she was packing three sets of clothes: one for exploring Paris on foot or in taxis; a second for dinners, plays, and shows with George or solo; and a third for special occasions. Perhaps they would rendezvous with Maurice Ravel at the Opéra, or dine with Nadia Boulanger at Maxime's. She also threw in novels to read during the crossings to and fro, and in Paris, as well as music-composition notebooks and a jumbo box of George's favorite Black Jack licorice chewing gum.

It should not be difficult to locate George, she assured herself. He was studying with Boulanger, whose offices were located at the Château de Fontainebleau. Nor did Kay wish to distract him. *Maybe Tuesday will be my good news day,* she hummed as she tossed a pair of camel calfskin gloves in the trunk.

She heard footsteps hurrying up the stairs. Andrea ran to her bedroom door, out of breath. "Mommy, Mommy, I got into the school talent show!"

Kay read pride and eagerness on her daughter's face. *Just like me, when I was her age,* Kay thought. *So proud of any recognition.* "That's wonderful, sweetheart! What will you perform?"

"For my audition, I played 'Für Elise.' But that's not what I'm really going to play. I'm going to surprise them with 'Liza.' "

" 'Liza.' Are you sure your hands are big enough?"

"I can do it, mom! But I'm not going to let you hear it until the talent show."

"And when is that, honey?"

"In three weeks."

It could not be. Kay knelt at Andrea's feet, taking her hands. "Oh, Andrea, I so wish I could be there. You see, I'm going to Paris. It's all arranged, darling. I fear there's nothing to do."

"Why?" Andrea pouted. "This is my first show!"

Kay caressed her daughter's head. "I know, sweet pea, and I'm so sorry! One day you'll understand. Now Andrea, I want you to know, I'll be thinking of you and your performance on that day. At the very moment you're playing, my thoughts, my heart will be right there with you. You give 'Liza'

350

everything you've got. Such a pretty tune. Maybe you'll win a prize! Please do try to understand, darling."

"I understand," said Andrea turning away.

Kay watched her go, her heart torn. She recognized so much of herself in her daughter, her sense of self but also of unfulfillment; her need to reach higher, always higher, and the anxious awareness that no matter how far she stretched — how much of life she gulped, how brilliantly she performed — it could never be enough.

Two mornings later Kay was lying on a walnut bed in her suite aboard the RMS *Olympic*, her nose in a poignant novel of romantic love, social class, self-deception, decadence, and despair. Pauline Heifetz had met Scott Fitzgerald's wife Zelda at one of Cole Porter's lavish parties in Venice and had found her charming and tragic. After reading *The Great Gatsby* she had passed it along to Kay. "Don't believe the reviews. Scott's style will floor you."

Kay had seen them. The critics agreed: *Gatsby* was "a dud," as the *New York World* put it. *Time* magazine called it "precious" in the most derogatory way. For H. L. Mencken, Fitzgerald's slim novel was nothing but "a glorified anecdote."

The story touched Kay, though, and not merely because it described the contours of a love triangle somewhat like her own. Any number of cheap romances might accomplish that. *Gatsby* was a good story, but it was more than that. It was a meditation on two opposite forms of love. Like Helen of Troy, Daisy Fay Buchanan hardly existed other than as an alluring object, crystallized in men's desires. She accepted this role, seemingly pleased to play the glamorous flirt. Jay Gatsby's idealization of her stemmed from indistinct memories of a long-ago tryst, as if no person or activity grounded in present reality could justify such passion. Her husband Tom's involvement with Daisy, in contrast to Gatsby's dreamy yearning, utterly lacked emotion. Until Tom realized he might lose her, she represented little more to him than an object of décor, real and corporeal but lacking mystery and depth. When these two opposing forms of love collided, *merely* ideal and *merely* physical, the inevitable outcome was catastrophe.

The character who intrigued Kay most was Nick, the narrator lurking in the shadows of the story. Modest, unassuming, and honest, Nick seemed bewildered by the shallowness, the complexity, and the perversity of those around him, but he was also impressed with them. Kay knew a few Jay Gatsbys and several Tom Buchanans, but she had never met a Nick Carraway.

In fact, Tom reminded Kay a little of Jimmy, the high-handed Ivy Leaguer with no concept of life beyond the bounds of privilege. And Gatsby's romantic desire for Daisy echoed her own elevated feelings about George. She wondered whether she was as ambitious, and as naïve and unknowing, as Jay Gatsby.

Finding these resemblances compelling but unbearable, she lay the book aside and exited her three-room suite for a stroll. She passed the pillared smoking room, the palm-tree-studded café, and the Grand Salon to the polished-wood promenade deck. Men in striped tank tops and cotton-belted shorts sat in high-backed lounge chairs around the swimming pool, discussing the stock market. Women in sleeveless jersey tops and short bathing trunks lay on chaises longues, deliberating the weather in Madrid and the latest styles in Paris. Kay walked to the prow and gazed over the Atlantic like Jay Gatsby staring across the water toward East Egg, the rippling sea reflecting and distorting his aspirations.

Julie Glaenzer's apartment was situated in the bustling center of Paris. His footman, Pascal, prepared her an *omelette aux fines herbes* and coffee. He spoke not a word of English but Kay remembered enough from three years of Opera French to get by. Pascal drew her a map and suggested attractions, but she implored him to drive her to the Château de Fontainebleau. They negotiated a compromise. Pascal suggested she explore the neighborhood while he concluded his morning's business on behalf of Monsieur Glaenzer, tidying up the apartment and forwarding correspondence. They would meet at the Café de Flore, a twenty-minute walk from the cathedral.

As Julie had explained, Notre Dame de Paris was indeed a two-minute stroll down the tiny Rue du Cloître-Notre-Dame. She entered the cool, dark cathedral, with its scents of burning candles, and strolled between the medieval pillars in the dusky blue-and-red filtered light. An organist was playing Bach's Fugue in G-Minor. The rousing melodies, evocative of floating seraphs, flitted through the cavernous space and bounced off the towering stone walls.

As she crossed the plaza, the sun emerged above Notre Dame's towers. She stopped, thinking of Victor Hugo's novel, *Notre-Dame de Paris.* She imagined the gypsy Esmeralda dancing and her deformed admirer Quasimodo watching, mesmerized. As bells rang, she shook off the vision.

Six days aboard the *Olympic* and now this invigorating, animated city! Tramways and motorcars, booksellers' stalls along the Quais de la Seine, cafés that spilled onto sidewalks. She crossed the Petit Pont and entered the Quartier Latin, populated with students of the Sorbonne, artists, and drunkards. She wandered down the Boulevard Saint-Michel to the Boulevard Saint-Germain and turned right, searching everywhere for George's face.

A half hour later she stumbled upon the Café de Flore, with its massive over-the-sidewalk awning; its small metal tables, abundant wooden chairs, and big windows; its young men and women engaged in animated conversations, gesticulating and interrupting each other. Pascal, sitting outside sipping a *café crème,* saluted her.

They rode in a taxi to the Quai de Bercy, where Pascal kept a Delage cabriolet in a padlocked wooden shed. Kay snuggled in the back seat of the long, maroon-colored convertible watching the tree-lined streets flit past and reflecting that the French had perfected the art of catering to the wealthy, educated classes. The corollary of which was an entrenched social hierarchy that the Revolutions of 1789, 1830, and 1848, and Paris's two-month experiment in pre-Marxian Socialism, the Commune, had failed to eradicate.

This impression was reinforced upon her arrival at the Fontainebleau Castle. Pascal took a seat outside a café in the quaint town, smoking and reading newspapers. A few elderly men were playing a *jeu de boules* on a grass strip nearby.

With her box of Black Jack chewing gum under her arm, Kay walked to the castle that had been the favored getaway of thirty-four French kings since the eleventh century. She passed through the Gallery of Francis I, decorated in 1528 by Leonardo Da Vinci's patron; the neoclassical Gallery of Diana; Marie Antoinette's fastidiously adorned boudoir; and the Emperor Napoleon's bedroom.

Exhilarated and sated, with a renewed respect for the opulent, decadent history of Europe's aristocracy, and excited at the prospect of surprising George, she arrived at the first-floor apartments of Nadia Boulanger's music school. She recognized the harmonies and rhythms of the famous *enseignante*'s piano, familiar from the compositions of Aaron Copland and Virgil Thomson. She sat in a gilded silk-upholstered chair next to one of Boulanger's students. When the lesson was over, she entered and introduced herself.

Haughty and severe in her pulled hair and round glasses, Nadia Boulanger dismissed her with a wave as if swatting away an annoying *mouche,* a French housefly. "Yes, Monsieur Gershwin visited, but I am afraid he is long gone."

Kay frowned. "I thought it was all set. He was going to study with you."

Nadia Boulanger raised her chin. "Who told you this? Ravel? Gershwin himself? I did not tell you this, did I, Madame?"

"Do you know where he's staying?"

"I am not a detective, Madame."

Deflated, Kay handed her the box of chewing gum. "A little gift from America," she said as she walked out of the studio.

CHAPTER TWENTY-TWO

Jimmy was standing at the mail table glancing through a pile of papers when Lionel entered from the kitchen. "Welcome home, sir."

"Thank you, Lionel."

"Did you have a pleasant trip?"

"The usual, Lionel. Thank you for asking." He glanced at the stairwell. "Is Misses Warburg in?"

"She's gone to Paris, sir."

Paris? Had she alluded to an upcoming trip to Paris, in any conversation? Not that he could recall. "Did she mention when she'd return?"

"Not to me, sir."

Jimmy nodded. In the pile of letters and flyers he came across the monthly newsletter of his daughters' school, announcing new teachers, ambitious projects and prizes, and faculty publications. He skimmed through it quickly, aware that its main purpose was to justify inflated tuition fees. But as he turned it over his eyes caught his daughter's name in a list of talent show performers. The event would take place this very evening. He visualized little Andrea performing on the school stage, small and alone, searching for a familiar face among the parents and friends in the audience.

And Kay, up to God knows what in Paris.

He glanced at his watch. Barely enough time but he had no commitments this evening and knew he would never forgive himself if he failed to try.

The Finch School was a tony, forward-looking academy for girls that de-emphasized etiquette and spotlighted literature, the arts, and music. The small auditorium was packed. Jimmy stood at the back, his arms crossed as he endured a four-part chorale harmonizing Bruckner's "Ave Maria," a young violinist's rendition of a Lully gavotte, and an amateur magician engaging a volunteer in a mind-reading game.

His thoughts veered to Kay. Her absence. Her unannounced voyage to Paris, probably to meet her lover. That she was enjoying an affair with Gershwin, Jimmy could understand. That she had fallen in love with him . . . well, that posed a challenge.

Bedroom dalliances were one thing, emotional disloyalty quite another.

Normally, a tightening of marital bonds accompanied the process of aging. No honorable man would leave his spouse for his mistress, discard his children for a new brood, or neglect his duties in business because he was lovesick. Only vulgar, *nouveau rich* saps — and, God knew, Jimmy had encountered his share of those — would comport themselves in such an indiscreet manner.

And here Kay had run off to Paris and was missing the recital of their sweetest daughter. The one who would shake him when he fell asleep reading her stories; who was convinced a ghost lived in their guest room; who had rescued a kitten and brought it to the veterinarian. Kind, eager Andrea.

Yes, Gershwin and Kay shared a passion for music. That hardly justified neglecting their daughter. He advised himself nonetheless to keep his anger in check. Despite Kay's dissatisfactions, despite her betrayal, his marriage — his family — remained all-important to Jimmy.

Finally, there she was, his daughter Andrea, bowing to the audience and then jazzing through George Gershwin's "Liza." Her performance impressed and troubled

Jimmy, not just for its audacity. For a girl of only seven, Andrea possessed an uncanny sense of Gershwin's harmonies, his melancholic and playful moods, his keyboard affectations. The bastard had left an imprint on Jimmy's little angel. *Well, I have only myself to blame,* he lamented inwardly.

He applauded as he never had before. The public reaction was more restrained. Most of the audience, surmised Jimmy as he looked at the other parents, was not convinced this kind of music held a legitimate place in the Finch School.

In the lobby after the show Andrea seemed surprised and thrilled to see him. "Daddy!" She ran to his arms and hugged him. "Oh, Daddy. You heard it all?"

"Wouldn't have missed it for the world," said Jimmy. "It was masterful. I would wager a penny you will not say no to ice cream."

"Let's get a banana split, Daddy." Andrea took his hand. "Oh, Daddy, I'm so glad you came."

They walked out to the street. *Whatever should happen between Kay and me, I shall always have this moment,* thought Jimmy.

CHAPTER TWENTY-THREE

With two weeks to wander Paris until her booked return, Kay explored the fragrant cheese and flower displays of Les Halles, the city's central market. The butchers' shops, where whole pheasants and pigs dangled from overhead ropes. The singsong calls of the vendors.

She climbed the steps to Montmartre, passed painters at their easels, and dined alone in a café of the Place du Tertre listening to a mournful *chanteuse* bewailing her heartbreak. She sat on a stone bench in the Parc Monceau finishing the novel Pauline Heifetz had given her.

Thus, one entire day.

The next morning she was chewing a crêpe suzette in a sidewalk cafe in the Rue Mouffetard when she realized: it was still last night in New York. Hours ago — probably around two in the morning, Paris time — her Andrea had played Gershwin's "Liza" in front of a privileged audience.

Kay had come all this way to meet George and had failed to find him. She had missed her daughter's début, and for what? She washed down her disappointment with *cidre breton*. She closed her eyes and focused as keenly as she could: *Andrea, I'm with you, darling. Mommy is with you. I missed your concert and I love you and I am with you.*

That night, with nothing better to do, she visited the Folies-Bergère, a cabaret music hall in the ninth arrondissement where Josephine Baker, a dancer from St. Louis known as *La Perle Noire,* The Black Pearl, performed a savage burlesque clothed only in a mock-African skirt made of bananas. A place George might well visit.

Beautiful and unchained, she twittered like a vireo. Her disciplined exuberance, the way she simultaneously expressed freedom and professionalism through her swivels, twists, tail-wags, reminded Kay of all she loved about home. Miss Baker's French audience cheered, whistled, smacked their tables, and reached for her thighs and breasts.

Later, Kay was sitting in a bistro listening to the rain and sipping a glass of raspberry *eau-de-vie,* wishing George was there, when

Miss Baker strolled in with a half-dozen couturiers, poets, and business advisors. No longer wrapped in her banana skirt but in a pale-blue silk evening gown and a big hat adorned with ostrich plumes, she strutted to a table at the center of the front window and ordered *une grande assiette de moules à la crème et au Pernod pour tout le monde.* Her flatterers and hangers-on talked at the same time, gesticulating and raising their voices.

Kay drained her snifter and rose to leave. As she was about to exit, her eyes caught those of the starlet and she decided to step over to her table. "I enjoyed your show tremendously, Miss Baker."

"Ah, *une américaine!*" warbled Josephine Baker. "Thank you, sweetheart. All alone here, in Paris?"

Kay nodded, smiling.

"Where are you from?"

"New York," said Kay.

"Come, sit here, *ma belle,* join us for some *moules,* will you?" With a wave, Josephine ordered another plate for Kay. "I do so miss New York."

Kay sat down, glancing at Josephine's devoted followers. "But you're a star here."

"Yes, I'm a star! I give them what they want. *La Bonne Sauvage,* they call me. Do you know what that means?" She punctuated her question with a full-throated laugh. Despite their poor understanding of English, her guests joined her in laughter.

As they dined, Josephine's friends chattered in French, much of it too fast for Kay to grasp. Occasionally Josephine broke off her conversation to respond to something one of them had said, triggering more laughter, and then resumed with Kay.

"You explain it, Emile," she ordered a friend who wore a goatee and a monocle. "What does it mean, in France, my being *une vedette* and all that. Tell her just like you told me, *mon chéri.*"

"It means," said Emile in his Gallic accent, "that mademoiselle must behave on stage like a — how do you say? — like a *singe.*"

Josephine laughed again.

"A monkey?" suggested Kay.

"Yes, a monkey with a playful and innocent disposition. A primitive," said Emile.

"Always making funny faces, jumping around, all that circus stuff," added Miss Baker, crossing her eyes. "You got to give your audience what they expect. And what the French want is to feel *supérieur.* That's really what this is all about. *N'est-ce pas, Emile?*"

"Eh, oui," agreed Emile dourly.

Is that what Chopin was doing, giving his audience what they wanted? wondered Kay. *Or Beethoven?* And then she thought, *maybe that was precisely what they were doing!* "But in the States," she said aloud, "they wouldn't even let you onstage, would they?"

"Some places would, some wouldn't," said Josephine. "But home is home, darling."

"We do long for home, don't we," confirmed Kay with a wistful smile.

"Never forget that," said Josephine. "Never forget where home is. No matter how far away you get."

Kay nodded, the words echoing in her mind. *Where home is.*

CHAPTER TWENTY-FOUR

Upon returning from Paris, she found a letter from George.

> Dearest Kay,
>   Today I wandered through the Buttes-Chaumont, a lovely park far from the usual tourist haunts, feeling lonely and thinking of you . . .

The date on the letter revealed that she was, in fact, nearby. But not quite near enough.

She rode to George's West Side residence, where Paul Mueller greeted her with a warm smile but told her, "I'm afraid Mister Gershwin is indisposed, Misses Warburg."

"What's the matter?" she asked, concerned.

"A terrible headache. The doctor saw him. He prescribed rest. And solitude. No work for a few days. There's nothing you can do."

"Please, Paul, let me see him."

Paul finally relented and allowed Kay to climb the stairs and see George sleeping. He looked pale. She kissed his forehead. He smiled without awaking.

Just a headache, she told herself. Of course George would have headaches. The man was under so many obligations. She yearned to be his pressure-release valve, if only she could. She felt worried and helpless.

Sitting in the back of her chauffeured car, rolling home, she made a decision. If all her yearning, all the scales and arpeggios she had practiced for so many years, all the music she had composed, and all her efforts to find happiness had led to . . . wherever she was . . . then perhaps it was time to visit Jimmy's psychoanalyst.

The cramped Upper East Side office of Dr. Gregory Zilboorg: Persian rugs; a sleigh-style ebony divan with paisley cushions; floor-to-ceiling asymmetrical bookshelves; and, scattered among the tomes, faceless sculptures in ivory and obsidian. Although he did not advertise it, Dr. Zilboorg specialized in the psychoanalysis of the wealthy and the famous. What fascinated him was not his patients' celebrity or money but their megalomania and narcissism, the personality traits that drove them to succeed or, perhaps, resulted from success. A diminutive man with a round face, a receding hairline, and an exuberant moustache, he viewed personality through the triple lens of fantasy, sexuality, and religion. He maintained that the role of the psychoanalyst was not merely to probe his patients' unconscious fears and motivations but to challenge their defense mechanisms. He wore costly silk-and-wool clothes in a slovenly manner, with the jacket falling off his shoulder, the shirt collar protruding above the jacket collar on one side, and his wire-frame glasses perched askew.

Because Jimmy had been consulting with him for years, he knew a great deal about Kay before she met him. He could hardly help seeing her, initially, through Jimmy's narrative. Nor was Zilboorg reluctant to discuss her weak maternal instinct, her emotional instability, and her mutable libido. Whatever that meant.

In his Ukrainian accent he urged her to pay attention to her dreams and to recount them in detail while reclining on his divan. It did not matter whether her descriptions were accurate since any associations and feelings that would bubble up through her words would hold as much meaning as the literal content of her dreams, if she allowed herself to relax.

She closed her eyes and remembered a dream. "I'm about to board an ocean liner. Massive, gray. It's night and the docks are crowded. Someone is singing somewhere. I feel this overwhelming sensation of dread."

Zilboorg asked Kay to free-associate about the melody, the singer's voice, and the ship's color. He also encouraged her to digress. She rummaged through memories of other gray objects including her father's typewriter and the dirigible that had floated above her mother's funeral. She remembered Al Jolson's gray jacket at the Cotton Club. "He made George famous, Jolson did, with 'Swanee.' "

"Yes, and?"

"And what?"

" 'Swanee'?" said Doctor Zilboorg.

" 'Swanee.' George . . ."

Zilboorg nodded.

"Why do you want to know more about George? I thought this was about me."

"It *is* about you. Your feelings. Your obsessions. Please, free-associate. 'Swanee.' "

Kay closed her eyes. "We were at a party. George and I. We met a jazzman. Luckey Roberts. They talked about 'Swanee.' Jolson's blackface makeup, which Luckey found offensive."

"Blackface," said Zilboorg, nodding. "Is it wrong, do you believe it is wrong, for a person to borrow a mask, an identity, that is not his or her birthright?"

"I don't know," reflected Kay. "Cultures borrow. Cultures enrich each other. But it can lead to misunderstandings. Hurt feelings. I guess one has to be cautious."

"And you," observed Zilboorg, "a Christian living in a Jewish world. Not just your husband, not just Gershwin, but so many of your acquaintances. The music you gravitate to these days. Broadway. Jolson, Gershwin, Berlin, Rodgers, Kern. Is there not a sense of cultural confusion?"

She looked at him, trying to understand the implication.

"Are you not wearing blackface every day?" asked Zilboorg.

Kay shook her head. "I'm not really Christian. And Jimmy isn't Jewish."

"We are not talking merely about belief," said Zilboorg, "but about history. Cultural history, it is passed down through generations. Just like genetic history."

Doctor Zilboorg was starting to sound like Reverend Ganter. She sat up on the divan. "Maybe you're talking about your own identity problem." She glanced at the Byzantine icon on a bookshelf.

"I don't think so, Misses Warburg." Zilboorg folded his hands on his lap. "Let's get back to that dream about the boat. Surely your id is telling you something."

Her identity, as she saw it, was not her most pressing issue. Instead she talked about her feeling of inadequacy as a mother. "I want what's best for my girls, of course. We are providing them with excellent caretakers. All and the same . . ." She finished her sentence with a shake of her head.

Zilboorg nodded. "You were raised in one segment of society, with its norms of parenting and so forth. Now you find yourself in another, where you don't feel quite at home."

Kay thought about this. "Maybe," she admitted.

"And where does Mister Gershwin fit in? More specifically, your obsession with him?"

"I suppose my feeling about him *is* a little crazy," she acknowledged. "The intensity of it. The way they hit me, out of the blue — out of the *Rhapsody in Blue.* Totally unexpected."

"And unreciprocated?"

"What we share is unique, and George

knows it. But he's cautious about commitment."

"What kind of commitment are you looking for?"

She removed a cigarette from her purse. "Commitment."

He leaned forward to light it. "So you have decided to quit Jimmy?"

She puffed. "Jimmy would never allow it."

"You don't need his permission." Doctor Zilboorg relaxed back into his seat. "You could go to Reno. In Reno a woman can get a divorce just for asking. And for a fee of course. I am telling you this so your decision is not a compelled one. But I am not suggesting you go to Reno. The best solution in a chicken coop involves breaking as few eggs as possible."

"I'm tired of the chicken coop. I need the sky."

"But are you not rather talking about flying directly into another coop?" asked Zilboorg. "Jimmy loves you very much."

"There's love, and there's love," said Kay. Zilboorg waited for more. "On the one hand, there's the emotion," Kay explained. "And on the other, what people call 'bonds of loyalty.' "

"Ideally," said Zilboorg, "marriage transforms the first kind into the second kind.

But perhaps marital union is not the kind of love you expected."

"Maybe I was expecting something that doesn't exist," said Kay. "But what can you do? Young women don't decide what to expect. Their expectations are shaped by others. They're told stories. Stories written by men. Passed down through our culture, which is shaped by men. 'Cinderella.' 'Sleeping Beauty.' Give your heart to a prince. Everything will be all right."

"Jimmy is the father of your children," said Zilboorg. "If you left Jimmy for George, might you not be exchanging one highly driven egotist, incapable of sexual loyalty, for another?"

"It's not their egotism," said Kay. "I don't hold that against them. In fact, I find it attractive. And I don't think egotism necessarily implies disloyalty, either."

Zilboorg adjusted in his chair. "Where does egotism come from? Where does ambition come from?"

"You make it sound like ambition is a disease."

"It is."

"Would you say I am ambitious?" asked Kay.

"Let's just say, you seem to be attracted to a certain kind of man."

"If my attraction for George, the fact that we share skills and interests, represents ambition, mea culpa," said Kay.

Zilboorg nodded. "You mirror each other."

"You bet we do." Kay snuffed out her cigarette. Glancing at the clock, she saw that the session was over. It was time to go home. And not a minute too soon.

CHAPTER TWENTY-FIVE

April 1929

The Little Show hearkened back to the first works with which George Gershwin had been associated, prior to the development of the musical play: collections of vaudeville skits loosely sewn together. And although George now preferred to write songs and orchestral settings for larger works, stories that unfolded through an entire evening, he attended *The Little Show,* appearing in the empty seat at Kay's left just before the curtain rose. Jimmy, seated at her right, noticed his arrival, smiled, and nodded. Despite everything, he harbored mixed feelings about George, admiring him intensely as a musician, somewhat less as a man.

The production included a scene called *The Still Alarm* by George S. Kaufman, a soliloquy by the comedian Fred Allen, and the bittersweet ballad "Can't We Be Friends?" by Kay Swift and Paul James.

Libby Holman, in a strapless carmine dress, stood alone between the closed stage curtains and twittered like a lark. George squeezed her hand. *This is your moment.* The audience exploded. "Can't We Be Friends?," in Libby's dulcet voice, drew them to their feet. Kay rose slowly, dazed. George clapped, shouted, and whistled. Jimmy grinned at his wife.

That night the cast, the creators, and the producers flitted from one party to another. To celebrate with Kay and Jimmy, Julie Glaenzer invited George S. Kaufman, Mark Connelly, Dottie Parker, Aleck Woollcott, and the rest of the gang, as well as the city's dissolute mayor Jimmy Walker, to his apartment. Luckey Roberts, recommended to Glaenzer by Gershwin, bedazzled them at the piano.

George shushed everyone for the toast. "Here's to the two new crown princesses of New York City." He held aloft his Mary Pickford. "Kay Swift and Libby Holman." He glanced from one to the other, sipped, and added: "And to Kay's terrific lyricist, Paul James."

Later, he introduced Kay and Jimmy to a slumped gentleman in a pin-striped suit. "Kay, Jimmy, or should I say Paul, I'd like you to meet Max Dreyfus, my publisher."

Dreyfus removed the cigar from his mouth. "That number, 'Can't We Be Friends?,' was the showstopper. Why haven't I heard of you before? Talent like yours, it's no London drizzle, it's a thunder shower. You're gonna make a ruckus in this town. Congratulations."

"Thank you," said Kay.

"With your permission I'd like to publish 'Can't We Be Friends?' Can't promise anything but I smell a hit." Kay wondered how he could smell anything past the stench of his cigar smoke.

She turned to Jimmy. "I never agree to anything right away," said Jimmy. "But yes." Dreyfus shook his hand, and then Kay's. "We have other songs," said Jimmy. "In fact, we're planning a full-scale show. It's called *Fine and Dandy*."

Dreyfus removed the cigar from his mouth and wiped a speck of tobacco from his lower lip. "*Fine and Dandy*. Nice title. Come demo your material and we'll take it from there." Apparently he had no idea Kay had already done so.

Three quick raps at the door. George pulled it open. "Fred, come in."

"Can I grab a shot?" asked a man with a big camera.

"How 'bout I join you?" Libby Holman

strolled over, holding her champagne flute like the winning bet at the Kentucky Derby.

"Of course," said George, making room for her. "What would a picture be without the star?"

Fred Astaire, George Gershwin, Kay Swift, Jimmy Warburg, Max Dreyfus, and Libby Holman slung their arms around each other. A lightning flash and a puff of smoke captured the happiest moment of Kay's thirty years.

With Libby Holman's performance of "Can't We Be Friends?," the dam broke. Played for music vendors by Max Dreyfus's army of piano pluggers and performed every evening by the bisexual, headline-grabbing siren from Cincinnati, the song's chirrupy lament pulled the city's emotions this way and that at the same time. Despite Jimmy's concerns, the stock market was still surging in the spring and summer of 1929 and no one was in the mood for a tearjerker. The upbeat melody of Kay's ballad commented ironically upon Jimmy's sad lyric like a friend reminding her jilted lover that the eaves are full of swallows.

Dreyfus called with the casualness and un-predictability of an uncle who sought to reinforce old bonds without wasting time.

"How's *Fine and Dandy* coming along? That sounds terrific but we need a few hits meantime to keep your names alive." Kay and Jimmy provided songs to be interpolated in *The Nine Fifteen Revue* and *The Garrick Gaieties.*

They celebrated at private parties and in clubs. An air of depravity, excessive wealth, drinking, explicit dancing, and promiscuity surrounded the new darlings of Broadway, enhancing their mystique and allure. Dick Rodgers and Fred Astaire now frequented Kay's home, as well as George Gershwin, Harpo Marx, George S. Kaufman, Alexander Woollcott, Averell Harriman, and the rest of their clique. The openly homosexual negrophile Carl Van Vechten, whose novel *Nigger Heaven* had made him a subject of adoration and scorn in literary circles, often popped in with Paul Robeson or Langston Hughes. Others, who could no longer walk down Fifth Avenue without being harassed by reporters and photographers, welcomed the freedom and release of the boozy Warburg salon. The goings-on of Libby Holman and Louisa d'Andelot Carpenter had become the focus of celebrity journalists. Harlem pianists Luckey Roberts and Willie "The Lion" Smith provided jangly entertainment. Kay sometimes spent the greater part of an evening watching and listening to their creations.

With leading cultural figures from myriad communities in New York — the Negros, Jews, homosexuals, lesbians, and others crowding their salon — with the accelerating power of Benito Mussolini in Italy and Adolph Hitler in Germany; with controversial decisions taken by the British Empire to split Transjordan, and then the Golan Heights, from the Palestine Mandate, it was inevitable that loud conversations would erupt about economics and politics, religion and race, national identity and ethnic pride. Woollcott inveighed against capitalism and what he described as "its first cousins, greed and imperialism," which, he claimed, had caused the Great War.

"And the Soviet Union isn't imperialist?" argued Averell Harriman.

"How so?" asked Gershwin with a frown.

Harriman seemed miffed. "You've heard nothing about the invasion of the Ukraine?"

"Sure I heard about it," said Gershwin. "The Russians say it's historically Russian. What do I know?"

Harriman shook his head. "Stalin is open about his plans. One state, one party, one ruler. Not just for Russia. For the world. The dictatorship of the proletariat and all that dross."

Gershwin thought this unfair. His parents had been born in the cruel regime of Czarist Russia, with its aristocratic excesses, oppression of workers, and pogroms. He took an intense interest in the young Soviet Union, which he considered an idealistic experiment struggling for survival. "Look at Stalin's achievements," he objected. "Equal rights for women. Full employment. Free health care and education. You don't need a PhD in number crunching to see that capitalism in America is rigged."

"Of course it's rigged," countered Averell. "So, for your information, is the music business. And so is the Politburo."

When conversation turned to Palestine, Jimmy expressed contempt for the Zionist movement, insisting that "the creation of a Jewish state will only reinforce the idea of dual Jewish loyalties. It's everything this world does not need."

Again, George objected. "Everyone's got dual loyalties. You think the Vatican's nothing to American Catholics? Or that Charles Lindberg doesn't feel Swedish? Or that Joe Kennedy could care less about Ireland? What the hell is wrong with being sentimental about the old country?"

Jimmy shook his head. "Two thousand

years. That's pretty damn old."

Meanwhile, Fats Waller sang,

This here spot is more than hot.
In fact, the joint is jumpin'.

And then, in mid-October, the city's white-hot financial elation finished erupting, leaving a smoldering Depression in its wake. The international economy melted. Banks evaporated. Stock traders sailed down from high-rise windows. Soup lines noosed city blocks. Small fortunes crumbled to dust and blew away. But for Kay and Jimmy, for George and many of their friends, the bubble never burst. In fact, it soared higher into the skies of New York. The entertainment industry was one of the few that continued to thrive. And six months before the crash, Jimmy had converted his stock market securities into government-backed bonds.

Even as the banking sector exploded, Jimmy's career as a wordsmith blossomed. He had once yearned to become a latter-day Lord Byron, free, romantic, and brilliant. He had toiled over one or two lines for hours and weeks, trying to squeeze significance and color into every syllable. All that striving and exertion had earned him no respect from the New York literary community. Now, having achieved success elsewhere, he was tossing off lyrics with abandon and hitting the target more often than not.

Kay, too, had honed her style, which featured gay, jaunty melodies and a bright orchestra replete with saxophonic tone color. In the title number, "Fine and Dandy," the starlet justifies her sexual straying. What else should her lover expect, when he travels so much?

When you're handy it's fine and dandy.
But when you're gone what can I do?

As Kay and Jimmy wrote and polished song after song, her confidence swelled. She understood Broadway now. If she had questions, she could rely on the best advisors, George Gershwin and Dick Rodgers, not to mention Max Dreyfus.

When they had buffed and glossed a dozen-odd songs, Kay's chauffeur drove her down Park Avenue to take tea with Dorothy Parker at the Waldorf. Looking through the car window at the depression-stricken city, she saw homeless people hunched in soup lines, beggars holding tin cups, old men sleeping on ratty jackets on sidewalks, and ragged boys chasing each other between passersby. Due to *citizen congestion,* a portion of East Fiftieth Street was closed to traffic, so Kay had to disembark and continue on foot. In her furs, she felt conspicuous and guilty — even while she stepped off the curb to avoid kicking a sleeping man, or offered a few coins to a woman whose toddlers clutched at her legs.

Her purpose in meeting with Dottie was to discuss the book for *Fine and Dandy.* Who would shape and flesh out the story line? Who would craft the dialogue? Like a watchmaker, Jimmy took pleasure in working with smaller structures — individual semantic units, metric schemes, rhymes. He had never learned, nor did he care to learn, to write characters other than himself, or to shape their conflicting fears and desires toward a climax and resolution.

Nor, as it turned out, had Dottie. "If I knew how to do that," she told Kay, "you wouldn't be financing my tea. And I wouldn't be sleeping in a Lilliputian walk-up. I'd be masquerading in the Venice *Carnevale* or dipping my little toes in the waters of Cap D'Antibes." Dottie frowned, leaned forward over the table, and whispered: "That man is staring at you."

Kay turned to look. Her psychoanalyst

was seated in a dark corner of the room. He smiled at her and turned his attention back to the man across from him.

"Oh, that's Doctor Zilboorg," said Kay.

"Hmm," said Dottie. "I've heard of him."

"What have you heard?"

Dottie looked at Zilboorg. "Oh, people talk. You know how people are. Anyone who's anyone. Anyway, I have a pal who will be perfect for your show. Donald Ogden Stewart. Stewie. A Yale man, with a light touch. You and Jimmy will adore him."

To avoid the squalor of the streets, Kay and Jimmy invited Stewie to dinner in their home, where they explained their concept. She had chosen a setting for their play, a small factory like the one her father had briefly owned, beset by labor-management strife. The B-Story would introduce a love-able, compassionate, hasn't-got-a-clue manager who so sympathizes with his workers that hierarchy crumbles. Jimmy invented the A-Story of star-crossed lovers who, despite their best intentions, cannot fulfill each other's emotional and sexual needs.

"A factory, that's fresh," agreed Stewie, tripping on his words and nodding. "Labor, management, boffo territory for conflict and satire. But —" he held up an index finger. "Caution! Nothing too vicious, political, or

386

cerebral."

Jimmy and Kay agreed.

"What we're after is laughs," said Stewie.

"Precisely," said Kay.

"And what's the triedest and truest laugh machine?" He answered his own question: "Vaudeville."

Jimmy scratched his cheek. "Vaudeville?"

Stewie nodded. "We're not looking for the bemused, patronizing grin of the New Yorker crowd."

"We're not?" asked Jimmy with a bemused, patronizing grin.

"The French term succès d'estime translates to American as 'failure.' We want guffaws," insisted Stewie. "We want them rolling in the aisles. And I know just the man to pull it off. Joe Cook."

Kay and Jimmy had seen Joe Cook perform. He was the last star of undiluted, unrepentant vaudeville, a man who understood like no other the power of absurdity paired with physical prowess; a fellow whose facility with silly seemed limitless.

They were skeptical. Was Stewie offloading the task of funnying it up? Did he intend to substitute antics for ingenuity? But after they read Stewie's droll, elegant published works they decided to let him take a stab at it.

A month later, motivated by Jimmy's down payment, Stewie delivered a draft that accomplished their objective: it demonstrated the humorous side of failure. It transformed misery into a smile. And then it tortured them with laughter.

Like their hit song, "Can't We Be Friends?," the effect of "Fine and Dandy" relied on its suggestion of desperate paradox, its evocation of artlessness in business and torment in romance through bumptious songs and zany antics. *Life is a train wreck,* it told its audience: *Enjoy!*

They hired Stewie to rewrite and polish the play. On his advice, they met with the vaudeville star Joe Cook.

Having learned a hard lesson with *Say When,* Kay involved herself in every aspect of *Fine and Dandy* from casting through décor. But when she recognized talent she gave it a long leash. Stewie was right in so many ways; not least, in his awareness of his own limitations. He knew how to craft an entertaining story but for guffaws he deferred to Joe Cook, whose virtuoso ad-libs and agile physical comedy reduced his audiences to mounds of jiggly Jell-O.

Rehearsals were arduous. One of the principals broke her ankle. A lead singer fell ill. Kay argued with the producers, on one occasion crumpling three pages of the score, throwing them in the air, and stomping off the set. Lyrics and melodies wandered off; other songs leapt in to steal their places.

But by the night of the dress rehearsal most of the scars had healed; others hid under ear-to-ear layers of stage grease. The actors' and actresses' faces glowed in the limelight as their voices traveled well-worn, engineered rails. While newly destitute families snored on sidewalks outside, the audience inside Erlanger's Theatre on Forty-Fourth Street roared with laughter.

Up in heaven, Kay thought, Sam Swift must be grinning. His daughter, the first woman in history to have composed the entire score of a musical play, to see it produced, and to experience the enthusiasm of a Broadway audience. Like Annie Oakley, Marie Curie, Amelia Earhart, and Dorothy Kuhn, Kay had proven that a woman could compete and succeed in a field reserved for men.

Max Dreyfus, Averell Harriman, Aleck Woollcott, Harpo Marx, Oscar Levant, and a hundred of their acquaintances guzzled Dom Perignon and swallowed *escargots au beurre persillé* at Julie Glaenzer's apartment, where Luckey Roberts now performed three or four times a week, attracting New York's elite sots and fox trotters, who treated the jewelry executive's penthouse as an exclusive club. Glaenzer, who considered the publicity a boon to his trade, slept at the Plaza hotel.

Kay found herself in conversation with Sam Rothapfel, the impresario and theater magnate, whom she had previously seen from a distance at a party or two. Known as Roxy to his friends, Rothapfel boasted about his newest project, the International Music Hall. "Culture is crowds," he told Kay. "Bigger room, louder laughs."

His enthusiasm reminded her of her erstwhile hero Wagner, who had once touted the merits of his Bayreuth project in similarly bombastic terms. But while Kay delighted in the hysteria that had filled Erlanger's Theatre earlier that evening, a part of her remained skeptical. The part that still responded to the quiet resonances of Chopin's nocturnes. The part that would never forget her father's contemplative, solitary, mournful side. The part of her that had failed.

Jimmy left early. Kay and George celebrated until about two in the morning. Then, instead of heading uptown to his apartment, or hers, she hired a horse-drawn carriage to trot them down Fifth Avenue to see the building that so inflamed Rothapfel's imagination.

At Fiftieth Street, construction of the RCA Building was not complete. The design, telescoping rectangular monoliths, oozed elegance and majesty, an art deco lighthouse looming high above the other buildings and the seas of the world, a symbol of the new American claim of cultural preeminence. The top floors, lacking walls, reminded her of a stack of pancakes against the moon. To keep out squatters, the construction crew had surrounded the site with plywood barriers, but Kay found a breach — a door at the side that was slightly ajar. "Over here!" she waved to George. They sneaked in.

A nocturnal jungle of steel, cement, and electrical vines. After their eyes adjusted they forged a path to the completed elevator shafts and slipped inside. Kay pushed the highest button. The elevator began whirring. It climbed and climbed. Sixty-four, sixty-five, sixty-six floors. They held their breath with anticipation. Finally it stopped and the doors slid open.

Steel girders, rivets, and hoisting cables. Giddy with wonder, they stepped onto a platform and looked west to the Hudson River and south through the center of Manhattan Island to the moon-streaked sea. The city below brightened by Edison bulbs, echoing the constellations. The headlamps of automobiles purring down Fifth Avenue. George pointed to a spot above the horizon, where a falling star streaked and vanished in the firmament. "Modernity," he whispered. "Mankind lighting the world. Us up here in the heavens."

He held her tight, listening to the buzzing and murmurs of the night. "We're all alone here, just you and me, Kay. Probably the first folks ever in this place." His eyes glowed.

"The workers are here every day, George."

"Maybe. But not every night. Not tonight. Tonight, this place is ours." His grip tightened. "Do you hear that?"

She listened.

"That music," said George, "blooming, like flowers."

She smiled. Yes, they were standing all alone, close to the sky, the stars, their dreams. Yes, she detected a celestial choir somewhere. A jazzy one. Her heart skipped a beat.

He kissed her with fierceness with the whole world below them. And while most of New York City slept they sank to the cold metal floor, embracing to the strains of *Fine and Dandy*'s romantic ballad "Can This Be Love?," which still resonated in their ears.

What can it be, can this be love —
this thing that I keep dreaming of?

"Listen to your heart," Father Ganter had instructed her. Well, she was listening now. And her heart was thumping.

CHAPTER TWENTY-SIX

April 1930

At the age of thirty-one, George Gershwin adored his parents and siblings with the uncritical love of a seven-year-old. Unlike Jimmy he felt a sentimental connection through them to the lore and melodies of their Russian forebears, all the way back to ancient Israel and Egypt.

Kay heard that linkage in the minor-key melodies and unabashed sentimentality of his ballads. The musical expressions that inspired him were the laments and defiant knee-slapping jubilations of downtrodden peoples. He borrowed pentatonic scales from strife-torn China and blue notes from the Mississippi Delta, percussive rhythms from Cuba and Mexico, warped notes and minor-key inflections from klezmer. When he tasted the melting-pot stew of New York City, what delighted him were the pungent chunks of lamb, onion, and hot pepper, not the smooth broth in which these flavors combined and dissolved. In this respect, George was Jimmy's opposite.

He decided to host a Passover seder that would illustrate his point, and invited Kay as well as his immediate family, in-laws, selected friends, and friends of friends. It was an elegant affair catered by liveried help. His sister, Frances, had married a violinist named Leopold, who in his spare time had invented a color film process known as Kodachrome. Frances and Leopold rode the train down from Rochester. Ira and his wife, Leonore, walked downstairs from the fourth floor; and their kid brother, Arthur, from the third. George's other guests included Duke Ellington; a bubbly Kansas City dancer named Ginger Rogers, whom George had hired for his new play, *Girl Crazy;* Carl Van Vechten; and three guests suggested by Van Vechten: the novelist Zora Hurston, who wore a red turban with a gardenia; the poet Langston Hughes; and the essayist George Schuyler, who sported a bow tie and an elegant suit.

"Mister Schuyler, I read your essay, *The Negro Art Hokum,*" Van Vechten gushed as Schuyler entered. "I thought it perfectly brilliant even as I took exception to every word."

"Thank you," Schuyler said. And then he turned to the woman at his side. "This is my wife, Jody."

The woman who offered her hand, not to Van Vechten but to Gershwin, wore a rose silk dress trimmed in jade green. But her most astonishing trait was her skin color. Although her husband was Negro, she was as white as Biloxi sand. Kay marveled at the fact that they had found a reverend or magistrate to consecrate such a union.

In all, twenty-seven people celebrated the Hebrews' crossing of the Sinai at Rose and Morris Gershwin's table that year. Over unleavened bread, wine, chicken soup with matzo balls, brisket, and stewed carrots they exchanged reflections on the Jewish people's memory of slavery and the trauma of colored folk in America, whom Rose called *darkies.*

"To this day, our bondage in Egypt remains the foundation of our identity," observed Ira. "That's what we share with American Negroes. And that is one damn powerful bond."

He looked to Ellington for a response, an affirmation of this putative affinity but it was the poet, Langston Hughes, who spoke up. "I just don't know. Maybe the Hebrews were slaves but that was so long ago. So many centuries of strife and cunning in the ghettos of Europe. And in between, the rise of capitalism. The Jewish success in business and entertainment." He glanced from Ira to George. "Whereas with colored people, it's a gaping fresh wound. We still have the smell of the cotton field in our nostrils, the sting of the whip on our backs, the wails of our women in our ears."

George nodded, tasting the soup.

"What you're saying is, you don't care a whit for my patronizing balderdash," said Ira.

"Precisely," said Langston Hughes.

"I believe Sigmund Freud has a term for it," suggested Zora Hurston, who had studied anthropology at Barnard. "It's called *projective identification*. The Jews want to see their reflection in the Negro. They, or many of them, want to play the role of sympathetic benefactor."

"I guess the question is, why?" asked Duke Ellington, looking at George as he sipped his matzo ball soup.

"Maybe to prove we're morally superior," said Ira, tasting the soup. "Since the Christians have always argued the opposite."

"There's plenty of projective identification to go around," said George Schuyler. "In fact, there's enough of it going on *within* both the Aframerican and the Jewish groups. In what sense was the slave experience your personal experience, Ira? Or yours, Langston? How about a peek at those stripes on your back?"

No one answered at once. Then everyone voiced their opinions at the same time, or so it seemed.

"By your logic, we colored Americans have no distinct culture at all," Ellington told Schuyler. "And no possibility of one."

"Precisely," agreed Schuyler.

"The lore gets passed down," said Zora Hurston. "Isn't that an inheritance?"

"The lore — and the music — get reinvented, too," said George.

"That doesn't make them less authentic," said Zora.

"Not at all," he agreed.

"I believe that lore you refer to," Schuyler told Zora, "comes from one sector of Aframerican society. My family never dwelled in the South. I grew up in Providence, Rhode Island, and upstate New York. A portion of my blood is Bavarian. Others of my forebears hail from the West Indies or directly from Africa. I may appreciate the blues but it remains as foreign to my experience as Tahitian conch-shell-and-nose-flute music. To imply that my skin color connects me to slavery is just as racialist as to claim that Mister Gershwin's earlobe or nose shape ties him to medieval usurers."

Gershwin nodded. Fascinated with the Adolph Hitler phenomenon, he was aware of the Nazis' attempts to define the Jewish *race* in terms of phenotype.

"But when white folk look at you," Langston Hughes told Schuyler, "they don't see Bavaria. They see Africa."

Shuyler shook his head. "I refuse to hand *them* the honor of deciding who I am."

"If only it were that simple," said Hughes.

"All right, shush all of you," ordered Morris Gershwin in his Russian accent. "It's time for the third *bracha.*"

"The fourth, papa," Ira corrected him.

"The third, the fourth," Morris waved away the interruption. "Either way, another glass of wine." He held up his cup, intoned a Hebrew prayer, and swallowed most of the wine in one gulp the way a Cossack might imbibe a shot of vodka before jumping onto his horse.

Through all this, Kay had contented herself with listening. But when George's mother started slicing the brisket, she touched her arm. "Please, Rose, let me help."

Rose jerked back as if slapped. "What, I'm

399

too old to slice the most tender beef in New York? Is my hand shaking?" She held out her hand.

"I didn't mean to suggest that," said Kay.

Rose resumed slicing, mouth pursed in discontent.

Kay looked at George. "What did I do?" she mouthed.

George shook his head, smiling.

Later, as she and George were about to leave, Kay heard Rose whisper to her son. "She's a nice girl. She dresses well. But for you?" Rose shook her head.

As soon as the door closed, Kay turned to George. "How dare she say *I'm not for you*? What does she know about me? I hardly piped a word!"

"She knows you're not Jewish." He escorted her up the stairs.

"Can't you stand up to that, George? Can't you tell her it's not her decision?"

"Kay, take my word: there's no point trying."

Kay believed him. What was the point of confronting Rose, as long as *she* remained married to James Warburg? But to leave Jimmy would be to break up her family and sacrifice her lifestyle. For what? In the hope that George would settle down and, against his mother's protests, propose to her? How likely was that?

In bed that night, she asked: "George, if I were to get divorced, would you consider — ?"

But he only mumbled something and turned onto his side.

During the Passover seder, George had spoken about his plans for *Porgy*. Zora Neale Hurston shared his interest in the book, and mentioned that she would be presenting a discourse about it, "from a psychological point of view." A few weeks later Kay and George located her apartment in Harlem, which was packed with neighbors, Columbia faculty, and students. "Du-Bose Heyward's fascination with the Gullahs," said Zora, "is of a piece with Carl Van Vechten's obsession with Harlem. And George Gershwin's," she added, noticing them entering.

"For context, you can think of Eugene Delacroix's North African period, Gustav Flaubert's novel *Salammbô,* Debussy's use of modalities derived from Indonesian gamelan music, Joseph Conrad's *Heart of Darkness,* and Stravinsky's *Rite of Spring.* All these works spring directly from the Romantic fantasy of the primitive, which one can trace back to Rousseau. This fantasy

401

incorporates two opposite poles of feeling: admiration and horror. Admiration for the innocence, freshness, and authenticity of primitive experience; revulsion at its cruelty and barbarity. But the underlying theme is the ego's fascination with the id."

Standing with George at the back of the room, Kay remembered her conversation with Josephine Baker. She understood that Zora's approach to the subject of Primitivism differed from Josephine's, just as Josephine's differed from the view that Luckey Roberts had expressed at Fats Waller's rent party. All were concerned, however, with how white people judged and misrepresented Negro culture, or how the self-described civilized world understood cultures they viewed as savage or pristine.

The problem, Kay knew, was crucial to composers like Gershwin, who thought of music as a means of communication between ethnic communities. If America was a melting pot, or rather a stewing pot that preserved the distinct flavors of all its cultures, and if that was what made America unique, then American music must celebrate it.

"Naturally the subjects of this fantasy," continued Zora, "be they Indonesian or Negro, fail to see themselves in these Romantic fictions and resent the colonial mentality that interprets them in a symbolic manner. I propose however that we evaluate *Porgy* not on its merits as anthropology, but as a novel that examines what is universal in the human condition through its detailed construction of a microcosmos. Let us start from the premise that no story is real in the sense of literal, but that great stories are very real indeed in the way that fantasies — and nightmares — are real. Perhaps more real, indeed, from the point of view of the psyche than reality."

"Let's hit the road," George whispered to Kay.

"This is interesting, George!" she whispered back. "Besides, she's your friend."

But he turned to leave, and she followed, and Zora saw.

"My beef with intellectuals," George explained in the back seat of the taxi, "is they pepper everything with references to other intellectuals, to prove their membership in the club."

"You're just expressing your feeling of inadequacy because you haven't read Rousseau," said Kay. "Admit it!"

His eyes crinkled with amusement. "Hey, let's hop out for a cream pie. Driver," he leaned forward, "drop us at the Café Edison, will you?"

"You got it, bud," said the driver.

Later, over key lime pie in the Café Edison, she tried again. "Zora's right, you know. The same way my mother, as much as she came to love Jimmy, couldn't understand the experience of his family — their history in Europe, how it still affects them — we can't really appreciate the legacy of slavery, how it affects people like Josephine Baker or Duke Ellington. The Duke can play the Cotton Club, but his own family can't sit in the audience."

George smiled. "If only my grandparents had suffered like Jimmy's." His smile vanished and he gripped her hand on the table. "Kay, we've got to get *Porgy* off the ground."

CHAPTER TWENTY-SEVEN

George began planning for the production of his as-yet-unwritten opera. He and Kay had visualized it on the stage of the Metropolitan. However, there was one glaring issue that had to be addressed at once.

Paul Mueller drove them down to Fifty-Third Street to meet with the Opera's general manager. The rendezvous took place at the end of the working day. The cigar lounge setting that the general manager chose was dim as a cave. Although women were not allowed, an exception was made for George Gershwin's *secretary.*

A tall, portly gentleman with an upturned waxed moustache, a matching wool vest under his long black jacket, and a heavy silver watch chain across his belly, the Italian-accented general manager explained the Metropolitan Opera's ban on Negroes. "This has nothing to do with my personal views, or with those of any member of the board." He offered George a cigar and started to offer one to Kay, then thought better of it. She lit a cigarette. "It is about tradition," the general manager added. "Audience expectations. Comfort levels."

"Comfort levels?" asked George incredulously. "How about challenging those comfort levels? Changing those expectations? How about making people squirm? Doesn't *Wozzeck* do that? Not to mention *Moses und Aron* . . ."

"Have you seen those operas performed at the Met?" asked Giulio with rhetorical equanimity, leaning back in his seat.

George glanced at Kay. "Great to see you, Giulio. We don't need to take more of your time. Thanks for the cigar."

Giulio tapped his ash into a crystal bowl. "There is a possible compromise. I would urge you to consider lampblack. The audience likes that."

"The entire cast, in blackface?" asked George.

"Why not?" Giulio spread his hands. "Now that would be a novelty we could all live with."

"One I can do without." George rose. "Come on, Kay."

As they rode uptown to George's apartment their conversation turned south to the show-business district. "We have no choice then but to produce *Porgy* in a Broadway theater," said George.

"How will Broadway audiences react to that style of singing?" asked Kay. "Nonstop music, curtain-up to curtain-down? A tragic ending?" Broadway shows were supposed to end in a joyous, tout-ensemble finale. It was the tried-and-true formula. It worked.

"How will they react? Moved, hopefully," said George.

"And then, there's the cost," said Kay. They both knew that *Porgy,* written and staged as George conceived it, with a large cast and a full orchestra, would be far more expensive to produce than any previous Broadway production.

"In our line of work, we take chances," said George.

Over the years some of his shows had lost money. Others had earned beyond expectation. Some songs flailed initially and later soared. Others leapt skyward, looped around, and plummeted down. Such was the nature of the arts.

During the ensuing days and weeks George and Kay discussed *Porgy* with representatives of the Theatre Guild, individual theater owners, and theater managers. George was the most celebrated Broadway composer, both domestically and internationally, and they all longed to work with him. But in the end, if he insisted on staging *Porgy* as an opera, he would have to guarantee thirty percent of the budget.

"All my liquid assets," sighed George. "And then some."

"We have to scale it down," said Kay, "or produce it elsewhere."

George shook his head.

Returning to George's apartment after a third meeting with the Theatre Guild, they found the playwright Guy Bolton waiting outside. He had written the books for several successful musicals, including a few of George's. Although Guy's parents were American, he had been raised in England and he exhibited his European patina like his gold-and-ruby tiepin, to establish his posh bona fides. At the same time, he offered a wink to those who detected his posturing, as if to imply *you and I know it's silly, don't we, old chap. The whole culture game, just a socially acceptable way to snuffle each other's behinds like bloodhounds confirming hierarchy.*

Dapper in his linen jacket with shoulder pads, his sky-blue shirt with a maroon and yellow club tie, and high-waisted, pleated, tapered pants, Guy kissed Kay's hand. "Heading off to sunny California. Palm trees, sand, starlets. Stopped to wave *adios* before hopping onto the transcontinental railway. And . . ."

They climbed to George's apartment and settled in the living room.

"And, well, I thought I might give your wrestling arm a gentle twist," Guy told George.

George glanced at Kay.

"We're setting up a picture," Guy resumed. "Top names, Janet Gaynor, Charles Farrell. You did catch *Seventh Heaven.*" It was a question, posed as a statement.

"Missed it," said George.

"Colossal box office. Sensational, actually. And with your music, and Fox's new Movietone technology, *Delicious* is bound to surpass it."

"Ah." George folded his hands on his lap.

Bolton leaned forward. "Crossed-star antics aboard a luxury cruise. That's the hook — the boat," he said in a low voice, as if divulging a world-changing secret. "What do they all dream of? The farm wife, the telephone girl, the factory man. Transatlantic voyages." And leaned back again. "And all this, over an orchestral setting, start to finish. Never been done before. You can deliver serious, romantic, upbeat, whimsical, all up to you, George."

"Guy," said George, "I know zero about movies. The culture, the art form, the process. It's thick as mud to me."

"There's gold in that thar mud, Georgie!" said Bolton in a mock-Western twang. "We'll tweak the story around your composition. The players are stupendous. So what do you say, old pal? Fourteen weeks of Eden and you come back pockets bursting. Opulent lodgings in one of the canyons," continued Bolton. "Tennis, great jazz at the Cocoanut Grove, and . . ." He glanced at Kay, then back at George. "Well, perks galore."

"Tell me, Guy," said George. "Does this production depend on my participation?"

"Would I pressure you like that?" Bolton smiled. His gold premolar flashed.

Guy stayed for a snack of cold smoked fish, onions, and cream cheese. George played him a song he had written for *Porgy,* a number he called "My Man's Gone Now."

"This is staggering, George. Phenomenal." Bolton slapped him on the collarbone. "Not one to disappoint, are you." He shook his head, half smiling. "An American opera!"

After he left, George and Kay fooled around at the piano. Finally he sighed,

410

"This one, I may have to take. For *Porgy*'s sake."

Kay mixed a Gin Rickey for herself and poured a glass of Chivas for him. "Do you really need to be gone fourteen weeks?"

He answered with a bluesy piano improvisation.

While Kay read through the music they had written the day before, George skimmed the mail. "That chord's a little soggy," he mentioned without looking up from the letter in his hand, or "let's invert that." She jotted the notation and moved on.

George opened another envelope. It was a request that he perform *An American in Paris* for a radio broadcast, after reading a short, scripted introduction. The remuneration offered was adequate but what George appreciated was the exposure.

He unsealed a letter from Paul Whiteman, asking George to perform in a movie he was producing about jazz. He set it aside, in the pile of mail that had to be answered.

A third letter was from Serge Koussevitzky, the music director of the Boston Symphony Orchestra and of the famous *Concerts Koussevitzky* series in Paris. Heralded as a bold champion of modern music, Koussevitzky had commissioned and performed works by Ravel, Prokofiev, Hindemith, and Stravinsky.

May I ask you to compose a piece for the Boston Orchestra? Next season we will mark our 50th Anniversary with a concert in Boston followed by a second in New York City and we would very much appreciate if you would write a piece for these occasions.

George balled up the letter and threw it into a trash basket. "Hell, I'd love to, but where will I find the time?"

His valet, Paul Mueller, retrieved it and carefully unfolded it. "Agree to the movie — *Delicious* — but insist on owning the rights. That way, you can reuse the score for Koussevitzky."

"You devil," said George, smiling.

"As long as Koussevitzky premieres it before the movie release, he'll be pleased as pie," added Paul.

"You know, that just may work!"

Kay did not like the idea. It made George's trip to Hollywood feasible. But she held her tongue.

Another letter: from Merle Armitage, the well-known impresario, suggesting an all-Gershwin concert at the Lewisohn stadium

— "an honor previously accorded only to Beethoven and Wagner," he read aloud.

"Make it a three-for-one," suggested Paul, on a roll. "Perform the same *Delicious* score. But only after you premiere it with Koussevitzky."

"Bingo," said George, shooting him with his index finger.

On yellow stationery, DuBose Heyward, the author of *Porgy,* invited George to travel down to South Carolina to soak in the local color, the dialect, the speech rhythms, and the gospel music of the Gullah people, who filled the tenements of *Porgy*'s Catfish Row.

A fellow named Lincoln Kirstein wrote that he planned to produce the American début of the great Ballets Russes choreographer, George Balanchine. Together, Gershwin's music and Balanchine's choreography would "dazzle."

George rubbed his chin. Finally he shook his head. "I can't do it."

The world's most esteemed composers had penned scores for Balanchine. Celebrated artists including Matisse and Picasso had designed his sets. "You're cracked," said Kay. "It's everything you want, wrapped up with a bow."

George looked at Paul Mueller, who nodded. "You are cracked."

413

"*Porgy* needs me," said George. "And *Of Thee I Sing,* my next musical. Not to mention *Delicious* and a million hassles. Just can't do it." He pointed to Kay. "But you can do this."

He picked up the telephone and connected through to the number on the letter. Kay heard him say, "Lincoln Kirstein? George Gershwin. Sorry, old pal, I'm booked from Monday to Mars. But I got an idea. Did you catch *Fine and Dandy?* Yes, it was. That score is by a lady named Kay Swift. No, not 'good,' Lincoln — brilliant. Why yes, that's right, James Warburg's wife. Of course we can."

He hung up and turned to Kay. "Next Wednesday, three p.m., six three seven Madison Avenue. And don't forget your cloche hat."

"My cloche hat?"

He cupped his hand around her chin. "They'll still see your *sheyna punim* but it will hide your feminine tresses." He kissed her.

"My *sheyna* — ?"

"Your pretty face," said George. "Yiddish."

George's proposal almost defied belief. George Balanchine. The Ballets Russes. The most innovative and respected dance troupe

414

in the world. Was it possible? she asked herself. Was she prepared? Would Balanchine take her seriously? Had she earned this privilege?

CHAPTER TWENTY-EIGHT

Jimmy. Berlin. Summer 1930

Another trip to Europe, another pause from the whirlwind of his marriage. Jimmy and Kay had long ago given up trying to maintain any pretense of happiness, balance, or normalcy. Even hope seemed a stretch at this point. At best, the tenuous status quo might last another year, or ten, until it snapped. Although he missed his daughters — and yes, his wife — Jimmy now depended on travel for reflection, reading, and refuge.

Wilhelm Kissel, the de facto chairman of Daimler-Benz, and Wilhelm Haspel, the head of the company's business department, had invited Jimmy to a cabaret in Berlin. *Haspels Frau ist Jüdin,* the letter from Stuttgart had explained. "Haspel's wife is Jewish." As if to say, *we're all family,* with a friendly Weimar wink.

A dank, crowded theater in the sweaty basement of a brick building in the red-light district. Panels of maroon-and-black cloth draped the walls and stage. Well-heeled businessmen, prostitutes, and a few *Hitler-Jugend* with their swastika armbands crowded the tiny tables, whistling and catcalling as heavily made-up, half-naked whores, homosexual hustlers, transvestites, and sadomasochists gyrated and pivoted, singing paeans to political dysfunction and social decay and acting out skits that glorified lust, dominance, and homicide. They mocked Paul von Hindenburg, the president of the republic, as a doddering stuffed shirt. They ignited and threw into the air fistfuls of paper money. In Jimmy's estimation the musicianship, singing, and dancing were semiprofessional at best. It all seemed a depraved parody of recent New York culture — risqué innuendo, kickline dancing, jazz.

"Some call it moral laxity," Haspel half apologized. "Others call it emancipation."

"And the authorities?" asked Jimmy. "What do they call it?"

"That gentleman over there," Kissel pointed at an obese man who puffed on a cigar and blew clouds of smoke into the air while fondling the adolescent girl on his lap — or was it a boy in lipstick? — "that is the chief of police. Of course we have laws against lewdness," he added as the waiter refilled their brandy snifters. "But who is going to enforce them? In the current social climate, such a person would be considered a *Spielverderber*" — a party-pooper — "and would rapidly be voted out of office. Germany is a democracy. We prize self-expression."

When they tottered down to the avenue to hail a taxi at two in the morning, the city was still buzzing. Jimmy observed posters slapped on stone walls that advocated for National Socialism, Communism, and other apocalyptic remedies. He saw adolescent boys and girls in garish makeup selling pleasure on street corners. A group of thugs kicked a man to a quivering pulp while others passed, apparently unconcerned. "Shouldn't we get this man to a hospital?" asked Jimmy, horrified.

"Don't even try. You would be killed," Haspel warned him. "I shall put a call in to the hospital when I arrive home. Of course," he added nonchalantly, "he will be dead by then."

"Perhaps now you understand Herr Hitler's message," Kissel slurred as a cab pulled to the curb and they climbed in. "His fight is against degeneracy. He names the perpetrators. His purpose is to exhume the German will."

Jimmy thought his logic confused, considering that they had just partied away their evening in a cavern of sexual exhibitionism.

Another night, Jimmy traveled to central Berlin to hear Hitler address a rally. The ceremonies began with a parade, which wound to a stop in the Alexanderplatz. As a brass band blew patriotic hymns, Hitler's uniformed soldiers lined up in rows under the flickering light of tall torches. All beautifully choreographed and lit: an answer to chaos and darkness.

Hitler began speaking. At first he sounded reasonable. Little by little emotion inflected his voice, carrying his vast audience up with him as if on a Messerschmitt fighter cruising toward a golden sunrise. The individual words did not matter so much as the overall message of purpose, resolve, and hope. But as Hitler's delivery grew impassioned, his tone rising all the way into high-yelp territory, Jimmy found himself dangling from a Made-in-USA parachute, floating back to earth.

Jimmy deplored the Austrian's demagogic style but, as he wrote to his father during the return cruise, still thought it prudent to accord Herr Hitler the benefit of the doubt. He agreed with Hitler on many points, after all, particularly in his skepticism about religion and his embrace of science. Recent findings of physical anthropologists, applying the objective measurements of craniometry and phrenology, proved that multiple races did indeed exist and displayed distinct characteristics. Hitler's rhetorical emphasis on the "hierarchical analysis of race" might well prove to be an electoral ploy rather than a rigid doctrine.

Nor was Hitler's professed hatred of capitalism an innovation. European priests and ministers had railed against *usury* and its practitioners — bankers — for centuries. Hitler's desire to eliminate Jews had taken root in this long-fertilized soil. Fancying himself a skilled surgeon of modern statecraft, he sought to excise the parasite race for the good of Germany and the world.

If Adolph Hitler was anything like other politicians, Jimmy reasoned, he would eventually reveal himself to be susceptible to negotiation. All politicians balanced on the shaky stilts of cheap ideology and public naïveté. Their Achilles' heel was and always would remain their need for a financial footing.

During the return crossing, Jimmy made the acquaintance of the publisher Alfred A. Knopf. They met at a backgammon table during a storm. The two men played to win and shared a passion for books. Relaxing over cigars and cognac, they discussed Willa Cather, Thomas Mann, T. S. Eliot, international finance, the upcoming presidential election, and of course Hitler. Knopf had seen *Fine and Dandy* and thought it fresh and delightful.

Within days, their rapport resulted in an informal agreement. *Paul James* would pen a book of poetry for Knopf. In a letter to Kay he described the meeting and his plans for the collection. The tone would be less solemn than his previous published efforts. That old seriousness had reflected the self-importance of youth. But these new poems would not be shallow, either. They would blend intimacy with irony. He spent so much of his time traveling these days, and pouring his heart into letters like this one, which he sealed with wax. Thus, he decided, he would call the volume *Shoes and Ships and Sealing Wax,* in a nod to the shape and substance of his life.

Kay sat at her desk, and picked up her Dunhill pen. "Dearest Jimmy," she wrote,

You saw Herr Hitler! What a spectacle you describe.
And now, on the return cruise, you're

421

playing backgammon with Alfred Knopf, who wants to publish your poems. Not the poems you once wrote, bursting with romance and bluster, but verse that's more playful, less high-toned. I suppose we've both learned a thing or two from our Georges, Kaufman and Gershwin. You're well on the way to realizing your dreams, Jimmy.

Do you remember when our marriage was a dream? I do. You were in Washington and I in New York, and the thought that we would soon be sharing our lives seemed too wonderful to be entirely true.

Which I suppose it was.

I'm so happy for you.

Love,

Kay

CHAPTER TWENTY-NINE

Fall 1930

Once upon a time, at the cusp of adulthood, Kay had convinced herself that she had discovered a kindred spirit in Jimmy. They had emerged from dissimilar childhoods and twisted a psychological tightrope from the strands of their differing hopes and expectations. They had crossed that high wire in tandem for more than a decade. It could no longer support them, but where was the safety net? With George she had found a pair of wings. Buoyed on the breeze of music, she might not need a cable. But now, with George far away in California, the wind had died and she was falling.

Walking to her appointment with Doctor Zilboorg, she paused at a newspaper kiosk. As her eyes wandered, a photograph at the bottom right-hand corner of the *New York Evening Graphic* jumped out and struck a blow to her plexus. The *Graphic* was one of those alchemical celebrity rags that transmuted scandal into gold, and this picture portrayed George Gershwin lounging with the starlet Paulette Goddard "at William Randolph Hearst's extravagant Mediterranean Revival love nest, a day's ramble and a world away from the City of Angels."

She studied the photograph. George's body turned toward the starlet's. Paulette Goddard laughing, her striking hazel eyes gleaming under her dark hair, her skin glistening under the sun, her hand on George's arm. His legs suntanned and toned. His smile.

Kay handed the kiosk attendant a nickel and skimmed the article, a hit piece that focused on Miss Goddard's "seductive and ruthless" movie star aspirations. Hearst had invited George Gershwin, Charlie Chaplin, and Harry Houdini, as well as Goddard and several "Hollywood nymphettes" for a frolicking weekend of tennis, movies, and feasts. The wily Miss Goddard, née Marion Levy — and "about as French as gefilte fish" — had eyes only for Mister Gershwin, who seemed to delight in her attentions.

The boy, looking over Kay's shoulder, whistled. "That Paulette Goddard, what a dish. Wooh!" He tugged on his collar for emphasis.

Kay winced. "I'll take them all."

"You'll take 'em . . . what?"

"This . . . this vulgar, indecent rag, the *Evening Graphic*. The pile of them."

The boy glanced at the picture again, straightened his cap, and frowned. "All of 'em?"

She nodded, fishing in her purse for her wallet.

"Wow!" he said.

Kay lugged the tabloids to the corner, where she stuffed them into a garbage bin.

"So there he is, enjoying himself in California," remarked Doctor Zilboorg, "while you are here, with only your husband to keep you company — for whom you no longer feel that libidinal zing."

"It's not just about that," said Kay.

But Zilboorg pursued: "I understand Mr. Gershwin has helped you, but so long as you remain emotionally knotted up with him, you will continue to suffer from waves of negative feelings, a sense of loneliness and abandonment. Has it occurred to you that your neurosis makes you vulnerable to being taken advantage of?"

"Does George take advantage of me?" asked Kay. "Do I take advantage of him? Did Jimmy take advantage of me?"

425

"Jimmy?"

"I don't know, for sex, for the prestige of being married to a classical musician? Did *I* take advantage of Jimmy's position, his wealth? You can look at it that way. But when both parties are giving freely of themselves, sharing, learning together, growing together, discovering . . . I'm not sure *taking advantage* is the right term. I see it as an exchange."

Doctor Zilboorg raised one eyebrow.

"Maybe that's something you noggin twisters get wrong," added Kay. "You think of love as desire, wanting to *get* something from another person, not as altruism, which is wanting to *give* something."

"This is playing with language, Misses Warburg. One of the ways the ego shields itself. Let us try another tack. Tell me more about Mister Gershwin. What is it about him that so fascinates you?"

"I don't know," said Kay. "Sometimes I think it's the music. Or his eyes, or the way he smiles. I wish I knew why I felt the way I feel." Uncomfortable with the way Zilboorg was looking at her, she adjusted her posture.

"Are you quite certain all you feel about Mister Gershwin is love?" he asked. "Maybe you are experiencing other emotions, as well."

426

"I also worry about him," she said. "He hears things. He smells things. One day, a headache will lay him low. Another day, it'll be a stomachache. No doctor can figure it out."

Doctor Zilboorg nodded. "We are speaking of a man with a great deal of psychic energy, repressed emotional turmoil, which he attempts to sublimate through his music, with limited success. What's left over finds expression in other ways."

"Do you think psychoanalysis would help?" asked Kay.

"It is essential," said Dr. Zilboorg. "In the meantime, though, with Mister Gershwin whooping it up in California, why don't you and Jimmy write some songs together, another show perhaps. The two of you are now an established team. This will be good for you and good for your marriage. Jimmy is back from Germany, is he not?"

"I'll discuss it with him tonight," said Kay.

Jimmy and Kay dined at Pail & Fork, a seafood restaurant on the East River, where he expressed his growing despair about German society. "The country is divided against itself. On one side, the Communists. On the other, the National Socialists. Each side hollering, neither listening. Meanwhile, the cultural middle class, or what's left of it, distracts itself with debauchery and toys with the romance of death. It's all spiraling downward like water into a sewer and if it continues, I fear another war."

"And Herr Hitler?" Kay cracked a crab claw.

"He's a symptom, not the disease." Jimmy sipped his Guinness.

"So what can be done?" asked Kay.

"I don't know if we can save Europe," said Jimmy. "But here in the States, we have to do everything we can to prevent the kind of out-of-control inflation that has ruined Germany."

"You can't fix the world all by yourself," said Kay as they walked home. "But you *can* write a darn good lyric."

"The world will survive without Paul James's songs. I have a book of poetry to write."

"Who reads poetry?"

"The bemused, patronizing *New Yorker* crowd," said Jimmy, quoting their friend Stewie. "Which is good enough for me."

Kay tugged at Jimmy's elbow lest he step on a sleeping man's leg. Even on the Upper East Side these days, entire families used concrete for mattresses and steps for pillows. "People need entertainment," she said, "maybe as much as money."

"That's easy to say when you have servants and several sets of porcelain you never touch," said Jimmy as he turned keys in the triple locks of their front door.

George's contract with the Fox Film Corporation included a provision for first-class transportation. Only twenty-six hours from Los Angeles to New Jersey in a five-foot-wide, wood-paneled cabin with a wet bar, a smoking lounge, upholstered seats, and nurses holding sandwich trays for fourteen privileged passengers.

So many innovations in such a short span of time. The motorcar, the washing machine, the telephone, the radio, the airplane, the moving pictures, and now the talkies — including the soon-to-be-released *Delicious,* with its first-in-history full musical score. Each invention carried the hope that mankind's burden would be lightened and each had, in one way or another, delivered on its promise. Still, all the technology in the world could not relieve loneliness, sorrow, or regret, Kay reflected as she stood in furs among journalists and family members on the recently paved Newark airport tarmac, her breath clouding in the chill.

The shiny, twin-prop Douglas DC-2 cut

through the sky, a speck stretching into a blotch, and descended in a rumble and a thunder, its nose raised, its hind leg dangling, a giant three-footed goose. The smartly uniformed airport crew wheeled a metal stairway to the door and George stepped out before the other passengers, beaming in a dark cashmere coat, toting a leather suitcase. Ira followed in a camel coat and a burgundy scarf. Journalists' flashes popped. Reporters shouted questions about the flight and how it felt to be back on solid ground.

George's amber complexion testified to hours spent on tennis courts and in the rear seat of a chauffeured Packard 906 convertible. Ira looked pale and greenish. At the foot of the stairs George set down his case. "Give us a minute, fellas," he waved to the photographers, who ceased snapping long enough for him to hug Kay.

They held each other until Ira pulled up his shirt cuff to glance at his wristwatch. The gesture was rhetorical since his timepiece was still set for California. "Come on already, it's cold in New Jersey," he grumbled.

As Kay's driver pulled into traffic, Ira apologized. "Sorry, Kay. The flight was noisy and bumpy and my stomach's still in my neck. Besides which, let me tell you, California didn't suit me one bit. Nothing there. No Broadway, no opera, no nothing. The Sahara. All anyone can blab about is B.O., by which they mean box office."

"How'd the show turn out?" asked Kay.

Ira loosened his tie and rolled down the window. "*Delicious*? It was . . . atrocious."

"According to the papers, you alligators had a time of it. Splashing around in Greta Garbo's swimming pool, horseback riding with Douglas Fairbanks, shopping with Paulette Goddard."

"It wasn't like that, Kay, honest," said George shifting in his seat. "It was, and it wasn't." He swung his arm around her.

"When George wasn't laid up with a headache, he was sulking," explained Ira.

"These movie-biz twits, they've got tin ears," said George. "The big cheeses do, anyway. But they hold the purse strings and they're convinced that makes them Toscanini."

"They think of music," elaborated Ira, "the way you might think of . . ." He looked out the window, searching for a metaphor. "A diamond choker on a work horse."

She smiled.

"And what they did to my *Second Rhapsody*!" groused George. "They chopped it up like confetti and glued it back together. They should be hanged for that alone. Shouldn't they, Ira."

"You got what you needed," Ira reminded him. "The *Second Rhapsody* is yours. You can return it to its virginal condition, dress it up, hand it to Koussevitzky, and début it in Boston, no apologies to anyone. Then you can perform it again at Lewisohn Stadium, and wherever else you like."

"And you got what *Porgy* needed," added Kay. "Wasn't that the point?"

"Yeah, yeah, great," agreed George. "We hauled off the cabbage. Just like farm laborers."

Their car turned into West 103rd Street. Looking out the window at his neighborhood market's sidewalk display, George smiled.

CHAPTER THIRTY

August 16, 1932

The Lewisohn Stadium stretched from 136th Street to 138th Street and from Amsterdam Avenue to Convent Avenue. Seventeen thousand tickets had been sold, a record-breaking audience. Thousands of spectators were turned away.

The day before the performance, George had been so ill that he thought he might have to call it off. He lay in bed unable to talk or even turn his head on the pillow without nausea and pain. Kay called his doctor, who knocked at the door, took George's pulse, and prescribed rest and aspirin. None of which seemed to help.

She spent that afternoon and night with him feeling helpless. George was unable even to swallow a spoonful of chicken soup. All Kay could do was to lie beside him.

The morning of the show, the pain lifted. "You know something? All that pain was worth it," said George. "It made me appreciate being alive." He sipped his orange juice. "I feel reborn."

In the afternoon, Paul Mueller drove Kay, George, Ira, and Oscar Levant to the stage entrance through a cordoned-off back alley. Kay had never seen such a crowd, brilliantly lit with arc lamps, chattering and laughing. Other composers, of the serious ilk, might have shied away from such a blatantly commercial venue, which drew not only the wealthy and sophisticated but also the common men and women who swarmed the standing-room-only area. But Gershwin reveled in the adulation.

Accompanied by the New York Philharmonic Orchestra, Oscar Levant delivered a sensitive and robust *New York Concerto*. "He plays the damn thing better than I do," George marveled.

"Far better," agreed Kay. While George played the *Concerto* and everything else with a free, improvisatory flair, shifting tempos and adding or subtracting flourishes at will, Oscar attacked it with bravura and rigor, as he would a piece by Brahms.

The orchestra followed with *An American in Paris* and then, as the audience cheered and whistled, George sauntered out to the stage, looking as graceful and dashing as ever despite his receding hairline. He bowed perfunctorily, sat at the piano, and released an energized *Rhapsody in Blue* as if letting a wild animal out of its cage. He followed with his *Second Rhapsody,* adapted from the long montage sequence he had composed for the movie *Delicious* and revised for Serge Koussevitzky. The spectators whistled, hollered, and stamped, demanding more and yet more. Looking at the crowd from the side of the stage, Kay pondered the phenomenon of mass hysteria, all this psychic energy focused on her beloved.

Of course there were the melodies. The razzmatazz playing. But none of that explained the giddy emotion she was witnessing. What they heard in his music was a resounding statement about America, *E pluribus unum.* From the blues and spirituals and cantorial chant and hayseed fiddle playing and south-of-the-border rhythms, as well as the residue of European high culture, America could forge a sound all its own, accessible, addictive, and modern. What these people saw in George Gershwin was the personification of their dream: an immigrant's son who had achieved wealth, American prosperity hammered in the factories of Tin Pan Alley, riveted with

Pittsburgh steel. The child of an alien ethnicity who had not only mastered the techniques and fashions of European High Culture, but who had helped reinterpret that culture, chipping away its pretentions for a rugged New World. Because he dared to be uniquely and truly *American,* without apology, he had earned the esteem of European composers and playgoers in London and Paris.

What Kay observed in that multitude of faces and heard in those cheers was not merely pride, but hope. Hope for a shared culture built on mutual respect. Richard Wagner had insisted that was the main purpose of art: to create and nurture the myths that fused a culture together. But Wagner had suffered from the European sickness. His vision of unified culture required the crushing dominance of one group to the exclusion of others.

For days afterward, it seemed everyone in New York City was talking about the Lewisohn Stadium concert. Several music critics and composers, rising stars like Aaron Copland and Virgil Thomson, now openly grumbled about the injustice of Gershwin's fame. Their journalist-critic devotees echoed and amplified their gripes, without specific attribution. The *New York*

Times noted that "critical opinion in many quarters expresses reservations as to Gershwin's lack of technical resources" and called attention to "the generally self-conscious manner in which the young composer utilizes the popular rhythms of the day in the development of his themes." The *New York World* offered a more nuanced, ambivalent appraisal: "Mister Gershwin makes the most gorgeous mistakes in orchestration."

Kay read this comment to George the morning after the show. He beamed. "That is the best compliment I ever received."

CHAPTER THIRTY-ONE

Thanksgiving 1932

Gershwin spent the holiday with Kay at Bydale savoring the success of his most recent Broadway show, *Of Thee I Sing.* Kay's friend George S. Kaufman and his new writing partner Morrie Ryskind had scribed the book, an absurdist mockery of American politics with Gilbert-and-Sullivanesque lyrics by Ira. They had modeled the character of Wintergreen on Jimmy Walker, the affable, not-too-bright, regular-guy mayor of New York City whom George and Kay had met at the Cotton Club and at a few of Julie Glaenzer's parties. Brooks Atkinson, reviewing *Of Thee I Sing* in the *New York Times,* wrote that the play was "funnier than government and not nearly so dangerous." Nominated for a Pulitzer Prize against Eugene O'Neill's *Mourning Becomes Elektra,* the Gershwin musical won, becoming the first Broadway production to earn such a distinction. Both its title-song spoof of jingoism and its romantic-depression ballad "Who Cares?" were fast-selling hits.

With *Of Thee I Sing,* Gershwin thought, the Broadway show had completed its journey from vaudeville spectacle through burlesque revue to full-blown theatrical satire, in which characters expressed their emotions, however ludicrous, in song and dance.

He had accomplished all he could within the show-business medium. His next step had to launch him beyond Broadway, beyond comedy. *Porgy* was commandeering his attention as well as Kay's.

Music now poured out of him in melodies and countermelodies that vied and tumbled, dissolved and reemerged like currents in a braided brook: racing xylophones and strings against a drawn-out two-note trumpet blast, swells and breaking waves of choral emotion, a vocal duet that started, stopped, and moved up and down like elevators sliding independently in side-by-side shafts. Kay notated his musical ideas, helping to organize them and suggesting ways to develop and interweave them.

The concepts themselves — the melodies, harmonies, and rhythms — were George's, not because Kay's melodic imagination was failing but because she avoided violating his boundaries. Since the age of fifteen George had devoted every jot of his time and energy to two projects, writing brilliant music and gaining recognition as the greatest living American composer. Although not born into the appropriate socio-economic class, although his parents had never heard of a conservatory education, he had always felt certain of his destiny.

Unlike George, Kay had never aspired to be *the greatest* anything. She only wanted to be the best pianist and composer she could be, and to live up to the expectations of those who encouraged her. It was not about superiority; it was about striving.

Midway through adolescence, George told Kay, he awoke from a dream. He had been standing on the top deck of a skyscraper watching automobiles, horses with buggies, and people running, skating, and jostling each other from narrow streets into a boulevard. In their midst, parades, strains of music. The airs of Mozart, Beethoven, and Wagner but also John Philip Sousa, Stephen Foster, Scott Joplin, the Negro folk singer, the choirs of Southern Baptist churches, klezmer and cantorial chanting. All flowing together into this magnificent celebration in the wide avenue. "Like Bach's

Mass in B-Minor in a thousand keys at once, mixed with African drumming and honking horns and thunder," he told her. "But you know what the feeling was, when I woke up?"

"Elation?" tried Kay. "Exhilaration?"

He shook his head. "Loneliness. Sadness. Like a taste of . . ."

"Of what?"

"Of my future, Kay."

"That future — your present — is hardly sad, George."

He shook his head. "Everyone wants to be loved. You want to be loved by as many folks as possible. But as that circle grows, the love . . ." His eyes wandered to the top of the wall, searching for words. "It loses its depth. Until it's flat as a shadow. And you realize you're all alone."

He said it with such gravity and finality, she shivered inside. She nestled her head in the crook of his neck. "You're not alone, George."

He looked at her as if emerging from that dream and caressed her cheek. She had joined him up there, at the top of the RCA tower. The thrill of the view was their reward. But for some reason she could not fathom, a dark fog was creeping over him. It took the form of loneliness and incapacitating headaches but its source was a mystery. She held him tightly as they lay in silence in the quiet night.

With George back in New York, he and Kay wanted to dedicate every moment and every ounce of their energy to *Porgy*. Still, he needed to attend to contractual work. He had promised Max Dreyfus a definitive compilation of his best songs, written out as he composed them prior to Ira's addition of lyrics: as solo piano pieces. It would be called *The George Gershwin Songbook* and again his purpose would be to blur the boundaries between so-called serious music and popular music. Instead of simplifying his pieces for the amateur pianist, he would capture on paper the flourishes and harmonic inventiveness he injected into them when he performed. Kay aided him, and he dedicated *The George Gershwin Songbook* to her. Not just out of gratitude, as he told her, but to shout to the world that she was the woman of his life.

If that's the best you can do, George, thought Kay, *I'll take it.*

Their lives were so intermeshed at this point, Kay did not know exactly where hers began or his ended. He depended upon her in so many ways, and she loved feeling indispensable. Perhaps, as Zilboorg insisted, this was not healthy, but her songwriting collaboration with Jimmy had apparently fallen apart and for the moment, George's grand projects had stolen all her attention.

The ballet for George Balanchine still seemed a distant hope, with little substance, although George insisted it was real. Lincoln Kirstein was searching for funding, and with the name Ballets Russes attached, he would most certainly find it. Kay began thinking about dance melodies and harmonies. George freely offered advice.

Other than contractual work, the main impediment to their productivity was his debilitating, unpredictable headaches. All Kay could do, when they struck, was to lie with him, reading a novel but feeling helpless and frightened.

In the hope of finding a solution, George finally agreed to meet with Doctor Zilboorg. Kay was not privy to their sessions but George told her that the idea of examining parts of his mind that were normally shut off to inspection fascinated him.

He had never grown up, he learned. This explained why he still lived with his family and his inability to commit to an adult relationship with a woman. The piano was his sandbox.

Kay threw her arms around his shoulders and searched his eyes. "That's a pretty nice sandbox. Far as I'm concerned, you can stay a kid forever. Except the commitment part, of course."

"We're working on that," George assured her.

Doctor Zilboorg insisted that George find a new home, to separate from his family. George objected that he needed Ira nearby since they worked together. "Fine," agreed Doctor Zilboorg. "Ira can be nearby. But leave your parents where they are."

Kay offered to find and decorate George's new accommodations. George had no time to spare and having grown up in the home of an apartment décor specialist, Kay savored the opportunity to channel her mother's creative spirit.

Lilly, Jimmy's secretary — whose brother dealt in real estate — helped Kay locate two penthouse duplexes at 33 Riverside Drive, one for Ira and one for George. Kay clothed George's in gray, black, silver, beige, and jade green, with Japanese-mat flooring and rice-paper partitions. She lined the walls with paintings by Picasso, Modigliani, Utrillo, Soutine, and Rouault, which George had bought in Paris, as well as two of George's paintings, one of his grandfather

444

and one of a graceful African woman.

While all this was going on, Kay too continued meeting with Doctor Zilboorg, probing the other side of the man-child issue. Why had she become involved with Jimmy Warburg in the first place, a man who considered himself, like a child, entitled to privileges far beyond the reach of other mortals? Why, later, was she so drawn to George Gershwin, who could be described in precisely the same way? Did she not detect a pattern?

It all originated in her childhood involvement with her father, Doctor Zilboorg insisted. They discussed Kay's recurring dream about the little girl in bows and ribbons playing the piano for workers in Sam's factory and slowly losing control of the music. This dream seemed as vivid as a memory and yet she was certain of its unreality.

"This fantasy is key," said Zilboorg. "This is why your psyche repeats it to you. Who was your father putting on display for his workers? Was it you, really? Or was it that little girl in bows, that master of the keyboard, that he wanted you to be? When did Sam abandon you? At his death or long before? Somewhere deep inside, you know the answer."

Perhaps she did know the answer, Kay reflected. Perhaps she feared it. If she had been living out Sam's dream her entire life, rather than her own, did that not make her life itself an illusion? Had Jimmy married a fantasy? And if so, what did that imply about her future?

If Jimmy had married a fantasy, he no longer really cared. He had plenty of hard reality to deal with. Since the death of his father, Paul, at the end of January 1932 — and without quite realizing it at first — he had become the most respected and powerful man in his family's financial empire. When voters in the United States, yearning for a path out of Depression, elected Jimmy's former boss in the navy, Franklin Delano Roosevelt, to the presidency, the new commander in chief offered Jimmy the position of undersecretary of the treasury. Jimmy declined but agreed to advise FDR on financial matters without title or compensation. He knew that his perspective on the banking system and on political developments in Europe was unique and he was eager to serve his adopted country without getting mired in the rough-and-tumble quid-pro-quo of politics and potential conflicts of interest.

FDR accepted Jimmy's terms, no money and no title, but insisted he relocate to Washington. He phoned Kay at George's flat to relay the news. "Why, that's marvelous," she told him. "A once-in-a-lifetime opportunity."

"I just don't know," said Jimmy.

"How can you think twice?"

"I'm married. I have children."

"Washington?" scoffed Kay. "A stone's throw."

They hung up without resolving the matter.

Three weeks later, Jimmy informed her by mail that he had taken up residence at the Carlton Hotel in Washington. He huddled daily in the Oval Office with FDR and his secretary of the treasury, Henry Morgenthau.

What he did not discuss in the letter was his love life. But Kay knew he would not remain alone for long. She played a major-dominant-seventh chord on the piano, followed by a tonic chord, signifying finality, perhaps the conclusion of the second movement of a sonata. "Well, that's that," she told George.

Standing behind her, George massaged the base of her neck.

"Mmm," she said, closing her eyes.

She flattened the middle note of the tonic chord, implying a key change. Perhaps there was a third movement to come, after all.

CHAPTER THIRTY-TWO

Summer 1934

George was digging clams with DuBose
Heyward on an island near Charleston in
South Carolina and attending Sunday
morning services in little churches. He
wrote to Kay about the spirited hymns, the
hand-clapped rhythms, and his fascination
with the Gullah people. He had also uncov-
ered a gift for building sand castles. "You
should see them," he wrote. "The towers,
the tunnels, the spiral stairs. If they had a
Pulitzer for sand castles, I'd have a shot at
it. Of course while I'm pushing mud around
I'm wrestling with *Porgy* in my head. Then
a big wave sweeps in and flattens it, which
makes it all the more precious."

George maintained that mental precom-
position was always beneficial. Like the
wave washing away the sand castle, leaving
behind a memory of its shape, the mind
rinsed away the inessential. All one remem-

bered of the precomposed piece was its essence, which was the best place to start. Thus, he had worked out the *Rhapsody in Blue* on a train from Boston to New York, and many songs while lying in bed.

At the Russian Tea Room in New York, Kay met for drinks with the ballet producer Lincoln Kirstein, the choreographer George Balanchine, and the young Harvard graduate who, Kirstein announced, was not only financing the project but writing the story: Eddie Warburg.

Eddie was Jimmy's cousin, a literature major just out of Harvard. Kay glanced at him. Eddie looked boyish, scrubbed, and eager, in a bow tie and a tight-waisted wool jacket. She realized Kirstein had used her name to acquire funding, just as he had used Balanchine's name in his effort to acquire Gershwin. Her world was starting to seem claustrophobic and incestuous — George Gershwin working with George Kaufman; Jimmy, George, and Kay all venting their misgivings and fantasies to the same psychoanalyst; and now, Jimmy's cousin financing and writing the book for her ballet.

I hope Eddie understands this opportunity, she thought. *What we're talking about is the possibility of creating a new style of ballet.*

American ballet. What Sherwood Anderson and Scott Fitzgerald had accomplished for the novel, what Gershwin was achieving for the concerto and opera, Eddie and Kay might realize for dance.

The Ballets Russes début of Stravinsky's *Rite of Spring* had marked a cultural inflection in Paris. That performance, in which a sacrificial virgin pirouetted and cabrioled herself to death, signaled the end of an age, the era of European dominance. That girl, expiring in splendor and exhaustion, was nineteenth-century, colonial Europe itself.

She wondered whether Eddie was up to the task. He possessed little experience writing for the stage, let alone for a ballet. But he was young, and supreme self-confidence is the privilege of those who have not yet learned better — as well as those, like George Gershwin, who are congenitally incapable of learning better. Eddie's easy smile conveyed enthusiasm; his banter, intelligence. Perhaps he possessed more depth than he cared to put on display.

George Balanchine, born Giorgi Balanchivadze, commanded attention. Tall, blonde, tailored, he balanced a cigarette holder at the ends of his delicate fingers, exhaling round puffs. His Ballets Russes were all the rage in Paris and though Russian by birth, he spoke English with a cultivated French accent. In America, he longed to direct a ballet that would be deemed quintessentially American. "Otherwise, what is the purpose? Why cross the ocean, to repeat what I have done?"

He visualized movement in fluid, orchestrated motions and sought the simplest story that could be told. "Let us begin with an image," he suggested. "Something no one would think of when they think of ballet." The original conception of *The Rite of Spring,* he recalled, began with the image of a primitive ritual — failing to mention that he had not yet become involved with the Ballets Russes at that time.

Eddie, Lincoln, and Kay brainstormed. They talked of vehicles — automobiles, trains, airplanes. But how to write a ballet about airplanes? They thought of the crowds on Fifth Avenue and Times Square. Kay suggested department store shoppers at Lord & Taylor or Saks Fifth Avenue. Balanchine appreciated this idea. They could construct a multilevel set, with moving stairs that would provide gasp-worthy opportunities for leaps and pirouettes.

"The only problem," observed Balanchine, "but it is a serious problem, I am afraid: we have such stores in Paris. Les Galeries Lafayette, La Samaritaine, le Bon Marché . . . No, no, this will not do. This is not enough uniquely American."

Eddy hit upon the idea of the Yale-Harvard football game. "Lots of movement," he said. "Not random but fluid and orchestrated, like you said. And a major event in American culture. One that everyone pays attention to. An absurdity, but an important absurdity. As American as mashed cranberries."

Everyone pays attention to the Yale-Harvard game? reflected Kay. *Maybe in your world, kid.* Nevertheless the idea of a football ballet was refreshingly counterintuitive, humorous in a way. An opportunity to poke fun at elite self-absorption.

Balanchine leaned over the table. "Please, tell me more about this."

Kay was already composing in her head. A resolutely modern score. A footballer leaping for the pigskin in slow motion and twisting to snatch it out of the air to the accompaniment of harps and celeste. A victory parade, the raucous, dissonant squawks and thumps of competing bands. She thought of interlacing college songs from Yale and Harvard into the score the way George had inserted American anthems into *Of Thee I Sing.*

"Kay?" she heard Kirstein repeat.

"Oh — yes."

"Can you work with this material?"

"I think so."

Returning to her apartment, she threw off her heels and ran to the piano barefoot. *Alma Mater* would not resonate with sadness and history like *Porgy*. But musically Kay would stretch far beyond *Fine and Dandy*. With George Balanchine at the helm one could expect originality and spectacle. Absurdly, the mere fact that she would be partnering with him placed her in a small, elite circle that included Igor Stravinsky and Sergei Prokofiev. In their fondest dreams, neither she nor her father had envisaged such a possibility.

Of course, Doctor Zilboorg had instructed her not to confuse her father's dreams with her own. *Well, it's too late for that, isn't it,* Kay told herself.

George was still in South Carolina when the package from Lincoln Kirstein reached Kay. Eddie Warburg had finished the story for *Alma Mater*. She sank into a leather armchair in her salon and read it. Eddie described a series of athletic and social scenes involving the Yale team, the Harvard team, their champion athletes, those athletes' girlfriends, and their rivalries, casting the Harvard quarterback as the hero and the Yale football star as the villain. The culture of Harvard was portrayed as all-American, strong, and conscientious, while Yale was populated with pampered, spoiled dolts. It was as tongue-in-cheek as it was sophomoric. Since they had decided the ballet would open in Hartford, halfway between the two colleges, Kay feared a backlash from music critics who were Yale graduates.

Balanchine's role ensured the project would receive attention. Splendid music and superlative dancing would offset any narrative affront. Lacking dialogue, ballet remained the ideal medium for a composer eager to demonstrate her prowess.

In short, she told herself, despite its potential shortcomings *Alma Mater* represented a breakout opportunity, the spring storm that would germinate the seed of the rest of her life. Kay would provide a dazzling score, entertaining, original, and quirky.

Yet she could not escape the nagging fear that the occasion might be squandered. Something did not feel quite right. She wondered whether she was not living out that recurring dream: given the occasion to display her musical brilliance and allowing the music to guide her, she might see the opportunity ignite and explode. She doubled down on her work, interrupting it only for piano lessons with her children, an occasional stroll in the park, or a Broadway show.

At the end of George's five-week adventure in South Carolina she met him under the clock at Grand Central Station. He looked ridiculous in white cotton trousers cut off above the knees, an untucked short-sleeve shirt, sandals, and a straw hat.

"No bags?"

"Paul threw everything in the Studebaker."

She hugged him.

"Zowie, that was another planet," he raved as they walked toward the exit hand in hand. "The cabins on the beach, the spiritual hymns, the people who'd rather give you the food off their plate than let you miss the fun. I fell hard for 'em, Kay. And of course they fell for me, too."

"Well, now you're back," she told him, lighting a cigarette. "And we'd better get you showered and into decent clothes or people will take you for a vagabond."

"If vagabond means wanderer, they'd be right!" They walked out to East Forty-

Second Street. "Let's grab a New York Sundae."

"You're not a wanderer, George," said Kay as they proceeded down the sidewalk. "Sure, you've spent time in London, Paris, Los Angeles, and Charleston. But you always come home, don't you."

"Speaking of Los Angeles," said George, "another offer came in. Two more movies. Fred and Ginger, can you believe it?"

She stopped, exhaled a puff of smoke, and looked at him. "You've already done that," said Kay. "You already got your DC-2 thrills, didn't you?"

He looked past her at a tin can blowing in the gutter. "This isn't a pair of wings, Kay. This is a tin can rolling down the road."

She shook her head sadly. "Whatever you say, George." She threw her cigarette to the ground and snuffed it with her heel.

"Anyway," George offered in a conciliatory tone, "it won't be tomorrow, if it happens. Maybe a year. Maybe two. Maybe never. Let's not think about it."

"Deal," said Kay.

He opened the door of Molly's Sweets & Sundries. Kay went in, anticipating a moment of sweetness and laughter.

CHAPTER THIRTY-THREE

December 1934

A Christmas tree now stood in Doctor Zilboorg's office, and in the spirit of the holiday he offered Kay an eggnog. "Rum, brandy, or bourbon," he asked.

"Brandy," said Kay with a laugh. She was surprised that a psychoanalyst would stock such libations, and said so.

"Libations?" he chuckled. "On the contrary, it is of utmost importance that you shed your inhibitions, your defense mechanisms. If alcohol helps, well . . ." He completed his sentence with a whirl of his hand. His mood seemed buoyant, perhaps an effect of the season. After handing her the drink he sank back into his easy chair, sipping. "Let's start where we left off, shall we?" He looked over his notes. "The important thing is to dissociate yourself, at least in this room, from both George and Jimmy."

"But I love George."

"There is nothing wrong with love. But let us try to dismantle whatever is weak in the scaffolding of your emotions. We are seeking the solid underlying foundation. You must avoid a repeat of your failed marriage. You will agree with that, I hope."

She tasted her eggnog, which was stronger than expected, with a bitter aftertaste. "That all sounds perfectly reasonable, Doctor Zilboorg, in theory. And every piece of music looks beautiful on paper. It's when the fingers hit the keys that the trouble starts."

He sipped his own drink, nodding. "No one claimed this work was easy. One has to tease apart the role of the libido, driven by the id, and the desire for self-aggrandizement, driven by the ego."

At his instigation they rowed their canoe toward the deepest part of the psychodynamic lake, where she peered into the water beyond her reflection. The forms that writhed in the depths aroused and frightened her. Nor was Doctor Zilboorg interested only in the "oneiric" portion of this activity — by which he meant, the dreamlike images that filtered through her consciousness. He asked which fantasies stimulated her most. "Feel free to close your eyes . . . Even to caress your thighs, if necessary, while visualizing."

To relax her defenses, he plied her with more eggnog. Kay hesitated, confused. Her mind raced as she tried to understand. The drink was causing her head to spin. What kind of brandy did this fellow use? A part of her felt flattered that Zilboorg was growing more relaxed with her. In addition to the patient-doctor relationship, perhaps a friendship was cracking out of the psychic egg. After all, Zilboorg knew her more intimately than almost anyone.

Even so, another part of her felt uneasy. She sipped again, listening to him drone on about the id and the ego. "These are the two dominant forces that power the emotion we call love."

Kay viewed herself as a modern woman, free of her ancestors' squeamishness. She questioned her discomfort. Zilboorg was trying to help. True, the idea of discussing her sexual fantasies with a slovenly, mustachioed Ukrainian in a tweed jacket and yellow shirt did not hold much appeal. But this specialist's reputation was sterling. She drained her glass and he refilled it.

She had never devoted much thought to her sexual fantasies. Nor had she broached the subject with anyone. She had hidden them even from herself. Now she confronted those secrets. Mysteries that had tainted her feelings about Jimmy since their first encounter, and earlier. What she had mistaken for a jigsaw of libertinism, jealousy, revenge, half-hearted reconciliation, and resignation revealed itself to be more complex and nuanced. She entertained the possibility that Jimmy's infidelities had not stemmed from a blend of egotism and sensuality but had been an unconscious response to something he had perceived in her, or a reaction to the emotional satisfaction that had eluded them. She had always thought him handsome and clever but despite his wooing and her best intentions, she had never truly desired him. Somehow he knew. Paradoxically her sexual distance, however much she had tried to compensate, kept her interesting and desirable to him, a perpetual conquest-to-be-achieved, an *unerfüllter Wunsch* as Freud might put it, rather than an acquired possession, *ein Besitz.*

For the first time in years she pitied her husband. Not usually given to tears, she broke down weeping in Doctor Zilboorg's office.

Kay learned that her libido, which should fly unfettered, had been trapped like an insect in amber. Doctor Zilboorg asked her to participate in an exercise that would liberate it. After her imagination and sensuality were freed, if she was still attracted to George Gershwin, she would discover that her love was purer and larger than she had suspected.

"Exercise?"

He smiled. "You need to set aside your defenses now. For this next step to be effective, you must trust me entirely. Your therapy has proved helpful so far, has it not? And yet, we have traveled only a short distance together."

He stood, pulled off his jacket, threw his tie over a chair, and unbuttoned his shirt. She watched him, confused. *He is accredited. Acclaimed. He has written books and addressed the American Society of Psychoanalysts. Other patients, including Jimmy and George, sing his praises.* "Any residue of Puritanism is pernicious," he explained, "and must be eliminated."

Distressed, she averted her eyes from his belly and the black curlicues on his chest and groin as he stepped closer. He forcefully guided her to the divan. She tried to squirm out of his hold. He pinned her on the sofa and lifted her dress. *This cannot be happening.* She heard a cry, the shriek of an injured bird. It burst out from a deep inner place and flew from her mouth. He shoved

462

and grunted. She had lost control of her arms and legs. She lay in his hands like a rag doll, passive and numb.

Then something broke inside her. She pushed away his torso, slapped his adipose shoulder once, twice, three times, and somehow recovered her voice. She screamed. He jumped off. She pulled up her panties, pulled down her skirt, grabbed her handbag and heels, and buzzed out low like a soiled, greasy horsefly burdened with fecal repast.

"Wait," Zilboorg called after her. "Let us talk this through."

Not a chance. Kay winged home barefoot and disheveled, bumping into passersby, dashing between cars. A honk here, an angry "lady, watch out!" there. Buildings around her seemed to waver, bow, and undulate. That damned eggnog! She had never before felt so disoriented, so vulnerable. Nor had she ever reacted to alcohol this way. And God knew she had imbibed quite a few exotic concoctions at wild parties.

Finally she turned the corner to her street. Did her building just move? Whatever had happened, now she was inside. She ran upstairs two steps at a time.

She plunged into a hot bath. She scrubbed

her arms, her breasts, her belly, her face, everything Zilboorg had touched. When the water cooled she stepped out and sprayed perfume all over herself but she could still smell him. She still felt his grasping hands. She closed her eyes and sat on the edge of the tub to exhale.

She stayed home for days, burying her head in her pillow, wandering downstairs only for booze, tea, or toast, trying to make sense of the Zilboorg nightmare, trying to put it behind her. She asked herself over and over what, precisely, had happened. How to define the event. It could not have been rape since she had acted as a willing partner, to a point. Nevertheless, she felt violated. She relived the repulsion, the powerlessness, the inability to act. She did not tell a soul. Who would believe her? Who would understand?

Doctor Zilboorg neither phoned to apologize nor attempted to confirm previously set appointments. He surely understood that he had alienated a patient and jettisoned any hope of future work with anyone related to her. And to think he cloaked himself, and his behavior, in the holy mantle of science and rationality. Just like the Nazis, with their shoddy *scientific race studies.*

She slept. She dreamed dark dreams. She came to think about her older dreams — the one about being lost in a train station, or about boarding a ship to nowhere — in a pre-psychoanalytical way, not as a message from her id but as a warning about the shape of her life. The forces of chaos, abstraction, and atonality warping a universe ordered by principles of classical harmony.

Months of psychoanalytic probing, capped with the trauma she had experienced at Doctor Zilboorg's hands, had left her rattled, drained, and isolated. She considered inviting Dottie Parker for lunch but while her friend might empathize, depending on her mood, how could anyone as chronically lovesick and notoriously libidinous as Dottie be capable of offering sound advice? She thought of meeting with Adele Astaire, even if it meant sailing to England. But Adele, in her zeal to help, would probably drag her into some frivolous adventure, and Kay was in no mood for trivialities.

She put a phone call in to St. Ignatius of Antioch. The receptionist, a weary-sounding lady with a Bronx accent, seemed not to recognize the Swift family name. She informed Kay that Father Ganter had retired three years earlier and asked whether she

465

would like to consult with the new reverend.

"No, no, that's perfectly fine," said Kay. "Thank you."

"Are you sure? He's a very nice man."

"No, thank you."

A knock at her bedroom door. She ignored it. Another knock, insistent. She reached for her father's pocket watch on the nightstand and accidentally brushed it to the floor.

Another knock. "Yes?"

It was George.

He noticed her disheveled appearance: her uncombed hair; the fact that she was lying in bed after noon, staring at the ceiling; her tired eyes. He sat on the bed, took her hand, and apologized as if he were responsible for her condition. "I know. I'm a louse. I should have called you. It's these headaches. They've been beating me up. I need to see Zilboorg again, and soon."

She studied his face. Finally she began, "I have something to tell you."

He waited for more but she hesitated. How could she explain this? How would George react? Would he assume she had encouraged Zilboorg? That she had not fought hard enough to stop him? Would he lose confidence in her? In a deliberate, uninflected tone, avoiding his eyes, she described her ordeal. All of it. She still was not sure how to label the event but whatever it was, she remembered every detail. She had relived it every day. When she brushed her teeth. When she ate. When she went to bed. First thing in the morning. She tried to avoid it but it stalked her, a memory that spattered sadness and shame everywhere.

He listened. He studied her face as she spoke. His response was unequivocal. His voice, emphatic. "The animal raped you, Kay. That's what it was. A rape." His voice softened "I'm so sorry."

For the first time since her ordeal, she let her sobs overtake her. He wiped her tears, kissed her wet cheeks, and caressed her head. He embraced her, tightening his grip long after her tears dissolved.

"Kay," said George after a time, as if remembering a business commitment, "you mind if I use your phone for a transatlantic call?"

Although transatlantic calls were a new phenomenon, and costly, she shook her head. George dialed the international operator. "I'd like to place an overseas call. The Ritz Hotel in Paris."

"What's this about?" asked Kay.

He shook his head. "Jimmy Walker, please," he said into the phone. Covering the mouthpiece, he told Kay, "Would you mind fetching me a cup of tea?"

Mystified, she went downstairs to the kitchen.

Jimmy Walker was no longer mayor of New York, having resigned in a haze of scandal. Rumor had it he was living in Paris with a Ziegfeld girl. But everyone knew he was still one of the most well-connected, powerful men in America.

When she brought George the tea, he was finishing up the phone call. "Thank you, Jimmy. Knew I could count on you."

"What was that about?" she asked after he hung up.

"Just some business," said George. "Let's grab lunch."

Three days later Kay noticed a small article in the *New York World-Telegram.* Doctor Gregory Zilboorg, the noted psychoanalyst, had tripped in a freak accident in his office, injuring himself badly, bleeding from his head, and losing consciousness. No one understood what had happened. His secretary had stepped out on lunch break. A neighbor had seen a male patient enter the building but was uncertain of the time. Zilboorg was discovered alone and was recovering in Lenox Hill Hospital. He was expected to survive. "Gruesome," Kay winced, handing the paper to George.

George perused the article. "Serves the bastard right."

Kay understood George would not consult Doctor Zilboorg again. Which dashed his hopes of finding a remedy for his migraines. Which darkened his mood further. She tried to reassure him. "There are other noggin twisters."

He shook his head, despondent. She wrapped her arms around his neck, bracing herself yet again for the unknown.

CHAPTER THIRTY-FOUR

They spent the following weeks in her flat and his, working in tandem and independently back-to-back at two pianos or together at one, drawing energy or at least solace from each other. Kay also composed while George painted. He had set up an easel and was blocking out a study of *Kay at the Piano* in somber, muted tones.

Three times per week Kay instructed her daughters, separately, at the piano. Thursdays were the most difficult. They were reserved for April, her eldest at fifteen, who made no effort to hide her lack of enthusiasm. "I can't stand the piano and I despise you!" she shouted through her closed door.

Kay tried to reason with her. "I understand why you would feel that way but I can't help being who I am, my love. I wish I could but I wasn't given that choice."

"Go away!"

"If you don't want to play piano," offered

Kay, "what *do* you want?"

"I want to live in Washington with my father."

Kay went into the salon, pulled out a chair, and stared at the window.

"Anything I can help you with, ma'am?" asked Lionel.

Kay shook her head.

Lionel was about to exit the room when the telephone rang. "Warburg residence. Yes, of course, Mister Warburg." He walked the phone to Kay. "Mister Warburg, ma'am."

James was calling from Washington. "Just checking in. How are my girls?"

They discussed their daughters' report cards. Andrea and Kathleen were progressing but April was stumbling. "Nothing I do works. I offered to take her to a play, to a museum. She wants to live with you."

"I know," said James. "How would you feel about that?"

"Demoralized," said Kay.

A pause on the line.

"And *Alma Mater*? Coming along?"

"I've been working hard on it. One moment, it's a masterpiece. The next, it's garbage."

"Maybe you should consider taking a break," suggested Jimmy.

"I'm afraid I'm already broken."

"Nonsense. Not you, Kay," said Jimmy. "You are indomitable. Let's just step back. Every river finds its sea."

"Whatever that means," said Kay.

"That's the Bible," said Jimmy.

Jimmy, quoting the Bible? "Thanks for calling." She hung up.

A week later, a police officer escorted April home from Central Park. "So sorry to barge in like this, Misses Warburg." Officer McGinty towered over April in the doorway — a made-up April, with thinned, arched eyebrows, mascara, and scarlet lipstick. The officer was clutching her shoulders. "The young lady here was smoking with a good-for-nothing scoundrel in the park and, I'll spare you the details, but I didn't want to risk any harmful prattling in the precinct of your good name, Misses Warburg, so I asked if I could accompany her home, and she graciously obliged."

"I did no such thing. Let go of me, you brute!" April wriggled out of his grasp.

Kay sighed. "Thank you, officer."

The door closed. Kay's tone changed. "Sit down." April mechanically complied. "Cigarettes." Kay sat across from her. "With a boy."

"As if you cared," said April.

"Pretty exciting, huh? Especially at fifteen."

"Don't you insult me, mother."

"Who's the boy?"

April crossed her arms, her lips tightening.

Kay leaned forward. "I don't give a damn who he is. You'll be far away from him soon."

April raised her eyes to meet her mother's. "You want to live with your father in Washington?" asked Kay. "You have my blessing. I'm tired, April."

"Not too tired for your parties. For your shows. For George."

Kay slapped her. Stunned, April brought a hand to her cheek, blinking. Tears pooled in her eyes, but she stared at her mother without flinching. Kay collapsed into her chair. "It's no use. We're done."

"Your marriage?" April asked.

"Who am I fooling?" Kay asked.

April shook her head, her eyes gleaming. "You are so selfish."

Kay closed her eyes. April was right. She was selfish. The price of passion and ambition. Kay thought, *it's not April's fault that she was born into a family that could not provide for her emotional needs, that she was not given parents who loved each other the*

473

way parents were supposed to — parents who were involved with their children before all else, as my parents were. She leaned forward and hugged her daughter. April felt so young, so slight, so tense, so lost. Kay tightened her grip and rubbed her daughter's back. April stiffened and freed herself.

Relaxing back into her seat Kay said, "I'm so sorry, April, that things have turned out this way."

"The hell you are."

"I wish I could be with you through the coming years. I know you'll visit me after things calm down."

"In your dreams."

"I hope one day you'll understand."

"I wouldn't count on that." April rose and ran to her bedroom, slamming the door.

Kay had filled *Alma Mater* with a modernism reminiscent in places of Ravel and in others of Stravinsky, as well as jazzy interludes and the blend of exuberance and irony that George Gershwin, Jimmy Warburg, and some members of the public were starting to identify as her signature style. She played the score three more times for George, improving it with each run-through, and declared it complete even though she could not quite dispel every nagging doubt. She

474

picked up the pile of papers from her piano and wrapped them into a package. "Could it be further improved? Maybe it could! Where do you draw the line?"

"Don't apologize for your work," George advised her.

"Who's apologizing? I'm just saying, I'm sorry. I'm sorry it can't be better." She unrolled several inches of a new sticky-ribbon product called Scotch Tape — "Isn't this stuff marvelous?" — and sealed the package.

"Hold your manuscript in your arms," George ordered her. "That's your baby. You're giving it up for adoption to the ballet. Hug the little sucker while you can." And with a wink he started playing a song he had composed for the opening of *Porgy.* Kay sang DuBose Heyward's lyrics:

Summertime and the living is easy.
Fish are jumping and the cotton is
high . . .

Kay kissed her manuscript and rocked it while George played. As the last chime-like notes hung in the air, he turned to her beaming.

"George," said Kay, "I'm going to get a divorce."

His smile fell away. "Jimmy okay with that?"

She sat down. "He knows it's inevitable. It's not like either of us wanted things to turn out this way. It just happened." Olga approached with a handkerchief. Kay dabbed her eyes. "I'm going to Reno," she said. "And then . . ."

"And then?" asked George.

"And then," she took his hand, "you're going to marry me."

He looked at her as if unsure what to say.

"We're practically living together, George. We work together. We play together."

"Then why let a rubber stamp wreck it? It's meaningless."

"Not to me."

He nodded.

"It's because your mother despises me, isn't it. Because I'm not Jewish."

"That could be fixed."

"You want me to convert, George?" And off his silence: "Why? It's not like you believe any of it."

George shook his head. "That's not what I'm saying."

"Do you even know what you want?" Kay challenged him.

He looked at her for a pensive moment,

476

and then offered her his beautiful, radiant smile.

CHAPTER THIRTY-FIVE

The way Jimmy did it. Could she ever forgive him? He came home one afternoon. He entered with his key. Well, the apartment was his.

Kay was in her dressing room selecting a hat, pearls, and white gloves for an evening at the opera. Puccini. A too-familiar tearjerker, but always entertaining. Hearing bustling, she stepped downstairs in her high heels.

He was dressed more casually than usual for a Wednesday in a camel-cashmere V-neck and houndstooth-weave wool slacks, with brown oxford shoes. The attire of a successful man, comfortable with himself, nothing left to prove.

"Jimmy!"

He noticed the pearls, the white gloves, the close-fitting dress, and smiled. "Lovely as always, Kay. I'm here to collect my girls."

"To *collect* . . . ? Right now? For what?"

He glanced at his wristwatch. The same wristwatch he wore at the Garden Pavilion of the Century Theatre so many years ago, when he proposed to her. "They should be packed by now. Olga and Lionel will accompany us, of course."

"Oh," said Kay, realizing. "April."

"All three," Jimmy corrected her.

Kay frowned. "All three? Do they —"

He nodded. "They didn't tell you?"

She slumped into a chair. "They didn't. You didn't."

"I'm sorry," said Jimmy.

He proceeded down the hall toward the girls' quarters. Kay tried to compose herself. Finally she rose, walked across the room, and dialed the phone. "Dottie. Kay. Listen, I won't make it to the opera. Invite whoever you want. The tickets are at Will Call. I'll explain later."

Jimmy reappeared flanked by Olga, Lionel, several trunks and suitcases — and Andrea, Kathleen, and April, all in their henceforth superfluous school uniforms. Olga stared at her feet. Lionel scrutinized the chandelier.

"This is what you want, honey?" asked Kay kneeling before Andrea.

Andrea nodded, tears streaming down her face.

Kathleen, in a lavender raincoat with a

matching broad-rimmed hat, hugged Kay's leg. "Goodbye, Mommy."

"It's not raining, darling." Kay stroked her hair.

"I know," said Kathleen.

An hour later, the girls — with Jimmy and Olga and Lionel and all their travel cases — were boarding the navy-blue first-class car of the Capital Limited in Penn Station. Kay stood on the platform trying not to weep.

Andrea pulled down the window of their cabin and reached out. "Goodbye, Mom."

Kay took her hand and kissed it.

The train hooted and began chugging.

Kay waved and blew a kiss. She watched the train leave and then watched the empty track as bells rang and whistles blew and people embarked and disembarked at other platforms. Finally turning to leave, she braced herself for an evening alone in her now-deserted home.

■ ■ ■ ■

PART THREE

■ ■ ■ ■

CHAPTER THIRTY-SIX

Every moral system must contain its antidote, otherwise it will consume itself and die. America — the screwed-down, practical, dominant strain of American civilization that had spawned Puritanism and Prohibition — held within its human apothecary two antidotes, an extreme one and a mild one.

The extreme antidote was gangland. Provocative stars like Mae West and George Raft had emerged from that basement jungle like fiends from America's id. But entertainment was only a side-business for the gangs. In the Park Central Hotel, unnamed assailants had gunned down crime boss Arnold Rothstein. At John's Restaurant on East Twelfth Street, at the behest of Genovese boss Giuseppe Masseria, a half-dozen gunmen had filled Umberto Valenti with lead. In the Hotel Claridge at Times Square the likes of Meyer Lansky, Lucky

Luciano, Bugsy Siegel, and Frank Costello ran a booze-and-cabaret outfit and helped engineer elections, including the one that had propelled FDR to the White House.

Kay chose the mild antidote. A resident of the Upper East Side who longed for liberation but contracted the heebie-jeebies at the sight of a bleeding corpse, and who might be willing to risk damage to her reputation but never to her body, headed not to gangland but to Grand Central Station, where she purchased a one-way ticket for the Capital of Sin. Reno, Nevada.

That divorce was sin, no one doubted. It was so reprehensible that it was unobtainable in the state of New York except in rare circumstances. If a man beat his wife daily, his behavior did not constitute grounds for legal disunion. If a couple lived apart and despised each other, they still did not qualify. The only exception was provable infidelity. *Provable* meant photographs or eyewitnesses. Even in those rare cases, the law imposed a one-year delay between the ruling and marital dissolution. In the meantime, both spouses' reputations withered. Especially, of course, the reputation of the one who was not the breadwinner.

In Reno, however, divorce was a red-hot industry. For those who could afford to travel and establish residency there, the wildest town of the West offered a greased escape from the shackles of marriage and motherhood, even from reputation. Among the wide range of acceptable pretexts: *impotence,* rarely demonstrable in court, and *mental cruelty,* a deliberately vague term. Proof was optional.

In the privacy of her Pullman roomette, Kay reflected on her seventeen years of wedlock. Marriage was supposed to bring joy, procreation, and fulfillment. But what did any woman at twenty understand about sexuality, its relation to human emotion, or parenting? At that age she had assumed that with all their charm, intelligence, and money, she and Jimmy would effortlessly surmount any obstacles. The idea that they would experience loneliness or sexual restlessness did not cross their minds. She reminisced on their dating, their verbal jousting, their sense of complicity. As for motherhood, the classifieds overflowed with nursemaids and nannies. In their milieu, everyone did it that way.

The train proved the best psychoanalyst. The rhythm of iron wheels *ba-bump*ing over track joints, the *clickety-clack* of car platforms banging against one another, the thud of footsteps in the corridors, and the opening and shutting of doors all contributed to a soporific rataplan that lulled her into contemplation and dreams. The train was speeding her not only from the metropolis but from every certainty and responsibility of matrimony. Her move was bold; it was rash; it felt inevitable; but she would miss certain milestones. That was the cost of freedom. She would not attend her daughter April's high school Christmas program. Alfred Knopf would be publishing *The Money Muddle*, a nonfiction follow-up to Jimmy's book of poetry that tried to explain the current crisis in international finance. Kay would miss the book launch party, probably much to Jimmy's relief.

Most momentous of all, *Alma Mater* would début without her. She opened the burled-walnut bar under the window, removed a bottle of Scotch, and poured herself a glass. She stood at the window sipping as Pennsylvania's forested hills and river gulches rushed by.

Beyond missed appointments, she would experience social sliding. Jimmy's bankers and investment managers would no longer recognize her. Who cared? She chanted Ira Gershwin's lyrics sotto voce to the wilderness:

My bonds and shares may fall
   downstairs.
Who cares? Who cares? I can't be
   bothered now.

Unlike George, Kay reflected, Ira viewed himself not as a creative whiz but as a craftsman. In his unassuming way, though, he was brilliant. During the last few years, Cole Porter had emerged as the most celebrated lyricist on Broadway. His songs "Let's Do It" and "Love For Sale" had stiffened, as it were, his reputation for urbane, risqué wit. In contrast, Ira never sought to call attention to the words. He wrote them rather to showcase George's music and its underlying emotions. It brought him joy when the audience applauded his brother. Ira Gershwin wanted none of that applause for himself. *What a dear, dear man.* She set down the tumbler, lay on the sofa, and gazed at the swaying crystal chandelier.

On the train one slept and woke at random moments. Time stretched and shrank. Memories and hopes rippled into one another, currents in the river of life. The landscape of America rolled past as the scenery of recollection flowed through one's mind. She could not remember a time when she had strayed this far from a piano for this long.

Who am I, without a piano? She picked up
Franz Kafka's novel, *The Trial,* which Jimmy
had recommended, having read it during
one of his transatlantic crossings. It occurred to her that the protagonist's sur-
name, K, sounded like the nickname Gershwin had assigned her. Like K, she was
caught up in a life-devouring process — in
her case a marriage, in his a trial — that
increasingly made no sense. The Twentieth
Century Limited rattled over the Mississippi River and into the great prairie, the
heartland of America. The air tasted fresh
and new.

*And then, just when you think you've found
your direction, life hurls a gust at you that
spins you around.* At the Reno station, a
reporter flashed a shot of Kay disembark-
ing. "Just a few questions, Misses Warburg.
Does this mean the end for you and James?
Is it true about you and George Gershwin?"

"Who are you?" she asked him as she
marched through the station. "What outfit?"

"*New York Times,* ma'am." The reporter
lifted his hat.

Kay spotted the horse and carriage of the
DB Guest Ranch and climbed up. "Let's
scram," she told the tan, weathered female
driver.

"Ho, ho, ho, gotta slow down, hon. You ain't in New York no more."

Seven miles outside Reno, the DB Guest Ranch, known locally as the DB Divorce Ranch, sprawled over twenty-three oak-studded acres. With a steep ravine, a corral, a swimming pool, and three stucco-and-wood houses that surrounded a brick court-yard with a fountain, the outrageously overpriced resort catered to eight socialites at a time, all female. The gimmick: no gimmicks. No facials, manicures, or mineral salt scrubs. No organized outings or campfire sing-alongs. Just the dry breeze that carried a sweet reek of horse manure and a month and a half of riding, reading, and rest.

State laws required that a woman seeking divorce reside in the area six weeks and pledge to remain. After thus proving her allegiance to the Silver State and obtaining the necessary papers, she was free to hop on the next train back to New York.

DB stood for Deb and Bill. These days, though, all that remained of Deb and Bill was Deb. Ironically, divorce had not caused their separation. Bill had perished consequent to a riding accident three years earlier, and to hear Deb tell the tale, none too soon, bless his heart.

Although Deb professed to be "only forty-two years young, honey," her ponytail was as silver as her cigarette ash, and even longer. She met guests at the station in a horse-drawn buggy, drove them to town and back, and oversaw the two Mexican laborers and three cowboys who cooked, fed and exercised the horses, and cleaned the stables.

The linens and flowered bedspread in Kay's room were clean. Worn copies of *The Virginian, David Copperfield,* and Douglas Fairbanks's *Laugh and Live* lined the bookshelves in the common room. The piano was not terribly out of tune. While Kay sauntered through Fauré's Ballade opus 19 or Debussy's "Rêverie," two or three guests lounged on the sofa and armchairs, chatting and thumbing through six-month-old copies of *Vogue* and *Vintage Antiques.* One of the cowboys, an athletic, tan man with deep-set gray eyes, who went by the unlikely moniker of Faye, leaned against the door sill.

"Yer somethin' else, ma'am," he said.

Kay turned and smiled. A couple of divorcees were watching him with appreciation. He did not seem to notice. *What a setup.* Eight women discontented with marriage, yearning for escape from their Beacon Hill or Streeterville penthouses, most likely deprived emotionally and sexually. Young, muscular ranch hands who probably agreed to sweep the stables for a pittance in exchange for a shot at erotic play. Kay shook her head, amused. She missed George.

But if Faye enjoyed impressionist piano music, or walking through the leafy gully talking about New York and show business, why not? As a sweetener, he knew how to manhandle an Arabian mare. He understood how to give her a workout until she was soaking. And he was always patient and encouraging.

Kay too rode hard these days. When they reached an open field she kicked her stallion into high gear. Her hair blowing, her horse huffing, she galloped as if Deb and Bill's were a competitive equestrian center rather than a leafy refuge. Faye slowed his horse, hand on hip, allowing her to overtake him.

"Where'd you learn to ride like that?" he asked after she looped around to trot back to the ranch beside him.

"You let me win, you scoundrel," she told him.

He laughed. "I didn't know we were racing, ma'am."

"Oh, come now, Faye."

He stayed for dinner. Kay sat at the far

end of the table, apart from the other women.

"Mind if I join you?"

Off her nod, Faye straddled the bench across from her. He topped off her glass with California burgundy. "Where'd you learn to make those keys sing like that, anyway?"

"New York. I've spent my entire life in New York."

The cowboy looked out the window. "You got oak trees in New York?"

"Some. I think. But not like here," she admitted.

"You got horses?"

"Not as many as when I was a kid, but yes."

"Rodeos?"

Kay savored a forkful of sweet pepper chili. "There you got me. I don't believe we have rodeos."

"Well that's a goddamn shame, you ask me," said Faye. "Ever been to a rodeo?"

"I'm afraid I haven't."

Faye took off his hat and placed it on the table. "What the piano is to you, that's what the rodeo is to me."

She gave this a moment's thought. "But what exactly *is* a rodeo?"

"It's where cowboys show what they're

made out of."

"You mean, their expertise?"

"I mean roping, jumping, steer wrestling, and my favorite, bareback bronc riding."

"What's a bronc?" asked Kay.

"It's a wild horse that ain't in the mood to have a man on its back an'll do just about anything to throw him off."

"I'd like to see that."

"Well you're in luck." He invited her to a rodeo where he would perform in two weeks. "I'll try to hold onto that bronco as good as you tinkle that piano."

"Say, play us some more Gershwin, will you Kay darling?" asked a freckle-faced beauty from Philadelphia. She treated them to parts of the *Rhapsody in Blue,* parts of *Alma Mater,* and other pieces she and George had written. The women talked. Faye listened.

After the other guests had retired to their rooms he resumed questioning Kay about New York, music, and show business. He seemed fascinated with the process of mounting a musical, the auditions, the ruthless revisions to script and songs, the impossibility of predicting an audience's response.

"That ain't what matters," said Faye.

"What matters?" asked Kay.

"It's that you wrote that score."

■ ■ ■ ■

The rodeo was, to put it mildly, an informal affair. Dressed in jodhpurs and white shirt she sat with other guests of the DB Guest Ranch in the first row of bleachers. Across from them, the corral fence, animal stalls, hitching posts, a parking area with automobiles and black ambulances, and the desert field.

Horses and bulls snorted in the pens. Men in loose pants with leather chaps, vests, neckerchiefs, and wide-brimmed hats herded a riderless horse into its stall. Once the corral was empty they opened a gate, releasing a calf that dashed as fast as its little stick-legs could propel it. Within seconds a cowboy raced up to it on his horse, waving a lasso, and flung the loop around its neck. The calf's momentum tightened the noose as the cowboy jumped off his horse, bounded over to it, wrestled it onto its back, and tied its feet all in a flash.

A second calf. A second cowboy. A failed roping. The rider hung his head in shame, his hat obscuring his face.

A third, successful but not as swift as the first. And a fourth, this calf larger than the others, which complicated the wrestling part. Kay saw it as ballet, a staccato dance to clopping hooves and drum-roll applause.

Following the roping exercises, the bucking bronc show began. This time, when the gate opened, a horse jumped out and proceeded to fling its rear and front ends alternately into the air kicking up dust, its tail leaping, its head bobbing. The cowboy held the reins with his right hand and waved his left arm for balance, flopping like a *Dean's Rag Book* doll shaken by a toddler, his head shooting backward and forward as if connected to his shoulders only by a string. Losing balance, the cowboy reached for the rein with his left hand before being thrown. He landed on his back and as he regained his feet, brushing the dirt off his chaps, Kay noticed a gash in his vest.

Three others herded the now-riderless horse into the pen. Another gate opened to reveal Faye, flopping on a second bucking bronc, his spurs dug into its neck, his body horizontal at times, at other times doubled over or flipping to the side. The horse lunged and danced. Faye flapped and snapped like a flag in a shifting wind. And then, *boom*! The bronc ejected him headfirst to the dirt. Kay caught her breath, shocked by the immediacy and drama of the moment. The horse quieted. Faye, the brave cowhand facedown in the dirt, struggled to raise himself. Other cattlemen rushed to him with a stretcher. Within minutes an ambulance was sirening him away. She felt his dismay and shame as if it were her own. His song — his audience-stirring belter, his impeccably rehearsed spectacle — had flopped.

She asked herself, what was it about performance that motivated people like her and Faye and George to test their dignity, to court heartbreak, to risk everything? Why could they not find contentment in the ordinary pursuits of the common mortal? In endeavors with predictable outcomes. Why were ordinary results — material comfort, social standing, happy children — not enough for such people? She grabbed her handbag and turned to Deb. "Let's go."

"What's the rush?"

"We're driving to the hospital."

Deb frowned. "You're askin' me to miss the whole thing?"

"I'm asking you to take me there. He works for you. Don't you care?"

Deb twisted her mouth in a knowing smile and touched her wrist. "Honey, don't fluff your wig for a hunky buckaroo. Swashbucklers like Faye? A dime a dozen 'round here."

Kay recognized the opening ploy of a

negotiation. She had already paid Deb plenty. "Drive me to the hospital, now."

It was a cottage at the edge of downtown Reno, beyond the zone where saloons yielded to bungalows, which in turn gave way to Jeffrey pines and rabbit brush. The emergency room housed five beds. In one, a drunk was rehydrating. Three were empty. Faye lay in the last, his feet sticking out past the end of the sheets, his sweaty hair plastered to his forehead. "Aw, this ain't nothin'. Just a coupla cracked ribs. Heck, I got twelve of 'em. How'd you like the show?"

"I hated the ending," said Kay.

"You didn't wait 'til the endin'," said Faye. "You walked out at intermission. You missed some of the best riders."

"Can you blame me for leaving?"

"Hell no. Just like any good show, it needs work."

Kay decided to return every afternoon. After all, she had nothing better to do at the DB Guest Ranch. Why not help nurse a poignant cowboy back to his natural bucking-bronc swagger? Then she reminded herself that all this, the horses, the bucolic charm of the ranch, the sense of freedom, represented nothing but a transitional passage in the rhapsody of her life. Nothing was to come of it except divorce papers.

When Faye was *all healed up* Kay and a couple of other soon-to-be-divorcées launched a party in his honor. Betty, a recent arrival, played an energizing jig on the fiddle; Kay accompanied her, and for once the cheap piano sounded just right. Everyone drank, told jokes, and danced, except the honoree. "Come on, you lazy gaucho, kick up those feet," Deb urged him, pulling him out of his chair. "You been lyin' on that mattress so long it's made a dreamer of ya."

The cowboy shook his head. "I'm a-sittin' here a-waitin' fer Kay."

As the jig wound down, Betty sawed a slow "Red Is The Rose." Kay and Faye danced alone to a violin ballad.

The *d-r-r-ing* of the telephone caused Kay to stumble. Faye caught her. Deb waved to stop the music. "DB Guest Ranch. Why yes, she's here. Who did you say? Why sure." She lowered the telephone and covered the mouthpiece. "Fer you, Kay. Person-to-person. Mister George Gershwin himself."

Only then did Kay realize: this was the night of the *Alma Mater* opening in Hartford. And it was three hours later there.

"George! How did it go?"

"Oh, Kay, it was beyond anything." Kay heard glasses clinking and laughter. "Everyone was just *wow*," gushed George. "You're missing the most jovial booze-fest since *Of Thee I Sing*. Archie MacLeish is here. So is Salvador Dalí. We had lobster and Spanish rice on the train from New York, now we're chugging chilled Veuve Clicquot, all care of Yours Truly. Hold on, Kay, there's someone asking for you."

Kay recognized the New England drawl. "Hello, Miss Kay Swift, this is Kate Hepburn and I just want to congratulate you on the positively delightful ballet you've written. It was simply sublime. Do come back to us soon so we can celebrate. Here's our darling George."

She passed the phone not to George Gershwin but to George Balanchine, who uttered a few words of commendation, English spiced with French, and passed it to Eddie Warburg, who sounded drunk. And so on through the New York Social Register. Kay listened to the huzzahs and merriment that zoomed through the wires all the way from Avery Memorial Theatre in Hartford, Connecticut. It seemed as remote, ephemeral, and immodest as firefly glints in a distant marshland.

"George Gershwin. Well, I'll be damned," remarked Faye when she hung up. "He yer beau?"

"I think so," said Kay. "I hope so."

The day after she collected her divorce certificate she stood railside at the Reno Station in pants, a blouse, and boots feeling apprehensive and optimistic. Packed in her suitcase were two envelopes: one for her wedding ring, the other stuffed with court documents.

She relived the last moments of her stay. That pause on the Virginia Street Bridge with Deb. As they crossed on foot over the Truckee River toward the courthouse, Deb stopped her. "This is where you toss the stone, hon." She touched Kay's diamond wedding ring and pointed to the water. "A Reno tradition. Brings luck they say."

"So you can dredge it out after I'm gone? No, thank you, Deb," laughed Kay.

"Huh-uh, I swear," said Deb.

Kay took off her ring and looked at the diamond and the inscription. She remembered the day Jimmy had proposed to her in the Roof Garden Pavilion of the Century Theatre. The day he had slid this ring onto her finger in her mother's apartment. *How young we were. How unknowing.* "My marriage may be over," she told Deb. "But the memories are here to stay." She pocketed the ring and with it, a large swath of her life.

The court proceedings themselves took less time than that pause on the Bridge of Sighs, and offered less drama. A judge named Murray, with a New York accent, asked her to verify that her husband, James Warburg, was guilty of *mental cruelty,* the most common pretext for divorce in Reno, and that she intended to reside in Nevada. He stamped a document, handed it to her, and called for the next case.

The Overland Limited to Chicago huffed and squealed to the platform. The conductor stepped halfway down the metal steps, blew his whistle, and called the passengers aboard.

CHAPTER THIRTY-SEVEN

Kay and George attended the sold-out New
York début of *Alma Mater* at the Adelphi
Theatre on March 1, 1935. Kay had attended rehearsals prior to her trip to Reno
but had not experienced the full show with
Balanchine's bold costumes, perfected
choreography, and lighting. Its tone impertinent, its musical style eclectic, her ballet
strutted and swanked across the West Fifty-
Fourth Street stage. George grinned. She
had tapped a vein of the musical mother
lode, that precious ore that alloyed entertainment and art. Kay tried to summon a
feeling akin to elation, or at least pleasure.
She had fulfilled her father's dream. *And
yet.*

It helped when she and George clinked
champagne flutes at Sardi's and a couple of
strangers stopped by. Most likely recogniz-
ing George, they gushed, "you must be Kay
Swift. Loved it."

The next morning, John Martin of the *New York Times* poured ice water all over her hangover. *Alma Mater,* he proclaimed from the top of his concrete-and-glass soapbox, was "really a revue sketch rather than a ballet." George Balanchine's new company, the American Ballet, was "a colossal waste of time and energy, and evidence of the decadence of the classic tradition as it is found in certain European environments, examples of what someone has aptly called Riviera aesthetics."

"What on earth is that supposed to mean, George?"

"Artists aren't allowed to eat prime rib, or ride in automobiles, Kay. Haven't you seen *La Bohème?*"

Kay reread the review. *What if John is on to something? Maybe the tone of* Alma Mater, *or the concept itself, is indeed snide or shallow.* She had always suspected as much. But contrary to Romantic myth, real artists did not labor in isolation, burning their overcoats to warm their garrets. Real artists in America today knew how to negotiate with the business people who could promote their work: music publishers, show producers, and stars like George Balanchine. When the world's most celebrated choreographer calls you, you pick up the phone. If he is bankrolled by a Warburg who, like Jimmy and others in their clan yearns to prove his mettle in the fickle domain of the arts, well, then, as Scott Fitzgerald observed, *where the money goes, there goes the culture.* Even an artist with the power of a George Gershwin usually had to write not what he wanted, and not necessarily what audiences expected, but what Broadway producers imagined audiences wanted. *Porgy* was an exception, but he would have to finance it himself. It amounted to an experiment, the riskiest venture of his life. She shook her head, emptied her cup, and entwined her fingers with his. "The audience liked *Alma Mater,* though."

"They were nuts about it." He glanced at the clock. "I have to clean up. *Porgy* tryouts. We'll need you at the keyboard." He could now play the entire score but he wanted to listen from the point of view of the audience. He frowned, sniffed, and looked around. "Do you smell that?"

"Smell what?"

"Something burning?"

She shook her head. George and his hallucinations.

George had already selected his Porgy and

his Bess but his producers, known as The Theatre Guild, were not comfortable with his choices. They had expected his name and clout to attract the likes of Paul Robeson and Josephine Baker, both of whom had auditioned in his apartment while Kay sojourned in Reno. Instead, he had picked two unknowns. Porgy was to be played by Todd Duncan, a young baritone from Indianapolis who taught at Howard University in Washington, D.C. Anne Brown, a pretty Juilliard ingénue, would personify Bess.

To demonstrate the astuteness of his choices George had invited Todd, Anne, and members of the Theatre Guild to his apartment. They sat on his Frits Henningsen sofas and armchairs, sipping Cristal Roederer champagne in Lalique flutes and munching on canapés. The singers faced them, sheet music in hand. Kay accompanied on the piano. Anne wailed a searing "My Man's Gone Now," Todd lit up the room with "I Got Plenty o' Nuttin'," and together they sang the love duet, "Bess, You Is My Woman Now," their voices slithering over unexpected, nonparallel paths. Neither Todd nor Anne sang in the grand operahouse manner of a Gitta Alpár or a Lauritz Melchior. Nor did they belt the tunes like Broadway headliners. They performed with the naturalness and simplicity of well-trained neophytes. Kay, representing the orchestra, participated in their dialogue, answering and adorning their melodies.

This was the first time that Kay and George heard professional singers perform the showstopper, "Bess, You Is My Woman Now." Long before Todd and Anne's concluding harmony faded, supported by a final high chord on the piano, everyone's eyes glistened. George glanced at Kay, who smiled back with relief.

CHAPTER THIRTY-EIGHT

On September 30, 1935, *Porgy and Bess* premiered at the Colonial Theatre in Boston. As the curtain fell the audience jumped to their feet and applauded for fifteen minutes. At their insistence, and the conductor's, George strolled onto the stage in his tuxedo and bowed, his eyes wandering to Kay. The ovation increased and resonated long after she joined him in the wings.

The show was an unqualified triumph, but later, meeting in their hotel lobby, the director expressed reservations about its three-hour length. He, George, and Kay decided which passages to excise or abbreviate. Kay and George worked all night, the following day, and the night after. They incorporated the changes in the third performance.

The director timed the audience's standing ovation. It clocked in at thirty seconds less than opening night. Still, he insisted, the cuts represented an improvement. In fact, he demanded more.

The version that opened in New York City ten days later therefore lacked some of the subtle connective tissue of the original. It made up for this loss in concision and verve. George thought it better. Kay was not certain but knew, her heart bursting with pride, that either way *Porgy and Bess* was an American masterpiece that would endure.

Most of the print reviewers cheered but some expressed puzzlement. Was *Porgy and Bess* a *musical* or an *opera*? It was performed in a Broadway theater, like a musical, but it lacked spoken dialogue, like an opera. In interviews George called it a folk opera. No one had ever heard that term. What did *folk opera* imply? George refused to provide a clear answer. He thought the question unimportant but many of the reviewers considered it crucial.

In newspapers and magazines, the debate exploded. Critics questioned the scene: an impoverished ghetto in Charleston, South Carolina. Broadway shows usually took place in iconic American settings: New York City, the prairies of Oklahoma, a steamboat on the Mississippi. Operas had always been set either in Europe or in one of the mythological realms favored by Wagner or Debussy. The America that Gershwin had set to music was not the nation many wished to display to the world, the industrial titan, home of great institutions of education and research, the hope and freedom of the wide-open plains. No, this Catfish Row had little to do with mainstream American culture or its European heritage. In their few appearances, white people were portrayed as oppressors.

And what to make of the dialect, officially known as Sea Island Creole English? It was neither grammatical American nor the cocky, colorful patois of Harlem. The idiom of the Gullah people combined English diction with syntax from the languages of West Africa and nineteenth-century plantation creole. It was difficult to understand, especially sung.

And those characters. A cripple, a drug dealer, a prostitute, a community of ardent Baptists. Were such people worthy of glorification? What, precisely, was Gershwin's intent?

But the thorniest issue stemmed from the fact that a handful of genteel white people, George, Kay, DuBose and Dorothy Hayward, Ira Gershwin, had appointed themselves the artistic interpreters of a culture not their own. In discussions of his novel, years earlier, DuBose had referred to his approach as *anthropological,* suggesting a modern, objective aesthetic. In place of the villains and heroes of the Victorian novel, which had presented itself as a medium for moral commentary, DuBose championed a narrative that depicted men and women as complex and flawed, often emotional, sometimes brave, and deeply ethnic.

But to many that very term, *anthropological,* also implied colonial arrogance. As the days passed, and then the weeks, reviews turned hostile. George's rivals, unable to deny the powerful appeal of his music, seized on the cultural issues. The composer Virgil Thomson led the charge. "Folklore subjects recounted by an outsider are only valid as long as the folk in question is unable to speak for itself," he wrote. "Which is certainly not true of the American Negro in 1935." Ironically, as George pointed out to Kay, Thomson himself was guilty of the charge he was leveling. A white man, he was advocating for the Negroes with this very comment, as if they could not speak for themselves.

Neither George nor DuBose thought of *Porgy* as social commentary about Negro culture in general. For DuBose it showcased one small piece of the American jigsaw.

George saw the story as an affirmation of humanity, a portrayal of the beauty and unseemliness, the simplicity and opacity of emotion and song, of shared humanity but also of the attitudes and idioms that lend a people its singularity. No one could credibly claim that George or DuBose did not love their characters, or that they reduced them to stereotypes or derided them. The denizens of Catfish Row were real, full-blooded human beings, with hearts bursting as they endeavored to forge a path through the muddle of life.

Theater patrons initially loved *Porgy and Bess,* but the increasingly hostile reviews sank it. Audiences dwindled. Every performance now lost money. *Porgy and Bess* closed after 124 nights. Not a good run by Gershwin standards, and a catastrophe for such an ambitious, costly production.

The night after the last performance Kay and George enjoyed a canard a l'orange with a blanc de blancs wine, prepared and served in George's candlelit apartment by Fred Boursier, the premier sous-chef at the Waldorf-Astoria restaurant. Just the two of them. "George," she told him, "mark my words. In fifty years, a hundred years, few people will remember Virgil Thomson. Even fewer will know the words of his arias. But everyone will know 'Summertime.' "

He smiled sadly.

The event that pained him most was Edward Morrow's interview with Duke Ellington in *New Theatre* magazine. The Duke's remarks sounded ad hominem and scathing. "The time has come," said Ellington, "to debunk such tripe as Gershwin's lampblack Negroisms."

Stunned, Gershwin read and reread the interview. For days he lingered in bed or moped around his apartment in pajamas and robe. Finally he called the Duke and they arranged to meet for lunch at Small's Paradise on 135th Street and Seventh Avenue. Kay accompanied him.

"Lampblack Negroisms," George read. He put down the magazine and wiped his forehead with his breast-pocket handkerchief. "Duke, there isn't a pot of lampblack in any of those dressing rooms. These are real people. Do you have any idea how much pushback I got for insisting on these singers? You've known me how long?"

"It's the dialogue, George. Do you know a colored person who talks that way?"

"Not here in New York, but in Charleston, among the Gullah people? You betcha. DuBose lived with them, worked with them, for years. His mother studied their language.

512

I prayed with them, Duke."

"Is DuBose colored, himself?" asked the Duke.

"Was Shakespeare colored, when he wrote *Othello*?" asked George. "Was Bizet a gypsy when he wrote *Carmen*? Was Rembrandt Jewish when he painted the Jews of Amsterdam — so respectfully that his portraits bring tears to my eyes? It doesn't change a thing what he believed or what color his skin was. Othello's a sympathetic guy. He's flawed but we root for him. Same goes for Porgy. No one's mocking him. This is no minstrel show, Duke."

"I guess you're sensitive to this," said the Duke, "having begun your career with 'Swanee.' "

"Damn straight I'm sensitive to it," said George. "Take a swing at the segregationists. But not at your comrades in arms."

"Duke," put in Kay, "when the novel *Porgy* came out everyone hailed it as a masterpiece. The *Herald Tribune*, the *Chicago Daily News*, everyone. Including the papers here in Harlem. They used the word *authentic*. Over and over. When the play opened on Broadway, same tune. No one objected. The dialogue hasn't changed that much. George just set it to music. And now it's inauthentic and condescending?"

The Duke salted his fries. "I didn't actually make that remark. Eddie made it up. And I'll say so publicly."

George glanced at Kay. The Duke could be hard driving and cagey. But a liar he was not.

"That said, I don't imagine you read *Porgy* the way I do," added Ellington. "Your *Porgy* isn't about the Negro tenement."

"I'm not following you," said George.

"All this promised land stuff," explained the Duke. "It's about the ghetto. *Your* people's ghetto."

George laughed. "You've never set foot in a church in South Carolina."

They finished their lunch and parted with a warm handshake. The Duke followed through, writing a letter to the editor of *New Theatre* magazine in which he stated that his comments about *Porgy* had been misrepresented. But the damage was done.

After *Porgy* closed, George faced financial ruin. His health deteriorated further. His headaches struck frequently and were more debilitating. He smelled burning rubber at the strangest times. Or it might be invisible trash bursting into flames, or human hair sizzling somewhere just out of sight. Kay feared it was his own life force that was being consumed in the furious flames of his ambition.

He caught a whiff of it when he and Kay watched workers remove the *Porgy and Bess* lettering from the Alvin Theatre marquee on Fifty-Second Street. As always, when Kay stood beside him on a New York sidewalk in daytime, she felt as if she were swimming in an aquarium. So many passersby looked at them in the intense yet restrained way of those who recognize a celebrity but pretend otherwise. "Why don't we just do it, George," she suggested slipping her arm through his. "Settle down somewhere in the countryside. Who needs this Coney Island roller coaster?"

"Kay, you're about the best thing that ever hit me," said George. "But I have to get back on my feet."

"You have a plan?"

"Another movie score. What choice?"

Kay fetched a cigarette in her bag. George lit it for her. "An offer I'm not aware of?"

He nodded. "*Shall We Dance.*" And then he chuckled. "Who knows, maybe it'll click this time. Fred and Ginger! Kicking up a storm out there. She's begging me. It's been too darn long since I've worked with either one of them." They walked up Broadway in the late summer afternoon. The colorful street thronged with vehicles and trams and smelled like asphalt and grease. Workers in smudged coveralls and neatly pressed suits trudged home from offices and factories, their heads low, their pace languid. "Don't worry, you'll have plenty of work, yourself," George told Kay with a sly smile. "You won't even have time to miss me."

CHAPTER THIRTY-NINE

1937

In the United States of FDR and talkies, largeness was all the rage. New York had surpassed London as the most populous city. It erected the tallest buildings in the newest art deco style. Its sparkling Radio City Music Hall offered the broadest range of entertainment to the widest audience. Featuring the world's biggest Wurlitzer theater organ, a full orchestra, and a choral group, Sam Rothapfel's Radio City aspired to be everything for everyone: the capital of wireless broadcasting; the biggest stage for musical revues, with the longest line of sublime leg-kickers; and the most expansive movie screen, where six thousand spectators could share laughs and tears offered up by the latest entertainment technology.

In the moviemaking industry, Thomas Edison's legendary rapaciousness had backfired, causing New York to lose its dominance. But what the metropolis lost in production, it made up for in consumption. Sid Grauman's Egyptian Theatre on Hollywood Boulevard, which seated almost two thousand spectators, seemed quaint compared to New York's Roxy Theatre and the Radio City, which accommodated not only larger crowds but also restaurants, art galleries, billiards rooms, and childcare facilities. The live orchestras played new song-and-dance numbers every week, with full-blown spectacles that preceded every movie. If America was the world's capital of industry, the American culture machine served up art on an industrial scale.

The task of writing the lyrics for Radio City, the hottest ticket for a New York versifier, fell to the Gershwin protégé Al Stillman. The equally enviable post of resident Radio City Music Hall composer, to Kay Swift. In this capacity, she wrote music full-time and heard it performed with little delay by esteemed musicians, many of them fellow graduates of her school, now known as Juilliard. In a phrase Ira Gershwin had coined, Who could ask for anything more?

The hefty workload distracted her from her loneliness now that George was back in L.A. She and Al shared an office suite halfway up the RCA Building and got along famously. Strolling to work in high heels, a leopard coat, and a matching hat, her clutch bag tucked under her arm, she was now "a recognizable fixture on Broadway," as *Popular Songs* magazine put it in a feature article devoted to her, with a picture on the cover under the banner: "She Is the Envy of Songwriters Everywhere."

Sometimes she worked all night. Other evenings, she brought her sketches home. Her apartment was so quiet these days. She fixed herself a martini and collapsed on the sofa wondering what George was doing at that moment.

Kay phoned Washington every week to ask about the girls, to speak with them and share sorrows and laughter. Andrea and Kathleen visited every month. They spent happy moments together in ice cream shops and concert halls — ironically, moments more joyous than before the divorce. But April refused any encounter. Sometimes Kay and Jimmy conversed, but like April, he did not wish to see her. "Perhaps in six months or a year we'll all get past the disappointment," he said.

From the tabloids, Kay learned about Jimmy's engagement to a certain Phyllis and of George's flirtations or possible affairs in

Los Angeles. *Plus ça change, plus c'est la même chose.* She ruminated about the future Mrs. Warburg's — *Phyllis's* — interactions with her daughters. She closed her eyes and listened to her breathing and then dived back into her work.

Late one night the phone rang. She was half asleep. A dreamless snooze. Who in her mad world could be calling her at this hour?

"Kay?"

She had not heard from him in weeks. "George! It's so good to hear your voice."

"I'm feeling droopy, Kay. So droopy and burned. This place is not home. I'm tired. How's life in the City? And you, how are things going at RCA?"

"You know me, George. Working. Coping. The city looks beautiful these days."

"These movie fellas, they can have their swimming pools, their motorcars, their starlets. It ain't New York. You can't even get a decent pastrami sandwich here."

She smiled. "On rye with mustard? From a guy named Meier?"

"I miss you, Kay." He said it with such gravitas she felt fearful.

Her voice softened. "Oh, George, I miss you too."

"Plenty of lookers here but you're one in a million."

"Ah, yes. Lookers!" said Kay. "Like that siren, Paulette Goddard and . . . who was it? Simone Simon. What a name!"

"Listen, Kay, I've been thinking."

"How are Fred and Ginger?"

"They're the new Fred and Adele. As I was saying —"

"— that I was one in a million? Only one in a million, George?"

"I'm through with it all. The dames, the games . . ."

"Is that a promise? What's your plan?"

"I'm beat. That's the long and short of it."

"I'm here, George. How are the headaches?"

"The other day it smacked me hard. Middle of the *New York Concerto*. San Francisco. The whole city was there. The mayor. Abe and Mabel Gump. Walter and Elise Haas. I'm about to play my cadenza and, *boom*! Everything's gone. I forget where I am, what I'm doing."

She missed a heartbeat. The phone line filled with sadness. She was lost in a dark field staring at a moonless sky.

"I'm finished, Kay."

She closed her eyes, biting her lips.

"You'll never be finished, George. Don't talk like that."

"Too much pressure. Too many years. What have I been trying to prove?"

"Whatever it is," said Kay, "you've proven it. But that doesn't mean you're finished. Just another phase."

"I just want to sew up this contract and fly home. To settle down. To write music at my own tempo. *Rubato.* Maybe in Valhalla, like Sergei. Would you like that?"

"Me? Wherever you like, George," said Kay.

" 'Cause if I get my way, you're going to be Misses George Gershwin." He almost whispered it.

She had given up hoping to hear these words.

"Kay? You there, Kay?"

A lump was obstructing her throat. She wiped her eyes, thankful he could not see her.

"Kay?"

"Valhalla, Peru, wherever you like. Oh, George, George, you rascal."

"Let's not waste any more time, my love."

"I'm ready," said Kay.

"It's late now in New York, isn't it. I didn't wake you, did I? What a knucklehead I am."

"The best wakeup call I ever received."

"Go back to sleep, then."

"Good night to you, too, George."

"Good night, my love."

She let her tears flow. She had reached a turning point. She had failed in many ways but succeeded beyond her dreams in others. Soon George and she would be reunited. This time for real. The girls would visit at their country house. They would ride horses. Certainly Andrea and Kathleen, and with time April, too. They would squabble. They would reconcile. They would delight in each other's company in a new place, at a new rhythm. She would atone for her sins. And all would be forgiven.

CHAPTER FORTY

July 11, 1937

In the distance, the rising howl of a siren, calling to mind the klezmer-style clarinet wail at the beginning of George's *Rhapsody.* And in that lament, so much humor, so much melody, so much pain. Kay opened the ashtray in the door handle of the black DeSoto and snuffed out her cigarette. The rain abated as she rolled into the Upper East Side. Fewer pedestrians here. "Shall We Dance" playing in her head. *Dah-da-daah, da da da dah dah. Dah-da-dah. Da da da deee.* So George. She closed her eyes to listen. *But why this dread?*

In her apartment the telephone was ringing. Apprehensive, she ran to pick it up. It was Ira. "Kay, where have you been?" His voice weak, unsteady. "I've been trying to reach you."

"I was watching *Shall We Dance* in the theater. What is it, Ira?"

A pause.

"It's about George," Kay heard herself say. She covered her mouth as if stifling a wail.

"George is gone, Kay."

She held onto the telephone stand. "What are you saying?"

"Last night," said Ira. "He . . . he passed away."

She swallowed. "But I . . . I just talked to him last night."

"I know. He called me. Couldn't stop talking about you. About settling down. A new phase. New songs. New everything."

The phone fell from her hand. *All her hopes. All their plans.* She heard Ira's voice in the distance. "He went to the piano. Wrote a song. For you, Kay."

She brought the receiver back to her ear. "Ira. Ira. What happened?"

"He must have stood up and passed out, just like that. Left the song on the piano. Never came out of it. Brain tumor."

Brain tumor? "How can that be? He was healthy. So much energy."

"He *seemed* healthy. But those headaches . . ."

"Oh, God." So it was not neurosis, after all.

"They called the White House. Tracked down the best surgeon in the country. Too late." Ira was sobbing. Kay leaned against the wall, trying to absorb the news.

The phone rang continuously but she ignored it. Nor did she venture out. She spoke only with Ira. They arranged to have George's body flown east. Olin Downes, long George's detractor, wrote the front-page obituary that appeared in the *New York Times:*

No other American composer had such a funeral service. Not a MacDowell, not a Chadwick, not a Stephen Foster or Dan Emmett or John Philip Sousa received such parting honors. Authors, editors, playwrights, and critics; national figures of the stage, the screen, the radio, the ballet; celebrated musicians, from Paul Whiteman to Walter Damrosch, composers as well as executants, gathered to say hail and farewell. This was eloquent of the place Gershwin held in the public esteem . . . He was a born melodist, with a native instinct for exotic harmonic effects and rhythmical ingenuity . . . Jazz gained a new consideration with Gershwin, and Gershwin, in turn, contributed individual genius to the form. When the tumult and shouting are over, he will have a secure place in the American tonal art.

Memorial programs played George's music from morning until night nationwide. Arnold Schoenberg, Irving Berlin, and Jerome Kern published tributes. The *New York Herald Tribune* printed details about the valuation of Gershwin's intellectual property. Some of his individual works were worth tens of thousands of 1937 dollars based on projected future sales. Of all his compositions and songs, the least consequential, in strict financial terms, was deemed to be *Porgy and Bess.* That entire score was valued at twenty dollars. In his will, George expressed the desire that it never be performed except by an all-Negro cast. No blackface.

Simultaneous funeral services were held on both coasts. The synagogues filled to capacity and thousands of mourners stood outside in the rain in New York.

Kay entered Temple Emanu-El. A sea of mourners filled the hall and side rooms. Paul Mueller led her down the carpeted central aisle. Midway through the synagogue, she felt a hand on her shoulder. She turned to see Jimmy. All three of their daughters stood at his side. "I am so sorry,

Kay." He blinked twice. She nodded. He embraced her and caressed her hair the way a father soothes his tearful daughter. They stood there for a long moment, indifferent to the gaze of others. Finally he moved to accommodate his daughters. Andrea threw her arms around Kay, crying. April pushed Andrea aside to hug her mother. She kissed her daughter's forehead. She patted Kathleen's hair.

At the front of the viewing line, she stood beside Ira. He squeezed her hand as he wept. George lay in his mahogany coffin dressed in his pin-striped gray flannel suit, his favorite — his hands clasped on his belly, his face serene, the hint of a smile on his lips. The mortician had pomaded his hair, rouged his thirty-eight-year-old cheeks, and inserted a red carnation in his lapel and a silk square in his breast pocket. *George would have hated the painted cheeks and the carnation.* Kay leaned down to offer him one last kiss, pulled the flower from his lapel, and threw it to the ground. No one reacted. She wiped her tears from his cheeks and whispered, "Good night, my sweet love."

On the bimah, Ella Logan sang George's last song. The one he was drafting after his phone call to Kay. The one he had dedicated

to her. Ira titled it "Love Is Here To Stay."
Looking regal and fragile, Kay Swift listened, her face drenched in tears behind
her dark veil.

> In time the Rockies may crumble,
>   Gibraltar may tumble,
> They're only made of clay,
> But our love is here to stay.

AUTHOR'S NOTE

History is the rough draft. Our minds do not easily assimilate its raw form. It is messy, often chaotic. We yearn for catharsis, and that is a matter of form as well as content.

A good historical novel differs from most good "narrative nonfiction" in three respects: gaps in the historical record are filled in; more emphasis is placed on subjective human experience; dialogue and thoughts are provided. Some historical novelists place a premium on entertainment value, others on authenticity, yet others on style. I think of all these aspects as interconnected and consider it my obligation to value them equally. Similarly, some write intimate novels that just happen to be set in the past, while others write epic novels that fill broad tableaux with names and intersecting story lines. Again, I try to provide both the small frame and the context, but in a streamlined and concise way.

The job of the historical novelist is to comb out the noise, find the dramatic arc, and shape events into a psychologically and emotionally cogent argument. Inevitably, this involves some reorganization of the raw material. I strive to modify the order of events as minimally as possible. However, storytelling remains paramount. As a result I have had to shift some events. Among these modifications:

◇ The meetings with Dr. Zilboorg (who, it seems, did assault Kay sexually) commenced later than as related in this telling, probably in 1934 or 1935. I needed this sequence to build slowly, rather than suddenly.

◇ Adele Astaire married Charles Cavendish in 1932, a little later than suggested here.

◇ George Gershwin moved to 33 Riverside Drive in 1929, not in 1932.

◇ The first time Kay visited George, Paul Mueller did not yet work for him. In fact, it was Kay who convinced George to hire a valet, and found Paul for him.

◇ George Gershwin dated Paulette Goddard during his second sojourn in Los Angeles, not his first.

◊ I'm not by any means sure Kay met Faye Hubbard in Reno. But it does seem to me that in certain ways her trip to Reno did set up her later marriage to him.

◊ I do not know that Gershwin had to provide thirty percent of the budget for *Porgy.* I have used this round number to dramatize the risk for him, which was considerable.

◊ The lyrics of "Little White Lies" have been lost, so I made them up.

Roanoke, Virginia,
January 6, 2020

ACKNOWLEDGMENTS

Jackie Cantor, my editor at Gallery Books, was enormously helpful and always a pleasure to deal with. My cousin Marc Kramer and my college pal Anne Russell read the manuscript and provided sensible, highly appreciated advice. Another college friend, Peter Russell, shared some of his vast knowledge of music, especially insights regarding *Porgy and Bess.* My wife, Annie, read every draft of the manuscript and offered indispensable comments every step of the way. My mother (who happens to be a professor of literature) also read several drafts and provided helpful comments. Thanks again to all, and to my wonderful friends in Los Angeles, Pittsburgh, Roanoke, Paris, New York, and elsewhere, who have always been there for me. A special shout-out to Jeff Sacre, who provided encouragement and support in a very different but equally important area of my life.

My gratitude to my wife, my children, Ariel and Zeke, and my "other son" Jack cannot be overstated.

My father's spirit inspired this novel. I will always remember him playing clarinet along with a phonograph record of *Rhapsody in Blue,* or with Mozart's elegant and ethereal Clarinet Concerto in A Major, or any of a number of Benny Goodman recordings. Thank you, Dad.

ABOUT THE AUTHOR

Mitchell James Kaplan is the award-winning author of the novels *By Fire, By Water* and *Into the Unbounded Night*. A graduate of Yale, he has lived in Paris and Los Angeles, and currently lives with his family in Roanoke, Virginia.